W9-ANX-342

DATE DUE

THE LAND

OTHER BOOKS BY DANA L. THOMAS INCLUDE

The Plungers and the Peacocks
The Money Crowd
The Story of American Statehood
Fifty Great Americans
Crusaders for God
Living for God
Living Adventures in Philosophy
Let the Chips Fall (A Political History of New York), written with Newbold Morris
The Living Biographies Series, Six Volumes, written with Henry Thomas

LORDS OF THE LAND

by DANA L. THOMAS

*The Triumphs and Scandals of America's Real
Estate Barons—from Early Times to the
Present*

G. P. Putnam's Sons, New York

To my Father
who gave me the tools of the trade

CONTENTS

Foreword

A decade ago the author wrote *The Plungers and the Peacocks,* a history of Wall Street and of the major speculators who made and lost fortunes on the New York Stock Exchange. Encouraged by the response of readers, he has extended his biographical approach to the subject of American real estate. Since land development embraces a wide variety of interrelated operations and every region has its own history, the present book is necessarily highly selective in its material. There has been no intent to write a systematic social history or to trace the development of the nation's public land policies per se. These have been extensively dealt with in a number of books. Indeed, the author has treated the subject in a previous volume of his own, *The Story of American Statehood.* The purpose of the present work has been to present the experiences of America's leading land barons, discuss their strategic methods, the manner in which they have accumulated—and dissipated—great wealth, and the impact of their financial maneuverings on their fellow Americans.

In the course of his research, the author has delved into a treasure trove of material, consulting books, memoirs, letters, and magazine and newspaper articles concerning the periods covered. (See Bibliography.) For more recent episodes he has drawn from his own investigations as a journalist on the national business scene.

DANA L. THOMAS
New York City, 1976

1

THE MAGNIFICENT BANKRUPTS

*The Founding Fathers Wheel and Deal
in Yankee Real Estate*

The oldest fortunes in America have come from the land. Unlike Europe, where most of the valuable acreage has been entailed for centuries by the nobility, American real estate has been open to virtually anybody with the daring and the ingenuity to possess it. From the moment the immigrants set foot in the New World and moved inward, the land jobbers followed closely on the heels of the explorers and the missionaries, plunging their money into promising real estate. The padishahs of landed wealth were a raffish crew who sowed mischief, as well as made valuable contributions, on a grandiose scale. Among them was one notorious gamester who triggered a nationwide financial panic. Another—a woman—held the city of New Orleans in her grip for years. Several land jobbers made fortunes seizing the "worthless" sand dunes of San Francisco and turning them into lucrative property developments. One promoter built churches next to his gambling casinos to appease God for his villainies. Another ran for the Presidency on his own ticket and, when beaten badly, threatened to become America's first dictator.

The great real estate clans—the Astors, Marshall Fields, Longworths, Flaglers—were hotbeds of fierce loyalties and smoldering rivalries, of fraternal scheming and counter-scheming. Yet for all their intrigues, the façade they presented to the public has been most seductive. They built homes that were replicas of Venetian palaces and medieval castles on the Rhine. They imported rare old Tudor tapestries and terrazos from Florentine villas. They shipped home entire Japanese gardens and plated their bathrooms and toilet bowls in gold. The wife of one San Francisco tycoon had two dozen gold toilets placed strategically in her residence so that her women guests could play whist in splendor while they gossiped.

The methods of the land jobbers in the days when America was young, and the land to be seized immense, were highly ingenious. They launched entire urban developments—Washington, New York, Los Angeles, Miami—and shaped the character of their growth for years to come. They exploited America's economic and social thrust for westward expansion and rode the boom in railroad building for their own aggrandizement. They bought the nation's press and pulpits, pressured entire legislatures into promoting their landed empires. They bribed, bullied, manipulated and seduced—and turned incomparable visions into dramatic reality. For all their faults, they carved a giant nation out of the wilderness. The physical appearance of America, the brick, stone and mortar of its houses, its factories and its cathedrals, are the handiwork of the landed panjandrums.

From the beginning, the most successful land dealers were even more fascinated by the gamesmanship than the money. They were intrigued with the challenge of solving highly complex deals. Hopelessly euphoric, they took a look at swampland and glimpsed the metropolis that one day would materialize out of it. They envisaged the industrial complex that would emerge from outlying farm acreage, the thriving tourist resort that could arise from a lonely sandbar. Psychiatrists, if they had existed in the early days, would undoubtedly have described many successful land peddlers as manic-depressives with outrageous highs and lows. Some of those who struck it rich and then gambled themselves into ruin were the kind of people who, on the deck of the sinking *Titanic*, would have sung "Oh What a Beautiful Mornin'."

And yet it made good sense to be a high roller in real estate during America's early days. There was no difficulty finding land. The country had a superabundance of it. The trick was to select property that was strategically located. The astute speculator bought property for a song on the outskirts of a town, estimating that it lay squarely in the direction the community would grow. If he guessed right and the village became a metropolis, its acreage wound up in the heart of the city, and by subdividing it into lots, he or his heirs became multimillionaires. Sometimes this happened within the lifetime of the original land buyer.

Real estate was then as now a highly volatile business marked by boom and bust. Most properties, much of the time, are either terribly undervalued or outrageously inflated. But land, unlike merchandise, cannot be quickly added to, and it takes an agonizingly long time to correct a situation. The most astute real estate operators have amassed their fortunes by moving in at precisely the right time. They are the first to sense when prices have reached rock bottom. Usually this is in the middle of a depression. The successful speculator is among the first to realize that hard times are coming to an end when everyone else is still immersed in gloom.

The successful operators in evaluating land can see beyond the use to which it is being put at the moment and realize its vast potential in other uses. The current worth of land might be meager, but if it can be developed in such a way as to change its employment dramatically, its value can be revolutionized. William Zeckendorf, who built America's biggest real estate imperium after World War II, explained his strategy this way: "I make grapefruit out of lemons."

The real estate operator venerates the tool of credit with the zeal a savage pays to his totem pole. The more money he owes, the less cash of his own he needs to put into a venture. The higher the leverage the greater the potential profits. The big swingers are never concerned with the appearance of their balance sheets. They are mesmerized with the future payoff. They are adept at adjusting to an unpredictable turn of events, for no scenario is more uncertain than the outcome of a complex real estate deal.

Land dealing is reminiscent of a story told about George M. Cohan, the eccentric Broadway playwright, who would frequently start writing a play without the slightest inkling of how it would end, and Cohan would put his actors into rehearsal before he had completed the final act. On one occasion a play was fed to the director and the cast in installments; the suspense mounted. The leading actor felt until the very last moment he was playing a romantic hero. On the day before opening night he was handed the final scene and did a double take. The hero turned out to be an escaped lunatic.

The experienced realty operator deeply appreciates the need of being able to handle every unexpected turn and twist of his script, and American history has been replete with challenges.

Historians have observed that a litmus test of a civilized society is the way it distributes the land to its people. Thomas Paine, William Godwin, and other progressive, liberal proponents of a "just, equitable society" maintained that a genuine democracy could be built only on the ownership of property by the masses of laborers, farmers, mechanics, and other folk of modest means. Henry George contended that privately owned land served no useful social function and that rents should be heavily taxed for the benefit of the whole community.

Throughout the nineteenth century, a group of populist politicians and social thinkers urged that the United States Government hand out its public acreage to the landless to provide "a safety valve" against an explosion of economic unrest. Social historians propounded the thesis that only the opportunity to migrate to the West deterred the financially struggling factory worker, the jobless machinist, the debt-ridden farmer from rebelling against America's economic system, and preserved the nation as a law-abiding society loyal to the concept of private reward for personal initiative.

From its beginning, the Government was split in its attitude toward property ownership, especially as it pertained to the public lands. When America, after its successful War of Independence, organized itself under the Articles of Confederation, and the Continental Congress passed the Ordinances of 1784-87, throwing open for settlement the territory of the old Northwest, a sharp debate arose as to how this land should be distributed. One faction of Congress wanted it sold to the wealthy, who could afford to pay the fanciest prices and thereby work off the national debt generated by the recent war. A second faction argued that the land should be distributed on the most liberal terms to anybody who wished to settle on it. Thomas Jefferson went so far as to assert that if the Government made it available to the masses for as little as a dollar an acre, the resulting demand would be great enough to pay off the debt in a reasonably short time.

In addition to the liberal and conservative ideologists, there were a handful of lone-wolf risk-takers who with little money but vast resourcefulness sought to latch onto the land as a private speculation. And these indefatigable jobbers consistently sabotaged the lofty visions of the social engineers who strove to remold the nation according to their personal predilections.

The fact was that aside from the political and philosophical theorizing the settlement of the United States was from the very beginning a gargantuan land speculation. The Spanish King Ferdinand, who subsidized Columbus' trip, looked upon the discovery of America as a huge opportunity to enlarge his real estate holdings. The monarchs of England and France who handed out charters to overseas land companies were literally jobbers expecting financial overrides on real estate hustling in the New World. The early land grabbers were found at the highest levels of American leadership. There is little question that King George III's attempt to stop George Washington, Patrick Henry, and Harry Lee from speculating in the western lands was a major factor in their antiroyalist attitude that eventually led to their joining in a war of rebellion against His Majesty. After the war the strategy of speculators remained essentially the same, namely to grab up acreage and unload it on others as quickly as possible. In this regard, a big business was done cozening America's overseas brethren—not the first or last time that they would be rooked by their American cousins.

American speculators figured that Europeans living under oppressive governments were straining at the leash to emigrate to America. Some heady optimists actually predicted that up to half of all the residents of Europe would one day occupy land beyond the Alleghenies, and they foresaw an enormous skyrocketing in real estate prices for those lucky enough to buy in on the ground floor.

But the sanguine speculators who grabbed up western lands hoping for quick profits found the problem of unloading them more difficult than they had anticipated. They were right in believing that the land they bought would zoom in value; they were wrong in their timing. It would take much longer than they had anticipated.

The early history of the Republic is replete with incidents that underscore the buoyant optimism of the land speculators, their capacity for self-delusion, and their vulnerability to going broke as, in the phrase of a modern playwright, they rode "on a smile and a shoeshine."

The first major example of this delusion and a prototype for the many manipulations that followed took place when the Continental Congress passed the Northwest Ordinance, throwing open the territory of the Old Northwest and launching the first large-scale public land development project in America. The lands comprised acreage originally owned by Virginia, New York, Massachusetts, and Connecticut, which had ceded their territories to the central government. The Ordinance set up the machinery for the organization of these territories and the admission of their inhabitants as states, setting a precedent for the entry of future regions. Settlers were invited to bid for the land as it was in the process of being surveyed into townships.

No one cast a more eager eye on the Northwest Territory than Dr. Manasseh Cutler, a New England clergyman who had for some time been toying with a dream of freeing workers from their urban impoverishment and leading an expedition to settle them in a new life on the virgin lands beyond the Alleghenies. He looked upon the opening of the Northwest Territory as a heaven-sent opportunity.

An astute and wealthy land hustler from New York, William Duer, got wind of Dr. Cutler's aspirations, introduced himself to the clergyman, and told him he would be happy to raise the money for his noble experiment if the clergyman transmitted to him and his business associates options on several thousand acres of the land he had obtained from the government. Duer wore two hats. In addition to being a land plunger, he happened to be secretary to the board of treasury established by the Continental Congress to supervise the financial affairs of the newly freed colonies. Accordingly, Duer was in a splendid position to ensure that Cutler received his public land grant, while privately reserving an option on part of the acreage. Before meeting with Duer, Cutler had petitioned Congress for a grant of one million acres on which the government had set a price of $1 an acre. (He had been frustrated in his efforts to raise the $1 million, but after being introduced to Duer, the gates swung open.) The latter suggested to Cutler that he increase his petition from one to four million acres. The money-hungry government would be much more anxious to sell four times as much land, Duer pointed out, and would grant Cutler extremely liberal credit terms to facilitate the deal. The additional three million acres could then be quietly assigned to a company Duer would set up and head, anonymously to be sure, since he was after all secretary of the treasury. Sure enough, under Duer's influence, the government announced its willingness to hand over four million acres to Cutler on the generous credit terms Duer had foreseen, and his syndicate gave the New England minister the $100,000 he needed to pay the initial installment for the land. Cutler then turned over to Duer an option on three million acres.

Duer distributed his shares in the option to land speculators in Boston and New York. They hoped to unload the title to the three million acres to wealthy speculators in Europe who had the necessary money to swing the deal. Indeed, the Duer syndicate planned to peddle this enormous tract bought at $1 an acre *even before they had acquired legal title to it.* All they had was an option, but once the land was unloaded, they figured, they would receive the profits out of which they would pay for the title. In oth-

17

er words, they were engaged in a massive short sale of real estate analogous to shorting stock on Wall Street.

Armed with their options, the Duer group looked for the wealthiest fall guys available. France was a promising breeding ground, and the Duer clique, to peddle its deal, sent over to Paris Joel Barlow, a Connecticut newspaper editor who was subsequently to become known as one of America's earliest poets of international reputation. One of the "Hartford Wits," he wrote *The Columbiad* and other works.

Barlow went around France lecturing on the real estate paradise the Duer syndicate had picked up in America's Northwest, but he found that cash was tight. It was the eve of the French Revolution, and the money market was extremely skittish. Realizing it was impossible to peddle the three-million-acre tract to one or several individuals, Barlow decided he would have to sell it in small lots to a large number of people who were prepared to embark for America and settle there. But when he wrote the Duer syndicate about his plan, it was appalled. It had expected to unload the tract in one fell swoop at a big speculative profit and it was unprepared to bring in settlers to America and put up any of its own money to build homes for them.

Indeed, Barlow, who had plunged into peddling the land in small lots to Frenchmen, soon became worried that he had bitten off more than he could digest. He wrote anxiously to Duer, "Don't for God's sake fail to raise money enough to put the people in proper legal possession of these lands I have sold them [otherwise] we are ruined. All our fortunes and my character will be buried in the ruins."

The first ship loaded with the unsuspecting French settlers arrived in Alexandria, Virginia, in 1790. Duer, anxious to keep their debarkment a secret so that it would not come to the attention of the government and land him in jail for selling land he had no legal title to, quietly sent an agent to meet the settlers, hustle them into wagons, and cart them into the wilds of Ohio where hopefully they would succeed in building a settlement without harassment from the Indians. But the settlers, whose expectations of the land they had bought had been inflated by the high-blown rhetoric and the brochures handed out by Barlow, were stunned.

They had expected to be greeted on their arrival, if not by a brass band, at least by a committee of leading citizens, furnished with the best French wines and viands, and escorted to a settlement of homes set amid lavish vineyards.

The émigrés constituted a motley crew. Some were high-ranking noblemen who, sensing that France was on the verge of a revolution, had sunk all their money into this American land investment, bringing with them workers to whom they had planned to sell subdivisions of the property they had acquired. Some arrived with a retinue of servants who had been recruited from French prisons for this opportunity of a new life. When this company reached the Northwest Territory and saw nothing but wilderness, it furiously denounced the real estate promoters who had misled it. A few of the settlers made their way back to New York and cornered Duer, threatening to disembowel him if he didn't return their money and provide passage home. The secretary of the treasury was equal to the occasion. He lavishly wined and dined his visitors, hinted broadly that thanks to his political connections he would enable them to unload their lands at a handsome profit to others, and consoled them with reports of another speculative deal on which they could make a really big financial killing. He had timberlands up in Maine, he said, that he was willing to give them a first shot at.

The colony of Gallipolis, as the Duer settlement came to be known, fared miserably. The French died in droves of hunger and disease. Only a few managed to get home. Meanwhile, Duer had plunged into a heavy new speculation in government bonds, lost disastrously, ending up a bankrupt in jail. Subsequently, the fortunes of this sharpie took a lively rebound; his son became president of Columbia University.

Another of the manipulators who came out smelling like a rose was Joel Barlow, the poet, who had used his considerable talent for rhetoric to inveigle a number of people into investing in the land swindle. Far from being hauled off to jail, Barlow rose high in political circles, becoming American minister to France. Barlow's poetry, if not his thievery, has outlived him. His *Columbiad* is required reading for students of early American literature.

One of the biggest land-jobbing deals in U.S. history was triggered by the founding of the City of Washington. After America won the Revolution, a number of the former colonies, seeking the commercial bonanza that would accrue to them if the capital were located within their borders, put in claims for the site. The debate was vigorous. Boston, where the first battles of the Revolution were fought, Philadelphia, where the colonial rebels had proclaimed independence, Yorktown, where Cornwallis had surrendered to lose the war, presented persuasive plans to the Congress. Finally, the politicians, to spare everyone's sensibilities, decreed that the capital would be located in none of these areas, but in the wilderness. Behind this decision lay sinewy political maneuvering. Alexander Hamilton had proposed a bill for the refunding of the Federal debt, that is, the redemption of the Continental script which had been used as currency by the Congress. Hamilton decided to push for redemption in order to reestablish the credit of the new government with the rest of the world. When news of this leaked to businessmen and bankers in the East, they sent agents out to canvass Revolutionary soldiers who had been given the script as pay, and who finding it had become virtually worthless, naïvely sold out to the business hustlers who paid them 10 to 15 cents on the dollar, on the gamble that it would be redeemed in full.

However, when Hamilton's refunding bill reached the floor of the Senate, it triggered a storm of protest by Congressmen representing the masses who had been fleeced of their paper money. The bill was fought to a stalemate in the House. Speculators, who had loaded up with the paper currency, began to sweat, fearing that Hamilton's plan would not go through.

But a compromise was struck in the Senate, largely through the overtures of Thomas Jefferson. Hamilton needed a single vote in the Senate and only five in the House to ram through his legislation. Jefferson was interested in a bill of his own. He wanted the new capital of the United States to be located as close as possible to his birthplace in Virginia. So a deal was struck. Hamilton got his redemption bill and Jefferson obtained his capital in a stretch of wilderness along the Potomac.

In July 1790, when Congress asked President Washington to

pick a site ten miles square on the Potomac, the engineer chosen to survey the territory and report on its suitability was Pierre Charles L'Enfant, a major who had fought with the American army. L'Enfant had grandiose plans for the capital of the infant republic. As a child he had been saturated in the atmosphere of Versailles, where his father resided as a court painter, and he believed that if the absolute monarchs of France had Versailles to display as a showcase, the citizens of the world's first democracy should be given a headquarters surpassing it in brilliance.

Thomas Jefferson, who besides being secretary of state was the superintendent of public buildings, heartily agreed with L'Enfant. The ground plan of ancient Babylon, he stated, was the finest the world had ever known, and the City of Washington should be built along these lines. L'Enfant envisaged a broad avenue of public buildings leading from the Capitol to the Presidential house. One would be a temple for a national celebration, he wrote, "such as public prayer, thanksgivings, funeral orations . . . and assigned to the special use of no particular sect . . . but equally open to all." The city was to be laid out in a series of public squares, each dedicated to a state that had entered the Union.

Once the area had been surveyed and the plans drawn, the land to be appropriated from its owners had to be paid for. The district, wilderness though it was, was held by a handful of wealthy landowners who had previously gobbled it up as a speculation, and now that their most optimistic hopes were about to be realized, they insisted vigorously on full compensation. There was a slight problem: the Founding Fathers may have envisaged a city that would beggar the splendor of Babylon and Nineveh, but the U.S. government was so broke it couldn't scrape up the cash to buy the land upon which this megapolis was to be built. Washington huddled with his associates to figure out a scheme for getting something for nothing.

What was hatched is disclosed in a letter the president wrote to Jefferson. "The terms entered into me on the part of the United States with the landholders of Georgetown and Carrollsburg are that all the land from Rock Creek along the river to the eastern branch . . . is ceded to the public on condition that when the whole shall be surveyed and laid off as a city . . . the present proprietors shall retain every *other* lot and for such possible land as may be taken for public use, they shall be allowed, at the rate of 25 pounds per acre, the public having the right to reserve such parts of the wood on the land as may be thought necessary to be preserved for ornaments.''

In short, the U.S. government got hold of 982 acres without offering a cent. *It planned to pay the owners for 541 of these acres out of the proceeds of a subsequent public sale of the property.* The President was confident that "everybody would acquiesce and show good will."

One half of the proposed tract was to be purchased by a committee of district commissioners for resale to the public. The other half would be kept by the original landowners.

In October 1791, President Washington and Thomas Jefferson repaired to a tavern in Georgetown to preside over the ceremony of opening the public bidding for these lots, which were priced by the government at from $150 to over $500 an acre. However, rank and file Americans weren't as enthusiastic over the prospects of this future Babylon as the politicians professed to be. All they could see were acres of nondescript forest and mud. Americans were extremely wary of buying anything from Uncle Sammy. Not so long before, they had been badly burned by accepting war certificates and seeing them dwindle in value to nothing. Moreover, the nation was suffering a business recession. Overseas the French Revolution had triggered a panic in banking circles throughout Europe. Stiffening credit lines had created anxiety in American financial quarters as well.

Only a handful of citizens showed up to buy the lots the government was peddling. So sluggish was the bidding that the embarrassed president abruptly broke it off to keep word from spreading how negatively Americans viewed the prospects of the nation's capital.

While the president called off the auction, he didn't give up trying. The city, which was named after him and on which he had staked his financial as well as personal prestige—he had bought a few lots on speculation himself—would be peddled to American land buyers, one way or another. A year later, when the cornerstone for the president's house was laid and the time seemed more propitious for real estate huckstering, a second attempt was made to auction off lots to the *Populus Americanus,* but again there were few nibbles. Realizing it was futile to try peddling a stake in the city of Washington to large numbers of individuals, the president and his crew decided that the only solution was to find a syndicate of big real estate operators with plenty of money to take over the financing.

At this point, the plight of President Washington and his cohorts came to the attention of Robert Morris, America's most majestic land speculator. During the Revolutionary War, Morris, as superintendent of finance, had fabricated a maze of banking deals, to raise huge sums of money and virtually single-handedly finance the Revolutionary War. Enjoying prime banking connections in Europe, blessed with an uncanny business sense and an insatiable appetite for the big gamble, Morris managed to wangle the necessary money to pay Washington, the Revolutionary armies, the salaries of the Continental Congress, and to keep the rebellion going during its darkest hours. When the Revolution was won and he left office, he continued to use his banking connections to enrich his own pockets. He plunged heavily into real estate transactions and wound up becoming the biggest land grabber in the new nation.

Indeed, even while serving as superintendent of finance during the war, Morris had been lining his purse. In 1780 he sent a letter to Silas Deane, the American commissioner to France, asking him to inquire of wealthy Europeans whether they would be interested in buying lands Morris had speculated in. An inveterate pragmatist, Morris figured that if America lost the war and he escaped hanging by the British, he could at least reap a financial windfall by peddling his properties to Europeans before the British seized them.

During the war Morris remained obsessed with the aim of marketing lands he had bought beyond the Alleghenies for pennies to buyers in Europe for dollars per acre. Like others of his estimable colleagues, Morris found himself up to his ears in options on lands he had grabbed for a down payment and not yet had title to. He was eager to pay off these options and grab the deeds before the actual transfers were made.

After the Revolution was won and England was removed from the scene, Morris plunged into land dealings on an even vaster scale. He owned or held title to seven million acres in half a dozen states comprising a baronial suzerainty whose magnitude has not been equaled in America since. Much of his land had been acquired from the Indians, and the redskins nicknamed their aggressive customer "the white man with the big belly," for Robert Morris's stomach was almost as wide as his ambitions.

During the heated political debate over where the new capital of the nation should be located, Morris got hold of three thousand acres along the Delaware River, and then having been appointed one of three commissioners delegated to select a site for the capital, he managed to push through Congress a resolution decreeing that the capital be located near the falls of the Delaware River— in the center of his land purchase. However, as noted, other politicians had interests of their own to promote, and the final site was located elsewhere.

When the government failed to peddle off to the public lots in the City of Washington, Robert Morris was ready to move onto the scene and pick up the pieces. Actually, he entered the venture at the recommendation of a business associate, James Greenleaf, who was a relative of the poet, Whittier. As a young man, Greenleaf had joined his family's shipping business. He was sent to Holland to represent the interests of his kin and he struck up a friendship with a coterie of Dutchmen who were speculating heavily in American land certificates. Upon his return to the United States, Greenleaf contacted Morris and suggested that they get into Washington real estate, promising that if they bought up the lots the district commissioners were holding, he would be able to unload them in Holland through his Dutch banking associates. Moreover, he added, he would be able to obtain from the Dutch bankers the loans necessary to buy the lots in the first place. The third speculator who joined the duo was John Nicholson, who as comptroller general of Pennsylvania had administered the disposal of public lands to war veterans, while pushing his own private speculations. Pennsylvania, whose treasury was bankrupt, had paid off its soldiers for losses suffered from the collapse of the Continental currency by handing them public lands. Nicholson, learning through his position as comptroller general where the most valuable acreage was located, grabbed it up at a discount from the war veterans. (It was the identical maneuver that other land jobbers had worked on soldiers who urgently needed cash.) While Nicholson amassed a huge tract of land this way, the financial burden of carrying it on speculation was so vast that he struck up a friendship with Morris, who was much wealthier than he and abundantly able to subsidize his operations. The two became aggressive partners in a number of profitable land deals.

Now this triumvirate, Morris, Greenleaf, and Nicholson, moved into the Washington arena with a highly astute scheme. They offered to buy up the unsold lots the district commissioners were stuck with and provide them with the funds to erect the necessary public buildings in Washington. As noted, the syndicate was counting on bankers in Amsterdam, not only to provide them with loans for the purchases, but also to help them find rich Hollanders on whom they could unload the lands. Had the strategy worked out as intended, American history would have experienced a fine ironic turn. The bulk of real estate in Washington, D.C., would have fallen into the hands of a clique of wealthy Dutchmen.

Acting on behalf of himself and his partners, Morris offered to buy seven thousand lots in Washington at $66.50 per lot, to be paid to the commissioners in installments. Moreover, to help the commissioners erect "magnificent public buildings"—the home for Congress, the house for the president—he offered to make them a loan of $2200 a month at 6 percent interest until the public buildings were completed.

Morris and his associates went blithely ahead with their scheme. It was a highly risky one, for they would not get full title to the property until they had completed their payments to the commissioners. Nevertheless, certain of being able to unload them easily, Morris was enthusiastic over the deal. "Washington building lots," he wrote a friend, "will continue rising in price for a hundred years to come."

President Washington, for his part, was delighted with the scheme—and not only for the patriotic reasons that money would be forthcoming to build the new Babylon. For the president was up to his periwig in his own land speculations. He had bought a number of lots in the capital for his personal account. (He purchased his first one on the west side of North Capitol Street between B and C streets. He bought a second lot in April 1794 in Square 21 of the City of Washington, and other lots in Square 632 on the west side of North Capitol Street between B and C streets.) Moreover, he advised friends to invest in lots of their own. (Some who took his advice plunged their life savings prematurely into Washington real estate and were wiped out.)

The Morris venture wound up disastrously, thanks to events the plunger could not foresee and over which he had no control. He had counted on getting loans from Dutch bankers and on unloading properties on Europeans, but unexpectedly the Napoleonic Wars broke out. Money grew extremely tight in Europe, and Morris' foreign banking sources suddenly dried up. Before its credit line was shut off by the Dutch bankers, the Morris syndicate had plunged heavily into debt on its purchases, issuing its own notes and signing for loans to be turned over to the Dutch banks. They hooked a number of buyers before it became known that the Dutch bankers refused to honor the drafts.

When the Dutch slammed the door, the syndicate tried to unload its properties on British buyers, and President Washington joined the promotion. With his own money at stake, the president induced his private secretary, Tobias Lear, to write a brochure which, issued in London, rhapsodized over the financial prospects of Washington real estate. The president had a double ax to grind. Not only had he put money into land all over the city, but he also had invested in a canal company which schemed to make the Potomac the principal artery of trade between the Atlantic Seaboard and the West. The growth of the City of Washington was a prerequisite to the success of both ventures.

With regard to Morris and his speculations, as with so many other real estate dealers before and after, the key to success lay in the timing. The problem was not only in evaluating the potential worth of the land purchased, but trying to guess the time span within which this value would be realized. Many speculators, obtaining land on steep margin and trapped heavily in debt, are unable to hold on long enough to have their realization come true and have had to yield up their land to others who reap the harvest they had foreseen for themselves.

Morris, in acquiring his lands, not only in Washington but even more particularly in the American West, had counted on the fact that Europeans would be eager to migrate to America, where society was a mobile, classless one in which they could move about freely, unburdened by the restrictions they suffered in Europe. The outbreak of the Napoleonic Wars and the invasion of the Continent by the French armies destroyed any hope of migration to America. The British fleet, in any event, blockading the Continent, would have made it impossible for emigrants to slip through. Moreover, the banking system was shaken up by the Napoleonic invasions, and the credit lines Morris had enjoyed during the Revolutionary War, and which he continued to depend on, suddenly evaporated. He found himself unable to carry his vast properties. Had Morris and his heirs been able to hold on for another generation or two, much of these lands would have quadrupled and skyrocketed in value for them. It would be another fifty years before immigration would swell to the proportions Morris had envisaged.

It was the disastrous Washington venture that broke the back of Morris's financial speculations. With the drying up of loans, the syndicate found itself unable to continue its installment payments to the district commissioners and it petitioned to be let out of its contracts. The lots were taken back by those worthies who were eased of their own financial predicament, at least partially, when the State of Maryland lent them $100,000 at 6 percent to enable them to continue erecting the buildings for Congress on Capitol Hill and the mansion to house the president a mile away.

Falling heavily into debt to the commissioners was only the

first of the misfortunes that toppled the financier of the American Revolution. Morris still held options on seven million acres of other land. He had gambled not to stay with it, improve it, and re-sell it, but to unload it as rapidly as possible on other gamblers. Inevitably, the chickens of his overoptimistic speculations came home to roost. In April 1795, the Bank of North America, from whom he had borrowed heavily, threatened to sue him unless he immediately paid off his loans. Since Morris was unable to bor-row further to carry his holdings, a pack of creditors closed in on him. Court actions were started on every side. Ironically, Morris had been one of the founders of the Bank of North America, which now was suing him; two other banks he had been instru-mental in founding, the Bank of the United States and the Bank of Pennsylvania, also joined the parade of creditors hounding him. The millions of acres of property he held were potentially worth a king's ransom, and yet under current conditions he was unable to raise a penny to prevent himself from being catapulted into bankruptcy.

Before the shadows descended, Morris made one final extrava-gant gesture. As the richest man in America (at least on paper), it was befitting that he build the nation's most ostentatious man-sion. He purchased an entire city block in Philadelphia for the site of his home, ordering sumptuous furniture from Europe, includ-ing sofas and tapestries from the chateaus of former French royalty. To warehouse the art and furniture that could not be crowded into the main living quarters, so numerous were his possessions, Morris had his architect, Pierre L'Enfant, build three stories underground honeycombed with passageways and vaults. As the plans for the house became increasingly elaborate, it took longer and longer to build. By the time Morris's debts had piled so high he was unable to continue to pay the architect, the marble edifice did not yet have a roof over it, its floors were only half finished and the masonry uncompleted. As the builder kept sending bills, Morris grew increasingly bitter and finally stopped his payments. The mansion lay half finished as crowds gathered around watching the rain pour into the unroofed rooms.

While his creditors pressed harder, Morris frantically tried to

28

unload his marble grotesquerie as payment for some of his debts, but his creditors refused to take it.

In those benighted days a man could be incarcerated for non-payment of his debts, and as the twilight closed in, the financier who had become the wealthiest real estate holder in America, sought refuge in his residence, called The Hills, which he turned into a fortress, locking the door against bailiffs to prevent being seized and carted off to prison. During 1797 and 1798, Morris was a prisoner in his home, held at bay by his creditors. John Nicholson, a partner in misadventure, who also went broke as a result of the Washington fiasco, was also hiding from his creditors, and a somber correspondence was carried on by the harried duo, their letters carried by a courier who sneaked through the lines of creditors besieging each house.

Morris didn't risk leaving the Hills, or even stepping outside his front door, for sheriffs were camped on the grounds waiting to nab him the moment he appeared. Morris wryly referred to his home as "Castle Defense."

He was bitter. He complained that any other nation, instead of hounding the man who had raised the money enabling it to win its independence, would honor him as its leading patriot. The bankers and other creditors who were so relentlessly harassing him might be hanging from gibbets, he observed, condemned by the British army if it weren't for him. The letters he wrote from Castle Defense to his associate Nicholson were interlarded with acid humor. Referring to the mass outbreak of litigation against him, he remarked, "A curse on all suits, say I. If they were good comfortable winter suits, one might dispose of them. The more the better. But these damn suits wherein a lawyer is the tailor are neither good for man, woman, child or beast." In another letter he observed, "God help us for men will not. We are abandoned by all those who want to get all we hold."

It was a quaint and terrible war of siege. Morris was like a fox surrounded by an army of huntsmen with loaded rifles and yapping dogs. To better observe the movements of his adversaries, he built a peephole in his kitchen and peered warily through it for hours at a time. On one occasion he wrote Nicholson, "I've been very busy this morning watching the man who was watching me. I rose early and lighted my fire . . . and casting my eyes towards the old peephole, there was my gentleman snug enough.''

Morris's fears weren't groundless. Hundreds of creditors, as a result of his numerous land deals, had come in person or sent lawyers or bailiffs to try to collect their debts. They formed an army camping around his property in tents, peering at his house through telescopes, watching for the opportunity to nab him should he open the door and emerge even for an instant. They tried all kinds of strategies to take Morris unawares. Some sought to bribe his gardener to open the door and let them in. One creditor, observing Morris appearing at the window, raised a rifle and threatened to shoot him if he did not hand over on the spot the money owed him. Surrounded on all sides and in constant fear, Morris became highly paranoiac. He accused his coachman of spying for his adversaries and refused to let him come near him.

Morris kept a dozen dogs on the property, and they were unleashed to roam the grounds and frighten away any bailiff who dared approach. Almost completely out of funds, he finally dismissed all his servants but one, his gardener, who acted as a one-man intelligence network.

One afternoon a sheriff appeared with half a dozen assistants. Three of them were stationed in a woods at the edge of Morris's property, armed with pickaxes and sledgehammers, prepared to rush the house when evening came. Morris, observing them from his peephole, beckoned to the leader of the party, and using all his talents of diplomacy, persuaded him to call off the attack.

From then on, Morris appeared frequently at the window to haggle with his creditors. He fended some off by improvising deals, assigning parcels of his property to be attached in partial payment of debts. He handed over one piece of furniture after another in his home. He bargained away all the shrubbery on his grounds—the plants, trees, and the orange groves he had acquired from the Orient. Finally, he handed over his silver dinner service.

Remaining shut up in his house for over a year resulted in severe discomfort for Morris. He was in his seventies and suffered from extreme corpulency. He was asthmatic, and the chimney which badly needed repairs, sent billows of smoke into his rooms, at times almost suffocating him. The windows were ill-fitting; the winter air seeped through, causing bitter cold. Yet he was afraid to open the door to allow any workmen to fix them. Once when a mechanic knocked to repair something in his kitchen, Morris in a state of extreme anxiety bid the man enter and then hurriedly bolted the door so that if the worker happened to be a sheriff in disguise, he would be locked in the house with him.

These continual cat-and-mouse maneuvers with his creditors undermined Morris's strength and sabotaged his will to resist. Resignedly, he adjusted to the fact that he must enter prison. In January 1798, he flung the doors open and let a bailiff enter, handing him a listing of the few of the possessions that still remained to him. His creditors had stripped him of virtually everything, leaving him only some clothing, bedding, several half-empty casks of Madeira wine, a few newspapers and books, a microscope, a single share of stock in the Bank of North America, which he had founded, and an antique watch that had belonged to his father. These he handed over to the sheriff to transmit to his creditors.

The following day, in the dead of winter, Morris entered the Prune Street Jail in Philadelphia, the prison he had once characterized as "a hotel with grated doors." Morris was neither the first nor the last real estate operator to go broke through the intoxication of his own optimism, but he was the only one who took the time from his incessant land transactions to save his brethren from George III's gallows.*

---

*Morris was released after three and a half years in prison, and he died in poverty five years later.

THE LITTLE FOXES
IN OLD MANHATTAN

*The Intrigues of the Astors in the City of
the "Big Drunk"*

As America left its colonial past behind and continued to fatten up its economic sinews, its land manipulators became more and more ambitious and increasingly adept at their financial legerdemain.

In the early days Americans acquired land beyond their original settlements simply by right of squatter's occupancy. They staked out as much territory as they could till. When other settlers joined them, boundaries were agreed upon through informal discussion. As the population grew, crude maps were drawn up and recorded with the community fathers so that titles could be substantiated in case of a dispute. Boundaries were delineated by elm trees, rivers, old farm fences, or simply stone markers often half hidden by ivy.

As the nation pushed westward and land allocation became more complex, the surveyor's trade burgeoned. An army of men skilled with compasses made a living this way. One of Abe Lincoln's earliest jobs was as a land surveyor in Sangamon County, Illinois. For each quarter section of land he measured, he received $2.50, and 25 cents for smaller town lots. Abe gained a reputation for being unusually accurate in his measurements and he was frequently called in to settle vexatious boundary squabbles. In one case he allowed his compassion to cloud his judgment. While surveying the town of Petersburg, Illinois, he surreptitiously laid out a street crookedly, since to have plotted it straight would have caused a widow he knew serious trouble. A section of her house would have fallen on the wrong end of the line and she would have been compelled to sell the property to allow for the digging of the street.

As the population increased and settlers pressed farther and farther westward, the need for efficient communications became increasingly paramount. The first links that tied the Eastern Seaboard to the lands west of the Alleghenies were roads built for military purposes during the French and Indian and Revolutionary wars. After the nation was launched, canal systems were dug to handle the increased commerce. At the close of the War of 1812, the nation embarked on a veritable orgy of canal building. Besides these "big ditches," Americans plunged into a road-building spree. In the legislation that admitted Ohio as a state into the Union, Congress for the first time authorized the Federal financing of highways, decreeing that part of the money received from the sale of public lands should be used to finance them. The first national road was started in the early 1800s. The initial stretch was built through Maryland, then extended into West Virginia and Ohio; a decade before the Civil War it reached Illinois, linking it to the rest of the Union.

Meanwhile, as opportunities for land acquisition burgeoned, the foundations were laid for the development of America's powerful real-estate families, many of whom have steadily expanded in influence. Indeed, no other business endeavor has been so dominated by family enterprises. While most industries are run by outside professional management, the real estate business to this day is largely a privately owned one handed down from father to son.

Although personal ambitions, frustrations, and irritations frequently trigger a clash between a son and his father, in most cases these are counterbalanced by one abiding consideration—pride in

33

the family succession and the desire of the clan to protect and perpetuate its holdings through the generations. Many land-rich nabobs, through skillful and devious ways, have managed to increase impressively their family fortunes. Although U.S. law specifically bans the outright entailment of large estates through the instrument of primogeniture (passing the estate intact from the founder to the oldest son, a device used for centuries in Great Britain), a number of landed dynasties have been able to circumvent this prohibition quite effectively, perpetuating their patrimony through elaborate trusts that allow the founder to exercise his control for a generation or more after his death.

Because of the sharp deterioration of the worth of the U.S. dollar, triggered by double-digit inflation and runaway prices, the strategy to preserve the family fortune has taken on new urgency in recent years. Confronted with today's sharp taxes on inheritance, heirs have been keeping their lawyers busy to the hilt fabricating new devices to hold onto what the family has accumulated. As Ferdinand Lundberg observes in *The Rich and the Super Rich,* "One of the surer ways of spotting truly big wealth is that it shows itself in huge public transfers of assets during the lifetime of the owner . . . many of the rich . . . die stripped of assets."

An especially skillful practitioner of the art of progressively stripping himself of his assets as he grows older is Henry Crown, of Chicago, one of today's richest real estate moguls. Now in his eighties, Crown has divested himself of millions of dollars over the years by distributing it among the members of his family. He spoke for many wealthy family heads when he recently told a reporter, "My objective is to make my net worth less at the end of any one year than it was at the beginning."

Despite the clannish loyalty of landed dynasties and their determination to preserve their possessions, there have been cases where the rift between fathers and sons has been sufficiently strong to tear the ties of family to pieces and completely redirect the employment of the inherited millions. The underlying tensions between a wealthy father and his heir can be enormous. As Harry Levinson, a professor at the Harvard School of Business points out, "The son resents being kept in an infantile role, always the little boy in his father's eyes—with accompanying contempt, condescension, and lack of confidence that frequently characterize the father's attitude."

In some instances the heirs have rebelled ideologically in an extreme fashion. An especially striking instance of a rebel who dismayed his family with his behavior was Rudolph Spreckels, heir to vast real estate and sugar properties in California and Hawaii who, at the turn of the century, took over leadership of the reform movement in San Francisco, bent on sending a number of wealthy associates of J. P. Morgan to jail for bribery. In attempting to "clean up the racketeering methods of Big Business," Spreckels was ostracized by his family and his social confreres who took their deposits out of the bank he headed and pushed him into financial ruin.

One dynasty, however, whose heirs have remained notoriously devoted to the ideals of its founder are the Astors of New York. Not only have the descendants of John Jacob I obediently carried on the lucrative job of adding to the family's real estate patrimony, but a branch of the family moved to England and showed how smitten it was with the worship of authority figures by behaving more royally than the monarchy itself. Ideologically in striking contrast to the latter-day Spreckelses, the Astors enjoy wealth that is older than the Spreckels fortune, for landed riches were accumulated along the Eastern Seaboard much earlier than in the West.

The wealthiest landowners in the East have sprung from New York, but it wasn't apparent until relatively late in the day that Manhattan real estate was destined to far outstrip in value the acreage of rival communities. Until the 1820s it was an open question whether the richest landholders would emerge in Philadelphia, Boston, or New York. For a number of years Philadelphia was in the lead. But when the Erie Canal was opened, New York forged ahead and became the top commercial center. The real estate sachems of Gotham eclipsed the shipping merchants in the magnitude of their fortunes. Enormous as were the latter, the shipping business was a hazardous one tied to the uncertainties of weather and the volatile fluctuations of cargo prices; and the shrewder merchants took the money they had wrested from the seas and put it into real estate.

Land was the pillar of Yankee wealth. The Declaration of Independence, which proclaimed that all men were equal, had very little effect upon the prerogatives of the wealthy landowners in the State of New York. The patroons for years after the birth of the nation continued to live as feudal lords.

While the founders of the great real estate fortunes in New York became the aristocracy of the new American Republic, their family trees were far from impressive. Fredrick Rhinelander and his brother William, started out as bakers on William Street. Peter Goelet began as an iron monger during the Revolution, before he made a fortune in Gotham real estate.

The second and third generations of Goelets were as pathologically miserly as their sweaty ancestor. Peter, the grandson, carried his penny pinching to such an extreme that, although he had accumulated $5 million in real estate holdings, he refused to pay a tailor to mend his pants. A colleague found him one day in his office of the Chemical Bank, laboriously patching them with a needle and thread. He maintained in his home a law library of ten thousand volumes, but he'd be damned if he'd pay a lawyer for advice he could get for nothing from his books. He kept a cow in a stable in his backyard to provide him with his daily glass of milk, and he tugged the teats himself to save the price of a servant.

As for Manhattan—the lusty little town in which these land holders wheeled and dealt their way to riches—historians point out that it was an arena of plunder long before the birth of the Republic. Some linguists aver that the name "Manhattan" was derived from a word in an Indian dialect meaning the "Place of the Big Drunk." Peter Minuit is said to have bought Manhattan for trinkets worth 60 guilders, or $24. It seemed at the time that the white man had wangled a remarkably shrewd deal, although considering the current state of Gotham's finances one can't be too sure that he really outsmarted the Indians.

Some historians charge that the Dutch robbed the Indians

blind, telling them they wished to buy only a few garden plots, but after the contract was signed, grabbing up the entire island. In any event there are more American Indians living in New York City today than when Peter Minuit bought it. (According to the 1970 census ten thousand Indians were residing in Gotham, representing sixty-five tribes, most of them originating from west of the Mississippi.)

From the beginning Manhattan was the breeding ground of inspired eccentrics. In the early 1800s, a carpenter named Lozier came up with an extraordinary notion. The city he feared was dangerously overweighted by buildings on its lower end and if any more structures went up there, it would sink into the Hudson River. To prevent this calamity, Lozier proposed to the mayor that a chunk of Manhattan's northern end be sawed off, towed down the Hudson, and attached to the southern tip so as to redistribute the island's weight. His honor was immensely impressed with Lozier's ingenuity and told him to go ahead.

Lozier advertised for an army of laborers to help him execute his plastic surgery. Five hundred men showed up one wintry morning. For several hours they stood in the cold, stamping their feet and blowing on their hands, waiting for the boss to show up. But the contractor had absconded the previous night with a bushel of money the mayor had handed him from the city treasury to finance the project.

The *hoi polloi* may have been excessively naïve to fall for this real estate swindle, but the municipal fathers were prey to serious miscalculations of their own. They scoffed at the notion that New York would ever extend beyond the limits of what today is Fortieth Street. One civic leader pontificated, "It is improbable that for centuries to come the grounds north of the Haerlem Flats [Harlem] would be occupied with houses."

Since he and his colleagues envisaged a city whose traffic would move chiefly between the East and Hudson rivers, they laid out numerous narrow streets running from east to west, intersected by only a few avenues running at right angles. The result was a nightmarish imbalance—a preponderance of narrow thin lines extending from river to river, crammed with houses facing north and south, starving from a dearth of sunlight. While Gotham has been labeled "Fun City," large areas of it can by no stretch of the imagination be called "Sun City," thanks to the blunder of its early engineers.

The man who reaped America's first great fortune was John Jacob Astor, the German immigrant who made his initial money trading Indian furs. Lowborn, uneducated, Astor never learned to speak English properly. To the end he carried on his business in an accent redolent of the Hamburg gutters. Yet this didn't prevent him from founding America's most elite family of blue bloods. Astor sold his skins all over the world, reaping, on a capital of one million, annual returns of half a million dollars. An especially lucrative market was China which bought his furs for cargoes of tea which reaped fancy prices in Manhattan. During the War of 1812, the price of tea doubled because of the British blockade. Astor's ships managed to elude the British navy and for a time he was the only merchant successfully to bring tea into New York at stiff prices.

Astor plunged most of his profits into buying up real estate properties in New York. In the first decade of the nineteenth century, "The Place of the Big Drunk" was a shabby little community. When Astor decided to put $300,000 into Manhattan real estate, his friends were aghast. Only a short time previously a Southern squire who had invested money in a tract on Manhattan was arraigned in lunacy proceedings by his distraught relatives. New York was the ugly duckling among American cities, not to be compared with Baltimore, Boston, or Philadelphia. The most that experts could envisage for New York was that it might extend its frontiers from the Battery as far north as Greenwich Village in the next century or so, provided that Manhattanites were willing to build homes that far north and spend two hours a day traveling to and from work. When Astor began buying property in 1804, no one could have foreseen that within twenty years a canal would be built—the Erie—linking New York by waterway with the Great Lakes and turning it into the number one commercial center of the nation.

Compared with his contemporaries, Astor's insight was prodigious. He not only envisaged that farmlands and cow pastures lying far north of Greenwich Village would ultimately skyrocket in value, but he had the patience to sink money that yielded no immediate interest into properties that might not be subdivided into lots for generations because the demand was not there.

However, the main thrust of Astor's initial buying was not in outlying farm lands—these were the long-term speculations; it was in the center of Manhattan that he made his first big coups. He received from city politicians (susceptible to Astor bribes) grants of underwater land at giveaway prices. In those days the banks of the Hudson and East rivers extended much farther inland than now, and the downtown area was mottled with streams of marshland. The recipient of a city grant got land under very shallow water and he filled it in with ground on which he built wharves and warehouses. Some land, handed over for a pittance, ultimately yielded hundreds of millions of dollars.

Astor operated like an expert chess player who was several moves ahead of his opponent. On one occasion he offered to sell a lot in Wall Street for $8,000. The price was low compared with what surrounding areas were going for. To an associate who expressed surprise, Astor confided, "You are astonished, but see vot I intend to do with that eight thousand dollars you gave me. The Wall Street lot, it is true, vill be worth twelve thousand dollars in a few years, but I shall take the eight thousand and buy eighty lots above Canal Street. I can buy them for a song up there vay out in the wilderness and by the time your von lot is worth twelve thousand *my eighty lots* vill be worth eighty thousand."

Astor was a tough bargainer. His neighbor Cornelius Vanderbilt, no business novice himself, once borrowed money from him on a mortgage. The date of the final payment slipped Vanderbilt's mind. The next morning he apologetically sent a servant around to Astor with the money. "I don't vant the money, I'll take de land," Astor retorted. While Vanderbilt held the mortgage, the property had appreciated enormously.

Astor tracked down promising properties with the single-mindedness of a bloodhound. He closely followed the affairs of one family whose farms sloped down the Bloomingdale Road to the

Hudson River north of what was to become Forty-second Street. The heir to the farm was a spendthrift who had wasted his inheritance and was on the verge of bankruptcy. When he turned up in chancellery court, Astor was waiting for him with an associate. They bid $25,000 for seventy acres of his farmland and got it. The partners divided their land, Astor taking the parcel nearest the Bloomingdale Road. A century later this acreage, which lay adjacent to what today is Broadway, was worth $20 million.

In one deal Astor became the owner of a valuable farm extending from Fifty-third to Fifty-seventh Street and westward to the Hudson River. He got the property for $23,000 by foreclosing a mortgage. It now lies in the very center of Manhattan.

To succeed, a real estate operator sometimes has to display the patience of Job. The greatest test Astor's patience was put to was waiting for an old widow to die. Mary Philipse Morris was a loyalist during the Revolutionary War who had fled with her husband to England when the British were defeated. Some years later it was found that Mrs. Morris held only a life estate in her confiscated lands and that upon her death they would revert to her children who had not abandoned the Revolutionary cause. Astor, who salivated at the smell of a bargain, was eager to pay the heirs for their right to the estate, but he had to wait for the old lady to die. She was seventy at the time. Astor waited for sixteen years. The widow refused to expire. Finally Astor petitioned the legislature to pass a law enabling it to buy the property and make a deal with him, but it declined to do so. When the indestructible widow reached the age of eighty-six, Astor still refused to give up hope, noting to a friend, "The life of Mrs. Morris is, according to my calculations, worth little or nothing, she being eighty-six years of age." But Astor was overly sanguine. The widow continued to the age of ninety-six. Then only after a complicated wrangle with the heirs was Astor able to gobble up the property.

Astor not only snatched undeveloped land but did some building of his own. In 1830 he bought all the property lying between Vesey and Barclay streets on Broadway to put up America's most lavish hotel. So that neighborhood landlords would not be alerted to his intentions and jack up the price for their lots, Astor executed his plan with the utmost secrecy. To divert attention from his real purpose, he took a trip out of the city, telling friends he needed a vacation. Meanwhile his agents secretly bought up the necessary lots at bargain prices. To leverage his investment, Astor borrowed heavily from the Chemical Bank.

At the time the Tremont Hotel in Boston was America's fanciest hostelry and Astor wanted to rival this with a rookery of even greater magnificence. To this end he hired Isaiah Rogers, the architect who had designed the Tremont. The cornerstone for the Astor House was laid on July 4, 1834. Built for $5 million, it was considered to be one of the architectural marvels of the day. (Hot water pumped by steam to the upper floors was a novelty in those times; only the Astor had it. Hot water, however, was only for washing one's face and hands for shaving. Technology had not yet reached the point where it could be employed for bathtubs and toilets.) The Astor House was lit by gas lamps instead of the customary candles, the hotel offered free soap for the guests, the services of a French chef, and keys for individual rooms—a rare luxury.

The final touch was the shop on the ground floor where guests could buy expensive Havana cigars peddled by a lissome lassie by the name of Mary Rogers. One night the counter girl mysteriously disappeared. The police discovered her body floating in the Hudson River. No clues were found and the cops were unable to solve the mystery. But a young journalist who had arrived recently in New York and read the newspaper accounts of Mary's death wrote a short story about it. Ingeniously reconstructing the crime, Edgar Allan Poe thought up a motive and means of murder that actually led to the arrest of the real killer. Poe's story "The Mystery of Marie Roget" was a striking example of Oscar Wilde's dictum that life is an imitator of art.

John Jacob Astor died in 1848, at the age of eighty-five, the richest man in America, possessing a fortune of over $20 million. He was roundly lambasted in the press. James Gordon Bennett, the publisher of the *Herald,* called him a "money machine" and declared that one-half of his property belonged to the people of New York from whom he had plundered it. Twenty million dollars was an unprecedented sum for those days, and many Americans refused to believe that a man could amass it honestly.

For years after Astor's death, bizarre rumors were spread about how he had actually become rich. One widely circulated story was that Astor had found the treasure that Captain Kidd, the pirate, had buried before he was hanged on an island off the Maine coast, and that the buccaneer's loot had financed his real estate dealings. One New Yorker, Franklin Head, claimed he had irrefutable proof that Astor, as late as 1799, was only a moderately successful furrier whose bank account totaled $4000. Two years later, Head alleged, more than $500,000 was deposited to Astor's account, representing the gold Astor had dug up from Captain Kidd's hiding place.

Another individual, Frederick Olmsted, insisted he was the owner of the island where the treasure was found and he sued the Astor estate for $5 million. Several other claims were made by aspirants who wistfully eyed the Astor inheritance. Eighty years after the founder's death, nine hundred members of an exceedingly fertile family, the Emericks, filed a claim for the Astor estate. The Emerick heirs produced a contract they said had been signed in 1787, establishing a partnership between their ancestor, John Nicholas Emerick, and Astor, giving Emerick a two-thirds share in all business enterprises in which the two might be involved. The stubborn clan of Emericks pursued this suit for years, producing documents left and right to support their allegations. They even dug up a will which they claimed was written by their ancestor in a spidery, ungrammatical hand. "I state John Astor was a poor boy. I loan him money and teach him the business." Despite this, the courts finally rejected the Emericks' claim and the Astors kept their cash.

Rich men hope to achieve some crumbs of immortality in passing their wealth on to the heirs. But Astor's oldest son, John Jacob II, hardly qualified as a worthy recipient. He was born an imbecile and the family kept him out of sight, confining him to a residence which functioned as a private lunatic asylum. All sorts of rumors spread about the occupant behind the high stone walls. Superstitious New Yorkers crossed themselves whenever they passed the gate. A physician had been hired at a salary of $5000 a year to care for the idiot who was a huge, powerfully built fellow. Whenever Astor erupted in fits of rage, going around smashing furniture, the doctor would grab him and shake him. "For God sake, Astor, behave like a man." Eventually the family complained it couldn't afford to pay the doctor his $5000-a-year salary and it tried to cut it in half. But the medico stood his ground. The battle over his wages went on until the deranged man ended it by dying.

The Astors, like other wealthy families, had a plethora of eccentric offshoots. One collateral descendant, a niece of Mrs. Astor, the *doyenne* of American society, married an oddball who cropped up in the press from time to time as a result of some embarrassing capers. He once beat the stuffings out of a fellow whom he charged with insulting one of his girlfriends. Then smitten with guilt for having attacked the man, he plunged the hand that had done the thrashing into a blazing fire, burning it to the bones of his fingers. It had to be amputated.

Another relative, John Armstrong Chandler, was a chronic lunatic who during his confinements in an asylum became a mystic. He developed a flare for automatic writing, turning out a novel which he claimed had been dictated to him by the spirit of Machiavelli and sonnets by Boccaccio and Petrarch. During periods when he was let out of the asylum, he walked the streets with a multicolored cockatoo perched on his shoulder which flung obscene language at passersby. He wrote several plays, delivered lectures on the Second Coming of Christ, and announced that he, Chandler, had developed an X-ray faculty which revealed to him the secret of the afterlife.

William Backhouse Astor, Jacob's second oldest son who inherited the family leadership, had a personality that was in stark contrast to his more exotic relatives. He was a drudge who kept obsessively adding to his father's millions without enjoying any kind of recreation, displaying the slightest *joie de vivre,* or uttering a single quotable syllable during his entire life. Although he was the richest man in America, he traveled nowhere. Only once upon graduating college he had made bold to take a brief vacation in Europe. But that was his first and final indiscretion. Remarks one biographer, "He sat in his office as if it were a house of detention, to which his father had condemned him for life."

William Astor was fifty-six when he took over his father's business. Previously he had amassed a fortune on his own through land and banking operations. He inherited another $500,000 from his father's brother, Henry, a prosperous butcher on the Bowery. By the time of his father's death, William was personally worth $5 million.

William Astor raised niggardliness to an exquisite art. While well-to-do New Yorkers rode to work in their carriages, William walked to his office and performed all his business errands on foot to save the fare. Like Alberich in the *Ring of the Nibelungen* he sat broodingly on his horde of gold, growing richer by the hour.

By 1875, Astor owned over seven hundred buildings and houses, besides numerous acres of raw land. He knew every inch of his property, every bond, contract, and lease that was registered in his name. No tenant could put in a pane of glass without his personal inspection.

Astor's method of operation was highly effective. Although he owned hundreds of lots throughout Manhattan, he took title only to the ground rents and permitted his tenants to erect their own buildings on leases which generally ran for twenty-one years. The lessee rented the building, paid all the taxes and assessments, and assumed the entire burden of upkeep. This strategy relieved Astor of the responsibilities of daily management, but enabled him to skim the cream of the profits. This same device was followed by the Goelets, the Rhinelanders, the Stuyvesants, and other successful realtors in Manhattan and has been carried on to this day.

As for unimproved lots, Astor held on to them until they were ready to rot before selling them. He took over from the senior Astor hundreds of properties above Fourteenth Street, put fences around them, and permitted them to decay under mountains of garbage. As the population of New York moved northward, these dung heaps developed into notorious eyesores, offensive to the businessmen and homeowners around them. Astor held on, knowing that his desperate neighbors would buy him out at outrageously high prices to keep the value of their own property from skidding.

As the Astor fortune grew (it reached over $200 million by the turn of the century), the family money wiped away the smell of its early lowly origins. William Astor II married into the impeccable old Dutch family of Schermerhorns, and the Astor name was consecrated with patrician blood.

In the meantime, intrafamily squabbles became increasingly devastating. One feud was directly responsible for a real estate investment that launched New York's most illustrious hotel. During the nineteenth century William Waldorf Astor III, the great-grandson of the founder, who was a misogynist with an abnormal streak of sensitivity and a craving for self-grandeur, aspired to be a leader of American society; but the spotlight was taken away from him by his even more ambitious aunt, the wife of his uncle, Mrs. William Astor known as *The* Mrs. Astor, who had clawed her way to become the queen of the beau monde. Poor William couldn't stand playing second fiddle to his overbearing aunt, especially since he was head of the family by right of birth and had as a wife a Mrs. Astor of his own. He decided to quit America and live among the British who appreciated "genuine blue bloods." But before going into exile, he was struck with an idea for getting even with his aunt. His mansion, located on the northwest corner of Fifth Avenue and Thirty-first Street, was next door to the residence of *The* Mrs. Astor. He decided to raze his home and use the site to build New York's tallest hotel. This he gleefully estimated would block off Mrs. Astor's vista from her magnificent garden, a view in which she took so much pride.

So William leveled his Fifth Avenue residence and plunged $7 million into building the Waldorf Hotel. In 1894, a year after the hotel opened, Mrs. Astor gave in. She engaged Richard Morris Hunt, an architect, to build her a new residence far uptown, away from the machinations of her nephew. In the grand manner of a medieval king of England undertaking a diplomatic parley with the king of France, as reported in a Shakespeare chronicle play, John Jacob IV met with his cousin William to see if they couldn't work out something to their mutual benefit. While these cousins hated one another, they shared one indestructible family instinct—a lust to amass more money. *The* Mrs. Astor's son agreed to erect on the site of his mother's former home another hotel even taller and more splendacious than the thirteen-story Waldorf being built on the adjoining lot. The cousins further decided that the hotels, the Waldorf and the Astoria, would be architecturally designed to be operated as a single hostelry; but John Jacob at the last moment couldn't resist giving his cousin the needle. He slyly inserted into the contract a clause providing that, if and whenever he so desired, every interior passageway uniting the two hotels could be permanently walled up. In short, if conditions between the feuding branches of the family deteriorated, John Jacob could shut his hotel off from his cousin's at a moment's notice.

The Astors put $13 million into the venture and William's revenge was sweet. He was not only quitting the country that refused to accept him at his own worth (in addition to his being upstaged by his aunt, New Yorkers had dared to vote down his bid for the governorship of New York), but he was leaving behind a hotel that would become celebrated around the world, and would perpetually remind New Yorkers of their folly in rejecting him.

Few Manhattanites were aware that the Waldorf and the Astoria had been built as separate hotels; that the Waldorf for years retained its own boiler and engine room equipment; that the hostelry was constantly threatened with being split in two if any friction developed between the cousins who owned it. Together the hotels were able to lodge a thousand guests and they dwarfed John Jacob's Astor House in splendor. The old gentleman had installed steam heating, a striking novelty for the day. The Waldorf Astoria had a private bath for each guest room. It was lit with electric lights.

The hotel became the choice place of America's *haut monde.* Its most celebrated area was a three-hundred-foot gallery that led off the main lobby where Wall Street captains of finance promenaded with their ladies, after a tipple at the Waldorf Bar and a banquet at the Astor restaurant, while New York's middle and

lower classes looked on like French peasants gapi\
eantry of Louis XIV's court. The passageway was a\
dubbed "Peacock Alley" in an era of elegant narcissi\
personal income taxes, when money was freely made an\
away. There is a story that William Waldorf, the moody a\
nifico whose anger at his aunt was responsible for this gh\
water hole, entered it only once during his lifetime, strode\
vously and rapidly along "Peacock Alley," his eyes cast dow\
the fancy velvet red carpet, hurrying into an elevator to avoid \
ing recognized by passersby. Then he left for England and neve\
set foot in America again.

The British Astors ultimately became more Royalist than the
monarchy, but unlike poor George III, they made sure to hold on
to their vast properties in America from which they had derived
the bulk of their wealth. Since they also escaped the stiff income
taxes the British government imposed on real estate in Britain after the First World War, the British Astors had the best of both
possible worlds.

For all their eccentricities, the Astors were highly pragmatic in
the one area where it counted. They were the biggest landlords in
New York. By 1900, when the family fortune had burgeoned to
over $200 million, quintupling in the last twenty-five years alone,
financial pundits predicted that it would snowball until it reached,
at the very least, $1 billion by 1920, and $80 billion by the year
2000.

In those days, the exponential curve of America's expectations
seemed limitless, for Manhattan was growing by leaps and
bounds. Its pace astounded even its most sanguine boosters. As
Manhattan stretched northward, a need developed to build a station serving as a terminal for trains steaming into the city. To
meet the situation, William Vanderbilt, the son of old "Corneel,"
and the chief owner of the New York Central Railroad, had the
notion of building a "Grand Central" train depot on Forty-
second Street. Realtors warned Vanderbilt that it was a ridiculous
idea, since the location was too far uptown to ever be used. One
newspaper carried an editorial wisecracking that Vanderbilt's station should be called "End of the World." The trip from the Bat-

tery which was at the time, still the center of the city, to Forty-second Street and back, was half a day's journey by horse and carriage. Yet Vanderbilt doggedly pursued his scheme. When Grand Central was completed, it was the only commercial building for miles around, surrounded by acres of meadows and pastureland. The financier used land just west of the station to pasture his favorite racehorse Maude, a celebrated trophy winner, and Vanderbilt enjoyed watching from his office window the gelding romp about in the pastures.

Vanderbilt had guessed right. The business center shifted northward. Within a couple of generations the train traffic into Grand Central became so heavy that the city, to prevent further pollution of the atmosphere, ordered steam engines entering New York to be changed to electric power and the New York Central to cover up its railroad tracks from Ninety-sixth Street to the station, by converting this approach into an underground tunnel for the trains. The pavement laid over the railroad tracks became Park Avenue, one of the world's richest thoroughfares. A massive new real estate boom was launched as speculators grabbed leases and put up luxury apartments over right-of-way property for America's wealthiest tenants. The Vanderbilt family and other major stockholders, who had at first bitterly objected to the cost of covering the railroad tracks, overnight found themselves in possession of one of the most lucrative acres on this planet.

All this however took place in a later era. Back in the 1860s the city was growing so rapidly it experienced a major traffic problem, and a crisis developed over its transportation system.

As real estate speculators began aggressively developing properties north of Fiftieth Street, they and other businessmen demanded a speedier method of travel than tramcars and horse-driven carriages. Various schemes were mulled over. One syndicate of landowners, which had speculated heavily in outlying properties and was eager to bring them within convenient commuting distance, came up with the notion of building a giant machine that would blast air against the rear wheels of a passenger car and send it shooting through a pneumatic tunnel like a sailboat skimming in the breeze. They figured that thirty thousand Manhattanites could be blown to work hourly from the tip of the Battery to Harlem.

Another syndicate promoted an alternative scheme—to construct a mammoth thoroughfare, thirty feet below Broadway, complete with sidewalks, lamplights, and tracks for steam trains. But John Jacob Astor IV and other rich landlords, fearing their buildings would collapse if digging was permitted underneath them, successfully blocked the scheme.

Thwarted from going underground, the city went into the air. A network of elevated railroads was built from the Battery to Central Park, via Sixth Avenue and over Second, Third, and Ninth avenues. Steam engines pulled cars along the elevated structures to the Harlem River at the chilling speed of twenty-five miles an hour, and they created havoc with city life. Horses reared and stampeded at the sound of the monster trains rattling overhead. At first few New Yorkers could be induced to travel in them. Urbanites were certain they would jump the tracks and crash into the street. One Manhattanite, a wild-game hunter upon his return from stalking lions in Africa, ventured on his first elevated train trip. When it swung into a curve on a trestle above Ninth Avenue, he grew violently ill and pleaded to be taken off and returned to the comparative safety of the African veld.

While the steam monsters rumbled overhead, traffic continued to increase at the street level, and the city wrestled with the problem of coping with mounting filth. An army of horses pulling carriages, buses, and tramcars unleashed mountains of manure that dropped randomly on lordly Fifth Avenue and slum alley alike. The lords of finance strolling with their grand dames were frequently showered with clouds of dried horse manure when a stiff wind blew, and they castigated the city fathers for not keeping the streets cleaner. Numerous attempts were made to do the job more efficiently, but the problem was not solved until Colonel George Waring, who had been a cavalry officer during the Civil War, was appointed head of the Sanitation Department. A psychologist long before the tribe officially existed, Waring organized his street cleaners into a brigade, put them into sparkling white uniforms, calling them, "Waring's White Wings."

Then Waring added a final touch. Instead of laboriously hauling away the manure a shovelful at a time, the "White Wings" were given little tanks on wheels to lug the stuff. It took more money from the city treasury, but productivity along with morale sky-rocketed. Each year, Waring led a grand parade of his white-uniformed group down Fifth Avenue. When the colonel passed the reviewing stand, he reined in his horse to face the mayor and other dignitaries and smartly sidestepped his way amidst the thundering ovation.

Meanwhile as Manhattan grew out of its knee pants and property values increased, the indulgences of some of its dealers in real estate became increasingly eccentric. The city teemed with bizarre land transactions that have stamped their mark on many a street corner.

For instance, Hyman Sarner, a merchant, owned several lots on East Eighty-second Street. He wanted to build apartment houses on one of his properties which reached almost to Lexington Avenue. Next to him on the Lexington Avenue side there was a lot only five feet wide which was too small for a building, but which would fit nicely into Sarner's plan if he could combine it with his other holdings. Sarner offered the owner, Joseph Richardson, $1000 for the lot, but the latter insisted it was worth $5000 at least. When Sarner refused to pay this, Richardson, a crusty old coot, slammed the door in his face. Sarner proceeded to build his apartment houses, arranging to have one view overlooking Lexington Avenue. When the houses were completed, Richardson, smarting over Sarner's refusal to buy him out, took his revenge. He told his daughter, "I shall build a house on my little strip that will block the view from Sarner's windows on the lower floors. He'll wish he had paid me the five thousand dollars I asked for." Richardson's daughter told her father he was crazy to think of building a house on land only five feet wide. But the old man was adamant. "Not only will I build the house, but I will live in it. Not everybody is fat. There will be room enough in my dwelling for folk who aren't sideshow freaks."

Sure enough Richardson built a house five feet wide and four stories high that blocked off the view from Sarner's apartment houses. Only the smallest furniture could be fitted into this Lilliputian dwelling. The hallway was so narrow a person, to pass another, had to dodge into a room until the other had gone by. The dining room was twenty inches wide. The chairs were proportionately tiny. The kitchen stove was a miniature model. Old Joseph Richardson lived gleefully in his "spite house," as the neighbors called it, to the ripe age of eighty-four, before he passed on to his presumably tiny reward.

New York was sprouting up in a haphazard fashion, dictated by the greed and whims of its real estate hustlers. And whatever beauty of architecture cropped up here and there was entirely fortuitous. H. L. Mencken once remarked that Americans seemed to have a positive "libido for the ugly. Here is something that the psychologists have so far neglected; the love of ugliness for its own sake."

Mencken who moved heaven and earth for a wicked witticism was perhaps being unduly nasty. Nevertheless, the architecture of New York and other American cities is hardly a towering example of happy aesthetics. This is because the overwhelming majority of real estate ventures have been launched as financial speculations. When a contractor sets out to build a structure, he hires an architect to do the designing for him. The contractor builds for as little cash as he can get away with and the architect on his payroll dutifully cuts corners and turns out, not what is artistic, but commercially practical.

William Zeckendorf, as noted, the biggest realtor in America after the Second World War, declared in a speech, "The rebel [architect] who would design only things of great beauty can find no clients or only a few . . . who are as crazy as he is."

Even if the contractor were bold enough to indulge in the luxury of sophisticated good taste, pointed out Zeckendorf, the banks and insurance firms who lend him his money would quickly disabuse him of this eccentricity. They are afraid of being criticized for lending cash on something that's never been done before. If it doesn't sell, their stockholders won't spare them. With the moneylender and the contractor manipulating the strings, the rank-and-file architect is a puppet who dutifully caters to the public's craving for aesthetic mediocrity.

Occasionally, however, an architect comes along who because

of his talents and influence breaks out of the economic shackles and transforms the grubby business of real estate huckstering into a serious profession and even a fine art. One such was Stanford White, a New Yorker who was unbeholden to builders or bankers because he had the ability to ingratiate himself with the wealthiest of American sachems who begged him to build homes and offices of distinction for them. White didn't have to come hat in hand to the moneybags, because J. P. Morgan, the biggest of them, was his personal friend.

For a brief golden moment, the architect transported the culture of the Old World into Manhattan, substituting for the crabby brick and granite of its traditional architecture the splendor of ancient Greece, Rome and Medieval Spain. White came of a distinguished pedigree. An ancestor landed in Boston as early as 1632. White's father, Richard Grant White, was one of the most admired scholars of nineteenth-century America. Born in 1853, Stanford, on the advice of John La Farge, the painter, abandoned the idea of becoming one himself and decided to be an architect. In 1872, at the age of nineteen, he served an apprenticeship with Henry Richardson, a leading American architect. White's five years with the Richardson firm gave him a solid foundation for his profession. Upon launching it he came to be lionized by New Yorkers, for almost single-handedly he transformed Manhattan into a visual lyrical experience. A wealth of public buildings and monuments came from his draftsman's desk.

The first important one, the Washington Arch, was built in marble and granite along ancient Roman lines, similar to the Arch of Titus. Located at the base of Fifth Avenue, and designed for the centennial celebration of George Washington's inauguration, it was the work that first made White nationally famous. Two years later, White designed the Madison Square Garden which became the most talked about monument of real estate in New York. A combined dining and amusement center, its architecture was a blend of Italian and Moorish styles set off by a magnificent central tower inspired by the Giralda in Seville, which White greatly admired. On top of this edifice was the ultimate soupçon—the naked statue of Diana, the huntress. Sculptured by White's friend

The Little Foxes in Old Manhattan

Augustus Saint-Gaudens, it raised the hackles of ministers, spinsters, and other custodians of public morals who were outraged at the audacity of placing a nude Diana on a roof to entice the throngs of passersby. The bluenoses accused White of perverting the education of little children with his "European tricks."

In addition to enlivening amusement centers with architectural gaiety, White clothed sober commercial buildings in ebullient attire. He designed the Bowery Savings Bank at Grand Street in the Renaissance style. He placed another Renaissance-styled bank on the northwest corner of Fifth Avenue and Thirty-fourth Street. He imparted the mood of fifteenth-century Italy to Russeks and the Sherry's Hotel at Fifth Avenue and Forty-fourth Street. He turned Tiffany's, the celebrated jewelry store, into a Renaissance palace. Its exterior was virtually a reproduction of the Palazzo Vendramini in Venice—an enchanting environment for the world's most extraordinary display of diamonds. For the mundane quarters of the newspaper, the *New York Herald,* White conjured up a replica of the Conciglio Palace in Verona.

Under James Gordon Bennett's stewardship, the *Herald* had become one of America's most conspicuous newspapers. When Bennett decided to move into larger quarters at the intersection of Sixth Avenue and Broadway, he retained Stanford White as the architect. The latter obliged by importing medieval Verona to Manhattan, and as a final touch he designed for the roof of the palace a huge bronze clock. Punctually, every hour, mechanical dolls emerged to strike a gong to the cheers of the sidewalk oglers.

White had a host of clients with elephantine egos, but none was more so afflicted than Bennett, the publisher. For years Bennett brooded over his death, speculating about his prospects for posthumous fame. While still strutting through the vale of the living, he commissioned White to build a mausoleum that would excite the envy of all the other rich hidalgos preparing for their ferry ride across the Styx. On Bennett's property in Washington Heights, White designed a massive marble tomb, atop which perched a stone owl 120 feet high. This bird of wisdom, meant to symbolize Bennett's career as a journalistic oracle, was to be scooped completely hollow inside to allow for a winding staircase to carry tourists up to the two luminous eyes of the owl from which they could peer out upon the city Bennett had amused for years with his high-handed eccentricities. The publisher had planned to plunge $1 million into this memorial.

But his plans were cut short by a change in Stanford White's own itinerary. The architect, who was a celebrated playboy, was murdered at the age of fifty-three by Harry Thaw, a Pittsburgh millionaire, over the affections of Thaw's show-girl wife.

White's murder was a severe loss to New York. Several years after the architect's death, Arnold Bennett, the British novelist, paid a visit to Manhattan. As he drove up Fifth Avenue, passing the mansions designed by White, he turned to a friend. "Fifth Avenue reminds me of Florence and The Strozzi . . . the cornices, you know." Passing Tiffany's on his journey of discovery, Bennett marveled over what a splendid re-creation it was of the palaces along Venice's Grand Canal.

If White had lived, some students of architecture believe, he might have prevented much of the ugliness that subsequently overtook Manhattan as real estate builders rushed in mindlessly to exploit the Skyscraper Era. As it is, the realtors didn't wait long to tear down most of what he had built. The last edifice White designed before his death, one of his most gracious, was Dr. Charles Parkhurst's church. Designed in the Georgian style, with elegant classical colonnades and an exquisitely shaped interior, it stood at Fifth Avenue and Twenty-fourth Street. Within ten years of White's death, a major insurance company, located next door, bought the land, razed the church, and erected a faceless office building that brought in higher rentals.

But even during White's heyday, there was another side to Manhattan, highlighted by the Astors who were typical of the real estate entrepreneurs who hired run-of-the-mill architects to carry out projects based solely on profits. While it is true that Mrs. Astor's Fifth Avenue mansion and the Waldorf-Astoria added some sparkle to New York's appearance, the bulk of the family's investment was sunk into commercial real estate, middle-class apartment houses, and slum tenements. And for several generations the business prospered hugely.

However, the values of real estate properties are determined by sociological and economic changes. Properties that once were lucrative have turned into white elephants because of the socioethnic transformation of the neighborhoods in which they are located.

A striking effect of this deterioration has been the dramatic decline of the Astor fortune, the first great one, derived from American real estate, that has been victimized by sharply changing times. In the early 1900s, as noted, the financial pundits figured that the Astor millions would continue to climb astronomically—into the billions—by the middle of the twentieth century. The reverse happened. Before the First World War over a quarter of a million immigrant families, mostly Jewish and Italian, moved into the Lower East Side and into many Astor-owned tenements. In the 1920s, as they climbed the financial ladder, these immigrants quit the East Side and moved to the Bronx, Brooklyn, and Long Island. Moreover, after the war, new restrictive immigration laws slowed down the European migration to a trickle. At the same time, the U.S. government, which had spent billions to finance the war effort, turned on the wealthy with stiff property taxes. Even in the decade before the war, the levy on real estate had risen to the point where 15 percent of the rentals generated from the Astor properties went into taxes. By 1929 this had risen to 21 percent, and in the 1930s to over 30 percent. In addition to rising taxes, dwindling immigration, and the exodus from the Astors' Lower East Side properties, the wisdom of the original John Jacob and his immediate heirs was not displayed by the later descendants. The early Astors had bought heavily on Fifth Avenue and Broadway and reaped a financial bonanza. However, by the 1920s, Fifth Avenue had passed the zenith of its price levels, and Times Square was becoming a honky-tonk district crammed with shooting galleries, hot-dog stands, and flea museums.

The later Astors hadn't been clever enough to foresee that the major expansion in residential and commercial districts would be along the upper East River and the Fifties, and they did not move in soon enough to exploit the booms. Instead they remained stuck in areas that were rapidly deteriorating.

Right after the First World War, the Astors, needing cash, began unloading some of their choicest properties. They sold the site of the present Paramount Building, the Longacre Building in Times Square, and the Waldorf-Astoria. Soaring taxes had turned the Fifth Avenue residences of most of the nineteenth-century multimillionaires into white elephants that no longer could be kept up, and one after another they were handed over to the demolition squad.

The later Astors strove to retain a semblance of their former glory. Although Vincent Astor sold the ornate family residence at 840 Fifth Avenue, and in keeping with the times, moved into more modest quarters in the East Sixties, he installed a replica of his father's study and bedroom done in the style of the 1890s. Vincent frequently slept in his father's lavish old bed surrounded by furnishings that were priceless museum pieces. After his father, John Jacob Astor IV, went down in the sinking of the *Titanic*, Vincent wore to his own death the antique gold vest-pocket watch the older Astor had always carried, and which was salvaged from the wreck.

One jewel of the Astor holdings was the family mansion built at 840 Fifth Avenue by John Jacob Astor and *The* Mrs. William Astor, society's *grande dame*. Erected in French Renaissance chateau-style, it had been a landmark of the "robber baron era." In 1925 Benjamin Winter, a Jewish immigrant who had risen from the slums of Hester Street and had amassed millions in real estate, bought the Astor residence for $3 million. Subsequently, he paid another $6.5 million for a lot at Fifth Avenue and Sixty-fifth Street, combined it with the site of the Astor mansion which he demolished, and built one of the world's most celebrated synagogues for the wealthy Jewish elite.

Meanwhile, the Astor fortunes continued to deteriorate. Ten years after the sale of the Fifth Avenue mansion to Benjamin Winter, the situation was even less bright. Vincent Astor, the latest descendant of old Jacob, had inherited fifty million dollars worth of Manhattan property, consisting of the St. Regis Hotel and an assortment of brownstones, office buildings, slum tenements on the Lower East Side, rundown apartment houses on the Upper West Side. Over a third of these properties were being operated at a loss, and the revenues from the portfolio as a whole were skimpy.

In 1942 Astor was called to naval duty when America entered the war. Unable to supervise personally his real estate holdings, he engaged Webb and Knapp, a top real estate firm, to reshuffle them in a series of buying and selling operations to upgrade their income. William Zeckendorf, a partner of Webb and Knapp, took over the job of reorganizing the Astor holdings. He operated shrewdly, converting mortgages into cash by selling Astor properties on the West Side and putting the cash into stronger properties, mortgaging them for additional money to buy up still more valuable properties at bargain prices.

Ironically, many of Zeckendorf's customers in this rehabilitation effort of the 1930s were German-Jewish refugees who had managed to slip out of Hitler's Germany with their life savings. They came to New York and decided to put their money into real estate. Not only was property a hallmark of stability, but the refugees felt that real estate prices were bound to rise during the boom that would be generated after the war was over. Some of these refugees were attracted to apartment houses on Manhattan's West Side, a number of which the Astor family owned, and Zeckendorf was perfectly willing to bait his offer to the hilt. The refugees, whose financial resources were limited, were anxious for their down payment to be kept to a minimum. Zeckendorf obliged by selling Astor-owned apartment houses on a small down payment in cash, but marking the total price much higher than he could have done otherwise if the down payment had been greater. The remainder of the contract he sold to a mortgage company and converted it into ready cash which he plunged into buying new properties in rapid-growth areas around the nation. So successful was Zeckendorf that after 150 deals he increased the wealth of the Astor portfolio by some $15 million.

The cycle had come full swing. Properties purchased originally by the heirs of the first Astor, a lowly immigrant from Germany, now went into the hands of the newest exiles from the Reich over 150 years after the first Astor had landed in America. In the course of these years, the Astors had become the bluest of blue-bloods, but now as their fortunes declined, they sold off their landed wealth to non-Aryans persecuted by a fanatical dictator.

Such are the ironies triggered by the economics of real estate.

3

"WHERE IN THE LORD'S NAME IS TUCSON?"

Flimflammery in San Francisco, New Orleans, Texas as the Land Jobbers Move in for the Kill

New York in the nineteenth century was a bastion of the Eastern Establishment of wealth and some of the biggest fortunes were accumulated directly through urban development. However, as the nation, after the War of 1812, moved westward across the Hudson, over the Alleghenies, into the Great Plains, and reached the Pacific Coast, as well as penetrating south to the Gulf of Mexico and north to the Canadian border, fortunes were raked in by ambitious, gutsy land operators who pushed into the wilderness following hard on the heels of the first explorers and missionaries.

Many of the real estate speculators who scouted for attractive land bargains were far more imaginative than America's statesmen. They were already out in Oregon on the trail of the first explorers, staking out their claims when Daniel Webster, that pretentious old politico, rose in the United States Senate in 1840 and brushed away the Far West as being at all worthwhile for Americans to consider owning. "What can we do with the Western Coast, a coast of 3,000 miles, rock bound, sheerless, uninviting and not a harbor on it? What use have we of such a country? I will never vote one cent from the public treasury to place the Pacific Ocean one inch nearer Boston than it is now!"

The land peddlers knew better. As one community after another was discovered by explorers and promoted by land merchants, the inhabitants proudly broadcast their achievements to the rest of the world. When the first locomotive roared into Tucson, Arizona, amidst the thunder of artillery fire and the booming of drums, the residents of the remote pueblo sent telegrams to the president in Washington and to the heads of nations around the globe, announcing the event. One message went to the Pope.

> The mayor of Tucson begs the honor of reminding Your Holiness that this ancient and honorable Pueblo was founded by the Spaniards under the sanction of the church three centuries ago, and to inform Your Holiness that a railroad from San Francisco, California, now connects us with the Christian world.

The following reply was received from Rome and read at a public banquet.

> His Holiness the Pope acknowledges with appreciation receipt of your telegram informing him that the ancient city of Tucson has at last been connected by rail with the outside world and sends his benediction; but asks for his own satisfaction, where in the Lord's Name is Tucson?

In most communities west of the Alleghenies, the land merchants received small protection under the local laws. The concept of justice ranged widely from territory to territory not only for landlords but for outlaws. Justice in the Oklahoma Territory immediately west of the Pecos River, for instance, was dispensed for years in a courtroom that doubled as a community store. One day a land speculator was brought before a judge and charged with the murder of a Chinese and the theft of a horse. "There is some doubt as to whether you committed your crime south of the Oklahoma border or north of it," the judge informed the accused. "However, I'm justice of the peace for both areas. Do you want to be tried according to Texas or Oklahoma law?"

The prisoner on a hunch replied he preferred to be tried by Oklahoma law. "In that case I find you guilty of stealing a horse and I fine you fifty dollars. I find you guilty of murder and I sentence you to be hanged for that."

"Your Honor," retorted the defendant, "I've changed my mind, I want to be tried by Texas law." The judge peered at him over his spectacles. "In that case I find you guilty of murder and fine you fifty dollars. I find you guilty of stealing a horse and I sentence you to be hanged."

Meanwhile, as the population migrated in increasing numbers toward the Pacific Coast, the opportunities accelerated for resourceful speculators. The laws passed by Congress for the first half century of the nation's existence favored Americans with ready access to capital. Until the passage of the Homestead Act in 1862 virtually all Government land apart from acreage given as a bounty to the war veterans was peddled to wealthy realtors and banking syndicates. And even under the 1862 law, which was designed to make cheap land available to all, rich absentee landlords sent out agents to grab up enormous acreage at the ridiculously low prices prevailing and parcelled it out at two and three times its cost to less clever newcomers.

As the nineteenth century progressed, the conflict between the land speculator and the squatter grew increasingly bitter. The bulk of settlers who moved westward were squatters seizing territory by right of de facto possession. They were so numerous it was impossible for real estate firms and their appraisers to keep up with them. By the early 1830s squatters were the largest landholders in most of the Midwestern states. In 1848 Congress passed a law changing the squatter from an illegal operator into a legitimate landowner. It offered him the right to buy his land at a decent price provided he lived on it permanently and didn't try to unload it as a speculation.

The squatters won the sympathy of rank-and-file Americans. The speculator was looked upon as a hit-and-run driver. His most useful role, if he stayed around long enough, was considered to be the developer of a new community. But in subdividing his lots he was accused of charging outrageously high prices.

The popular attitude was in many respects hypocritical. As the westward movement gained momentum, there were numerous new territories where virtually all the male residents were jobbers hoping to reap a financial killing from real estate. The most respected citizens started out as hustlers. If a man gambled with land and went broke, he was condemned by the pious for being a "horrid speculator." If the acreage he seized turned into a thriving community, he became a highly venerated founding father.

The evolution of California from a colony of Spain into a full-fledged American state provided a particular *embarras de richesses* for land speculators. A flourishing new market for huckstering was opened up as early as the conclusion of the Mexican War in 1848, when the American armies seized a huge expanse of Mexican territory. Under the laws passed by the Mexican authorities to prevent the development of land monopolists, no single settler was permitted to acquire a grant of more than forty-eight thousand acres. When it became obvious that Mexico's armies would be defeated and its power in North America broken, Pio Pico, the Mexican governor of the Territory of California, saw a quick way to line his pockets before he quit. He started issuing, at a stiff price, fraudulent land grants for colonists that superseded the forty-eight-thousand-acre limit, giving out huge tracts of a hundred thousand acres or more left and right. What Pio Pico didn't have time to do, American land speculators finished for him. They forged titles wholesale, handing over jumbo tracts to themselves by signing the Mexican governor's name.

When California finally fell into American hands, $150 million worth of Mexican land grants were presented for validation to U.S. officials. The United States attorney general reported to Congress that the Mexican archives, "furnished irresistible proof" there had been an organized system of fabricating land titles in California. The making of false grants with the subornation of witnesses, he declared, had become a routine business.

Many of the cities and towns of present-day California originate from these Mexican land embezzlements. Their bastard origins are shrouded in historical intrigue. After the Mexican War, Washington was bombarded by land speculators and their agents lobbying to have their crooked grants legitimized by Congress. Key Congressmen had a heavy personal interest in these grants. One indefatigable sponsor of the petitions was Senator William Benton of Missouri, whose relatives held one grant under a Mexican title and another purchased by bribery from the Mexican governor.

Many of these bastard grants were upheld by Congress and the U.S. courts. The City of Oakland was founded on twenty thousand acres of land swindled from one of Spain's oldest, most aristocratic families, the Peraltas, by a crook named Horace Carpentier.

Bitter disputes over grants mushroomed up in Northern California, particularly as miners, frustrated in their hunt for gold, poured into San Francisco and Sacramento, hoping to pick up land. They found when they tried to buy it that the bulk of the real estate was already claimed by operators holding Mexican grants. A savage struggle broke out as militant miners moved onto the land as squatters, defying the Mexican land speculators to drive them off. For years the title to large hunks of California were battled over in the courts by the squatters and the Mexican grant holders. During this period of prolonged litigation, the banks refused to accept land titles as security for loans, and when the holders of disputed titles went broke waiting for a court decision, an army of lawyers and loan sharks took over their estates by default.

During these unstable times, an inimitable crew of dreamers and schemers did a land-office business peddling their fantasies. One highly successful picaroon was Count Agoston Haraszthy, an Hungarian who, caught in an uprising of workers against the monarchy, fled to America. He entered politics as a Republican and, in return for services to the machine, wound up as director of the Federal Mint which was opened in 1854 in San Francisco. Under his stewardship, $140,000 worth of gold bars vanished mysteriously. Questioned by the district attorney, the count explained that during the process of smelting the gold, slivers inadvertently escaped through the flue of the furnace and disappeared into the air. An awful lot of slivers must have vanished through the flue, since $140,000 worth couldn't be accounted for. Incredibly the investigators accepted this explanation and the count went scot-free. With the money filched from the mint, he bought land in the Sonoma Valley and entered the wine business. He traveled all over Europe sampling fine vintages and came home with a bundle of cuttings culled from the best foreign brands. Importing Chinese laborers to plant eighty thousand vines, the nobleman who had robbed the U.S. Mint wound up as the father of California's wine industry.

Several other hustlers have become enshrined in California real estate history. There was Henry ("Honest Harry") Meiggs who grabbed land along the northern shoreline of San Francisco, plunged his own money and all he was able to coax from others into a huge property development in the North Beach area. But Meiggs made a blunder. He calculated that the future expansion of San Francisco would be northward, while, in fact, the city developed in a southern and westerly direction. Meiggs went bankrupt but he had the foresight to get himself elected to the City Council and embezzle $1 million worth of city notes. When the police closed in on him, he fled to Brazil.

Another sharpie who went broke trading in California land was "Horseface" Stearns, who bought up vast ranch properties with money he had made in the gold mines. But the climate turned sour. Stearns's cattle died in a drought and he was pauperized.

One of the oddest San Franciscans to make a killing in land among other things was Christopher Buckley, an Irishman who emigrated to California in his youth. Buckley opened a gin mill for sailors on the waterfront and for a time he was his own best customer. He was an insatiable tippler who gargled his pipes virtually all his waking hours. He literally drank himself blind.

He made the rounds of doctors, consulted leading specialists in America and Europe, tried every possible treatment, but it was useless. Acute alcoholism had destroyed his sight. But Buckley had a keen instinct for survival. He stopped drinking and henceforth swallowed nothing stronger than mineral waters. Sharpening his remaining faculties, he developed an uncanny memory for names and voices. No matter under what circumstances an individual was introduced to him, Buckley, after once hearing his voice, never forgot him. People were brought to him rapidly, haphazardly introduced, and all they had to say was, "How do you do, Mr. Buckley," and he would address them by their name forever.

Blind though he was, Buckley climbed rung by rung up the ladder of city politics. Developing a genius for delivering block votes, he became a precinct captain, then a ward boss, and finally clawed his way to become the chief of San Francisco's all-powerful Democratic party machine.

Buckley wielded this influence, despite his handicap, thanks to his neat scholarly mind and an obsession for facts. He had painstakingly amassed dossiers of incriminating evidence on the public and private lives of scores of politicians, businessmen, and assorted San Franciscans.

Combined with his formidable knowledge of city affairs, and all the legal loopholes available for assorted knaveries, this blind virtuoso developed a public manner that exuded sophistication combined with disarming candor.

As his intrigues grew more complex, requiring increasing vigilance, Buckley gave up tapping on a cane like an old blind Pew and began going around on the arm of "Brother Henry," an ex-convict whom he hired as his "Seeing Eye."

Thanks to his control of the city, Buckley reaped a fortune from lucrative real estate dealings. He freewheeled in raw land options and pounced upon valuable commercial and residential properties. He used the San Francisco Fire Department's ordinances to drive into bankruptcy the owners of properties he coveted for himself. Buckley went into the contracting business as a silent partner, awarding himself all the major building and road construction projects and pocketing the franchise for cleaning the streets.

Once he had San Francisco and much of the rest of California in his hip pocket, Buckley set his sites, metaphorically speaking, on the national scene. The Democratic party was battling over the nomination of Grover Cleveland for president, and Buckley figured he could be a leading power broker in the naming of the candidate. He was shocked to find that he didn't wield as much influence at the national convention as he expected. The delegates from other states didn't rush over to bend their knee before San Francisco's all-powerful political boss. The California delegation was off on its timing; it didn't seem able to vote the right way at the right moment. It gave only half its strength to Cleveland when everybody else hopped on his bandwagon, assuring that California would have very little influence in Washington for the next four years.

Henceforth, Buckley's grandiose chicanery became too much for even easygoing San Franciscans. The press stepped up its barrage of criticism. Reform opposition snowballed, and in 1891 a grand jury prepared to investigate Buckley's reign of terror. The boss was smart enough to realize the jig was up. Clutching the arm of "Brother Henry," he fled to Europe for "an extended vacation." He carried all the money he could stuff into his suitcase, but he couldn't lug away his vast real estate properties, and these went under the auctioneer's hammer, to be snapped up by aggressive bidders. Several of Buckley's holdings, in the downtown area, along the Bay, and extensive ranchland north of the city, have been handed down in families for generations, vastly enriching the lucky holders.

One wealthy landowning family whose members were as ruthless in their way as Buckley had been but who, unlike him, survived to establish a glittering social dynasty was the autocratic clan of Spreckelses. The fortune was founded by Claus Spreckels who arrived in San Francisco a penniless immigrant from Germany. He went into the grocery business, moved into the sugar industry, and wound up in control of all the cane sugar refined for San Franciscans. Then he reached out to Hawaii, snatched up valuable real estate and most of the plantations growing raw sugar, and became the richest and most powerful landowner on the islands.

Spreckels had four sons who turned out to be as savage as he. Once when the *San Francisco Chronicle* carried a story insinuating that Claus Spreckels was manipulating securities of the sugar empire in shabby Wall Street dealings, Adolph, the youngest son, barged into the office of Michel de Young, the newspaper publisher, whipped out a pistol, and shot him. Fortunately De Young survived. Spreckels was arrested, but so influential was his family that he was acquitted.

John Spreckels, another son, inherited his father's pugnacity. He wheeled and dealed through a maze of transactions outside of San Francisco to become San Diego's biggest real estate owner. He clinched his first deals when San Diego was an infant community, and most of the land in what is today the downtown section was selling for under 25 cents an acre. Spreckels was overwhelmingly ambitious. To cash in on the haulage of freight to Southern California, he built a railroad into Mexico. The tracks had to be laid over difficult mountainous terrain. One stretch, the Carriso Gorge, was government-owned property, but Spreckels filed a homesteader's claim for right-of-way through it. The agreement required that the work be performed within a specified time. But because of the delay in constructing the railroad, Spreckels' claim became void by default. To prevent someone else from preempting it, Spreckels resolved the problem simply. He bought the entire mountain range outright from Uncle Sam.

The Spreckelses were notorious for their intrafamily squabbles. The sons fought bitterly with their father. One battle broke out over the sale of the senior Spreckels' Hawaiian sugar and real estate holdings which had been dwindling in profitability. Claus Spreckels and John and Adolph, his two older sons, wanted to sell the properties; Rudolph and Gus, the younger sons, argued that they could revive them into a lucrative operation. Old Claus was enraged by his sons' presumptuousness. He sold the plantations, severed all ties with the young rebels, and sent a message to every banking house in San Francisco, warning them they would suffer severe reprisals if they dared lend his fractious offspring as much as a penny. The sons went around from one bank to another, receiving a cold shoulder. Finally, Rudolph and Gus managed to wangle money from a maverick who had the guts to defy old Claus, bought back their father's plantations, rebuilt them into lucrative enterprises, and peddled them at a price that made each independently wealthy.

Rudolph Spreckels, when he was in his early twenties, engineered this *coup de maître* against his father. Before he was thirty he had become a multimillionaire in his own right, and he swelled his fortune by investing in clever real estate deals throughout the San Francisco area. He moved into a baronial residence on Pacific Avenue, maintained an estate in suburban Burlingame, and bred thoroughbred racehorses that became trophy winners.

Since the family hassle over the Hawaiian plantations, Rudolph had not spoken to his brothers, John and Adolph, although the former resided only a couple of blocks from him; as long as they lived, the brothers never again exchanged a word. Not only did Rudolph Spreckels challenge his father over the best way to run his plantations, he clashed with him in another financial brawl that set Frisco agog. Two gas utilities, one financed by Rudolph the other by his father, fought bitterly for control of the San Francisco market. The utility Rudolph subsidized beat old Claus's firm and became the top dog. Spreckels, Senior, yielded. "Only once did anybody ever get the better of me in a deal and that was my own boy," he confessed, beaming with pride.

The real estate fortunes of the Spreckels and other tumultuous dealers were launched in a city that was as restless and Faustian-minded as its millionaires. Like Australia, which began as a convict camp, San Francisco started out as one of the toughest, noisiest, bawdiest communities this side of Devil's Island. It reeked of the whiskey and violence of a typical mining camp. Along the saloon- and brothel-packed Barbary Coast, Market Street, and the winding ascent to Nob and Telegraph hills, over a thousand murders were committed in the seven years between 1849 and 1856, but only one killer was sent to jail. The situation was so wild that the law-abiding elements formed a vigilante committee, dispatching members to corral thugs and hang them publicly to the tolling of church bells. For a time vigilante lynchings were as common as ham and eggs for breakfast. Then apathy set in. One news editor who dared to attack a thieving politician was gunned down by him in a public park. A few citizens looked up casually from their newspapers and then went back to the important news.

The city, launched on a gold boom, grew rapidly. Steam shovels scooped up the dunes, and mountains of sand were hauled away and piled up on acres of downtown shoreline to lift it high enough to withstand the rolling sea. Rows on rows of stores, saloons, and brothels were reared on busy docks that stood on piles above the seabed, catering to the needs of incoming ships and sailors.

In the mid-fifties, San Franciscans built their homes and offices for the sole purpose of living to a ripe old age and dying in bed. (Or at least in the corner saloon.) They put up doors and windows of the heaviest cast iron to prevent the entrance of thugs. To cut down muggings, they lit their streets at night with the best illumination science could buy—gas shipped from the coal mines of the North.

Money, aesthetic purists to the contrary, spells culture. Fed by the millions reaped from gold mines, railroads, and real estate and the rapid rise of wealthy families anxious to develop an instant aristocracy, San Francisco turned into the West Coast's leading center of the arts—and this at a time when other frontier towns were still cultural dunghills. By the mid-seventies, San Francisco had more schools, more newspapers, more libraries than the rest of the country west of the Mississippi. It was the one place sophisticated enough to welcome Lola Montez, the king of Bavaria's mistress, who in addition to being a celebrated dancer and whore, was an *avant-garde* champion of women's liberation. Lola received as hearty an ovation here for her wit and wiggles as she had ever attained in Paris. San Francisco was smartly bohemian. Its journalism was sparkling and raunchy. Unbowdlerized Shakespeare was played to crowded houses.

The money from real estate built mansions of brassy ostentation down to the solid-gold-plated bathrooms and toilet bowls. Parvenu magnificoes imported entire villas from Europe, and when some of the more tasteful nabobs went native, they reared mansions with the exteriors of elaborately sculptured white stone and curlicues that, standing on the heights overlooking the Bay, looked like castles out of Hans Christian Andersen.

There was a strong Southern flavor in San Franciscan society. A number of ex-planters, ruined after the Civil War, emigrated to

69

San Francisco, made money in real estate or oil, and built mansions that exuded the mood of antebellum Dixie plantations. There was also a liberal sprinkling of Jewish families who made money from the land. "Crazy Adolph" Sutro, who reaped a fortune buying up sand dunes and became Frisco's leading property holder, holding one-tenth of the city's real estate, was a Jew from Hungary. Michel de Young, the publisher and rich landowner, was another scion of the city's Jewish aristocracy.

But whatever the origin, Southern, Jewish or dyed-in-the-wool Anglo-Saxon, much of Frisco's elite turned up surprising misalliances. The city was celebrated for its French-style restaurants which served Parisian food downstairs in the lavish main dining room. Afterward a husband who took his spouse to dinner kissed her good-bye, summoned the carriage to take her home, and went upstairs to bed with a high-priced whore who specialized in the latest tricks from Paris. From some of these after-dessert specials, alliances sprang up that turned into marriages, and several of San Francisco's most austere dowagers counted at least one bordello as their ancestral home.

San Francisco was a veritable cornucopia of real estate wealth, but there were other areas along the length and breadth of the rapidly growing United States where dreamers and gamesters turned their visions into money in the bank.

Just as the Spreckelses rose to financial power in San Francisco, so aggressive hustlers like Nicholas Longworth became wealthy and influential through pioneer land manipulations in the Middle West. Longworth became the largest landowner in the area and the richest tycoon in America after John Jacob Astor by snapping up acreage in what developed into the City of Cincinnati; and he lived to see his fortune grow as Cincinnati expanded its boundaries to become the Queen City of the Middle West.

Indeed, Cincinnati, because of its location athwart the Ohio River, became an early cynosure for a covey of land hustlers and developed into a lusty community while Chicago was still swampland and Cleveland an obscure outpost. The site of Cincinnati was discovered through sheer serendipity. A trapper in pursuit of robbers paddled up the Ohio River into the Northwest Territory.

The countryside seemed so fertile and the location so strategic, he determined to put his money into developing it. Since it was public domain, he petitioned the Continental Congress and managed to get a million acres of land between the Big Miami and the Little Miami rivers for 60 cents an acre. He gave the government a down payment and advertised the lands for twice the price he contracted for.

Meanwhile, another syndicate petitioned Congress and received permission to buy 2 million acres along the Ohio River. A third syndicate, also sensing the value of the region, bought 750 acres, paying next to nothing for it in Continental script that eventually became worthless. This group chose more shrewdly than the others, for it was its location that ultimately became the City of Cincinnati. The first settlers shelled out the equivalent of $3 an acre for a town plot. One hundred and sixty years later a single plot in Cincinnati, located in those original acres, was worth a minimum of $3 million, and some of it was going for three times that amount.

Nicholas Longworth's ancestry meandered through centuries of English history. One forefather, Francis Longworth, owned a home near Shakespeare's Globe Theatre in London. With a landlord's instinct for protecting his property values, he protested to the authorities over a business enterprise that had been launched in the neighborhood—a carnival where trained bears danced and cavorted to the delight of children. Longworth complained about the noise, the crowds, the smell from the bears; Queen Elizabeth responded by granting him land in Ireland as far as possible from the stench of bears and shouts of applauding small fry. Longworth took up residence in Craggan Castle from whence two generations later his grandson sailed to New Jersey where he raised a family fanatically loyal to the king even after the Revolutionary War broke out. The family had bet on the wrong side. When America won the war, it was dispossessed of its property and socially ostracized.

Nicholas, the third child, had no inheritance to look forward to and figured he might as well go West to launch his career. In 1803 he started off by flat boat for the Northwest Territory, sailing down the Missouri with a few pennies and a battered leather trunk. His boat tied up at a spot between the Miami rivers where a tiny outpost had grown into the community of Cincinnati under the protection of guns mounted at Fort Washington, a fortress built for defense against the Indians.

A clever individual could advance rapidly on the frontier, but Longworth's rise to affluence was spectacular even by the standards of his day. Deciding upon law for a career he apprenticed himself to a judge, brushed up on his Blackstone, and hung out his shingle.

Longworth entered the real estate game quite accidentally. One of his clients was a man charged with horse stealing. Since a horse was a necessity of life on the frontier, conviction of stealing would have meant the execution of his client. But Longworth persuaded the jury to acquit him. The client had no money to pay his legal fee but he had two old whiskey stills. Longworth took the stills in lieu of cash and sold them, in exchange for thirty acres of his land, to a tavernkeeper who planned to go into the whiskey business. The tavernkeeper was an honest fellow and he confessed to Longworth that the land he was handing him was "not worth shucks." Longworth took it on a gamble. The acreage fifty years later was worth over $2 million.

With that deal Longworth was on his way. The fees he took in as a lawyer he invested in land on the outskirts of the village of Cincinnati for as little as $10 per lot. Longworth sensed the immense future to be enjoyed by the waterway which linked Pittsburgh with the Gulf of Mexico through the Ohio and Mississippi rivers. The first steamboat had not yet landed at the wharfs of Cincinnati when Longworth plunged his cash into land speculation. By the time he was in his forties, he was a multimillionaire.

Some of his friends shook their heads cynically, attributing his success to sheer luck. "You couldn't throw Longworth into the Ohio River," remarked one of them, "without his rising to the surface holding a rare specie of fish in one hand and a fresh-water pearl in the other hand."

As immigrants poured westward and Cincinnati prospered, the value of Longworth's property boomed. The population of Cincinnati in the twenty years between 1830 and 1850 grew from 25,000 to 173,000. By the middle of the century Longworth had become the wealthiest man in America after John Jacob Astor and he paid the second highest property taxes.

The more money Longworth accumulated the more eccentric he became. He took malicious delight in turning society's most cherished values topsy-turvy. He handed out piles of money to bums, vagrants, and ne'er-do-wells. A friend of his, also a wealthy man, scolded Longworth for giving cash to the town's social dregs. Longworth retorted, "You must find giving money only to those who are irreproachable citizens a very economical method. . . . My charities are for the Devil's poor because I'm the only man of the city imprudent enough to help them." The alcoholic and the thief always got a handout from Longworth if they came with a heartbreaking enough story of their tumble into ruin.

Once a friend of a widow who had been left destitute after her husband's death asked Longworth to give her money. "Old Nick," as his friends called him, asked if the widow was a deserving woman. "I have good reason to believe that she bears an excellent character and is doing all in her power to support a large family of small children," the friend told him. "In that case," retorted the tycoon, "I shan't give a cent. Such persons will always find plenty of people to relieve them."

Once while Longworth was walking along a street, a beggar approached and pointed to his shoes, showing bare toes gaping through. Longworth took off one of his own and invited the hobo to try it on. When he saw it fit, Longworth kicked the other one off; then he sent a servant to buy him a new pair of shoes, but he warned him to get the cheapest available.

Longworth's acts were open to suspicious interpretation by skeptical people. Once he donated a four-acre lot for the site of an astronomical observatory. The land was one of the most valuable properties he owned, and a business competitor charged that Longworth had given it not for reasons of philanthropy but because he realized that once the scientific installation was erected, his acreage lying around it would sharply rise in value. Long-

73

worth replied to his critic that if he would deed a similar piece of his own land, he would be glad to underwrite the cost of building another observatory on it equal to the size of the first. His offer was not taken up.

"Old Nick" was extremely penurious. An ardent horticulturist, he tended his own garden dressed in shabby old clothes. He appeared in the streets and in the drawing rooms of his rich friends looking like a tramp.

Once Abraham Lincoln, then an obscure prairie lawyer, came to Cincinnati for a court trial. Having time on his hands, he rambled through the town seeing the sights. Longworth's gardens were considered one of the wonders of the area and Lincoln decided to view them, if the owner had no objections. As he passed through the entrance to the estate, he found, weeding the shrubbery, an insignificant little fellow dressed in filthy overalls and a shirt whose oversized collar hid his ears. Taking him to be the gardener, Lincoln asked permission to tour the grounds. "My master is a queer duck," replied the fellow. "He doesn't allow strangers to come in, but he makes exceptions. He will be glad in this case to consider you a friend, sir, but before viewing the garden perhaps you would like to taste this wine." It dawned on Lincoln, as the conversation continued, that he was speaking to the master of the estate, and he apologized for his error. "Not at all," replied Longworth. "I'm quite used to it. In fact you are the first to find me out so soon. Sometimes I get ten cents and sometimes as much as a quarter for showing visitors my grounds. It is the really only honest money I've ever made, having been by profession a lawyer."

Longworth died at eighty-one, leaving $50 million to his heirs, including the ownership of numerous properties lying in and around Cincinnati. As the town developed into a premier city of the Middle West, the $50 million was vastly multiplied by Longworth's descendants into one of America's greatest fortunes.

Unlike their unconventional ancestor who gave shoes to a beggar and thumbed his nose at society's conventions, Longworth's descendants became the most cerulean of blue bloods. One of his grandsons, Nicholas, added glamorous tinsel to the family tree when he married Alice, the daughter of President Theodore Roosevelt. Young Longworth was a rising young Congressman; Alice was a stellar member of Washington's upper crust who kept the columnists busy reporting her social frolics. The marriage proved to be a most fortuitous merger of wealth and political influence.

Not only were fortunes amassed by the Longworth family and others in the Middle West, but money was reaped from the soaring value of acreage a thousand miles to the south in the vast Panhandle of Texas, where gamesters achieved a financial killing from the day Texas entered the Union and even before, during its history of solitary independence and as a colony of Mexico.

Here, however, there was no Nicholas Longworth to tower over the real estate scene in the extent of wealth and influence. The profits from Texas soil were divided among a score of aspirants who first grabbed up ranchland, and when the maximum revenues had been squeezed out of the cattle business, turned the acreage into farmland and residential real estate to wrest still more profits.

Texas in the 1870s, as always, demanded the best of everything, and when Austin was chosen to be the capital, its citizens decided to build the largest statehouse in the Union, taller than the Capitol in Washington. The problem was how to scrape together the money to erect the edifice.

The state fathers studied the fine print of the treaty which brought Texas into the Union and came up with a solution. So anxious had the United States government been to corral the Lone Star State into its family, it accorded Texas something no other territory was offered, the right to retain her public lands. Texas was given control of millions of acres, much of which lay in the area known as the Panhandle. Accordingly the Texas fathers came up with a bright idea—why not finance the building of their showpiece capitol by paying a contractor not with money, which was in short supply, but in acres of grass and dirt, which Texas had in abundance?

In 1882 the Texas Legislature voted to appropriate three million acres in the Panhandle to whoever would build the state-house. The announcement was widely publicized throughout America, but builders didn't stampede to snap up the offer. Indeed when the deadline expired, only two bidders had shown up. The legislature awarded a contract to one of them, a syndicate consisting of John Farwell, who was one of Chicago's biggest dry-goods wholesalers; his brother, Charles, a congressman, who was ambitious to enter the White House; Amos Babcock, another big wheel in the Republican party; and Abner Taylor, the president of the contracting firm which a decade previously had rebuilt Chicago after the great fire that had destroyed three-quarters of the city.

Shrewd as the Farwell Syndicate was, it was taken over a barrel by the slick Texas politicos. So certain was it of the value of Texas land (like other Americans it had been thoroughly brainwashed about the virtues of the Lone Star Utopia) the syndicate assumed it had purchased the crown jewels of America's real estate. It undertook the job of building the statehouse without thoroughly investigating the acreage it was receiving in payment, relying on the report of the Texas land commissioner that it was of substantial potential value. Actually the land lay almost a hundred miles from the closest settlement that could be called a genuine town. The Texas government itself had not conducted a detailed survey of the land, but privately it was convinced that much of it was uninhabitable, and of no more use than a desert.

Austin politicians congratulated themselves on making suckers out of their Yankee cousins, but some more scrupulous natives, suffering a twinge of conscience, charged the legislature with perpetrating a fraud. Based on the projected cost of building the statehouse the contracting syndicate was paying Texas over a dollar an acre. The state had previously tried to sell off the most fertile part of this tract privately and had been offered only half that price.

Shortly after the contractor commenced operations, it realized that it had bought a dud. It was forced to build a railroad to haul marble from quarries that were a considerable distance away; moreover it was hit by a labor shortage and, unable to find enough skilled American masons, it had to send to Scotland for granite experts, only to be dragged into court by Uncle Sam on the charge that importing labor under a contract was an indenture transaction that was outlawed by the Constitution.

The work ran into such difficulty the deadline had to be extended. But when it was completed it seemed well worth the effort to the Texas politicians. The statehouse was highly impressive-looking. It stood taller than the Capitol in Washington and boasted a huge gilded dome on top of which perched a figure representing Justice that peered ostentatiously down on the inhabitants of the town.

The statehouse was dedicated in a lofty ceremony attended by most of Austin's citizenry. In the middle of a stem-winding speech by the governor, the dome—that gilded, globular marble supporting the statue of Justice—as if struck by an earthquake collapsed with a thunderous crash.

Harried by costs that were more than double what they had originally estimated and furious over the shabby dealings of the Texas fathers, the contractors had gotten back at them. They had employed cheap stone instead of the promised granite, cheated on the amount of mortar, and sheeted the dome with an inferior material.

It was a case of poetic justice, but to avoid further embarrassment the Texas politicos revised their contract, offering the contractors more favorable terms. The latter rebuilt the capitol with the material originally promised, and the honor of Texas was restored.

The Farwell Syndicate was delighted to find that the land was in much better shape than the Texas fathers had supposed, and it decided to sell the bulk of it off as ranchland. To raise the capital for ranching on the scale required by three thousand acres, it turned to that fountain of capital markets—England. The Farwell Syndicate set up an English subsidiary, Capitol Freehold Land and Investment, Ltd., to sell bonds, and a number of prestigious Britishers were hired as directors. The Duke of Aberdeen, a Scottish blue blood, became trustee for the holders of the bonds; the marquis of Tweeddale, governor of the Commercial Bank of

Scotland, was named chairman of the board. Other directors included a member of Parliament and a leading London merchant. One hundred and fifteen million dollars was raised to convert the Texas land grant into a jumbo ranch. Over a hundred thousand head of cattle were stocked on the three-thousand-acre tract which was fenced in with six thousand miles of barbed wire, enough to run from New York to Los Angeles and back with a few miles to spare. The British investors figured they couldn't miss. Weren't the Americans big beefeaters? Weren't cowboys a legendary institution in the States? But the ranch called the X I T turned out to be a dud investment.

Severe blizzards hit the Panhandle, the cattle died in droves. The Capitol Syndicate's American manager, afraid of reporting the loss to the British investors, carried on his books thousands of cows and bulls that were deceased. Not for nothing did the term "watered stock" originate in the cattle industry, for ranch-land investors were able to teach the bulls of Wall Street a few things about flimflamming. When the British syndicate finally realized it was being swindled, it dispatched an agent to America to see that books were henceforth kept more honestly; but its emissary wasn't the wisest choice. He found very little time to supervise ranch business in between swigging whiskey at the ranch house and shooting crap in Dascosa, a nearby town.

By 1901, the X I T Ranch was faced with bankruptcy. The gullible British syndicate went broke. The American partners, notably the Farwells and their descendants, managed to salvage something from their investment. They formed a real estate trust—Capitol Reservations Lands—to take over the property for real estate management after the cattle had been sold off. The widow of Amos Babcock, one of the original members of the syndicate that built the Austin statehouse, brought a suit against the others, charging they had sold the ranch to promote their personal profits. A lawyer hurried over to the ranch demanding to see the financial books, but the manager saw him coming, swept the records into a safe, and cocked his Winchester rifle.

The courts decided in favor of the Farwell Group, which, after selling off its cattle, set up a promotional agency to entice Texas colonists into buying ranch lots and converting them into farming. It was through the promotional efforts of Farwell and other bankrupt ranch owners that much of the Texas Panhandle, originally devoted to ill-starred ventures, was salvaged for small farmers and landowners who wound up colonizing much of present-day Texas.

So much for the Farwells, the Babcocks, the Taylors, and the vicissitudes of the X I T Ranch. Other lucrative land manipulations took place in the early days of the Republic in the burgeoning Southland to the east of the Lone Star State, notably in the Louisiana Territory purchased by the Jefferson Administration from France, and especially in the flamboyant, coruscating City of New Orleans.

As Nicholas Longworth dominated the real estate business of Cincinnati, so Myra Gaines, a tiny, birdlike woman with a will of steel, hovered over the city of Creoles, holding the key to its real estate fortunes in her grip for a span of sixty years. The power Myra Gaines had over an entire city is vintage drama, yet the story has remained an obscure footnote of Americana.

The United States Congress gave President Jefferson $15 million to buy the Louisiana Territory from Napoleon. Within a decade, thanks to their aggressive speculations, the combined wealth of a handful of land hustlers exceeded the total price the Federal government paid for the tract. One of the largest fortunes to emerge from the frenetic dealings in the territory was made by Daniel Clark, a young Irishman who settled in New Orleans in 1784 when it was still a Spanish province. Clark plunged into the lucrative trade that was carried on by the city's merchants with the United States, France, and Spain. To expand his influence, Clark went into politics and developed important contacts within the U.S. Government. It was largely through his intimate knowledge of Louisiana and the advice he proffered the Jefferson Administration that it was induced to purchase the territory. In the course of amassing one of the largest fortunes in the new region, Clark became the biggest landowner in and around New Orleans, buying up seven hundred acres adjacent to the city and valuable acreage in the city itself, including a vast slice of territory that had been awarded by Congress to General Lafayette for his contributions to the American War of Independence, but which the general, subsequently tumbling into debt, was forced to sell to raise money. Clark also bought up the grants of numerous others at bargain prices when they fell upon hard times. Clark had an active political as well as financial career. By the time he was thirty-three he was a multimillionaire and a congressman with substantial influence in Washington; at the same time he was a close personal friend of Aaron Burr, and some historians believe he played a key undercover role in Burr's ill-starred scheme to seize Mexico and turn it into his personal empire—a venture for which Burr, as all the world knows, was tried for treason.

At his death, Daniel Clark owned half the city of New Orleans involving property worth over $50 million. He had written a will in which he directed his huge holdings to be administered in trust for his elderly mother. (Clark was ostensibly a bachelor and had no other relatives.)

Fifteen years after the realtor's death, in 1834, a young woman, Myra Davis, turned up in New Orleans and astounded the public by charging she was Daniel Clark's daughter, demanding title to his real estate holdings.

Daniel Clark, asserted Myra Davis, had fallen in love with a French Creole woman who bore him an illegitimate daughter. He subsequently married her, but because the woman was socially beneath him, and he feared that the marriage would interfere with his career, he had kept it a secret, secluding his young wife in a country house outside of New Orleans. Clark's will had made no mention of a marriage or a daughter, but Myra alleged that this will written in 1811 had been superseded by a new one drawn up by Clark just before his death in which, experiencing twinges of conscience, he had left his property to her. Business associates of Clark, according to Myra, got wind of this will and tore it up, preferring to administer the property in behalf of Clark's mother, an elderly woman whose affairs they could dominate.

Before his death, Daniel Clark transmitted all his New Orleans and other vast real estate holdings, claimed Myra, to a close associate, Joseph Bell-Cheise, under the confidential terms that he would administer them for the use of his daughter until she came of age. She was brought up by a guardian, a Mr. Davis, in ignorance of who her real father was and didn't discover the truth about her inheritance or that her father had been Daniel Clark, the celebrated politician and multimillionaire, until she became an adult.

The arrival of Myra Davis in New Orleans with the claim that she had legal title to much of the city triggered tremendous anxiety. Was this story Myra Davis told a true one or was this woman an impostor who had concocted a claim to bilk New Orleans' residents out of millions of dollars in real estate? Many of Daniel Clark's properties had been sold and resold to others. Not only were large numbers of people involved, but the vastness of the claim boggled the mind. Clark had bought up much of New Orleans on a shoestring. And, in subsequent years, the price of his properties had increased as the city grew in population and commerce. The foresighted Clark had plunged his money into properties that lay in the center of the city. Moreover, he had put money into Esplanade Avenue on the outskirts which became New Orleans' most fashionable residential area. By 1860 the value of Clark's downtown and Esplanade properties alone were worth over $30 million, at a time when the *total* assessment of real estate in all of New Orleans was only $100 million. One single piece of property which Myra Davis laid claim to extended on both sides of Canal Street from Dauphine Street to the Mississippi River and constituted the entire shopping center of the city, featuring block after block lined with wealthy stores.

The properties Myra claimed had been turned over, titles and deeds transferred again and again. And all of these transactions were now put into jeopardy by Myra Davis's allegations. Moreover, Myra turned out to be an exceedingly contumacious woman. In one year alone—1866—she sued over 150 people who she insisted were illegally occupying properties that belonged to her. A year later she launched suit against 70 others, and the following year, against 250 more victims. "By and large," writes one historian, "the whole population of the city came to feel itself in jeopardy as long as Myra Davis roamed at will through the halls of justice seeking whom she might devour."

Myra's lawsuits paralyzed the business life of New Orleans; if a buyer wanted a desirable lot, he insisted (since Myra was claiming virtually the entire city) that the owner guarantee him that he could return the property without damages if Myra won her suits. One story circulated about a buyer who told him it wasn't necessary to give a guarantee since the property lay definitely outside the area of Myra's claims. The owner showed his customer a map which demonstrated that the lot was not part of Daniel Clark's holdings at all. Nevertheless the buyer remained anxious, and before he signed the deed the owner had to ask Myra to sign a guarantee that she would not claim the property. Myra cheerfully agreed to do this—for a $500 fee.

The politicians and business community called Myra "Public Enemy Number One." So bitter was the feeling of New Orleans' residents toward Myra that she couldn't appear in the streets without the risk of being assassinated. Whenever she left her house to enter a carriage, she was besieged by angry mobs. But Myra ordered her coachman to whip the horses and plunge through the crowd to get her quickly out of the dangerous situation. One citizen fired a gun point-blank at her, and for years she carried around as a prized possession the silk bonnet with a hole in it where the bullet had entered inches from her scalp.

Myra Davis's legal battle turned into the longest recorded in American judicial history, lasting over sixty years, bouncing back and forth between the lower and the higher courts of the nation and reaching the Supreme Court on twelve different occasions. The contretemps involved virtually every prominent lawyer in the country.

The judges who first heard the claim were long dead when the case was still being argued before other judges who bequeathed their records to still others before they passed on. Among the prominent attorneys who participated against Myra was Daniel Webster, who by then was an old man; he was secretary of state to boot. (In those days such side business was not considered a conflict of interest.) A descendant of Myra's observed that to

some women life means a man to love, a home, a family, or a career, but to Myra Davis, "life meant litigation. She had learned to
accept it, use it, and finally to revel in it through the long years
she went on fighting for her rights while the whole country
watched." Her lawsuit became an *idée fixe* with Myra, and in pur-
suing it she read numerous law books, becoming an expert in every item of the Code of Louisiana, and she wound up being a better lawyer than most of the attorneys who worked on her case.

It took a substantial sum of money to pursue the litigation, and
at the outset of her battle in the courts, Myra married a wealthy
retired officer of the U.S. Army whose funds provided her with
the means to prosecute the suits during the early years. General
Gaines died in 1849, leaving one-third of his fortune to his widow
while the rest went to his children by an earlier marriage. The
$100,000 Myra received was a comfortable enough inheritance
for a woman to live on in those times, but Mrs. Gaines was far too
obsessed with the litigation to let go of it, and in a few years the
money was swallowed up by her lawyers.

From then on Myra lived frugally, spending only on the bare
necessities of life. Every dollar she could save she put aside for
her litigation, living in run-down rooming houses in slum areas of
town. Hovering over the city like an ominous bird of prey, hoarding every penny to continue her case, Myra went from court to
court, year after year a tiny, bony, four-foot, eleven-inch under-
sized woman. Even when she reached her sixties, she wore her
hair dyed red in little curls like a young Southern belle. She
dressed in black from head to toe, wore black gloves, and carried
an oversized black suitcase crammed with legal papers involved
with her litigation.

The issue of whether Clark had ever legally married the French
Creole mother Myra claimed to be the daughter of, and whether
Myra was entitled to $50 million worth of New Orleans real estate
couldn't be resolved by the nation's finest judicial minds. The
question as to which will was the legitimate one, the will of 1811
which was in existence or the one of 1813 which was unavailable
but which witnesses for Myra swore Daniel Clark had written to
supersede the first one, eluded the attempts of numerous courts

to adjudicate. When a justice of the lower court found against Myra, she would immediately appeal to a higher court which decided for her, only to have the verdict reversed by still a higher tribunal. As one historian observes, one usually believes that a decision by the Supreme Court is one of the fixed, decisive things in the American judicial system. Not so, in the Myra Gaines case. It was brought before the United States Supreme Court *no less than twelve times.* On eleven occasions the court reversed itself one way or another. In 1848 the Court upheld Myra. In 1851 the Supreme Court, with the same Justices sitting, upset their previous decision and ruled against Myra. Their Honors simply couldn't decide whether Daniel Clark and the Creole beauty, Zulime, had actually been married or if Myra had fabricated the story and was a brazen impostor. Before the case was over, thirty Justices of the Supreme Court, not to mention the numerous judges of State and Federal courts, had sat in on it. The final time the case was submitted to the Supreme Court it took two massive trunks to ship from New Orleans to Washington the legal papers that had accumulated over the years; when they arrived the Chief Justice confessed that the documents were too numerous to be read. He and his Associate Justices, he declared, would merely scan through them to get the gist of what had taken place. Seventeen of Myra's lawyers died in the course of her litigation. As the suit dragged on and on, Myra became an institution familiar to generations of Americans who were born long after the case had begun.

The initial fury of the New Orleans citizenry had long since turned into a spirit of resignation. Myra's claim to receive all the "rents, fruits, revenues and profits" on numerous properties in and around the city was looked upon fatalistically, "as a civic problem like drainage or flood control." Landlords refused to be concerned; the city had authorized their title deeds; let it see to it that they were clear.

The indomitable little woman in black continued to exist only for her courtroom appearances. It became an obsession with her to endure and outlive her opponents. If she couldn't win against them, she could at least outlast them. When she was in her sixties, referring to the city politicians who were adamantly refusing to hand over half of New Orleans to her, Myra wrote acidly: "No doubt their calculation has been to wear me out, so consequently at my death the suit would be abandoned; but lo and behold, hundreds of my principal enemies have passed away and I do not feel older than when I was 30 years of age. I have indeed great cause to be thankful to my heavenly father."

Meanwhile she continued to endure severe deprivation. On one occasion while living in a roach-infested boardinghouse in the dreariest part of the city, kept alive only by her staunch conviction that $50 million worth of property was rightfully hers, Myra wrote to a friend. "For nearly a week I've not had one cent. I've had to borrow ten dollars from a lady in the house." On the day she wrote this, Myra instructed her lawyer to refuse a compromise suggested by her legal opponents. She insisted on fighting for 100 percent vindication.

In 1890, sixty years after Myra Gaines launched her first suit, the Justices of the Supreme Court, after huddling for the umpteenth time, handed down a final ruling in favor of Myra, arguing in their august wisdom that the proof of burden was on the defendants to prove that she was *not* a legitimate heir of Daniel Clark and that they had failed to do so. The jurists decreed therefore that Daniel Clark had *indeed* married the French Creole, Zulime, and Myra was their legitimate daughter. Justice Wayne, who wrote the landmark decision, had been born in Vermont four years after Myra had first launched her case in the courts. In handing down his opinion, the Justice took suitable note of the legendary reputation of the case and its place in American history. "Those of us who have borne our part . . . will pass away, the case will live. Years hence, as well as now, the profession will look to it for what has been ruled upon its merits and also for the kind of testimony upon which these merits were decided."

Because of the endless, complex property transactions that had taken place since Clark's death, it was undesirable, indeed impossible, even to attempt to give back to Myra all the property she claimed. The Court settled upon returning one major tract that had been purchased by Daniel Clark located in the Esplanade

Avenue section between Canal Street and the Mississippi River—a region that was now part of the wealthy residential center of the city. This tract, involving 140 acres, had along with Clark's other properties been bequeathed in his will of 1811 to his mother, and executors of his estate had subsequently sold it to a buyer for under $5000. Thirteen years later the latter sold it back to the city of New Orleans for $25,000. Now, in recognizing Mrs. Gaines's title to the tract, the city was ordered to pay $2 million—the value of its appraised appreciation now, forty years later, plus accumulated interest amounting to $500,000.

But there was a final twist of irony. The Supreme Court's decision came too late to be of any use to Myra Gaines. Worn out by years of litigation, the indefatigable claimant made the trifling miscalculation of dying in her sleep in her shabby rooming house a few months before the verdict was handed down by the Supreme Court. Most of the $2 million awarded by the court was divided up among her numerous lawyers, and the relatively meager sum that was left was distributed among her grandchildren living in New York. Myra Gaines received not the slightest advantage from her long obsessive battle in the courts. Had she dropped the case instead of squandering her husband's inheritance, her grandchildren would have received about the same amount of money in the end. But then the law annals would not have inherited one of the rarest chapters of judicial curiosa in American history. And more than that, historians would have been deprived of the opportunity to debate to this moment whether Myra Davis Gaines was indeed the rightful heir to Daniel Clark's property or whether she was a fraud.

So much for the adventures of Myra Gaines. One eccentric with a drive as obsessive as Myra Gaines's but who unlike Myra struck it rich in real estate, two thousand miles north of New Orleans, was George Francis Train who became known as the Father of Omaha, Nebraska, thanks to his pioneer land buying in the future meat-packing town when it was merely a wilderness. Train not only bought up five hundred acres and paved the way for an extensive residential development that for years was called

"Train Town," but he built the Herndon Hotel which became one of the most celebrated hostelries in America.

Like Jay Cooke, the banker, Train made money in real estate, thanks to the launching of a railroad that overnight enhanced the value of his land holdings. What did the trick in this case was the Union Pacific which formed the western branch of the first railroad to span the continent. By masterminding the financing of the road, Train was in on the inside discussions when it came time to select the eastern terminus for the stretch of the road being built from California eastward. Learning that the terminus would be located in Omaha, Train rushed out to the wilderness area and bought up all the acreage he could lay his hands on at dirt-cheap prices.

The debate as to where the terminus should be located had been a bitter and protracted one. A group of investors headed by Abe Lincoln, while he was president, had fought vigorously to have the terminal located fifty miles to the south where the Lincoln group had quietly invested heavily in land. But the Train Syndicate won the day.

The financing of the railroad had been highly troublesome. In July 1862, Congress authorized a charter which provided for an initial investment of $100 million worth of stock and $50 million in bonds. The stock issue was to be bought by private interests in hundred-thousand lots of $1000 par value each. If this were accomplished, the government promised to underwrite another $50 million through bond issues. Once $2 million had been raised privately and 10 percent of that amount—$200,000—had actually been paid in cash, the corporation could go into business.

The problem was how to raise the initial $2 million and get the gigantic project going. Despite the enthusiasm of the promoters, wresting $2 million in front money from America's wealthy proved remarkably difficult.

Train, who was chosen to troubleshoot the deal, approached the Vanderbilts, Astors, Goelets, and other scions of New York's plutocracy without success. Then he tried a gimmick; it was, as he described it, "the pint of water that started the great wheel of the machinery." He remembered that years before, while he was

87

on a business trip in Paris hobnobbing with Prince de Polignac and other financiers, he had become intrigued with a new concept for raising capital developed by two banking brothers, Emile and Isaac Perier. France, under the Emperor Napoleon III, had been experiencing a brisk commercial boom, and the brothers, realizing that old-time methods of raising capital were no longer adequate, organized a syndicate they called "The Crédit Mobilier," which provided loans based on the collateral of real estate. The French government enthusiastically endorsed the scheme, and thanks to it Baron Haussmann was able to borrow money to rebuild Paris comprehensively into today's beautiful capital.

Train decided to apply this French money-raising idea to the task of scrounging up cash for the U.S. railroad. Turning about in his mind how to organize his vehicle under U.S. law, this real estate genius with an encyclopedic memory recalled that Duff Green, a businessman, had in 1859 succeeded in pushing a bill through the Pennsylvania Legislature to enable him and associates to reap a financial killing in a tariff swindle worked through the Philadelphia Custom House. (The intent of the conspirators was unmasked and the charter provided by the bill lay unused.) Realizing that this charter, which was a license for operating a commercial banking business for placing loans and raising money on stocks, would provide an ideal vehicle for a legitimate (as well as a crooked deal) Train sent a lawyer to Philadelphia to burrow through the historical archives; and he found to his astonishment and delight that he could buy Duff Green's charter, lock, stock, and barrel, for a piddling $25,000. Train changed the name of the Pennsylvania charter to "Crédit Mobilier of America," and this became the financial mechanism which launched the railroad.

By the fall of 1863 the $2 million needed to get the venture rolling was accumulated, but Train was too restless to attend to the grubby details of day-to-day operations. The task of administering the project was turned over to Thomas Durant, a Boston financier, and Train freed himself to conjure up new schemes, picking up valuable real estate along the way as the tracks inched across the country.

The land gamester addressed public meetings to whip up enthusiasm and bring money into the coffers of the Union Pacific. When the ground was broken to lay the first mile of track beyond the Missouri, the ceremony took place in the little community of Omaha in the territory of Nebraska. Train dug the first pile of earth with a silver shovel and stirred up the crowd with his rodomontade. He predicted that the most gigantic land boom in history would be triggered by the building of the railroad and that this would result in the creation of a chain of cities linking the Atlantic to the Pacific Coast. "Before the first century of the nation's birth is over, we may see in the New York Depot a strange Pacific Railway notice; 'European passengers for Japan will please take the night train; passengers for China, this way.' " The transcontinental railroad, Train prophesied, would, in short, serve as a highway linking together Western Europe, the Orient, and America. "Ten millions of immigrants will settle in this golden land in twenty years. If I had not lost all my energy . . . and enterprise I would take hold of this immigration scene," he added tongue in cheek, "but the fact is I've gone too fast and today I am the most played-out man in the country." The crowd roared.

To underscore his belief in this exuberant scenario, Train took a speculative plunge in the locality where he delivered his address. Omaha was an insignificant patch of semiwilderness, but it was to be the eastern terminus of the Union Pacific, and Train knew a good deal when he saw one. He grabbed up five hundred acres in Omaha at $175 an acre in what today is the heart of the city, spreading from Twentieth Street to the Missouri River, south of the tracks of the Union Pacific. He purchased an additional eighty acres in the northeastern section.

When the railroad was completed, Train reaped a fortune on his real estate dealings, only to wind up losing every penny because of a peculiar quirk in his personality. Most successful land hustlers are dreamers as well as schemers, but Train was one who carried his dreaming a little too far. He was a visionary, a Faustian gambler with a streak of madness. As he grew increasingly rich, he became odder in his behavior.

The wealthy realtor began signing the letters he wrote friends and the cards he sent out on Christmas "The Great American

Crank." When he met people he refused to shake hands with them, explaining he had developed profound psychic powers and to touch the hand of another human being would destroy the energy linking him with spirits from the Great Beyond. When Train was introduced to anybody, he would ceremoniously shake hands with himself. He wrote notices to the newspapers informing them he was living in a time sequence apart from the rest of mankind. He had given up the chronology introduced by Christianity which divided history into B.C. and A.D. As far as he was concerned, he declared, he was living in a new Psychological Era, basing his chronology on the date of his own birth and his current age. When he reached fifty, he marked his letters P.E. 50.

Resting from his peripatetic business ventures, Train settled down in New York which was the breeding ground of other inimitable eccentrics like himself. In Wall Street, not far from Train's office, two young women, Victoria and Tennessee Claflin, had started out as spiritualist mediums and wound up as the first female stockbrokers on Wall Street, enjoying the financial and personal patronage of no less a personage than Commodore Vanderbilt.

Beside exchanging stock market tips with the Commodore and bouncing in and out of the arms of lovers from coast to coast, Victoria did a thriving side business: she published a magazine that was literally a blackmail sheet. She collected titillating gossip about financiers and other stalwarts of the community and sent them the galley proofs of what she had written, threatening to publish them if they didn't come through with hefty contributions to her magazine.

Finally Vickie struck the juiciest target of all—Henry Ward Beecher, America's most venerated preacher, and the brother of the author of *Uncle Tom's Cabin.* Vickie launched a series of front-page articles, charging that the minister had a penchant for recreations that were not exactly to the taste of Mrs. Grundy. After his Sunday sermons in which he called down the wrath of God on sinners, Vickie charged, the minister would retire to an anteroom in the church behind his pulpit and copulate with the fair-sexed members of his congregation who eagerly lined up for this benediction.

When the stories appeared in Victoria Claflin's magazine, they hit Wall Street and Fifth Avenue with a sharp impact. The vestrymen of Beecher's church and other pillars of propriety were aghast at this attack on America's beloved *beau ideal*. They had a warrant sworn out for Vickie's arrest on charges of indecent slander.

Vicki's imprisonment made headlines, and George Train, an irrepressible champion of eccentric causes, leaped to the bait. He promptly fired off a statement to the press, expressing his outrage at the imprisonment of Victoria Claflin on an obscenity charge. Obscenity was no business of the court, the police, or the legislature, he thundered.

To demonstrate his point, the real estate mogul went through the Bible, selecting the most erotic anecdotes, scenes, and references he could dig up in the venerable tome. He culled racy references to the sexual athletics of the patriarchs who begat one child after another long after other men were long past their tumescence, and he recorded all this whoring, adultery, and lust in a journalistic fashion, using banner headlines as if they were the latest news flashed by a daily tabloid. He issued this as a mimeographed newspaper and followed the first issue with a new one every few days replete with spicier and spicier episodes from the Good Book.

The Solomon Grundys were outraged at this real estate archmagnifico turning moral arbiter. Train was arrested on a charge of slander and clapped into the Tombs Prison, a foreboding edifice that housed thieves, pickpockets, and assorted rascals. He was locked up in cell 56 on Murderers' Row where twenty-two New Yorkers were reluctantly awaiting a meeting with their Maker. Across the way from Train sat Edward Stokes, a broker who had shot Jim Fiske, the financier, over the love of a show girl as the latter was in the act of ascending the grand staircase of the Park Central Hotel while New York society stood gaping in the lobby. In the cell next to him sat Jim Sharkey, an early prototype for

Brecht's "Mack, the Knife." A killer, pickpocket, and all-around scamp, Sharkey escaped the electric chair when his sweetheart, Maggie Jordan, the same size as he, sneaked into his cell one night and changed clothes with him, leaving the warden with a female prisoner on his hands.

Train's spirit wasn't at all dampened by his imprisonment. He organized the twenty-two murderers into a social club which elected him president, and they whiled the hours away with anecdotes and toasts over imaginary bumpers of champagne.

The district attorney and assorted authorities didn't realize what they had gotten into when they arrested Train. They figured they would clap this obstreperous troublemaker into prison for a few days to shut him up and then quietly release him. However Train astounded them by insisting that the issue over which he was arrested be squarely met and that it was his constitutional right to have a public trial to decide whether the Bible was, in fact, an obscene book. This was the last thing the authorities wished. Neither they nor the followers of Beecher nor any of the pietists of the New York Establishment had the slightest intention of putting the Bible in the prisoner's dock. They blanched at the vision of audiences packing the courtroom listening to arguments on whether the Holy Scripture was a dirty book.

When the implications of Train's arrest dawned upon the state authorities, they rushed him into court to go through the formalities of releasing him with as little publicity as possible. He was brought before a judge to enter his plea. The clerk asked Train a routine question. "How do you plead? Guilty or not guilty?" "I'm guilty," roared Train. His Honor hastily interceded. "Enter a plea of not guilty; remove the prisoner!" But Train argued so vociferously he had his plea of guilty restored before he was dragged off to his cell.

Anxious to get rid of this oddball, the prison officials showered him with hints to get off their backs. The guards stopped patrolling the corridor outside his cell and left his door open for hours, hoping he would walk out. Attendants taking him for exercise in the prison yard suddenly vanished, leaving him alone with only a wall to scramble over. But Train resisted all enticements to escape.

For fourteen weeks he remained in the Tombs while the stalemate continued. The court authorities were furious at this "dreadful person who obstructed business, distracted judges and made a travesty of justice uttering his vaporings and trumpetings."

Then the district attorney, after burrowing through the statute books, came up with a brilliant scheme. It was out of the question to put the Bible on trial as Train demanded as his constitutional right, but there was another solution. The court could declare this "obstreperous obstructor of justice" legally insane. Under New York State law, if a man were ruled crazy, no indictment could be brought against him; ergo, no trial could be held. Declaring Train legally crazy would effectively eliminate the need for bringing the Bible into the courtroom.

Accordingly, the state won an order confining Train to a lunatic asylum. The court didn't really believe Train was crazy and had no intention of committing him to an asylum. It had won its objective of keeping the Holy Book from going on trial. Train was set free, but remained technically a "legal lunatic," a permanent ward of the court. He was forty-three when he was placed under the ban; he lived under it for thirty-three years until he died. Free as a bird, he was *legally* as crazy as the Mad Hatter.

The court order had inevitable consequences. Put under an order of insanity, which meant that the judge didn't consider him capable of managing his affairs, Train was stripped of all his wealth. He was shorn of the titles and deeds to his vast real estate holdings in Omaha where land values had skyrocketed at the completion of the Union Pacific. Millions of dollars worth of his holdings went into the hands of trustees who divided up the profits. In addition, Train lost a lavish villa which for years had been one of the showplaces of Newport. Former financial associates slammed their doors on Train. Nobody wanted to do business with a man declared legally insane.

Defiantly, Train continued his eccentric behavior. Impover-

93

ished, abandoned by most of his wealthy friends, when the few associates he had left chided him for persisting to behave queerly, he retorted, "I am a legal lunatic. Why shouldn't I talk out of my head?"

He bombarded the press with crank letters predicting that he would turn up yet as America's first dictator. Like the *Mikado* of Gilbert and Sullivan, he had plenty of people on his list who never would be missed. First, he warned, he would hang the murderers, next the thieves, then the nation's top politicians, and finally all of Congress. Once Train was picked up by a sheriff who had been sent by creditors to extract money he owed them. When the judge asked him his name, he replied, "George Francis Train, more commonly known as the Champion Crank." Asked his occupation, he retorted, "Aristocratic Loafer."

Only to children, those avid acceptors of myths, did the erstwhile real estate tycoon show any affection. In his final years, destitute and living the life of a tramp, Train sat from sunrise to sundown on a park bench in Union Square in Manhattan feeding the pigeons and relating by the hour tales from his eventful life to the neighborhood kids who flocked around him.

Train died in 1904 in his seventy-sixth year, which resulted in the last and greatest irony; for his death restored him from obscurity to temporary eminence. Suddenly people forgot the "transgressions" of the real estate prestidigitator and remembered him with affection. New Yorkers stormed the funeral parlor to pay their respects. The mayor ordered the flags of the city to be lowered to half-mast. The mayor of Omaha, whose northeast section was still being referred to as "Train Town," sent the pioneer real estate plunger a cross, woven from a bouquet of flowers. The Omaha Real Estate Exchange wired a message that the city had lost "one of its earliest and most enthusiastic friends." Cables came from Britain and France where Train had made extensive real estate investments. President Theodore Roosevelt sent a special emissary to the funeral.

Before burial, a noted alienist had the brain of the Great American Crank extracted, and found that, sane or crazy, it was among

94

the heaviest ever weighed. Prominent psychologists of the day were preaching that a man's intelligence was in direct proportion to the weight of his brain, so this Yankee oddball had the last laugh after all.

One more episode must be added to the assorted doings already recorded in the nineteenth-century real estate arena. San Francisco, Cincinnati, Oklahoma, and Texas were exploited and cultivated by rough, aggressive, Caucasian, land jobbers whose ancestors came from Europe. But during the land boom that erupted after the Civil War, a new and entirely different sort of aspirant strove for property ownership, and his attempts launched a curious chapter in American history.

This candidate was the newly freed American black man, who insisted that he be given title to the soil he had tilled for others for over two hundred years. When the Russian serfs were freed by Czar Alexander II, they were given the rights to the land they had cultivated for their masters. The same was done for the French, Italian, and German peasantry. The American blacks wanted similar treatment.

In the maze of double-dealing that transpired during the Reconstruction Era, the blacks kept their eye on the ball, never swerving from their demand for land. Despite the rhetoric of Northern politicians and finely worded proclamations of freedom, the black man, illiterate though he was, realized that land ownership was the key to being genuinely liberated. He knew with the instinct of all people who have worked the soil that he who owns the land possesses the power.

The U.S. Government treated the matter very gingerly. On the one hand abolitionists like Charles Sumner and Thaddeus Stevens argued that blacks must be given land as an outright gift or for a nominal price and that this should be paid for out of taxation or as a war reparation exacted from the South. However, industrialists in the North were loath to hand over the land of the defeated planters to their former slaves. They looked forward to the South's early re-emergence as a market for Northern capital, machinery, and consumer goods. Moreover, Yankee businessmen had no intention of setting a precedent in America of confiscating the land of the ruling classes.

One British economist observed: "All that is now wanted to make the Negro a fixed and conservative element in American society is to give him encouragement to and facilities for making himself by his own exertions a small land owner; to do in fact for him what we have sought to do for the Irish farmer. Land in America is so much cheaper and more abundant that it would be infinitely easier to effect the same object there."

However, the white planters who failed in their rebellion against the Union now argued it was unjust to punish them by handing over their land to the black man. And many Northerners agreed that such action by the Government would be the worst sort of petty vengeance.

Oddly, one experiment in black land ownership was tried during the war itself. The Government momentarily let its guard down and handed over to the astonished black man the key to the sacred temple of property rights. When General Sherman marched from Atlanta to the sea, cutting the Confederacy in two, Edward Stanton, the secretary of war, went to Savannah to observe at first hand the situation of the newly liberated Negroes. Thousands had been handed the gift of unemployment as the first bonus of their emancipation. Thrust from the plantations where they had been chattel property but at least had no financial worries, they now found themselves without jobs, facing starvation.

To cope with the embarrassment of having America's new freemen starve to death before they could be presented to the world as an example of Yankee idealism, Stanton and General Sherman propounded a novel scheme. In January 1865 Sherman issued a field order decreeing that the Sea Islands, extending from Charleston south to Port Royal, and all adjoining lands running along the rivers for a distance inland of thirty miles, together with territory adjacent to the St. John's River in Florida, be handed over to the American blacks who had followed Sherman's Army through Georgia. These lands, amounting to 485,000 acres, had been owned by Southern planters who had not paid federal taxes on them for four years.

General Rufus Saxton, one of Sherman's aides, was made inspector of settlements and plantations and assigned the task of dividing up the lands among black families. Forty thousand black men accepted the opportunity with alacrity. But the job they faced in cultivating the land was not easy. Before facilities could be acquired for transporting them to the Sea Islands, the planting season was far advanced. The blacks had no animals, pitifully few agricultural tools, and it was difficult to procure the necessary seed for planting. Nevertheless they set out eagerly for the Islands and, through diligent work, managed to clear the land and plant thousands of acres of cotton. Almost thirty thousand blacks were settled on the Sea Islands, and within twelve months seventeen thousand were earning enough money from the cotton they grew and exported to be entirely self-supporting. They established a community savings bank and deposited over $240,000 of their profits in it.

But the role of realtor was not destined to last long. With the ending of the war, many Southern planters, bereft of their property, vigorously complained of the "injustice" done them. True, they had lost a war of rebellion, but this was a piddling thing next to the stark reality that, bereft of their land they would have to work as laborers for a living. Andrew Johnson, the president, lent a ready ear to their complaints. He granted a pardon to the rebellious planters and along with it the restoration of all their property except their former chattel slaves.

When the blacks realized they had been handed a joker and given only a temporary possessor title, not permanent ownership of the land, they were furious and threatened to resist eviction. The planters retorted that they had better go back to Charleston and work there; and if they could do nothing else, pick oysters for a living.

Washington became uneasy. General Saxton, who had originally been assigned to hand out the land, was dismissed. In his place Washington dispatched another high-ranking general, Howard by name, to explain to the benighted folk what the situation was. The general felt it incumbent on him to pour the balm of oratory upon their wounds. He rose to speak but the words stuck in his throat. To hide his embarrassment he blurted out, "Why don't we all join in a song?" An elderly black woman in the rear piped up, "Sure 'nough. Let's sing 'Nobody Knows the Trouble I've Seen.' "

The stricken landholders drew up a poorly spelled petition to the president of the United States expressing their "sad feelings" over his proclamation and pleading with him to distribute an acre and a half of land to each family. But Johnson, who before the war had declared in a table-thumping speech that "the great plantations must be seized and divided into small farms," was now deaf to their request.

Thousands of blacks who had been landlords for perhaps the briefest span in recorded history upon being evicted went to work as common laborers. Many poured into Florida looking for jobs in factories or tilling other men's crops. Two thousand five hundred migrated in disgust to Liberia.

From time to time in the following years the Government attempted to turn some black men into landlords by condemning and confiscating Southern property for unpaid taxes. The Freedmen's Bureau took title to almost eight hundred thousand acres of farmland in Virginia, South Carolina, Georgia, Louisiana, Kentucky, Tennessee, and North Carolina; but a million acres was not enough to transform an entire class of former slaves into landholders.

While Washington slammed the door on the black masses, exceptionally able and shrewd individuals managed to grab title to land on their own. Overcoming social and legal obstacles, blacks in Virginia in the late 1860s and the 1870s accumulated up to one hundred thousand acres. A few became wealthy farmers controlling up to one thousand acres. Some maneuvered their way into the ownership of large city properties in Virginia. Georgia blacks scooped up four hundred thousand acres of land assessed at $1.3 million. To this they added other city and town real estate holdings valued at $1.2 million. In Arkansas by 1875 two thousand of forty thousand blacks voting in the state owned a house, a farm, or property in town.

They had managed to acquire their holdings through shrewdness, perseverance, and because the land was so inexpensive they could buy it on a relatively large scale if they could scrape up the cash for a small down payment. For the crowning irony was that the value of the land in the South had depreciated so enormously when slave labor was overthrown and the industrial system collapsed, it had become cheap enough for even a former chattel to acquire it. In 1860, just before the war, the assessed property of the South, including its slaves, was valued at about $4.5 million. By 1870 it had shrunk to $2.1 billion.

Since the Emancipation Proclamation, no black family has emerged with a fortune to challenge the Longworths, Astors, or Fields, but given time, there may yet be a black landed aristocracy, especially if devotion to the soil and the fruits thereof is any criterion for success.

4

"I BELIEVE
IN THE NORTHERN
PACIFIC
AS I BELIEVE IN GOD"

Boom, Trust and Bust in the Age of
Westward Expansion

Historically, many of America's largest real estate fortunes
have been triggered by the growth of the nation's transportation
facilities. Millions of dollars have been won—and lost—by land
speculators playing the massive boom in United States railroads
that, after the Civil War, linked America from sea to sea.

The Vanderbilts, for instance, not only amassed their fortune
from railroad freight, but also from the land which was handed
out by the government along the routes of their roads, and they
added frosting to the cake when they converted the tracks running into New York into Park Avenue, the world's single wealthiest residential strip. Henry Flagler in Florida and the Van Sweringen Brothers in the Middle West similarly made millions by using
railroads as an instrument for boosting the value of their real es-

tate holdings. The communication needs of the growing nation played spectacularly into their hands.

Indeed, building railroads was to most American investors only a secondary aim. The main lure was the chance to speculate on the handouts of land that accompanied the road grants. From the start the entrepreneurs who schemed to span the continent with iron spikes were aware they could not lure speculative money on the prospect of a return from the railroad traffic. The lines were to be laid in sparsely settled areas—in many cases outright wilderness—west of the Mississippi, and it would be decades before enough people would arrive to make freight haulage profitable. The major magnet for attracting capital was the land offered by the government along the prospective tracks, acreage that could be turned into a rapid profit through a speculative rise in prices.

Mark Twain in his *Gilded Age* writes of the speculative mania in land buying that accompanied the railroad boom after the Civil War. One of his characters, a stock promoter by the name of Mr. Bigler, is enthused over building the Tunkhannock, Rattlesnake and Youngwomenstown Railroad, which he predicts will be a superhighway to the Far West. "We'll buy the lands," rhapsodizes Mr. Bigler, "on long time backed by the notes of good men; and then mortgage them for money enough to get the road well on. Then get the towns on the line to issue their bonds for stock. . . . We can then sell the rest of the stock on the prospect of the business of the roads. . . . And also sell the lands at a big advance, on the strength of the road."

Like the imaginary Mr. Bigler, the avarice of flesh-and-blood railroad investors was fired by the prospect of rocketing real estate prices.

One early prospectus for a road to be built through Indiana in the 1830s explains, "Were the company to purchase a million acres of the lands adjacent to the work, the increase alone in the price of the lands would, before the work is half completed, pay for the entire construction of it. Once the location of the route is announced, the price of every acre of land within two miles of it will triple."

The profitability of real estate charters the government handed

101

out to entice the railroad builders became notorious. One British businessman traveling in the United States wrote home about the Illinois Central Railroad, which was in the process of being launched. "This is not a railroad company, it is a land company."

As the building of the railroads turned into a speculative jamboree, the rail-*cum*-land barons used their franchises as a weapon with which to strangle a community or let it live. They would announce with a fanfare of publicity that they were prepared to locate their route near a certain community. Privately they would contact the leaders of the community and ask for money as a token of its gratitude for their decision. If the municipal fathers were reluctant to come up with the cash, the barons hinted they would bypass the town and let it strangle to death commercially. Since the value of its real estate—indeed the entire financial future of the community—depended on its being on the rail line, the municipal fathers usually were quick to pay the extortion money.

Sacramento, San Francisco, Stockton, and other towns to receive the blessing of being located along the route of the Central Pacific Railroad were blackmailed by its owners into giving huge sums of money in order to survive as commercial centers.

The historian Matthew Josephson graphically describes the tactic. "A railroad company approaches a small town as a highwayman approaches his victim. The threat 'if you do not accede to our terms we will leave your town two or three miles to one side' is as efficacious as the 'stand and deliver' when backed by a cocked pistol."

The rail barons rapidly became the financial powers of the nation, using their possessions of real estate in a gigantic chess game to outmaneuver roads who were contesting their fiefdoms. Like the medieval Italian *condottieri* and ducal princes, writes Josephson, they seized "one valley or the passageway to it by setting their castles upon the heights overlooking the rivers . . . or closing the mountain passes."

And in the course of the struggle the rail barons became fabulously rich from the millions of acres of ranchland, timberland, and vineyards which became enormously valuable.

One businessman who saw the supreme advantage of linking

102

land speculation with building a railroad was Jay Cooke, America's leading banker, celebrated for having masterminded the campaign to float bonds to finance the Civil War. (The Lincoln government had found it politically more expedient to raise the money for battlefield operations by shunning tax-raising measures and calling upon citizens to subscribe voluntarily to bonds.) Cooke managed to coax enough greenbacks from Yankee pockets into the government treasury to subsidize the entire war and reap a hefty commission for himself.

Cooke had an impeccably trimmed beard and piercing blue eyes. He looked like a saintly peddler of the Gospel, and indeed he was a missionary, highly adept at converting other people's dollars into his own bank account.*

Once the war was over, the venerated banker-patriot looked for further ways to line his pockets. Alert to the opportunities for making money by exploiting patriotic causes, Cooke realized that building railroads was an especially promising pursuit. It delighted the heart of all Americans eager to link the nation from sea to sea, and it had enormous possibilities for personal aggrandizement. Cooke was cognizant of the power a prospective railroad had on land speculation. He had plunged into real estate operations as a stockholder of the Philadelphia and Erie Land Company, which owned properties along the route of the railroad. Having picked up his winning chips from the Philadelphia-Erie game, Cooke was attracted by the possibilities of the then American Northwest because of its potential for becoming one of the nation's great commercial centers owing to its proximity to the Great Lakes. Duluth, a growing community in the northern end of Minnesota, especially whetted his enthusiasm, located as it was at the head of Lake Superior. Duluth had only seven wooden frame houses, a schoolhouse, and the inevitable land office where local real estate hucksters were hustling town lots.

Cooke sent a business agent, Rice Harper, out to Duluth to size

*Sources on Cooke's machinations include E. P. Oberholtzer, Cooke's *Collected Papers, Reports of the Northern Pacific*, etc. (See Bibliography)

up the community, and the latter wrote him, "I give it to you as my firm conviction that if Duluth becomes the terminus of a railroad on Lake Superior, it will attain a larger growth in five years than any other city in twenty."

Heartened by this appraisal, Cooke bought up forty thousand acres of land in and around Duluth. He and his partner snapped up timber for the sawmills that would inevitably be built to provide supplies for the Eastern lumber manufacturers once the land around the Great Lakes was connected by a railroad. Preparing for this eventuality, Cooke continued to amass land. Rice Harper was sent out a second time to Minnesota—in April 1869—to make more investments.

The journey was a rough one. Harper proceeded to Lake Superior and, trapped in a blizzard, was marooned for a week before he was able to cross the bay to Duluth. Because Duluth's harbor was icebound, the boat had to land several miles from the town. Harper struggled into Duluth in subzero weather, but undeterred by his experience he plunged his cash into lots in the heart of the future city. Prices had already risen to the point at which lots were selling for $600 an acre.

Loaded up with vast properties in the Northwest, Cooke now more than ever needed a railroad to turn his speculation into a commercial success. He canvassed rail promoters from coast to coast, scrutinized their various plans, and came across one highly promising venture. A New England syndicate headed by a Boston wool merchant, who had made a fortune speculating in Maine timberland, was planning a railroad to run from Lake Superior to Puget Sound, connecting the Mississippi with the Pacific Northwest. Cooke decided that this projected line, the Northern Pacific, was just the tool he needed for his land speculation. The Northern Pacific Corporation had already been formed, and its stock was trading on Wall Street on the prospects of its getting a land grant from Congress. Cooke began buying up the stock, whose price was rising and falling like a yo-yo as traders waxed alternately bullish and bearish over the firm's chances of getting the land permit. Cooke quietly accumulated enough shares to become a substantial shareholder, and in December 1869 surfaced, announced his holdings, and offered to take over the job of selling the company's bonds to the public. To this end Cooke wangled an agreement with the company founders under which they would take half of the profits, Jay Cooke and company the remainder. The owners were delighted to become associated with America's paradigm banker, who had such highly influential friends in Washington. When Cooke's announcement that he would assume the task of raising money for the Northern Pacific was flashed over the telegraph wires, one of the directors of the company wrote to the banker, "I flung my hat to the ceiling. Smith [the treasurer] and I congratulated each other's arms off with protracted and increasingly furious handshaking."

Once he had assumed the job, Cooke went assiduously to work. Bribe money was handed out liberally to key Congressmen. As a result the Northern Pacific Railroad was chartered in July with a government grant of a million and a half acres.

In a rare burst of generosity, Uncle Sam handed over more than twenty-two thousand acres of land for every mile of road to be finished by its entrepreneurs. This amounted to more than fifty million acres of prime agricultural land, timberland, and mineral resources extending from Wisconsin through the richest parts of Minnesota, Dakota, Montana, Iowa, Oregon, and Washington to Puget Sound. The grant to the Northern Pacific amounted to more territory than the six New England states with Maryland added. It was almost seven times larger than Belgium and four times greater than Holland. The land alone, the Northern Pacific syndicate figured, would provide a fortune for the insiders. If they unloaded it to the public at only $5 an acre, this would provide an income of $140,000 per mile against a cost of only $40,000 per mile to build the railroad.

This extraordinary giveaway had not been obtained without a bitter hassle in Congress. Every pressure had been put on the Washington politicos to persuade them to hand over the fifty million acres, and the most energetic lobbyist was Jay Cooke himself, acting through his brother, Henry, who ran the Washington branch of Jay Cooke and Company. In charge of pushing the bill through the Senate was Senator Alexander Ramsey of Minnesota, representing one of the states that would benefit hugely by its passage. While the bill was being considered, Henry Cooke wrote to his brother, "We have been at work like beavers and have whipped the enemy on every vote so far—in most cases three or four to one. We let the other side do most of the talking and we do the voting."

An amendment was introduced to the measure by Senator Simon Cameron of Pennsylvania, who came from a major iron and coal state and insisted on a provision that "American iron or steel only shall be used in constructing the track." Once this amendment was inserted, the bill was passed by the Senate in April 1870 by a vote of 40 to 11. It then went to the House "with," as brother Henry reported to Jay Cooke, "the prestige of a four-fifths majority."

At this point Representative William Wheeler of New York, the chief sponsor on the floor of the House, made the tactical blunder of trying to ram it through without a debate. This aroused anger and there was a tempestuous scene on the House floor on May 5. Launching a filibuster to block the measure, a small group of Congressmen railed against it, calling it "an outrageous extension of the policy of land subsidies," and berating the "spectacle of the government's surrender of a mighty land empire into the clutches of private speculators." "There has never before been such a grant," charged one Congressman. "It leaves no land for another road in the whole northern part of the United States, and provides a single syndicate with a monopoly of the wheat fields, pastureland, forests, fisheries and mines of the Pacific Northwest."

Despite these accusations the House passed the measure on May 6 by a vote of 107 to 85. When the news was received in Duluth, the price of real estate jumped 10 percent within an hour. There was one detail to be attended to. President Ulysses S. Grant had to sign the bill. However, this was not considered a problem. The Chief Executive was counted safely in Cooke's camp.

Indeed, a few weeks previously, Jay Cooke had taken the precaution of sending a fishing rod to the president's small son,

Jesse, and the president's wife had written to him that the gift had become Jesse's favorite possession. Hearing this, Cooke invited the president to come with his son for a week's fishing at his estate. Grant accepted, but the time had to be reduced to a single day because of the president's "pressing engagements."

When the Northern Pacific bill arrived at the White House, Grant held a Cabinet meeting and discovered there was brisk opposition to his signing it. The day after the meeting Henry wrote his brother, ". . . . the bill was met with violent opposition, but as this is told me in strictest confidence, you must not allude to the fact. . . . General Grant was firm as a rock, and my information is that the bill received the sanction of the majority of the Cabinet."

The president remained loyal. There was more at stake than a fishing rod. He had received substantial personal loans from Cooke, and he wasn't about to turn on his benefactor.

Grant signed the bill, and on July 1, 1870, a mortgage was executed by the Northern Pacific Company to cover all the land the firm had received from the grant. While technically the company could not take title to any of it until actual trackage had been constructed and it was inspected and approved by government engineers, Cooke and his associates were not bothered by this detail. Ultimately the land would be theirs legally, Cooke reasoned, so why not execute a mortgage beforehand, using the land as collateral, since this was the biggest selling point the company had in raising the capital needed to get the project going?

Congress, be it noted, had not provided the actual operating money; it had offered the land to enable the company to generate the cash by issuing bonds on it. To raise enough seed money to start building the road, Cooke decided he would organize a "pool," offering the select group of insiders a chance to get in on the ground floor. Then, using this land as collateral, he would launch a nationwide bond campaign to promote a mass infusion of money from the public to complete the project. As the public was lured in, the pool members would be able to unload their holdings at a heady profit.

Holding out this tempting prospect, Cooke wrote to his leading financial colleagues, inviting them to subscribe to a one-twelfth interest in his pool in "man-fashion." They couldn't lose on the deal, he pointed out, since the price of their shares was bound to rise as they were dumped on newcomers.

Those whom Cooke approached were exuberant at being selected. Among them was Schuyler Colfax, who as a sideline happened to be serving as the vice president of the United States. He and other influential figures were asked to come in without putting up a penny of their own, since their influence was such they would help Cooke's promotional effort to wheedle further cash. Cooke contacted Salmon Chase, the chief justice of the Supreme Court, and offered to cut him in to the deal. Chief Justice Chase replied that he reluctantly had to refuse. Not that the ethics of the matter bothered him. In the jovial era of post-Civil War finance, there was no thought of discriminating against a chief justice of the Supreme Court and preventing him from reaping the profits of a boondoggle. In a democracy dedicated to equal opportunity for all, the highest officials of government had just as much right as anyone else to clean up on the American public. Chase felt he had to refuse because he was in his sixties. "Though the prospect of future profit is very inviting," he wrote, "it is rather too remote for one who does not expect to live longer than I do. I wish I could be connected in some way with your magnificent undertaking but I do not see how."

Cooke replied that Chase had apparently misunderstood his offer. There was no question of his having to put up any of his own money to get the securities. Cooke would carry him on his own account. Then, when the public was lured in and the price of the bonds skyrocketed, the profits would more than absorb the cost and provide a windfall as well. At this clarification, the chief justice accepted with alacrity.

Having joined the promotional team, Chase overflowed with the juices of revivified youth. The more he thought about the financial high jinks of the scheme, the more excited he became. He became so enthusiastic that he wrote Cooke in August 1870, saying he would love to be appointed to the board of the Northern Pacific Company. He had no idea of course of giving up his august post at the Supreme Court, but he hinted he would be extremely grateful for the chance of serving as chief executive. "I think I would make a good President of the Northern Pacific and my . . . reputation would justify a good salary."

Upon hearing about this request, a business associate of Cooke's remarked to the banker, "I think the chief justice had far better retain his position at the head of the nation's Judiciary. He would find it much more difficult to efficiently manage a railroad."

The chief justice continued to kick his heels. "Hurrah for the Northern Pacific!" he wrote Cooke after visiting Duluth to see for himself the prospects of the rapidly growing town. "I wish I was able to take four times as much bonds as you've assigned to me."

Indeed, there was such a scramble by influential Americans to get into the pool that Cooke had to establish stiff requirements for entrance. In January 1870, Governor Smith of Vermont wrote the banker, pleading to have a million dollars worth of subscriptions reserved for him and his friends. Cooke replied that the entire amount needed had already been over subscribed and he was slamming the door on further entrants. He felt sorry, Cooke added, but the governor and his friends were just "too slow" in presenting their applications.

However, other candidates who applied late were told they would be accepted. Actually this Aesopian banker had set aside shares from his own large reserve which he continued to hand over to those he wished to accommodate. Like a ticket agent who always has a few pasteboards to spare for a hit show, Cooke had shares for anybody who was an asset to him. He realized that his railroad- and land-speculation scheme depended for its success upon an astute public relations program. He had to brainwash the public into accepting the project in the spirit of the Second Coming of Christ, since the whole bag would have to be dumped ultimately onto rank-and-file Americans.

Cooke was far ahead of his time in understanding how to manipulate public opinion through media promotion. He paid careful attention to newspaper journalists who were in a position to reach the masses. Chief among the scriveners was Sam Wilkeson, a veteran newsman who was brought into the pool by Cooke on a free subscription. Wilkeson had wide contacts, and under Cooke's direction approached Horace Greely and Henry Ward Beecher, two contemporary celebrities. Beecher, the nation's number one evangelist preacher, was invited into the pool with a subscription of $15,000, and Horace Greeley, the powerful editor of the *New York Tribune,* was asked to come in for $20,000 worth of bonds, both receiving their securities without putting up a cent, being permitted to pay back over long, easy installments. Like Chief Justice Chase and others, they were told that by the time they had to kick in the bulk of their money, the price of their securities would have risen so substantially it would not only cover their cost, but also provide them a lively profit.

Beecher and Greeley avidly accepted. The former was editor of the *Christian Union,* a religious newspaper with a wide circulation. He invited Sam Wilkeson to write a series of articles for his paper, describing in glowing rhetoric how the Northern Pacific would bestow untold blessings on America.

Having won over Wilkeson and the pages of the *Christian Union,* Cooke went after other news journalists. He gave the editor of the *Philadelphia Press* $5000 in return for printing his publicity handouts. In the meantime Wilkeson worked on a public relations brochure, the finest professional hucksterism could concoct. A colleague reported to Cooke how the pamphlet was prepared. "Mr. McCullouch, a newsman, wrote a version which read like the Declaration of Independence; Mr. Sheppard [another reporter] wrote a version which read like Disraeli's novels. I gave them all to Sheppard and had him boil them down. I then scratched out about half of what he had written, and after a good deal of twisting and turning, the result was arrived at."

Cooke's publicists arranged for a team of lecturers to take to the hustings, giving talks on the glories of the Northwest. One lecturer on the pool's payroll—a newsman, Coffin by name—prepared a lecture called "The Seat of Empire," which he dutifully delivered over and over again at town meetings throughout New England. Sam Wolf, recorder of deeds at the Library of Congress, was hired as a lecturer to extol the Northern Pacific. Wolf was a linguist especially skilled in German, and it was his mission to whet the appetite of Teutons to emigrate to the American Northwest. In the spring of 1871 Cooke's agents organized a town meeting at the Academy of Music in Philadelphia to acquaint people with the blandishments of the region. Four thousand people crammed into the hall and hundreds were turned away. Wrote Sam Wilkeson, the Pooh-Bah of the public relations crew, "I believe in the Northwest as I believe in God."

One of Wilkeson's hirelings took a trip to the Red River Valley and wrote a notice for the *Boston Journal* calculated to inspire young New Englanders to rush to the West, settle on the land, and start jacking up those real estate prices for Cooke's coffers:

Think of it, young men; you who are measuring off tape for young ladies, shut up in a store for long and wearisome hours, barely earning your living; throw down the yardstick and come out here if you would be men. Can you hold a plow? Can you drive a span of horses? Can you bid goodbye to the theater and turn your back upon the crowds in the street? Can you accept for a while the solitude of nature, bear a few hard knocks for a year or two? Can you lay aside paper collars and kid gloves and wear a blue blouse and work with calloused hands? If you can, there is a beautiful home for you out here. Prosperity, freedom, independence, manhood in its highest sense, peace of mind and all the comforts and luxuries of life are awaiting you.

Amidst the hoopla to raise money there were some disquieting notes. There was one dissenter within Cooke's official family, a Mr. Harris Charles Fahnestock, who suffered twinges of conscience over the plan to raise $50 million from the American public. The government, Mr. Fahnestock reminded Cooke, had made no financial guarantee and had handed out land whose future was uncertain. "I do not hesitate to say," he wrote Cooke, "that the present actual condition of the Northern Pacific if it were understood by the public would be fatal to the negotiation of its securities." Cooke, pointed out Fahnestock, had assured the public in his publicity broadsides of the intelligence, vigor, and efficiency

111

of the management. But, observed Fahnestock, "we know that it [the management of the Northern Pacific] has been inefficient, distracted by other engagements and extravagant to the last degree. You have assured them [the public] that the lands are unparalleled in climate, soil, timber and minerals, and are superior to those upon which Massachusetts has become wealthy and great. We know that a large portion of the lands from Lake Superior to the Mississippi are practically valueless either for cultivation or for lumbering and that the residue are less valuable than the public has been led to believe. . . . Too much dependence has been placed upon the names of the promoters." Fahnestock pointed out that the price of the bonds was highly inflated, was not based upon the solid accomplishment of the company but upon the razzle-dazzle publicity that had been unleashed over America.

Fahnestock further pointed out that the bonds once bought by the public could never be used in an emergency as collateral to obtain loans from banks because the bankers knew that their value depended not upon the intrinsic worth of the company but upon one man's ability (Cooke's) to make them good. Their chief asset depended on the salesmanship of a financial showman. The only guarantee Cooke pledged the public was his own name and reputation, Fahnestock warned. "You have the most delicate responsibility of the trusteeship, making you morally liable to every man and woman holding the bonds for the proper and economical application of all the monies received and for the verification of all the statements contained in our publications which have endorsed the bonds . . . as the best and safest security for widows and orphans and trust funds and as good as United States bonds."

Undeterred by Fahnestock's objections, Cooke proceeded with his plans. Five million dollars had already been subscribed by the pool. Another fifty million of public money was needed to get his project going full swing. But it was important for its success to keep the price of Northern Pacific bonds steady. This meant that the members of the pool who had been invited in on the ground floor must be warned to hold on to their bonds, although it was tempting for these charter members to dump their holdings on their country cousins. A premature unloading by the insiders could result in a down break in price that would be fatal to his plans.

To make sure they would not unload prematurely, the banker who kept a record of the numbers on the face of each bond he had issued his pool comrades threatened that if any of them sold their holdings, he would trace the malfactor and strip him of his syndicate privileges.

Cooke had gotten into the Northern Pacific primarily to facilitate his land speculations and he never lost sight of this aim. The building of the railroad was window dressing for his real estate manipulations, but to get his land prices soaring, he had to persuade large numbers of people to come out to the Northwest and settle there.

Cooke trained all his promotional guns to this end. He provided as an inducement an early version of the modern installment contract applied to land buying. The company offered to sell lots for a 10 percent down payment in cash, 10 percent to be paid within one year, 10 percent in two years, 10 percent in three years, and 15 percent annually thereafter, with the final payment to be made within seven years.

To handle the migration, Cooke opened a central office in New York with branches throughout the Northwest Territory. Reception houses were built to receive the settlers and lodge them without cost until they were able to purchase their farms. Immigrants leaving from New York and other eastern points were to be met by company guides who would advise them as to the cheapest, most convenient way to travel. If there were over five in a party, they could obtain bargain rates on the railroads. Once they had reached the tracks of the Northern Pacific that had already been laid, they were to travel free to their designated property site. They were told how to build their cabins, how to buy their household implements and farming equipment at the lowest possible prices, when to begin plowing, what to plant.

Meanwhile, as plans for the immigration were publicized, the price of Duluth real estate rocketed. Several of Cooke's associates moved into the town to set themselves up in business and prepare for the commercial boom they felt was inevitable.

One of Cooke's colleagues wrote home to him, "It is not the

Duluth of a little more than a year ago, with its 105 inhabitants and its fifteen or twenty rude buildings on a strip of land between the unbroken wilderness and the waters of the greatest of lakes."

Another reported, "The progress of this town is remarkable. It quite equals that of San Francisco for the time and under the circumstances."

By the summer of 1872 two thousand homes renting for $40 a month and up had been built, and there was already an acute housing shortage. As the tracks of the Northern Pacific inched toward Duluth, a large influx of people rushed in to settle in the town and adjacent territories. Many were the rag and bobtail sort, for along with the boom came the liquor trade, gambling, and gunfighting. Over thirty whiskey shops were opened to serve the workers on the railroad during after-job hours. The more enterprising whiskey peddlers beat their competitors to the choice locations by loading up boats with liquor and navigating a hundred miles ahead of the railroad laborers to be ready for them when they arrived.

As more and more settlers poured into Duluth, the speculative fever accelerated. Fortune hunters grabbed up land, expecting the population to double monthly and the price of their acreage to climb at an equal pace. These speculators were the most vociferous in demanding that the Northern Pacific directors announce as quickly as possible that Duluth would definitely be the eastern terminus of the railroad, but these Duluthians were challenged by a community located across the Minnesota line, Superior, whose land hustlers, headed by the governor of Vermont and a clique of New England businessmen, were pressing to have the terminal located in Superior, not Duluth. The two towns plunged into a bitter rivalry. Duluthians ridiculed the settlers of Superior who lived on low flat ground, calling them "swamp-jumpers." The townsmen of Superior retaliated by calling their neighbors on the higher ground "hill-climbers" and "cliff-dwellers."

Life was difficult in Duluth and Superior. The climate was harsh. In November 1872 a violent storm swept across the lake, wrecking the boats that were lying in anchor near the towns. The storm was followed by a severe cold spell lasting until the following April, with the ice on the lake remaining fifteen inches thick until May, bringing all navigation to a halt.

Meanwhile, the business climate in which Cooke launched his public bond issue was also turning cold. The economy had been shaken by the attempt of Jay Gould, a stock market manipulator, to corner the nation's gold supply, which had triggered a panic almost toppling America's entire financial structure. Shortly afterward a fire had broken out in Chicago, leveling three-quarters of the city. This was followed by another one that almost totally destroyed the commercial center of Boston. These calamaties underscored in many minds the uncertainty of real estate as an investment.

Meanwhile, the boom in railroad building had become tarnished. A scandal had erupted involving the operations of the nation's first transcontinental road, the Union Pacific, involving numbers of Congressmen who had lined their pockets on land speculations.

The Northern Pacific itself was having difficulties. The laying of its tracks was proceeding with excruciating slowness. Cooke, in his ambitions to expand operations, had encouraged the board of directors to buy a controlling interest in a trunk line, the St. Paul and Pacific, paying over $1 million for the franchise. The road had run into financial trouble. The price of its bonds had dropped below par, damaging the market for Northern Pacific's own bonds. Finally Cooke was forced to sever his relationship with his ailing subsidiary.

From all over America the banker's agents sent in ominous reports. The Northern Pacific bond issue—the so-called Seven-Thirties—was selling slowly. Agents complained it was virtually impossible for them to keep their price at par.

With domestic funds laggard in coming in, Cooke, to drum up money, followed the strategy of Robert Morris and other predecessors. He set his cap to lure foreigners into his venture. His first port of call was the illustrious House of Rothschilds. Cooke's emissary, William Moorhead, called on the head of the London branch lugging prospectuses with scintillating reports about the Northern Pacific. Old Baron Guy de Rothschild accept-

ed him courteously and listened to Cooke's offer. The baron and
the four sons affiliated with him in the business discussed the matter for several days, and then Cooke received a cable from his associate, "The old gentleman said the Rothschilds never engage in
anything that required risk or trouble in the management."

Undeterred, Cooke pressed on with his scheme to wheedle
money from European bankers. His idea was to induce foreign
financiers to raise money for him by issuing bonds to the public.
To a continental associate, Robert Thode and Co., and other
bankers he had previously done business with, he assigned
specific territories for merchandising the bonds. The bankers
were offered an interest in the pool, together with liberal commis-
sions on the sales they made.

To induce the bankers, Cooke dispatched agents to give their
pitch all the way from Scandinavia to Italy. One wrote home enthusiastically, reporting on the round of business dinners he had
addressed: "I always . . . toast America, the flag of the Union,
Jay Cooke, Northern Pacific Railroad, their countrymen in America, myself, wife and children, and so forth, and then I . . . allude to the happy homes along the Northern Pacific awaiting to
receive Europe's millions of landless people and so forth. When I
mention what you did for the Union (during the Civil War) I stir
them up to a terrific point and they generally give you three
cheers and sometimes three times three."

To soften up resistance to the Northern Pacific, Cooke resorted
to a technique he had used so expertly in America, bribing the
European press to serve as a propaganda machine for him. It was
vital to buy up key newspapers since a group of European bankers was stubbornly warning its countrymen to stay away from the
Northern Pacific bonds. Europeans had already been cozened
badly in investments in other American railroads and in land
schemes dating from the American Revolution. The board of governors of the Berlin Bourse asserted that the Northern Pacific
bonds were a risky adventure because the American government,
while granting land, had given no specific financial guarantee.

When reports of this opposition reached Cooke, he fired off a
letter to the board members of the German Bourse. "My name

and that of my firm are not, I presume, unknown to you. I will not here refer to our connection with the government as its main financial agent during the recent war, but I desire to state that for over thirty years as a banker in Philadelphia I've been engaged in fostering the building of American railroads and in disposing of securities, and I've never yet sold the bonds of any company, the interest upon which has not been punctually and regularly paid and the principal made more secure from year to year."

To counter the rising hostility, Cooke tried an astute promotional ploy. He leaked to the American press the disclosure that Germany's revered elder statesman, Chancellor Otto von Bismarck, was planning to visit America and stay with him as his guest. The news was false when he released it, but Cooke in an attempt to make it come true wired a formal invitation to the chancellor who in Germany occupied a throne just a little lower than the kaiser's. It was almost a year before the chancellor got around to answering the banker. "Dear sir, your letter of the 13th of June last reached me on the 11th of July. If you remember how shortly that date was followed by the declaration of war [the Franco-Prussian War] you'll excuse the otherwise unpardonable delay in answering so kind an invitation. Being about to embark on a diplomatic campaign very likely to lead to an armed conflict, I felt doubly impressed with the charms of your secluded island and your delicate hospitality. Peace is now happily restored, but a great deal remains to be done at home and I do not know whenever it will be given to me to satisfy my old longing for your country." Signed, v. Bismarck.

Attacks in Europe continued to be launched against Cooke's enterprise. One newspaper editor who had somehow avoided being hooked onto Cooke's payroll castigated the "ring of greedy operators" of the Northern Pacific and their "huge robbery of the public domain." Fumed the editor, "Not since the celebrated South Sea Bubble, when so much money was plunged into wild hazard," had there been such a brazen scheme as Cooke's.

Most annoying to Cooke was the fact that the foreign outcry was fed by a dissident newspaper at home—the *Philadelphia Public Ledger*—whose publisher and editors had refused to take

117

Cooke's bribes. His inability to silence the *Ledger* infuriated the banker. He wrote his brother Henry, "It is the greatest outrage any journal ever committed upon decent citizens. We are pitching into them and if it is necessary and it is thought best, I will establish a penny paper equal to the *Ledger,* reducing the expense of advertising fifty percent. If this man continues to fight us as he has done, I will fight him."

What made the attacks of the *Ledger* especially embarrassing was that George William Childs, the publisher, had developed an affiliation with the powerful *Financial Times* of London which interchanged news with it and which was influential not only in Britain but all over Europe since it was subscribed to by all the major banking houses, stock exchanges, and top business firms on the Continent.

Unable to muzzle the *Ledger,* Cooke wired his agent in Britain, George Sargent, to see if anything "could be done with the London *Times.*" Sargent replied, "All the press in England can be bought for about a three thousand pound [$15,000] expenditure excepting the *Times* which must be arranged for separately." Sargent added wryly that the only way Cooke could prevent the *Ledger*'s articles from being reprinted in the London *Times* was to sink the ship that carried the copy over.

Finally, Sargent managed to wangle an introduction to Henry Sampson, the lordly financial editor of the *Times.* The editor had the reputation of a man who couldn't be bought, but Sargent was highly optimistic, for, despite his modest salary, Sampson lived in princely fashion and had sumptuous tastes. Sampson invited Sargent to his home in Hampton Court where he entertained him for two days in his usually elegant style. While he waited for Sargent to propose a suitable deal, the editor broadly hinted he was ready to change his mind about the Northern Pacific and support it under "certain conditions."

"This is the hole I have made him crawl out of," Sargent wrote Cooke, "and I shall have his hearty cooperation on terms that must never be known but to you, to him and to me." Sampson was supposed to be unreachable at any price, but obviously Sargent had named one that succeeded in seducing this pillar of journalistic respectability. In addition to arriving at the right price dollarwise, Cooke sealed the bargain with a gift. He had heard that the editor's sister was a collector of fine stones, and Cooke purchased one of the rarest amethysts to be found on the shore of Lake Superior, sending it to the woman.

Sampson was a highly valuable man to have in one's pocket, for it turned out that in addition to his position as financial pundit on the newspaper, he had managed to become a major stockholder in a big brokerage house, the General Credit and Discount Company. In the twinkling of an eye, as soon as Sampson joined the Cooke team, the broker house received a contract to act as the banker's agent for issuing Northern Pacific bonds not only in Britain but throughout Europe.

Once the *Financial Times* was sewed up, Cooke contacted a banking house in Darmstadt, Germany, hoping to induce it to raise 50 million marks through a bond issue to the German people. Cooke ordered Sargent to hurry to Darmstadt to complete the negotiations, but Sargent postponed the meeting for two days to attend a dinner given American diplomats by British financiers in honor of the Fourth of July. As a result of these festivities, Sargent, instead of meeting with the Darmstadt bankers to sign the contract on a Wednesday, didn't arrive until Friday.

This forty-eight-hour delay proved highly costly, for in the interim a diplomatic crisis which had been slowly seething between Louis Napoleon, emperor of France, and Bismarck, the chancellor of Prussia, suddenly erupted. During these critical forty-eight hours, political negotiations between them collapsed. Bismarck ordered the Prussian armies to invade France.

The outbreak of war caused a stampede on the European stock markets and in the banking houses. The sale of bonds for an American railroad suddenly was out of the question.

But Cooke pressed on. Stymied by his efforts to raise money from abroad, he redoubled his efforts to use the American public as his cornucopia.

Despite all the promotional razzle-dazzle, the bond issue, as noticed, was selling slowly in the States. A less skillful legerdemainist might have concluded that since the bond issue was not going well, the way to step up sales was to increase the interest rate. Not Cooke. This audacious necromancer of finance decided that the best way to revive sales was not to increase *but to decrease the interest on the bonds.* They were selling at 7.3 percent per annum, and people weren't lining up in droves to snap them up. Cooke decided the solution was to call in the 7.3 bonds and reissue one bearing 6 percent interest. It was all a matter of psychology, he figured. The public would reason that no board of directors would be foolhardy enough to lower the interest on their bonds unless they had inside information that the financial strength of their company had changed substantially for the better. A company which no longer needed to borrow its money at so high an interest rate couldn't be on the verge of the collapse that had been so widely predicted for the Northern Pacific. If a firm showed such confidence, it must know something that the man in the street wasn't aware of.

Moreover, Cooke calculated, when the announcement was made to call in the higher interest bond at a designated date and issue a lower interest bearing one, "alert" investors who sensed a bargain ahead of others would rush in to snap up the 7.3 percent bonds before they disappeared from the market. These bonds were now selling at 90 cents below par, but the announcement was bound to send the price smartly above par, Cooke reasoned. Investors would then buy them faster than they were now taking them and those who had them would hold onto them with a firmer grasp.

When Cooke directed the Northern Pacific board of directors to proceed with this stratagem, they expressed astonishment at its brusquerie. They argued that if the bond issue were to be closed on this basis, it should be done as quickly as possible and with a "tremendous whirl of publicity." Observed one director, "It is our only salvation before we go into bankruptcy."

Cooke as usual was aeons ahead of his colleagues in his thinking. He was planning not one but a dozen moves in advance to turn adversity into opportunity by spinning a new skein of speculation upon the shaky foundation of the old. His strategy for floating the 6 percent bond issue was to organize a new closely knit syndicate of pool members who would get in on the ground floor to reap the anticipated ride-up of prices as the appetite of the public was whipped up for the bonds.

With the Northern Pacific in a tight financial squeeze, with the 7.3 percent bonds doing badly, and rumors spreading throughout the country that the company was losing money, the new bonds had to be issued as quickly as possible while there was still an enterprise left to operate. Cooke decided to call in the bond issue when it reached a $30-million point in sales. At the time the 7.3 percent bonds had been issued, Cooke had boasted publicly that he would raise $50 million. But despite the merchandising efforts of fifteen hundred agents, sales of the 7.3 percent bonds were lagging at the $16-million level. Another $9 million in bonds had been distributed to members of the pool.

The plan to close one issue and launch a new one was not without risk, for it meant that Cooke would have to disclose publicly the miserable results of his financial efforts up to the present. Before the new bonds could be registered, Cooke would have to reveal that despite his vast promotional ballyhoo and his army of fifteen hundred bond agents traveling throughout the country to drum up business, sales were struggling at the disappointing volume of only $16 million.

However, the more the banker contemplated the subtleties of his scheme, the more his appetite was aroused. He would put together a pool of insiders with the sleight-of-hand levitation he had exercised for the first pool. Only the exterior details would be different. He planned to offer the bonds to ground-floor subscribers at eighty-five dollars net with a 50 percent bonus in company stock. Along with the $9 million worth of bonds, the pool members would get $4.5 million of paid-up stock. This $4.5 million worth of stock, plus the cash discount on the bonds that would be realized as they rose in price above $85, would amount, Cooke figured, to about $4.5 million after deducting expenses for publicity and advertising. Once more, as before, Cooke warned the pool members to hold onto their bonds and not dare to sell below par if they wished to entice the public. "It is the prettiest speculation that I know of," Cooke boasted to a politician he invited into the syndicate.

Cooke felt no obligation to inform the public at large of the uneasiness felt privately by his colleagues and himself regarding the prospects of the Northern Pacific. When an elderly investor, retired from his job, wrote asking whether it was advisable to put the few dollars he had managed to save up into Northern Pacific bonds, the venerable banker instructed his secretary to reply, "You are a splendid fellow for an old gentleman of sixty-four. Mr. Cooke desires me to say . . . that he has perfect confidence in the Northern Pacific bonds. They are receivable for lands at any moment at ten percent better than you can buy the said lands for greenbacks. Your own good sense will show you that a bond thus secured and thus receivable cannot be a bad investment, even though the skies should fall . . . Mr. Cooke himself personally would not hesitate to put all that he has in the world into Northern Pacific."

To another anxious investor, Cooke wrote, pointing out that the Northern Pacific venture could not possibly be risky because of the land that it held as collateral, "There is not the slightest probability of there being any cessation in the legitimate demand for land unless the world comes to an end."

At one point a rather awkward situation arose. Horace Greeley, the journalist who had been invited into the pool, died suddenly a year and a half later and his will was contested by his heirs. One of the assets mentioned in it were his shares in the Northern Pacific pool and the legal question arose as to how his interest in the pool should be valued.

Sam Wilkeson wrote to Cooke in consternation, "I have got to go to White Plains or else be carried there under sub poena. Among the questions that will be asked me is what is the value of Mrs. Greeley's interest in the Northern Pacific Railroad enterprise. My testimony will be reported of course and published throughout the country, and I can conceive that every word I say about this enterprise had better be well weighed. So, my friend, considering the interests of your pool and everything, tell me, what do you think Mrs. Greeley's $10,000 interest is worth."

It was one thing for Cooke in peddling bonds to the susceptible public to inflate their value to whatever heights rhetoric could raise it. It was another thing to come into court and swear before a judge as to what he *honestly* felt was the value of an interest in the Northern Pacific Railroad pool.

But the imperturbable banker was equal to the occasion. He wrote to Wilkeson, "Yours of the 30th received. It will do you good to go out to White Plains provided you don't swear too hard about anything." If the Greeley widow were to return the bonds to him now, Cooke added, he would be willing to give her $10,000 in exchange for her husband's interest, and if she wanted cash, he would also insist on taking back the stock bonus that had been handed Greeley. "We'll give ten thousand as it stands but no more."

Meanwhile, as Cooke launched his new bond issue, the nation's business climate was continuing to deteriorate and money was growing increasingly tight.

Since the end of the Civil War, America had plunged into a mammouth railroad-building orgy. Within three years after the end of hostilities over forty thousand miles of track had been launched. In the five years from 1869 to 1873, twenty-eight thousand lines of track were added at a cost of $1.4 billion. By the time Cooke issued his 6 percent bonds, over seventy-five thousand miles of track had been laid for almost $4 billion in bonds and stock. The amount of money borrowed by the railroad companies was substantially greater than any return that could be hoped for in the conceivable future.

Afterward in retrospect, Clarence Stedman, a broker and historian of the money markets, pointed out that no sensible businessman provided a supply of a product or service in advance of the demand for it. But the speculators in railroads promoted their projects, scrambled for money, and laid tracks all over the place long before the demand could reasonably be expected to catch up with their supply. Observed Stedman, "Sound policy would have permitted the population to make its own way over the Great Plains beyond the Mississippi and then when it became necessary to supply these regions with modern rail transportation, the time would have been ripe for the investment in the laying of tracks."

In August 1873, when Cooke unveiled his new bond issue, the Northern Pacific company had laid 455 miles of track. Over $18 million had been offered in stock and another $25 million issued in bonds. The company had a floating debt of almost $7 million, and it had spent $28 million on constructing the road so far.

Cooke, as head of the nation's leading banking enterprise, had been making heavy advances of money for his railroad operation. This cash had come in from bond issues and the deposits of individuals and banks in almost every state of the Union. Now, with money growing tighter, a number of bondholders and depositors were growing uneasy about the rising cost of living and had withdrawn their deposits from Cooke's bank and his network of affiliates. In 1873 the aggregate deposits of Cooke's bank fell from over $4 million to less than $3 million.

Cooke became increasingly the victim of this temporary cash squeeze. While the Northern Pacific Railroad had substantial assets, largely in real estate with a high potential value, the bulk of these wouldn't pass into the hands of the company until the tracks had actually been laid. While its fifty-million-acre land grant looked fine on the books, Cooke and his associates increasingly needed cash to meet the demands that his depositors were making on him. Only 1 percent of the land included in the grant was actually under the legal ownership of the company, and of that only a fraction, forty thousand acres or so, had actually been sold to generate cash.

Cooke was in a classic straitjacket. He was rich on paper but he couldn't translate his enormous land assets into immediate cash to meet the sudden unexpected demands on him. The trick in real estate dealings is to be able to hold onto land for the long haul so as to cash in on its appreciated value, but there may be long periods of time when properties are not easily marketable, and if the property holder has sudden cash demands, he can be in deep trouble.

In the spring of 1873 the money market, as noted, had become ominously tight. Gold, that infallible barometer of public pessimism, soared in August to a price of 119⅛, the highest level reached since the summer of 1870. Financial trouble was brewing in international circles. In May, after several years in which the Austrians had been speculating heavily in wildcat securities, the bubble burst, and the Vienna Bourse was plunged into panic. The stampede touched off disturbances in stock markets all over Europe. Stocks plummeted on the London, Amsterdam, Frankfurt, and Paris exchanges.

The U.S. money market continued to tighten in the fall, and on Wednesday, September 17, the interest rates on currency climbed to 25 percent. Investors in growing numbers were hoarding their cash, and stocks on the New York Exchange began to tumble. Most financiers in their statements to the press continued to profess no anxiety about the future. The *New York Herald* proclaimed in an editorial there was no reason whatsoever for worrying because "the country is too prosperous and wealthy to be seriously disturbed." However, old Commodore Vanderbilt, who was heavily involved in the railroad business as head of the New York Central, remarked privately to a reporter, "Building railroads from nowhere to nowhere at public expense is not a legitimate undertaking. Men are trying to do four times as much business as they should."

On the evening of September 17, Jay Cooke entertained a special guest at his country estate just outside of Philadelphia: the president of the United States. It wasn't unusual for Grant to come by and spend a day or two with the nation's top banker. On this occasion the financier had a special treat for the Chief Executive. He had recently received a box of expensive Havana cigars from Cuba. They were wrapped in a glass case upon which Cooke's name was spelled in gold letters, and when the two finished dinner, they retired to the sitting room. Cooke brought out his Havanas for the president, who was hopelessly addicted to cigars. When Grant had smoked a Corona to its dregs, he pulled out another cigar from Cooke's box and lit it with the butt of the first one. He continued absentmindedly to chain-smoke, lighting one cigar on the butt of another as he conversed with his host past midnight, unaware that he was obsessively emptying the box.

A private telegraph wire had been installed on the estate to connect it with the outside world, and dispatches poured into Cooke's study as the evening progressed, warning of growing anxiety in financial circles. The two men talked into the early hours of the morning. They slept briefly and took a carriage to the railroad station at Philadelphia where they parted. Cooke boarded a train for the city where he had his offices, and the president started for Washington. At Tyrone, Pennsylvania, a half an hour out of Philadelphia, the president's train took a turn too rapidly around a curve and narrowly missed being wrecked.

Cooke turned up at his office on Third Street. Shortly after he sat down at his desk, he received a wire from Fahnestock, who was head of the New York branch of the banking firm. Fahnestock, as noted, had long been critical of Cooke's policies with the Northern Pacific. He had resented the banker's pouring so much of his financial resources into the railroad. He had whipped himself into a state of high provocation. After mulling the matter over for weeks, Fahnestock now decided to pull the plug under Cooke by calling in his partnership share of the firm's funds.

Fahnestock telegraphed Cooke that his New York depositors were putting heavy pressure on him for their capital and he needed to have a substantial sum of money wired immediately to keep his bank open. The telegram reached Cooke at 11:00 A.M. Cooke replied by cable that he would make every effort to raise the money as soon as the financial houses on Third Street were astir. (Businesses opened later in Philadelphia than in New York.) Cooke had no idea of how urgent and ominous Fahnestock's request actually was.

There was a tragic failure of communication between these partners who were located only 100 miles apart and linked together by telegraph wires.

The minutes went by. An hour passed. When there was no response from Cooke, Fahnestock called in several of his vicepresidents and remained closeted with them. Then he summoned the press and announced that he was closing down the doors of Jay Cooke and Company in New York City. Fahnestock explained to the newsmen that he was temporarily closing down because of the rapid withdrawal of deposits and the massive drain that had been made upon his cash resources because of the company's involvement with the Northern Pacific Railroad. The clock had not yet struck noon as he briefed the reporters.

When the wire reached Cooke that his partner had closed the doors of the New York office, he was stunned. With his New York financial base cut off, he had no way of tiding himself over his temporary cash crisis. He stared blankly at the wall. The doors of the Third Street bank in Philadelphia swung shut and the bank's branch in Washington, the First National Bank, closed its doors an hour and a quarter later.

The impact on the public was sharp. Jay Cooke was the nation's largest, most prestigious banking house. It had been the government's partner in financing the Civil War and was considered by Americans to be as solid as the U.S. Treasury. The *New York Tribune* headlined its afternoon edition, "A Financial Thunderbolt." The *Philadelphia Inquirer* described the closing of Jay Cooke and Company as "a thunderclap in a clear sky." Exploded the *Inquirer,* "No one could have been more surprised if snow had fallen amid the sunshine of a summer noon." Said the *New York Herald,* "We couldn't have been more flabbergasted if the Bank of England had collapsed."

Weather-wise the day was a gloomy one in New York. The sky was black and rain had been falling since dawn, turning the streets of the downtown financial district into a quagmire of mud. As the news of the collapse of Jay Cooke spread, crowds gathered on Nassau and Broad streets, lining the sidewalks from the Post Office to Exchange Place. They overflowed the steps of the Sub-Treasury Building, surged around the statue of George Washington.

As soon as the announcement of Cooke's bankruptcy reached the New York Stock Exchange, messengers scooted from the exits and down the stairs on their way to broker houses with the tidings. Stocks began to tumble. Western Union, the bellwether of the list, fell from 89 to 54¼, and the New York Central, the second favorite, slid from 104 to 89 within an hour after the announcement.

Hundreds of stock traders who had bought on heavy margin

and no longer had the money to answer their calls crowded around moneylenders on the sidewalks along Broad Street and Exchange Place, haggling to fix a rate for borrowing cash. They pleaded with the shylocks, bidding hysterically until the price of money touched 0.5 percent per annum over the legal interest rate.

One professional lender, after digging into his pockets and shoveling out $30,000 worth of greenbacks at 0.375 percent over the legal rate, held up his hands and announced that was all he would dole out, but the demand was insatiable. Traders threatened with bankruptcy seized him, begging for more money. The shylock reluctantly admitted he had $20,000 dollars left in his pockets, but he wouldn't let go of it until he discovered how high a rate his colleagues were getting. As he started to walk off, he was mobbed by twenty petitioners blocking his path. They held onto him desperately until he agreed to distribute the $20,000.

All that day the crowds surged around the building of Jay Cooke and Company, cursing and waving their fists. They peered into the windows and dared the partners to come out and face them. Not until evening had settled down on Wall Street did the crowds finally break up. Only then did the higher echelon of the Wall Street branch risk sneaking out of the building to go home. Left hanging over the desk of the branch manager was an ironic sign, "Buy Northern Pacific 7-30 bonds. As good as government's. Secured by mortgages and land grants."

At the Philadelphia headquarters of Jay Cooke and Company the mood was equally somber. At the rumors of bankruptcy, the board of governors of the Philadelphia Exchange catapulted into Third Street and sped toward Number 1114, the old graystone building that served as headquarters of Cooke and Company, to find out if the news were true. Along the way a newsboy was shouting an extra, "All about the failure of Jay Cooke." Police grabbed him and took him to a station house. These cops had not yet been apprised of the bankruptcy and figured the kid was yelling a phony headline and causing a stampede merely to drum up trade.

Washington was thrown into similar turmoil. Clerks scampered out of government offices to snatch up newspapers and confirm

128

the story for their bosses. A murder trial was abruptly halted in the Criminal Courthouse as the judge, the lawyers, the witnesses, and the spectators grabbed their hats and rushed into the street to join the crowds surging around the Cooke building.

Throngs remained all afternoon and into the early evening, refusing to leave. They stood before the great walnut doors of the nation's prestigious banking house through which hundreds of millions of dollars had poured to finance the Union armies fighting the Southern rebellion. When night fell and the crowd dispersed, a reporter pushed his way to the front door of the bank and banged the knocker. The door was opened a crack by a janitor who peered out warily. The newsman asked to be let in to see Jay Cooke. The janitor replied that Mr. Cooke had gone home for the night. There was no one left in the building but this workman, the scrubwomen, and the huge cellar rats which scurried through corridors into the chambers where the heads of the financial empire once had made decisions affecting the nation's economy.

The impact of Jay Cooke and Company's bankruptcy was by no means confined to a single house. Numerous banks across America used Cooke as their clearing agency for all their business activities. The Northern Pacific Railroad was a multimillion-dollar operation, and its bonds and securities had been placed in homes of Americans from coast to coast. As the nation's financial bellwether, the collapse of Jay Cooke was profoundly traumatic.

On Thursday, September 18, when Cooke announced the closing of its Philadelphia headquarters and its branches in New York and Washington, the repercussions were immediate. Within a couple of hours two other banks closely affiliated with Cooke, the First National of Philadelphia and the First National of Boston, folded, and several other banks, which had kept their accounts with Jay Cooke and Company, were reported to be in deep trouble. Throughout the afternoon rumors spread in financial circles that Thomas A. Scott, a broker house, which was heavily involved in underwriting the Pennsylvania Railroad, was on the verge of going under. In New York, Richard Schell, a broker close to the Vanderbilt crowd, went to the wall.

The following day, Friday, dawned with skies threatening rain.

The atmosphere in New York was tense. People wondered whether this would be another Black Friday, remembering the day in 1869 when Jay Gould tried to corner the nation's supply of gold and triggered a Wall Street panic.

The answer came quickly. Shortly after nine in the morning the celebrated broker house of Fisk and Hatch, which had been Jay Cooke's leading agent in his Civil War bond campaigns, was reported to be in financial distress. It had been involved in raising money for the Chesapeake and Ohio Railroad and had borrowed heavily to finance its operations. During the first hour after opening for business, it was deluged by depositors with calls for $1.5 million. Unable to meet them, it shut its doors. Shortly afterward word was flashed that the National Bank in New York was in danger and within an hour it folded. Before the day was over, thirty-five broker houses and banks announced they were unable to meet their obligations and collapsed.

The dominoes continued to fall. Before nightfall on September 20, the third day of the panic, twenty-six more banks and broker houses tumbled in New York. Twelve financial institutions shut their doors in Philadelphia, and banks went busted in Chicago, Albany, Washington, Saint Louis, and as far away as Toronto, Canada.

The Fidelity Trust Company in Philadelphia, a house which had close connections with Cooke, was engulfed in turmoil. A throng of people had converged on it early in the morning of the twentieth, filling Chestnut Street from Fourth to Third. The police were called out to keep order. When the clock on the statehouse tower struck nine and the bank opened for business, people surged into the marble colonnaded hallway, queuing up before the tellers' cages. The bank's president, N. B. Brown, was prepared for the run, and the tellers were instructed to pay depositors upon demand. Within a couple of hours almost $2 million were distributed, but the withdrawals continued to mount. Yet the bank continued to serve all newcomers. The lines dwindled as word was passed that Fidelity had sufficient cash in its vaults. When the day was over it was still open for business.

However, the Union Banking Company, a few blocks down,

was not so fortunate. Within two hours after opening its doors, it posted an announcement that it was busted. The mob hurled rocks and smashed windows. The police were called to keep the bank from being broken into. That same day the Franklin Bank in Chicago went under. The majority of teachers in Chicago's public school system were depositors of the Franklin and they were wiped out.

On Saturday, September 20, the president of the New York Stock Exchange announced that trading would be suspended indefinitely to save stocks from collapsing further. The closing of the Exchange ironically saved the financial skin of Jay Gould, the gold ring manipulator. Gould had been victimized by his own excessive avarice. When Cooke collapsed Gould had gone heavily short, selling a wide number of stocks. As the prices tumbled, the financier began purchasing the stocks back halfway down the decline in an attempt to cover his contracts—only to discover that when he tried to get title to his borrowed securities, the brokers who had bought the stock for him no longer had the money to keep them and had dumped them on the market. Gould, panic-stricken, sent a message to the president of the Stock Exchange announcing he had been forced into bankruptcy, but when the messenger arrived, he found that the Exchange had been closed down minutes before by presidential decree. Accordingly, the announcement of Gould's suspension was not made public. The Exchange remained closed for ten days before resuming trading, and this provided Gould with the necessary time to rally his financial resources and bail himself out. He survived to engage in further dubious manipulations, shearing countless unwary sheep.

There was no letup. On September 21, the fourth day of the crisis, two more banks and two trust companies collapsed in New York. The Lake Shore Railroad was unable to pay back a loan, and the Union Trust Company, which was closely associated with the Vanderbilt interests, shut its doors after resisting a prolonged run by depositors. Just before the Union Trust went under, Colonel Vanderbilt, the shaggy, spindle-legged multimillionaire owner of the New York Central, was seen, by the crowd which peered through the windows from the sidewalk, shuffling

131

with his cane through the corridor of the bank, and the rumor spread that the elderly nabob had left a sickroom to shamble down to the bank to withdraw $1 million from his account. The manager of the Union Trust indignantly denied the report, but it was fruitless. A run developed as depositors poured in demanding their money. Within several hours the bank folded.

The truth as learned later was that Vanderbilt, who had received a $1.7 million loan for the expansion of the Lake Shore Railroad, one of his subsidiaries, had been pressed by the bank in its hour of need to pay back the money, but the venerable geezer was either too straitened in his finances or too plain ornery to comply. This intensified the bank's plight and led to its smashup. Uneasiness was increased when a report got out that Charles T. Carlon, the secretary of the bank, had not been seen in his office for several days, and that $250,000 had disappeared from the vaults. One newsman reported that Carlon had been observed hurriedly boarding a train at the Grand Central Station. That was the last glimpsed of him.

When the Union Bank announced it was shutting down, a delegation of Manhattan ladies angrily paraded up the stairs, banging on the door for their money back. To reporters who covered the action, a leader of the demonstration reported they were insisting that the bank give them, if not their savings, at least the interest on them. The ladies were met at the front door by the manager who refused to admit them to see the president. Rebuffed, they marched off, grumbling about "the dishonesty of taking savings that had required years of labor to accumulate and squandering it on the altar of speculation."

The Union Trust announced that it would reopen shortly, and a crowd of depositors stationed itself for three days and nights outside its doors, anxious to be the first to get inside when the bank resumed operations. The throng attracted speculators who persuaded a number of depositors to assign their bank books to them at 75 cents on the dollar. These sharks were themselves cleaned out, for the Union Bank never reopened.

On Monday, September 22, when the new business week started, the chain reaction triggered by Jay Cooke's collapse continued to gather momentum. The run by depositors, which had hitherto been confined to the commercial banks, spread to the savings banks throughout New York. Also the National Life Insurance, one of Manhattan's giant institutions, went into bankruptcy. The National Trust Company, another financial pillar, found itself in a dangerous situation. Lying in its vaults were $800,000 worth of government securities, but it was unable to borrow a penny on them since they had not reached their maturity. Like a gourmet who is unable to enjoy a banquet because his store teeth hadn't arrived, National writhed in frustration and went bankrupt.

New York remained the focal point of the panic. On Saturday, the twentieth, President Grant and Secretary of the Treasury William Richardson rushed to Manhattan to provide whatever emergency help they could. These government bigwigs set up office quarters in the Fifth Avenue Hotel. Sunday, Grant and his advisers met a delegation of Manhattan bankers and merchants who pleaded for immediate relief. That night President Grant sent a telegram in cipher to his personal secretary in Washington, General Orville Babcock, instructing him to order the Treasury to buy up $12 million worth of New York City's banker bonds as a first step to alleviate the situation.

Meanwhile, an association representing the New York banking community agreed to pool its dwindling resources and issue clearinghouse certificates receivable in settlements of balances to be distributed to any clearinghouse member on approved collateral, the bank obtaining them to pay 7 percent interest. Twenty-six million dollars worth of these certificates were issued over the next few weeks. At the same time the banks instituted a period of forty days during which they agreed to suspend all currency payments to depositors except for a few small drafts.

Within the next few weeks as the financial crisis continued to accelerate, it spread from financial and banking circles into the nation's much wider business and industrial community. On October 27, a month after the suspension of Cooke and Company, the Dutchess Print Works and several other manufacturing concerns in upper New York State shut their plants, throwing thousands of men out of work. A leading leather manufacturer in Boston suspended business. Its senior partner, Horace Conn, mysteriously vanished; his worried family begged the police to search for him, but he was never found. The United States steel industry went into a decline, and the metal furnaces in Pittsburgh shut down, sending fifty thousand people onto the streets. Sprague Concerns, Inc., a network of companies owned by Senator William Sprague, which produced cloth, sewing machines, and operated car lines, went broke. The firm had been speculating heavily in real estate in New York and the Midwest. Ten thousand workers lost their jobs.

Through November the panic continued to mount. In Philadelphia six thousand mill employees were dismissed. The prices of real estate properties plummeted in New York and Chicago. The New York Coast Steamship Lines and the New York Central Railroad reported a 50 percent tumble in freight business. By mid-November forty thousand people were out of work in Manhattan. The city, unable to meet its payroll, discharged seven hundred government workers.

The winter of 1873-74 was one of acute suffering. The unemployed held meetings and labor leaders in New York, to call the attention of other citizens to their plight, got permission from the Board of Police to hold a mass rally at Tompkins Square; but two days before the demonstration the Board of Parks got cold feet and revoked the permit. The workers defied the edict, marching through the streets of Manhattan and into Tompkins Square. The police surrounded the demonstrators and moved in swinging clubs. The mob resisted. A dozen workers and bluecoats were killed.

What had started as a real estate speculation engineered by an ambitious private syndicate ended up plunging the nation into the worst recession in its hundred years of history. It took five years for America to recover from Cooke's ministrations. Meanwhile the ministerial-looking banker with the impeccably trimmed beard was bombarded with letters from people who had trusted him and had been wiped out. One elderly gentleman wrote him in February 1874:

"I Believe in the Northern Pacific as I Believe in God"

At the request of Eliza—a poor blind woman who holds a five hundred dollar Northern Pacific bond which her friend advised her to buy from you—I write to state to you that this bond is all her earthly wealth and the loss of it will oblige her to go to the poorhouse. I thought perhaps you could do something for her in her destitution. Her case is not an ordinary one. She is without father, mother, sister or brother and made what she had by honest labor. She told me with tears running down her cheeks that if she could only see to work she would not care. As you are by nature a benevolent man, I hope you will do something to relieve this destitute woman in her hour of extremity. For the sake of humanity let this letter receive your attention. It would call forth in her prayers on your behalf and awake such grateful emotion as to assure a reward.

That same month another investor who had been lured by the siren beckonings of the banker wrote, "I wish you would try and make up the money that you owe me, three hundred and sixty dollars. I worked twenty-eight years to get that little sum together. I have to support an insane husband and I'm a poor woman. You told me and my little girl when we went to the bank to get out our money that all was safe and if anything happened you would let us know. Did you do it? My number is 1127 Vine Street. I shall look for the money, for of course it is a little bill to you which you could pay out of your private purse and make us comfortable."

So far as Cooke and his coterie of associates were concerned, things were not nearly as bad as for the rest of the nation. Although his banking and railroad empire went broke, the foxy old banker managed to recoup a generous proportion of his private wealth.

Unlike Robert Morris, who had raised money for the American Revolution and went into bankruptcy through his real estate speculations, this banker who had financed the Civil War remained solvent, largely *because* of his real estate manipulations. He had been strapped by a temporary shortage of cash, unable to meet immediate demands, but he held title to vast acres of land, much of which, although it couldn't be converted into cash immediately, had enormous potential value.

135

There was nothing wrong in Cooke's prediction about the ultimate worth of his land. Although a bankrupt, legally unable to manage the affairs of Cooke and Company or the Northern Pacific Railroad, the banker nevertheless continued to give unofficial advice to his associates, and he advised them, together with the creditors who were formed to reorganize the affairs of the railroad, to exchange their stock in the railroad company for the land in the Pacific Northwest itself. (New preferred stock had been issued in a reorganization of the line and it was redeemable in these lands.)

Three years after Cooke went into bankruptcy, Duluth, the city where he had first plunged into real estate transactions, was finally, under new management, linked by rail to the Pacific Northwest. Cooke personally was able to convert the real estate he had stubbornly hung onto into cash, and this put him financially on his feet again. Moreover, other shrewd speculators who bought up the bonds of disgruntled Northern Pacific investors and converted them into land holdings at from 50 cents to $2 an acre within twenty years could have sold out, some of them multimillionaires, at from $40 to $60 an acre.

For the Pacific Northwest was destined to become a prime agricultural and mineral heartland of America. Minnesota and the Dakotas emerged as a lucrative wheat belt with yields of bushels rising steadily over the next fifty years. The timberland of Oregon and Washington became the focal point of the nation's lumber business, and the waters along Puget Sound developed into a major center of fisheries.

Cooke's dissident partner, Harris Fahnestock, had been wrong in his jaundiced view about the Pacific Northwest. After the Depression of 1873 while the greenbacks, printed at the behest of government politicians, continued to flood America, driving the nation further and further into an inflationary spiral that cut the ground from under investments in paper securities and money instruments, the handful who were foresighted enough to hold onto acreage in the Pacific Northwest came out substantially ahead. Once again God's green acres proved to be a powerful hedge against the decline of the dollar.

5

THE GRAND DUKES
OF CHICAGO

Marshall Field, Levi Leiter, Potter
Palmer Take Over the Bawdiest Town
on Earth

The development of a great city has always served as a spring-board for the accumulation of land and realty fortunes. The Astors made the bulk of their millions dealing in Manhattan real estate as the city grew from a village to a colossus. Nicholas Longworth and his heirs amassed a fortune from the growth of Cincinnati into a leading metropolis of Middle America. The fortunes of the Van Sweringen brothers were closely linked to the burgeoning expansion of Cleveland. The Spreckels family became wealthy from the skyrocketing of San Francisco land values. Similarly, Chicago, the mighty metropolis of Middle America, provided the lucrative setting for three of the most skillful land prestidigitators of all—Potter Palmer, Levi Leiter, and Marshall Field. The audacity of their maneuverings, played out in one of America's most turbulent communities, is a highly provocative story.

The growth of Chicago in the nineteenth century was faster than any other metropolis of a million people or more at any time in history. In the span of a single century the population climbed from fifty to three million people, a level that took Paris two thousand years to accomplish. During this period the real estate values of the Windy City grew enormously. Its 211-square-mile area rose in assessed value from $2,000 to $5 billion, an amount that was three times greater than the Jefferson Administration paid for the 370 million acres of the Louisiana Purchase in 1803 and more than the value of all the farmland in twenty states of America in the 1920s.

The origins of this muddy little patch of wilderness were humble indeed. The Indians had called Chicago, "Chickaguew," meaning "Bad Stink." It was wilderness when John Kinzie, an Indian trader, came to the spot and put up a cabin in 1804. The Windy City initially developed at a glacial pace.

In 1830 its entire area consisted of twelve log cabins. The previous fall, commissioners had authorized the laying out of the town. By 1832 there were only twenty-eight voters, and the tax list amounted to $148.29.

Chicago in the 1840s remained an obscure watering hole. Cows grazed within sight of City Hall. Hogs roamed through the business area by day, and wolves ran wild at night through the downtown streets. Entire sections of the town were perennially sunk in mud that was notorious for "stickiness, color and smell." One contemporary account describes how a villager had sunk so deep in the muck of the streets that only his head and shoulders emerged. A passerby asked if he needed help. "Hell, no!" he retorted. "I've got a horse under me."

In the middle 1830s, the city fathers covered this ubiquitous mud with wooden-planked streets in the downtown area, but the garbage was left standing for weeks on end, for no one had figured a way to cart it off. (The town was located below the level of Lake Michigan and gravity couldn't be used to drain the sewage away.) Engineers concluded the only thing to do was to jack up the buildings and put hard grading under them. Since the inhabitants were desperate enough for any experiment, every single building in the town was hoisted on jacks to the level of the lake, a task that took five years to complete. The biggest difficulty was with the Tremont Hotel, a six-story brick building that was the showplace of the town. Skeptics insisted it couldn't be lifted without tearing the bricks apart. But one contractor promised he could hoist the hostelry eight feet above its muddy foundations without shattering a single windowpane. He hired a thousand men who set huge jacks under the Tremont and took turns turning the jacks, inching the hotel up to the desired level. This hoisting was done at night, gently, imperceptibly, so that the sleeping guests were completely undisturbed. Only when they looked out in the morning did they realize they were at a new level.

Despite the resourcefulness of its engineers, Chicago continued to be mired in mud which rendered its streets impassable for weeks at a time. One visitor reported, "I have seen empty wagons and drays stuck on every block on Lake and Water streets." Passersby put up whimsical signs. "No bottom here." "This way to the lower regions."

On humid summer days, garbage larded with dead rats and excrement stank under the wood-plank sidewalks, making walking an ordeal. The traffic was chaotic. As late as the 1860s Chicago had no right- or left-hand traffic lanes, and carriages and tramcars careened at random through the streets.

During Chicago's humble beginnings, real estate dealings were highly apathetic. Settlers were not attracted by the cheap land offered by the government—for $1.50 an acre. In 1833 the Pottawattomie Indians thought so little of the area's potential that they sold the government twenty million acres of land they owned in and around Chicago for 6 cents an acre and thought they were getting a huge bargain. John Kinzie, who built the first cabin there, was so unimpressed with the promise of the region that he didn't bother to exercise his rights on sixty other acres lying at the forks of the river on which he had bought an option. *In 1830 a farsighted speculator could have bought all the land comprising the present city of Chicago for about $170,000.*

A visitor from the East who came to Chicago in the 1830s reported, "I would not give sixpence an acre for the whole of it." Charles Dickens, who visited Chicago in 1842, was no more impressed with the inhabitants than with the scenery. "I was surprised to observe that even steady old tobacco chewers are not always good marksmen here . . . Several gentlemen called on me who in the course of conversation frequently missed the spittoon at five paces, and one who was certainly shortsighted mistook the closed sash for the open window at three.''

The city was frequented by gamblers, con men, and other criminal fugitives from the East. One of their favorite gathering places was the Lone Star Saloon located on a street called Whisky Row. The bartender, a chap named Mickey Finn, served his patrons a drink that was laced with a white powder obtained from a voodoo doctor. It would lay the imbiber low, allowing Finn to strip him of his belongings and toss him into an alleyway where he remained unconscious for up to forty-eight hours before reviving. Over the years the "Mickey Finn" became the label for the most powerful drink resourceful bartenders could concoct, endowing the Chicago saloonkeeper with an imperishable immortality.

Gradually as the town began to flourish, defying the mud and periodic floods, land speculators began swarming into it. Prices were especially stimulated in the mid-1830s by rumors that a canal would be dug to link Chicago with traders from the East. As the strategic position of the town suddenly dawned on the public, fast-talking lawyers made $500 a day writing land deeds in Chicago and the surrounding area. Operators who had nothing but wooden stakes, a hammer, and plenty of gall platted towns and cities that existed only in their imagination. The speculation took on boom proportions. "If you had sense enough to eat soup with a spoon," one observer remarked, "you were smart enough to get rich."

In February 1834, the rumor that a canal would be dug to connect Chicago with the East became a reality when the Illinois legislature authorized the governor to pledge the canal lands and tolls to raise $500,000 and launch the project. Moreover, a new state bank was chartered, capitalized at $1.5 million, to issue notes of up to two and one-half its capital to further subsidize the scheme. A branch of this bank was established in Chicago, providing liberal credit, and a government land office was opened, attracting a new army of speculators.

In the mid-thirties, Harriet Martineau, the writer, reported, "I never saw a busier place than Chicago . . . The streets were crowded with land speculators hurrying from one sale to another. A Negro dressed in scarlet, bearing a scarlet flag and riding a white horse with housings of scarlet, announced the time of a sale. At every street corner where he stopped the crowd gathered around him, and it seemed as if some prevalent mania affected the whole people. The gentlemen of our party were bombarded by storekeepers who hailed them from their doors with offers of farms and land lots, advising them to speculate before the prices rose higher."

It seemed as if every male adult was busy selling lots, if not as his main business then as a sideline. The story went the rounds about a leading doctor in town who was prone to getting his two lines of activities mixed up. (He did a thriving side business peddling real estate lots.) Once while calling on a sick lady, he made his diagnosis and wrote out a prescription. The patient looked at it. "Doctor, you don't say how I should take the medicine." The physician looked over his shoulder as he was about to leave. "Oh, Canal terms of course. One quarter down and the balance in one, two and three years."

Reports of real estate fortunes being made in Chicago reached the East, and Chicago lots were sold at public auctions in Manhattan. Speculators poured money into Chicago from as far off as Scotland. By 1835 the rise in prices was extremely rapid. Lots at the corner of Lake and Dearborn streets that could have been bought "for a cord of wood, a pair of boots and a barrel of whisky in 1832," as one businessman observed, now were valued at a sum of money "that would fill a warehouse with such commodities." Dole's, a lot eighty by a hundred feet at the corner of Dearborn and South Water streets, was sold for $9000 in March 1835 and resold for $25,000 in December. A hundred thousand dollars was offered and refused for Hogan's Block at 272 Lake Street. By the following summer, the total sales value of land in Chicago had increased from $168,000 in 1830 to $10.5 million, a jump of over 10,000 percent.

Chicago became the haven for an influx of capital from Southerners and residents of the Border States. It developed into a Mecca for war profiteers and draft dodgers who plunged barrels full of cheap paper money into land deals. Since the Windy City was strategically located between the lush coal deposits of the Mesabi Range and the trade waterway of the Great Lakes, it became a thriving hub of the nation's postwar commercial boom. The completion of the Union Pacific and the Central Pacific railroads across the continent in 1869 turned Chicago into a major freight terminal. In 1882 direct rail communications were opened between Chicago and New York, and the time for the trip was cut from seven days to only thirty-six hours. By then the city had become the nation's leading meat-packing center.

This prosperity had a sharp impact upon real estate values, opening vast new opportunities for alert manipulators. The three most successful who were to amass the largest fortunes in the Windy City were Potter Palmer, Levi Leiter, and Marshall Field.

Potter Palmer, the first of the triumvirate, arrived in Chicago from upper New York in 1852. At twenty-six he had accumulated $5000 from business dealings in the East. With this capital he opened a dry-goods store. A clever business manipulator, Palmer made his first millions from the Civil War. In the early days after the Union defeat at Bull Run, many businessmen grew panicky about the prospects of the Union and unloaded their merchandise at cut-rate prices. Palmer bought bales of cotton, muslin sheetings, and flannels thrown onto the market at depressed prices, loading his warehouse to the rafters. He borrowed, plunged heavily into debt, to accumulate more and more inventory, and his gamble paid off. The Lincoln Administration had floated an ocean of greenbacks to finance the war effort, and the North went on a spending spree. As a result, wholesale prices of goods began to skyrocket. Enjoying a large inventory of cheaply bought merchandise, Palmer was able to sell it lower than any of his competitors, raking in substantial profits. To the astonishment of his rivals, he did not pocket the money but plunged it into building new inventory.

Palmer's competitors seriously miscalculated the astute young man from New York, and he made a ten-strike on his strategy.

He continued to buy up inventory as prices tumbled, cashing in on a rebound of prices. By underselling his competitors, he swept the field clean, emerging as the front-runner. In addition to his Chicago store, Palmer engaged in operations in New York, where he bought additional amounts of inventory, held onto it for several months, and without so much as moving it out of the warehouse, unloaded it to others at rising prices. By the time he was thirty, Palmer was a multimillionaire. He took part of his fortune and plunged it into Chicago real estate, gobbling up some of the choicest properties to swell his income further.

Just as Palmer reached his stride in real estate dealings, another man arrived on the scene, ten years younger—Marshall Field—who was to follow Palmer's strategy in turning a dollar and wind up even richer than the master.

Field was born near Conway, Massachusetts, and as a youth clerked in a country store. When he accumulated $1000 in savings, he quit and left for the wide-open territory of Chicago, figuring the chance to make money there was greater than in the East. He joined the dry-goods store of Cooley Wardsworth and Company as a clerk at $400 a year and so impressed the owners with his business acumen that within several years, when one of them withdrew, the others invited him to become a partner. However, this was not sufficient for the ambitious young merchandiser. He wished to strike out for himself though he had only turned thirty.

Casting about, Field received an offer from Potter Palmer to sell his business. His health was bad, Palmer explained, and his doctor had recommended a vacation. Moreover, Palmer offered Field a loan to cover part of the purchase price. Friends of Field's were skeptical about the offer. Palmer was a devious fellow, they pointed out, who had made his first millions buying merchandise on falling prices when everyone thought he was crazy. Now a rumor spread that having continued to accumulate merchandise on a market that had suddenly turned unfavorable, Palmer had become overloaded with an inflated inventory and, with prices starting to tumble and a period of postwar deflation setting in, Palmer's offer to Field was simply a device to unload his merchandise on an unsuspecting young man.

143

However, Field went ahead, despite his friends' warnings, taking in as a partner a hustling young business associate, Levi Leiter, accepting Palmer's loan, and raising additional money to buy the business.

Sure enough, prices which had been declining at the end of the Civil War suddenly began a precipitous drop and shortly after starting in business, the new firm, Field and Leiter, sustained a loss of over $250,000. However, thanks to a series of resourceful maneuvers, it managed to survive while others went to the wall. The economy revived and by the end of 1865 each partner was enjoying a 30 percent dividend on his investment.

As for Potter Palmer, he continued to amass money in ingenious ways. On quitting his store business, the canny New Englander turned his talents to buying and selling properties in the volatile real estate field. He hit upon an idea for a grandiose land speculation which called for the complete transplanting of the main retail business district of Chicago from Lake Street to State Street. State Street at that time was a crabby little lane winding between blocks of run-down boardinghouses and cheap saloons. By contrast Lake Street was Chicago's leading financial and retail center. At the close of the war, for instance, the corner of Clark and Lake near the Field-Leiter store was considered the best acreage in the city and was selling for $2000 a front foot.

However, with the shrewd eye of the expert land speculator, Palmer was convinced that Lake Street, hemmed in by both river and railroad, was doomed to deteriorate since it couldn't expand in any direction. Also State Street had a tremendous advantage over Lake since a trolley line coming from the South Side met a line from the West there. Potentially it was one of the most convenient areas to reach from every section of the city.

The region, as noted, was a slum. Politicians for years had proposed measures to improve it, but nothing had been done. However, Palmer was quick to appreciate the fact that the shabby little single-track streetcar line that wound through the area would eventually provide key linkage with trunk lines from all over Chicago.

Quietly Palmer bought up a slew of run-down properties along

State Street until he held title to virtually all of the frontage extending for three-quarters of a mile.

Then he made another bold move. The way to turn this into a major commercial area, he decided, was to widen the twisting narrow lane into a boulevard. To do this he would have to demolish every property he bought and rebuild each far enough back from its original site so that the lane in front could be widened into the thoroughfare he desired. Businessmen scoffed when Palmer hired architects to move back the boardinghouses, grog shops, and tumbledown meat markets he had purchased. Palmer had to finance his real estate venture out of his own pocket, for he could not persuade any banker to back his "crazy" scheme. But Palmer was a persistent man. He went around the neighborhood inducing the local property owners to follow him and put their money into relocating their properties in the rear so that the twenty-foot-wide lane could be broadened into an avenue.

Then to entice the fashionable shopkeepers and other business establishments located on Lake Street into his new area, Palmer tore down one row of shacks he had bought on the southwest corner of State Street and Quincy Street and built a hotel standing eight stories high that became the most lavish hostelry in Chicago. On the other end of State Street he erected a six-story store fronted in marble. Before he was through, Palmer had plunged almost $2 million into his gamble to transform the ugly duckling State Street into the Cinderella center of Chicago.

Coaxing and cajoling other property owners, he led a stampede from Lake Street into the State Street area. The effect of this shift by business merchants had a sharp impact on the values of the real estate that Potter Palmer had so shrewdly accumulated at the beginning of his operation. A lot near the corner of State and Madison in 1860, when it was still a run-down area, sold for $300 a front foot. Six year later, thanks to Palmer's gamesmanship, the price rose to $500 a front foot, and by 1869 to $2000. Other speculators moving in with Palmer reaped a heady windfall. All the downtown streets in the new area surged in prices. In 1868–69 alone, the advance was so rapid it was possible to buy land in the State Street area one day and garner a hefty profit the next.

Potter Palmer had turned the classic trick of the virtuoso real estate manipulator. He had selected run-down property, bought it for a song, refurbished it, and lured others into buying surrounding properties so as to enhance his own investment, enabling him to make a killing on the rise of prices.

Then suddenly in 1871 Palmer's long-range plans ran aground. He was tripped up by an even shrewder manipulator than he— nature.

A family by the name of O'Leary lived in De Koven Street on Chicago's West Side. Patrick O'Leary was a construction laborer, the father of five children. The O'Learys were extremely poor, and to increase their income, Mrs. O'Leary kept in a barn in the backyard half a dozen cows which she milked each day, peddling the output to neighbors.

One Sunday evening in October 1871, a friend of Patrick's, "Peg Leg" Dennis Sullivan, a coachman with a wooden leg, visited the O'Leary family, but when he knocked on the door, he found they had gone to bed. That Sunday was a dry, windy night. There hadn't been a touch of rain since July 1, and newspapers reported that the ground in and around Chicago was so parched and the timberlands so dry, there was cause for considerable anxiety.

As Dennis Sullivan turned to leave the O'Leary home, he saw flames rising from the barn a hundred yards to the rear. He rushed into the barn, grabbed a young calf whose hair was on fire, beating it out with a blanket and lugging the struggling animal to safety. Despite his wooden leg, Sullivan was an agile man, but as he plodded through the smoke, his peg leg got trapped in a crack in the floor. Hurriedly he unstrapped his leg, and hopping around on the other, he waved the blanket, smothering the smoke, driving the remaining cows out of the barn. He emerged from the flames hopping down the street yelling, "Fire! Fire!"

Dennis Sullivan's shouts aroused neighbors who reported the fire to the watchtower on Court Street. A lookout guard was mounted on a twenty-four-hour basis alert for a fire breaking out in any part of the city. On receiving an alarm, their job was to order engines to rush immediately to the emergency area, but on receiving the reports of the fire in the O'Leary barn, an inexplicable mix-up occurred. The guard, instead of signaling to the five fire engines located closest to the area of the flames, summoned a company of engines a mile and a half away. Meanwhile, the fire had spread out of control.

For forty-six hours previously the wind had been blowing with unusual violence from the southwest. The flames from the O'Leary barn leaped to adjoining sheds and engulfed a row of houses, driving the people into the street.

A wake was being held for a recently deceased woman. The family and relatives fled in panic, leaving the corpse to be burned to ashes. Between Canal Street, which the fire reached rapidly, and the river, there were a number of coal- and lumberyards. Piles of coal and cordwood were set ablaze like fireworks, turning the night sky scarlet. As the fire roared ahead, indiscriminately devouring commercial buildings, houses, and shacks, a member of the City Council, James Hildreth, suggested that buildings in the path of the blaze be dynamited in an attempt to stop the flames. A keg of dynamite was rushed to the basement of the Union National Bank which stood barely a hundred yards from the advancing fire, but the blast only shattered the windows of the building and didn't topple it.

As the fire advanced unchecked, human nature displayed itself in a variety of ways. A pedestrian by the name of Drake, passing a hotel on Congress Street, which the flames had not yet reached, approached the owner and offered to buy the hotel lock, stock, and barrel on the spot, waving a thousand-dollar-bill as a down payment. He was willing to snap it up at this bargain price on the gamble that it would escape the onrushing fire, and he tried to persuade the owner to take the money rather than risk losing his entire investment. The panicky owner yielded and the deal was made over a handshake in the lobby. Drake, the buyer, figured he had a fifty-fifty chance of salvaging the hotel from the holocaust. He won his gamble. The hotel escaped the fire, but after it was over and he came to collect title to the hotel, the owner reneged on the deal. Drake had to press his case at the point of a revolver before the reluctant hotelman handed over the deed.

The fire had erupted at ten o'clock in the evening. By midnight, driven by the wind which was blowing at gale proportions, it reached the Chicago River, jumped it, and entered the South Side of the city. The heat of the flames was so intense it melted cast-iron columns three feet thick, in seconds. It turned the iron wheels on streetcars to molten hubs and car tracks into smoking wreckage.

The owner of a popular restaurant hired men to haul several hundred barrels of champagne and whiskey from his wine cellar down to the lakefront to prevent them from being destroyed. Several dozen whiskey barrels failed to make it; a mob hijacked them, smashed them open, and drank themselves into a stupor.

At the Chicago Club, an exclusive aerie of rich society, a jolly company was having a champagne breakfast when news of the fire arrived. The party did not pause in its revels, for, as one afterward reminisced, it did not believe that "God would strike his best supporters." The flames reached the club just as the members lifted their tumblers for the twentieth round of toasts, and they scooted out carrying bottles of vintage champagne along with cartons of cigars.

Steadily the fire advanced from section to section, threatening to engulf the entire city. Because of the prolonged drought, the wooden tenement buildings, lumberyards, and sidewalks were as dry as paper and burned easily. Starting from the O'Leary barn, the flames had rapidly devoured all the buildings on the east side of the street, proceeded into neighboring Taylor Street, then to Canal Street and the river, demolishing the bridge and leveling to ashes the sprawling factory of the Chicago Hide and Leather Company.

Within an hour the whole area between Jefferson Street and the river north of Polk and south of Van Buren was a sea of flames. Teams of firemen posted themselves in the path of the blaze, struggling to arrest it. But they may as well have tried to hold back the wind. It and the fire had combined into a titanic force. Propelled by the wind, burning brands were carried far ahead of the mass of fire, wreaking havoc and softening up resistance to the advance of the main column.

A blazing board carried by the wind fell upon a cluster of shanties where the roofs of several formed a junction at Adams and Franklin streets east of the river and a third of a mile from burning buildings of any size west of the river. In moments, the wind whipped the blaze into a raging inferno, trapping the city between two columns of advancing flames. The torches of fire were carried by the wind in advance of the main flames, and wherever they fell they produced subfires. Throughout the night and early morning several distinct, widely separated fires burned simultaneously, trapping large areas of buildings between them. The central column followed, overtaking these advanced conflagrations, gathering new fury from them.

By eleven-thirty the fire had penetrated as far as Van Buren Street on the frontier of Chicago's South Side, and had there been no more than an ordinary wind, it would have burned itself out at this point since it already had consumed everything in its path. When it continued on, crossing the river, it became obvious that the fire was not going to be contained in a single section of the city. A general alarm was rung all over Chicago.

By midnight the North Side was completely laid waste with nothing left for the fire to consume except the Nelson Grain Elevator which unaccountably remained unscathed. Far off to the northeast between the two rivers and the great structures of hotels, banks, and wooden warehouses, beyond the brick and marble houses of the wealthy, stood the Central Water Works which was the only agent left that could possibly save Chicago from total annihilation, and toward that critical area the conflagration of wind and fire now bore down. When the flames reached the waterworks and the great engines ceased to pump, the city's last means of defense crumbled.

Amidst the hysteria, macabre things occurred. One woman, found dead near the charred ruins of her house, clutched a fistful of government bonds which she wouldn't let go. The fire displayed a curious sense of selectivity. Virtually all houses in downtown Chicago collapsed, although here and there were walls and fragments of walls supported by partitions. One three-story brick house stood with a wall intact. In an upper room there was a mantelpiece with a clock whose hands had stopped at twenty minutes to ten in the evening. In front lay a ladies' exquisitely hand-painted fan. In the wreckage of another house a locket was found unharmed, containing a wisp of hair and an engraved inscription, "Lock of George Washington's hair cut in Philadelphia while he was on his way to Yorktown, 1781." The locket was the property of a woman who died in the fire, bequeathed to her by an elderly relative in Philadelphia whose mother had given George Washington a haircut while he was passing through the city with the Continental Army.

The survivors identified the remains of dead relatives in various ways. One father recognized his child through a photo album that lay near the body. Another man who spent a day and night looking for his wife was led to the body by the lid of a trunk he recognized. A set of dinner plates told one survivor that the ruins he stumbled on had been his home. One man who lost his entire family spent two days and nights looking for them. The third morning he found his wife's old sewing machine and his little boy's jacket. Then he came upon the body of his wife. He knelt and caressed her face, speaking to her as if she were alive until someone led him away. He sat on the bank of the river, talked to himself for a while, then rose and vanished forever into the countryside.

The news of the fire shocked America. Crowds hovered around newspaper bulletins in cities from coast to coast, seeking word about their next of kin, but no lists were released. The fire had wrecked communications into Chicago.

Emergency morgues were set up all over the city. As soon as corpses were identified, they were placed in shrouds and shoveled into the earth. Those not immediately recognized were kept for forty-eight hours to give relatives an opportunity to make an identification from records of whatever personal belongings were recovered. Schoolhouses all over the city were converted into mortuaries. Bodies were laid across the schoolchildren's desks until it got so crowded they had to be piled on the floor. Soldiers with bayonets kept the mob from stampeding into the morgues to learn if their parents, wives, and children were there. The soldiers insisted people file in singly or in pairs.

After the flames subsided, looting was widespread and there were rumors of wholesale lynchings. One telegram from Chicago, when comunications were restored, reported, "The mob has just hung a man to a telegraph pole for cutting the finger of a dead woman in order to get her ring." Rioters pounced on the corpse of a woman wearing a pearl necklace. Her body was in rigor mortis and they had to sever the head to tear the pearls loose.

On the second day of the crisis martial law was declared in Chicago. Troops were sent in by the governor of Illinois. Private William Young, a soldier of Company C, Fourteenth Regiment, of the State Guard, sat resting between rounds of duty on the bank of the Chicago River. Small fires had broken out across the river, and the authorities had ordered a Catholic church and other buildings still standing to be dynamited to prevent the flames from spreading. As the church collapsed into a heap of bricks, the private rose and walked into his tent. Captain Nesbitt, napping in his headquarters, was awakened by a shot. Running in the direction of the sound, he found Private Young sprawling on the ground, the muzzle of his rifle resting against his head. The suffering around him had so depressed the spirit of the high-strung young soldier, he had killed himself.

The living valiantly picked up the thread of their lives. One minister held a service for his neighbors and the soldiers who had been sent in to patrol the streets. His pulpit was a wooden crate box which had been emptied of its merchandise. "I hunted a lot of time yesterday for the foundations of my home," he told his audience, "but they were swept away like the faces of the friends who used to gather around my table. But God doesn't own this side alone, he owns the other side too and all is well. Are your dear ones safe? The only answer is whether they trusted in God or not." The gathering sang a chorus of "Jesus, Lover of My Soul."

The minister continued, "Cora Moses, who used to sing in our church choir, sang that beautiful hymn as she died. There was only the crashing of the buildings between the interruption of the song on earth and its continuation in heaven."

In Chicago, as the survivors returned from the countryside, riots broke out over the outrageous prices some grocers were charging for food. A mob broke into one shop, seized the flour a gouger had been asking $5 a sack for and distributed it free. Another grocer, to prevent a similar break-in, guarded his store with a shotgun. The workmen who had been recruited to clear up the streets struck in the middle of the job, demanding higher wages.

The Chicago fire lasted thirty hours; it was the greatest natural disaster to befall America until the San Francisco earthquake of 1906. It destroyed an area twice as big as the Great Fire of London in the seventeenth century during the reign of Charles II, and it burned out a larger area than the burning of Moscow when Napoleon invaded the Russian capital in 1812. Three and a half miles were totally destroyed. Out of a population of 320,000, five hundred were known to be dead. Many more Chicagoans were not reported as casualties since their charred bodies were never recovered from the wreckage. A thousand families were left without shelter. Over seventeen thousand homes and buildings were demolished. The cost of destroyed property was over $200 million.

Many of the gutted buildings were architectural models of their kind. Among them was the *Chicago Tribune* office which was one of the nation's most elegant newspaper establishments. It was a four-story stone structure built only two years previously at a cost of $250,000. The *Tribune* building had withstood the holocaust until McVicker's Theater nearby caught fire, spreading the flames to its premises.

Another victim was the Crosby Opera House that had been closed during the summer and fall for renovation. Its owner had spent $80,000 to refurbish it in a lavish new decor. It was to have been reopened to the public the night after the fire erupted, and on Sunday evening only an hour before the catastrophe, it was lit up for the first time so that its furnishings could be admired by gaslight. Its carpeting and upholstery had been made expressly for it in France. Bronzes had been imported from Italy. Adjoining the auditorium dedicated to opera, there was a concert hall that sat fifteen hundred people and an art gallery, most of whose paintings were saved from the flames.

McVicker's Theater was one of the fanciest playhouses in

America. Like the opera house, it had been closed for the summer and remodeled at considerable expense. Woods Museum on Randolph Street was another victim of the fire. It housed one of the finest ornithological and entomological collections in America, together with a zoo containing a number of rare animals, all of whom perished. Also lost in the fire were Farwell Hall, the home of the Young Men's Christian Association; Metropolitan Hall on Randolph Street where Adelina Patti once had sung and which was intimately associated with the leading musical events in Chicago; the Academy of Design, whose loss was a particular blow to the art world for it owned three hundred important paintings, foreign and domestic, most of which were destroyed.

When the fire had exhausted itself and the survivors surveyed the extent of the ruins, a dispute broke out in the newspapers and the pulpits over who or what was to blame for the tragedy. Shortly before the fire the voters of Chicago had rejected a proposal by clergymen to shut down the saloons on Sunday. Now Fundamentalist preachers thundered out that God had incinerated Chicago to punish its citizens for their sins.

For years one legend was perpetuated that the fire had started when one of Pat O'Leary's cows kicked over a lighted candle. Another rumor was that boys in the neighborhood had gathered in the O'Leary barn to smoke cigars, and one of them had accidentally set fire to the hayloft. The fire marshal and the police made a thorough investigation and never found the actual cause.

The Chicago fire opened up opportunities for hefty real estate speculation. Properties housing multimillion-dollar buildings that were demolished overnight plunged in value to virtually nothing. A bearish mood toward real estate investment permeated most Chicagoans.

However, as always, there were a gutsy handful of plungers ready to risk their cash on optimistic hunches when all around them were steeped in gloom. With much of Chicago destroyed, an unusual opportunity opened up for snapping up damaged, devastated parcels at bargain prices to speculators who dared to gamble.

The fire had destroyed a number of banks along with the deeds to property titles that lay in their vaults. Crooks moved into the city, forged their own titles to lay claim to properties that belonged to others. Adventurers flocked in, laying out fictitious plots, selling them to people who did not bother to inquire into the titles in their anxiety to get hold of the plots.

When the fire erupted, Potter Palmer, the real estate maestro, happened to be visiting New York and he learned that thirty-two of his buildings had burned to the ground. Displaying the same gambling spirit with which he had bought merchandise for his store when everyone else was selling, Palmer plunged money into rehabilitating his properties, hoping that, encouraged by his optimism, real estate prices would rebound.

Marshall Field, Potter Palmer's leading tenant, who had become almost as wealthy a land dealer as the former, was not above a little speculation himself to take advantage of the chaos caused by the fire. Field's store had been destroyed, but he carried over $2 million in insurance on it.

After the flames were extinguished, Field began searching for a site upon which to rebuild his store. He found for temporary quarters a two-story brick barn in which the Chicago City Railroad Company had once quartered the horses for its trolley cars. Field leased the building for $9785, moved whatever merchandise he had salvaged into it, and immediately began planning for a more permanent site.

Selecting this area, Field had followed the strategy of his old friend and master tactician, Palmer. Instead of choosing property in what had been a fashionable district, he settled upon the shabbiest section possible, a slum littered with burned-out boardinghouses and whiskey shops for sailors. The area was occupied by poor Irish who lived in ramshackle shanties. Several of these homeowners became wealthy when prices shot up as a result of Field's surprise move, for having bought the land cheaply and put up a store, Field induced other leading merchants to follow his lead and settle near him.

Field continued to wheel and deal, using his power as a merchandiser to give him leverage in his real estate operations. (Subsequently, he moved back to State Street, once again catching realty values and business trends with perfect timing.) Actually, Field had been putting his surplus wealth into real estate from his early days as a merchant prince. "The future of real estate here is tremendous," he wrote in 1870 to a London banking associate.

After the fire, Field and his partner Levi Leiter increasingly devoted their energies to real estate investments. They displayed an uncanny zest for the game and a sharp nose for bargains. As they stepped up their buying of parcels of land and buildings, their speculations had an increasingly important impact upon Chicago's property values. Newspapers watched the ventures of the two men closely, and whenever they made a purchase, the fact was widely publicized.

But a rift ultimately developed between the two plungers. Their temperaments were at opposite poles and they fought continually. Field had started out as a salesman riding on a shoeshine and a prayer. Leiter was a cautious, penny-pinching bookkeeper who managed the credit operation of the store but lacked Field's bold merchandising vision. Despite their bitter wrangling, they managed to accumulate over $5 million worth of real estate, of which $2 million was owned jointly by them.

But as the years passed the relationship between them became increasingly strained and a rupture was inevitable. Field seized the initiative in breaking off the partnership with typical cunning. He took five junior partners and key executives aside and asked each privately, "Would you stay with me if I decide to buy out Leiter and carry on alone?" Each of the individuals replied in the affirmative. Leiter was a cranky man, difficult to work with, and he had few friends.

Armed with these confidential promises, Field called Leiter into his office one morning and told him he wished to discontinue their partnership. It was time they broke off. Leiter was caught by surprise. Before he could respond, Field continued: "I'll name you a price for which I'm willing to buy your share or sell my share of the business, whichever you wish." The price Field quoted was amazingly low—only $2.5 million, ridiculous for a business that was generating annual sales of $25 million. "I'll give you first choice," offered Field, "you can either buy or sell." Leiter, enticed by the low figure, eagerly offered to become the buyer. Only after committing himself did he discover he had been booby-trapped. When he contacted his junior partners to sound out their loyalty, he discovered they had promised to stay on only if Field remained the sole proprietor. Without these key personnel Leiter feared the business would disintegrate.

This astute manipulator had been conned by an even more subtle operator into agreeing to a preposterously low price for a sellout. Nevertheless he had committed himself to the price and he went through with it. "You win," he told Field, "I'll sell."

The details of the breakup of the partnership were supposed to be handled with the greatest secrecy, but Fred Cook, one of the *Chicago Tribune*'s most enterprising reporters, received information through a leak and he wrote about some of the juicier aspects of the rupture, revealing in the course of his exposé the enormous extent of Field and Leiter's property holdings. "Individually and collectively," wrote Cook, "Field and Leiter are the largest real estate owners in Chicago."

Leiter was hardly pauperized by the rupture. He left the firm, as noted, with $2.5 million in cash, plus millions of dollars worth of real estate. While he had parted from Field in anger, circumstances were to bring them together again years later.

Levi Leiter's son, Joe, in his twenties, was a compulsive gambler. He played high-stakes poker and he took daring risks in the stock market with his father's money. In 1897 Levi gave his son a present of $1 million to spend as he desired. Joe set out to achieve the dream of all commodities speculators—cornering the wheat market. In the winter of 1897–98, he tried to buy up all the contracts of wheat he expected to be harvested. His strategy was to buy cheap, hold, and when the inevitable shortage developed through his holding off the wheat, he would be able to name his own price for selling it and make a killing. Joe bought all he could get his hands on, on margin, and by May 1898, he almost accomplished his goal.

But he ran up against P. D. Armour, the meat-packing tycoon, who was a rough operator, and sharp speculator in grains. Armour needed nine million bushels of grain immediately to cover his own contracts. When Joe refused to release his wheat, trying to force the price still higher, Armour ran his young adversary into a trap. It was the height of winter. The meat-packer secretly rushed a fleet of ice tugs to Duluth to crush the floes in the frozen Soo Canals. The tugs pulverized the ice. Dynamite finished the job. Armour was able to ship in not only enough wheat to deliver to his own accounts, but nine million extra bushels which he proceeded to dump on the market.

Young Joe was caught unawares. He had counted on a shortage of supplies, aggravated by the ice-locked condition of the canal. He never dreamed that wheat could suddenly materialize in the dead of winter. Leiter's corner was smashed. The $10 million he had rolled up in paper profits were wiped out. He went down under the tidal wave of Armour's cheap wheat, his debts climbing to over $20 million.

At this juncture Levi Leiter tried to rescue his son from his colossal misadventure. By selling off a number of his real estate holdings, he was able to raise all but the final $2 million needed to pay off young Joe's debts. One property the senior Leiter owned at the corner of State and Madison streets, occupied by Schlesinger and Mayer, the department store, would provide the money he needed if he could find a buyer. He had bought the property years ago for only $200,000 without any intentions of ever parting with it. Its value now had snowballed to at least $2 million. Urgently needing the cash, he was ready to let it go. But times were bad; money was tight. There was only one man in Chicago whom Leiter knew had the ready cash—his old partner, Marshall Field. However, the two men hadn't spoken in fifteen years.

Leiter swallowed his pride, contacted a mutual friend, and pleaded with him to see Field and find out whether he would be willing to buy the Madison Street property. When Field was approached he responded, "Tell Leiter he'll have to come and ask me himself."

The next morning Field's old partner walked into his office. The two men were closeted for half an hour, then Field emerged and told his secretary, "Have a check made out to Mr. Leiter for two million dollars. I'm buying Schlesinger and Mayer." It was not only a good business deal for Field, but it would help a father square the accounts of his son. It was one of the rare times Field displayed any sensitivity toward another human being.

Steadily, Field enlarged his real estate holdings until he had much of Chicago in his grip. He bought a number of buildings adjacent to his store. He gave Hetty Green, the wealthy woman realtor and Wall Street plunger $350,000 for a chunk of choice property she owned on Wabash Avenue. With the fortune generated from his store and the additional millions harvested from real estate, Field became the biggest property owner in the city, with title to seventy-four corner lots and income-producing buildings that, by his death, had generated a worth of $40 million.

Chicago's wealthiest realtor was a generally cold, aloof man, incapable of communicating any warmth to others. He was just under six feet, eyes a steely blue-gray beneath shaggy eyebrows, and a prominent forehead. His face was melancholy, his handshake flabby. One finger of the right hand was stiff as a result of a boyhood accident and he had a tendency to keep it in his pocket as if he were embarrassed by it. He walked with a slightly bowlegged gait, and as the years advanced, he grew increasingly roundshouldered. Although worth over $100 million, he had no *joie de vivre*. He lived a highly rigid life. His tastes were frugal. He hadn't an iota of sensuality in his makeup.

Field was driven to work each morning by a British coachman behind a team of elegant black horses. The driver always stopped several blocks away from the department store, and Field got out and walked the rest of the way so that the clerks and the doormen wouldn't be envious of him. One of his associates observed that Field "had an infallible talent for making money and no talent whatever for spending it or enjoying it."

His business strategy was out of *Poor Richard's Almanack*. "Never mortgage yourself in real estate. Do everything strictly on a cash basis. Never borrow a dime. Don't buy a share of stock on margin and never give your note on a loan." For all his $120 million, Field was fantastically tight with a penny. One day he was playing golf with a journalist who fancied himself a wit. Field took a brisk swing and missed the ball. "How would you like to hit it a mile?" asked the writer. The scribe took a greenback out of his wallet. "Wrap this around your golf ball. You can make a dollar bill go farther than any man I've ever met."

Field had few friends, and his closest associate was even more frosty than he was—George Pullman, the developer of the railroad sleeping car. These two tight-lipped, bloodless individuals had a strong affinity. Nobody else could have stood each other's company.

Not only was Pullman Marshall Field's closest friend, but the latter obviously had a large say in the affairs of the Pullman Company; when Field's will was probated, it was found he had a huge position in Pullman stock.

Pullman was one of the nastiest men who ever raked in a dollar from the free enterprise system. He had bought up acreage south of Chicago and built a city to house his workers. It was a quintessential company town. Pullman's workers bought food in the Pullman-run stores. They resided in Pullman houses whose rentals were automatically subtracted from their wages. Pullman City was a remarkable venture in real estate and gall. When Pullman's workers, overwhelmed with indignities, finally struck, the boss called in government troops and terminated the uprising as ruthlessly as if it were a foreign guerrilla operation.

Pullman was so hated by his employees and by the general public, who sympathized with them, that when he died the disposal of his corpse became a major problem. The funeral services were held secretly behind heavy security guards in the dead of night. To prevent the body from being stolen, the mahogany casket was lined with lead and plastered over with quick-drying asphalt. Then after it was lowered into the grave, heavy concrete was poured in to turn the casket into a sealed-in, immovable object. Over this were laid steel rails bolted together and embedded in more concrete. One newsman remarked when he heard of the burial measures, "It's clear the family is making sure the son of a bitch doesn't get up and come back."

The precautions were by no means unfounded. When Pullman's will was opened, it was discovered that the multimillionaire had left the princely sum of $3000 a year to each of his sons. Thereafter these heirs visited their father's grave once a year to urinate on it.

Field, like his friend, was a difficult man to live with, and his marital life was abrasive. He continually wrangled with his wife in public to the embarrassment of everyone present. The couple were severely mismated. Unlike her husband, Mrs. Field had bohemian tastes and loved the company of artists, writers, and other unconventional people. Her invitations to actors and music hall singers shocked Field deeply.

The final years of Field's life were marked by tragedy. When his wife, Nannie, died in the south of France after several years of separation, Field was in his late sixties. He ended his loneliness by taking a new wife, Mrs. Arthur Caton, a neighboring widow. There was irreverent gossip the two had carried on an affair while Mrs. Field was alive and lived with her husband in their Prairie Avenue mansion. According to rumor a tunnel had been dug connecting the Field house with the nearby Caton house, and the aging lovers had met there surreptitiously.

Nineteen hundred and four was the year when Mrs. Caton's husband died and Field married the widow in London. Hardly had the couple completed their honeymoon when disaster struck Field's only son and male heir. Marshall Field II, who had lived in a mansion next to his father, had been a severe disappointment. Unable to adjust to his role as the heir to Chicago's richest man, he worked for a while aimlessly in his father's store, then quit, marrying the daughter of a wealthy Chicago brewer. His health was poor and he spent most of his time traveling abroad with his wife, seeking out a round of doctors, treatments, and health spas to cure his ailments. The fact that Marshall Field II was unable or unwilling to fit into his father's mold and carry on the family business was a bitter blow to the older man. The heir obviously had profound problems. His father was incapable of a display of affection for him. His parents were constantly quarreling. His home life, for all its outward splendor, had been a painfully unsettling one. Field had developed into a high-strung neurotic, terrified of not living up to the standards set by his father.

Late one chilly afternoon in November 1905 the younger Field put a gun to his temple and killed himself. It was just before six o'clock in the evening. For several days previously Field had been severely depressed. During that day he had been unable to make up his mind whether to take his wife and children on a holiday at a New Jersey resort or go on a hunting trip alone. Unable to come to a decision, he instructed the butler to stop packing until his wife arrived home from shopping and made up his mind for him. In the meanwhile he retired to his dressing room, presumably to put on his evening clothes for dinner. A shot rang out. The servants rushed into the room and found Field had slumped to the floor, his hunting rifle alongside him.

Rumors spread through Chicago that the shooting had not taken place in the Field mansion, that Marshall Field II had been cavorting in Chicago's most elegant brothel, the Everleigh Club, and had been shot during a quarrel with a prostitute, and that to avoid the scandal, Field had been carried out of the back door to his own home on Prairie Avenue where the public was informed he had been shot.

The rumor that the only son of the austere multimillionaire had been shot in the arms of a whore was to persist for years despite family denials passed *sotto voce* around the tables of socialite gatherings and in shabby saloons. However, biographers of the family point out that while it is possible young Marshal occasionally or even frequently visited the Everleigh Club—it was a brothel that catered to the most prestigious families in Chicago—the evidence is overwhelming that the shooting took place in Field's home. For one thing, the hour at which it occurred, at six o'clock in the evening, was not one in which patrons normally gathered at the club.

Young Field was thirty-seven when the tragedy occurred. A cable was sent to Boston where his father was honeymooning with his new wife. The senior Field commandeered a private train, reached Chicago in nineteen hours, and rushed to the hospital where his son lay fighting for life.

The meeting was poignant. As Field left the hospital, shaken with grief, reporters and cameramen swarmed around him and flashbulbs popped. Shaken with fury Field raised his cane. "Here, you stop! Aren't you ashamed?"

The young man lingered on while his wife helped to nurse him. On the fifth day he died. The funeral was private. Flowers were discouraged. Shortly afterward the young widow, Mrs. Field, left alone with three children, made a striking commentary on the agony of being the rich son of a formidable father. "American wealth is too often a curse."

The senior Field insisted that his son had not committed suicide but that his hunting rifle had gone off accidentally while he was cleaning it. He blocked all attempts by the police to investigate the incident and refused to allow detectives to enter the house. The servants, under his orders, refused to talk. However, evidence Field suppressed from the public pointed strongly to suicide. The death gun, for example, was an automatic weapon which Field, an avid gun connoisseur, had bought for his collection. It was virtually impossible to discharge it accidentally since it was tightly locked. One news reporter investigating the incident secured a duplicate weapon, cocked it, and threw it on the floor repeatedly, discovering that it would not go off when locked automatically, even when slammed to the ground. In any event, Field was a veteran hunter, thoroughly expert in handling firearms. It was highly unlikely that he could have shot himself by accident. The reporter who investigated the gun was not permitted to print his story. Indeed, none of the Chicago newspapers pressed an investigation, contenting themselves with accepting the family's version. Marshall Field was the major advertiser in Chicago newspapers, and if he withdrew his business, it would be a financial calamity, so publishers and editors acquiesced in the conspiracy to conceal the truth from the public. Not only did the press meekly accept the family version of what happened, but so powerful was Marshall Field in the city's affairs, the Police Department quickly dropped its investigation without seriously attempting to accumulate evidence.

After the death of the younger Field, the father was no longer the same man; his self-confidence was completely gone. He walked hesitantly, bowed in grief. On New Year's Day, 1906, less than two months after the death of his son, he played a game of afternoon golf. It was snowing and the old man decided to golf in the storm, using red balls to stand out in the drifts. He played eighteen holes with Stanley Field, his nephew, and Robert Todd Lincoln, the son of President Lincoln, with whom he had become friendly. As he finished the eighteenth hole, Field complained of a sore throat, but he did not go to bed and rest. Instead he visited his store, attending to business matters. A heavy cough developed, but the doctors could not persuade him to stay in bed. He left by train with his wife for New York where he had business to attend to at the Grand Central Company of which he was a director. By the time the train arrived in Manhattan and he reached the Holland House, Field was so sick he was unable to walk to his suite. He had to be carried to bed. He had caught a severe case of pneumonia. His temperature soared to 107 degrees, and the day after he arrived he died.

The death of Marshall Field triggered an outburst of eulogies from ministers in the pulpit, newspaper editors, and solid citizens from coast to coast who extolled the virtues of this prototype American capitalist. Observed the *Chicago Tribune,* "Field was a man who by legitimate means built up a great fortune in the pursuit of which he has never lost the confidence and trust of his fellowman." In this era before World War I, the wealthy entrepreneur who had never been caught overtly with his hand in anybody else's pocket was considered a paragon of the breed. Field had his faults of course; a man who paid the lowest wages in the nation and was a business confrere of George Pullman, wasn't exactly perfect.

One rainy morning four days after Field's death, the funeral was held with the trappings that would have been appropriate for the president of the United States. All Chicago's business establishments were closed and flags flew at half-mast throughout the city. Thousands of Chicagoans stood in the rain paying their respects as the cortege went past.

The bereavement reached a neurotic pitch. One of Field's employees, a certain Pierre Funck who had worked at the store for forty years, was the archetypical loyal servant who worshiped authority, and Field was his hero. After the burial services Funck failed to show up at the store for the first time in four decades. Other employees looked for him and found him at the cemetery sitting by the grave of the boss. He remained there for hours, resisting all efforts to take him home. He never entered the store again but paid frequent visits to Field's grave, plodding through snow, ice, and rain. His obsessive grief lasted for twenty-four months, and then early in the spring he paid a last visit to the cemetery and went home to die. The doctors could find nothing physically wrong with him.

The widespread aura of good feeling toward Field that had triggered the wave of eulogies accompanying his death was ironically short-lived. While the multimillionaire's body was still warm in the burial plot and the rhetorical phrases hot upon the lips of his admirers, Field's will was published, and the entire nation was stunned to learn of its terms. Filed on January 24, 1906, it turned out to be one of the longest wills ever written, over twenty thousand words, and one of the most extraordinary in the history of the genre. It was legally airtight in what it aimed to accomplish—perpetuate the old man's fortune after his death, allowing him to hold onto it from beyond the grave without disbursing it. Field gave virtually nothing to charity. He left $1 million each to his wife and daughter-in-law, $6 million to a daughter, and he distributed a few hundred thousand dollars among distant relatives.

But the bulk of his fortune, over $120 million, was left to the two male children of his son who had died prematurely. The boys were ages twelve and ten. But according to an extraordinary provision of the will, these heirs would not receive their inheritance at the age of their majority, twenty-one, as was usually the case. Their acquisition of the money would be delayed until they reached fifty, which meant among other things that the state could not collect the inheritance taxes normally accruing after a reasonable lapse of time. It would have to wait for the heirs to reach middle age before it could get a penny in taxes. Field explained in his will that the heirs must wait until such time as "they will have such experience as men of fortune as to be unlikely to dissipate the vast wealth that they will then become possessed

164

of." The old fox was going to ensure that the adage that great fortunes accumulated by the founder didn't remain in the family for more than two generations before it was dissipated would not apply to him. "If the estate is conservatively managed," Field predicted, "it will then be among the largest private fortunes in the world; and its owners will be men of fixed habits and large experience."

Field had managed to outwit the state, his heirs, and to accomplish, in a sense, what mortal men have always dreamed of but never succeeded in doing—to perpetuate their own eternity. A major provision of the will was Field's instruction that one-half of his $120 million estate be continuously invested in real estate. He had a healthy confidence in the steady appreciation of his realty properties and figured they comprised the finest channel for the further growth of his fortune. He forbade the trustees of the estate to lease any of the property "unless the lessee contracts to put up substantial modern buildings." He preferred, he wrote, long-term leases to short-term ones. Indeed, he charted a very conservative policy of real estate investments. It was obvious that Field hoped his heirs would display the same sagacity he had shown for buying and selling land, and that the estate would continue to expand by grabbing up the finest properties available in Chicago.

Marshall Field's will when it was publicly released created a wave of dismay and resentment. The idea of tying up the bulk of a $120 million fortune for the next forty years without any of it being recovered in taxes or spent for the benefit of the community outraged many socially minded Americans. The governor of Illinois and other state politicians were so infuriated that the State General Assembly at its next session passed a law outlawing any future will that delayed the acquisition of money by an heir after he reached twenty-one. This triggered a series of other changes in Federal and state inheritance tax laws around the country. Anger coupled with admiration for the ingenuity of Field's plan cropped up in articles from time to time over the next twenty-five years. One newspaper editorial predicted, "No piles of money are ever going to be amassed again in the United States . . . and should anyone attain to the ranks of the very rich by ingenuity or miracle, he won't be able to pass on his savings to anybody else. It looks very discouraging for any young four dollars a week dry goods worker who has ideas about becoming a millionaire.''

William Bole, the lawyer who drew Field's will, was a specialist in advising wealthy fortune hunters how to avoid taxes, and he devised numerous, ingenious testaments. He was convinced the Field will was his masterpiece, the fruition of a lifetime of experiment. Over the years numerous attempts were made by relatives and collateral descendants to break the provisions of Field's will without success, so foolproof was its legal strategy. At one point, five different parties paid nine law firms $1 million to try to change the will—in vain. One effort involved a long legal wrangle in which Elihu Root, the celebrated attorney, represented a Field relative. After his failure, he observed, "One cannot but be amazed at the astonishing completeness of Field's scheme in tying up his property. He seemed to personify the accumulation of wealth for the sake of accumulation.''

Like the Astor family in New York, the Fields had their share of black sheep members who popped up, doing scandalous things to embarrass it. For instance, Marshall Field III's younger brother, Henry, at the age of twenty, while studying in England, fathered an illegitimate child. The family hushed it up, paid the unwed mother a sizable sum. Henry was shipped back hurriedly to America and married to a respectable society girl who was the niece of the British Lady Astor. Henry died a few years later, leaving Marshall Field III the sole heir to his grandfather's fortune. The mother of the bastard child took legal action and tried to get some chunk of the Field millions for her son, but the courts decided against her.

According to Field's will, Marshall and his brother, the grandsons, were to be taken care of by liberal handouts from the trust until the age of fifty, when as noted, they would receive the principal. But when Henry died, the entire fortune went to Marshall Field III. Under the steady appreciation of investments in real estate, stocks, and bonds, the fortune had grown from the $120 million at the time of the senior Field's death to about $300 million.

Marshall Field III came into possession of one of the single biggest family inheritances on earth. While the Rockefeller and Du Pont family holdings were greater, Field had more wealth under his personal control.

Marshall Field III grew up with severe psychological handicaps. First and foremost was the trauma caused by the suicide of his father. The boy was ten at the time, playing in his bedroom, recovering from a recent bout with the flu. He heard the shot ringing out from his father's dressing room down the hallway. He heard his father's cry of pain; then a panicky maid rushed into the bedroom, took the boy in her arms and carried him out of the house to relatives. Bewilderedly he asked questions and got no answer; but the cry of his father, the grief of the servants who hustled him from his home, haunted him during his years of growing up. At twelve, labeled by the newspapers "the richest boy in the world," young Marshall was sent off to England to acquire a British education. He went through the *de rigueur* training of an heir to vast wealth. He attended Eton and Cambridge and strengthened his sickly, delicate body with rigorous athletics.

When Field returned to America at the age of twenty-one to serve as a trustee of his grandfather's estate, Chicagoans were curious as to what the potential inheritor of the Marshall Field millions was like. Resentment had been expressed at his mother's decision to send him to England to acquire an education. The trustees were especially embittered. When Mrs. Field asked for money for her son's schooling, they retorted that Marshall the First had desired his heir to be educated as an American. "He is being raised as a gentleman," replied Marshall's mother. "Yes, as a *British* gentleman."

When Field returned to the States wearing English tweeds and sporting a British upper-class accent, he was severely criticized in some quarters as being a nondescript, ineffectual playboy. Carl Sandburg, a reporter for a Chicago paper, referred to him as "physically and mentally a sort of nobody who travels on his grandfather's name and memory." On the other hand, when Field enlisted in the army during the First World War, the *Literary Digest* ran an article expressing delight at this democratic gesture of the wealthy princeling who acted just like any other young man in America's emergency.

Receiving an income running into millions from the trust as well as his deceased brother, Henry's share of the money, Field plunged into the life of an international playboy, hunting with the hounds, breeding prize Guernseys, raising thoroughbred horses, flying his own amphibian plane. He purchased four adjoining mansions on Sixty-ninth and Seventieth streets in Manhattan, converting them into a town house. On three thousand acres of Long Island countryside, he created Caumsett, a country establishment that exuded the elegance of the stately homes of England. The estate, one of the most magnificent in America, was a notorious example of conspicuous consumption. Eighty servants were needed to operate it. It had its own water supply, electric power facilities and fire-fighting apparatus, formal gardens, a zoo featuring three jackasses imported from Abyssinia, twenty houses merely to accommodate the staff of workers. There were private beaches for the servants as well as the guests. Anchored in the Sound, Field kept a steam yacht for his guests' pleasure and a stable of automobiles for them to drive along the thirty miles of private roads inside the estate. Field spent his days shooting skeet and pheasants, fishing for trout, playing polo, flying his amphibian plane around the world. Life was flamboyant and lived alfresco.

Amidst this, there was tragedy. Field's marital experience was stormy. He separated from his first wife in 1930. She took the train to Reno, telling newsmen she and her husband "were as far apart as the sun and the moon." Field gave his ex-wife his $3-million Manhattan town house and an income of over $1 million a year. He took for a second wife the former Audrey James, the widow of a wealthy British industrialist and goddaughter of King Edward VII. This marriage ended no more happily than the first.

The second Mrs. Field plunged into her husband's extravagant life-style *con brio*. The press reported the Fields yachting in the Mediterranean, hunting with the Prince of Wales, remodeling an antebellum Virginia plantation, leasing a Wyoming ranch for a single house party.

When the Depression struck, Field's wife continued her ostentatious party-giving. In the dark days of 1932 she decided to touch up the dining room of the New York apartment, an event which one gossip columnist chronicled enthusiastically: "Taking their cue from Sir Philip Sassoon's London music room, Marshall and Audrey have mirrored walls, and on the mirrors are painted the most wondrous collection of our feathered friends upon which my optics ever have gazed . . . The birds are the work of no less a genius than Étienne Drian, who came from Paris especially to ply his brushes on the Fields' dining room mirrors, and his bill . . . resembled nothing so much as the national debt of Albania!" Stories like these in the press were in sharp contrast to the dreary accounts of unemployment and breadlines which filled the newspapers.

In September 1943 Field finally received the bulk of his $300-million inheritance. But long before he received the principal, he had become moody, introspective, increasingly dissatisfied with the divertissements of a playboy. His lavish entertaining on his three-thousand-acre estate, the private plane trips he took around the world,the yachting cruises, the aimless, witless life which was all surface and glitter with no real content, this flaunting of his millions at a time when the nation was mired in a deep depression and millions of Americans were out of work standing on the street corner selling apples and lining up at soup kitchens—all this profoundly disturbed him.

His life was affording him no real happiness. His second wife after several years of marriage had gone off to Reno like the first—in 1934—and received a divorce. Field fell into a deep depression. "I don't know why the newspapers keep calling me a playboy," he observed to one reporter. "God knows I'm not having any fun at all." Something was dreadfully wrong.

Deep in his psyche there remained the memory of a shot that had rung out in that somber mansion on Prairie Avenue when he was playing in his bedroom as a child. He had pondered for years over the terrible death of his father. Convinced that it was a suicide, Field was haunted with an agonizing question. His father had been born to a life of gaudy opulence. He had the power to

169

achieve instant gratification, to possess all the glamorous things he desired. Why, then, at thirty-seven did he kill himself? How painful was his rootlessness, his search to establish his identity?

The suicide of Marshall Field II and the agonizing reasons that drove him to this drastic step had become the nightmare of Marshall Field III's life. He was obsessed with the need to understand his father, to articulate through his own life the purpose behind the tragic interruption of his father's existence. Marshall Field had from his earliest years felt deeply guilty about money and the sorrow it brought. When he was only twelve, shortly after his grandfather's death, a news reporter asked him, "What will you do with your grandfather's money?" And the child replied, "I don't want it. I'd rather not have it. Mother might have it, but of course if Grandfather wanted me to take it, I'd have to do it."

Field felt he had been marked for painful destiny. The inheritance of $300 million was an obligation he preferred to avoid. Now in middle age, Field plunged into a period of black despair, and he turned for help to psychoanalysis. He sought out Dr. Gregory Zilborg, an exotic individual outstanding even among Freudian psychoanalysts for his idiosyncrasies. Zilborg had been a Russian revolutionary in the period before the Bolshevik uprising. Subsequently, he had been appointed an official in Kerenski's provisional government. He was a man of penetrating culture and mesmerizing personality.

One of Dr. Zilborg's great preoccupations was with the motivations of suicide, and Marshall Field represented a classic case history for him to investigate. Field remained in therapy with Zilborg for over a year. Some critics claimed that the Russian psychoanalyst exerted an unhealthy influence. What chiefly interested him, they charged, was the golden opportunity to manipulate the allocation of $300 million by instilling in his patient a set of values and purposes that were a mirror image of his own. From the time Field first met Zilborg, wrote a journalist for *Time* magazine, "the Russian revolutionary and psychoanalyst flitted in the background with the evanescent quality of a Cheshire cat."

Despite these unkind charges, Field emerged from his therapy adjusted to his wealth and prepared to do something constructive with it. He was freed of the haunting memory of his father's suicide, freed from the compulsive need to find out the reasons why, and from the guilt he subconsciously shared in the killing. Significantly Field allocated a substantial sum of money to help Dr. Zilborg establish a committee for the study of suicide. Described by a newspaper as "being financed by apparently limitless funds," the committee was staffed by seven psychoanalysts and psychiatrists. Zilborg, before meeting Field, had written several professional papers discussing the motivation of civilized and primitive men who had been driven to take their lives. With Field's money Zilborg continued his studies in greater depth, analyzing the cases of several thousand suicides. The committee came out with a report presenting findings that the act of self-destruction is by no means impulsive as had been thought. The will to commit suicide is latent in the majority of people. It is the culmination of a series of unconscious desires and drives going back to childhood.

Field emerged from his psychoanalysis in his early forties a changed man. The result was as decisive in its way as the conversion of Saint Augustine who also had led a free-and-easy, hedonistic life until he converted to a profound religious faith. The insights Field had acquired, he dramatically put to use. He withdrew from the investment banking business, severed his associations with most of his former financial friends and socialite playfellows. He acquired an interest in liberal causes and social problems. He delivered a lecture before the American Public Welfare Association. "I happened to have been left a great deal of money. I don't know what is going to happen to it and I don't give a damn. If I cannot make myself worthy of three square meals a day, I don't deserve them." A lifelong Republican, Field withdrew his financial support from the Republican candidate for the presidency in 1935 and joined the camp of that "traitor to his class," Franklin D. Roosevelt.

The uses Field now put his wealth to would have turned his grandfather, Marshall Field I, purple. The senior Field had written an ironclad will designed to keep control over the course of his fortune after his death. And now ironically when it finally got into the possession of his grandson, the money was spent for so-

171

cial causes that were diametrically opposed to everything old Field had stood for. Marshall the First had been an archconservative, who kept his laborers on a leash of appallingly low wages, who grew apoplectic at the thought of labor unions and helped his friend, Pullman, break a railroad strike in a series of bloody battles that had horrified Chicago. His grandson now visited the slum areas of Chicago and was so appalled by living conditions, he spent money to buy up the land, demolish the decrepit tenement houses, and erect as housing for the neighborhood poor, apartments to rent for $45 a month.

Field's transformation from a wealthy dilettante into a backer of left-wing social causes sent tremors through the community of America's wealthy blue bloods. His former playfellows on Long Island shook their heads. One of them observed that the only possible reason he had become crazy was "because of being whacked over the head with polo mallets too often." One society dowager exclaimed, "Why, only last fall I saw him ride point-to-point at the hounds. I can't believe this has happened to him." Referring to his remarks that he had no use for worldly possessions, John D. Rockefeller, Jr., retorted, "Marshall Field may not care what happens to his money but I care what happens to *mine*." One observer of Field's predicament as the vilification mounted commented, "A very rich man who decides that he will carry the banner of the common people is in a hell of a spot. The rich will hate him and the poor will suspect him."

Upon emerging with his new philosophy, Field plunged a fortune into financing *P.M.*, a New York newspaper which promoted left-wing social causes and refused to accept advertising for most of its life before it folded, leaving Field with a sizable deficit. Field also moved to Chicago, the town where his grandfather had amassed his fortune, and in an attempt to break the monopoly of the right-wing *Chicago Tribune*, plunged a barrel of money into setting up a rival newspaper, the *Chicago Sun.*

The *Chicago Tribune* was run by the irascible Colonel Robert R. McCormick, descended from the wealthy family whose founder had invented the reaper. When Field invaded the newspaper field, McCormick blasted him mercilessly in a broadside of editorials. He charged that Field launched his newspaper solely for the purpose of evading taxes. "For each million dollars he spends in Chicago, his tax will be reduced by eight hundred thousand . . . taken away from the national income to buy planes, tanks, battleships and the pay of soldiers."

Ironically, it was Marshall Field I's financial backing that launched the *Tribune* and made possible the job that Colonel McCormick now held. Joseph Medill had approached Marshall Field, asking him for money to permit him to buy the then struggling little newspaper, and thanks to this loan, Medill made the purchase. One of Medill's daughters married the father of Robert McCormick, and hence the position of power from which the colonel now lambasted the grandson of the senior Field.

The grandson continued to spend his inheritance in ways his grandfather would never have dreamed of. Having launched the *Chicago Sun* and then bought the *Times,* the afternoon newspaper, to merge with it, Field also purchased the controlling interest in Simon and Schuster, the publisher, and in Pocket Books—which he disposed of later.*

Meanwhile, the fortune accumulated by old Marshall Field continues to grow. Much of it remains in accordance with the wishes of the founder in lucrative real estate, although the realty holdings are smaller than they used to be because the trustees have been liquidating some of the properties to raise income for other ventures. The crown jewels of the real estate portfolio include a number of commercial buildings in Chicago's downtown area, including the forty-three-story Field building and the La Salle Theater building, along with a number of properties that combine stores on the first floor with apartment houses above.

The single biggest real estate transaction launched by the successors of Marshall Field I has been the building of the world's largest commercial edifice—the Merchandise Mart. In addition to housing the wholesale and manufacturing divisions of the Marshall Field store, the Mart was designed for leasing space

*Field died of brain cancer in 1956. The current head of the family is his grandson, Marshall Field V.

to representatives and manufacturing agents. It also housed the world's largest restaurant and biggest radio broadcasting studios and the ninety acres of area it covered could have held much of the population of Chicago.

As the years passed, the Mart ran into financial difficulties. Marshall Field & Co. had put $30 million into building it primarily to house the store's merchandising business. But during the Depression of the 1930s, as the store lost money, the wholesale division was eliminated and new tenants had to be found for the vacated space. Times were hard and only the U.S. government was willing to sign up as a tenant. As a result, by the 1940s, over half of the Mart was occupied by government agencies who paid low rentals. While $30 million had been put into building the Mart, it was valued at only about $20 million. Marshall Field & Co. had a huge funded indebtedness and by 1945 it was anxious to sell off the Mart to pay off its bond obligations.

At this juncture Joseph P. Kennedy, the father of the future president, appeared on the scene. After making millions on Wall Street and from the movie and whiskey businesses, Kennedy had, after World War II, turned to real estate. He had built up a heavy cash position during the war because he had been bearish about American's economic position; so he had plenty of money to put into property deals. Nevertheless he proceeded cautiously.

Thanks to the excellent pipeline Kennedy had into the highest circles of government, he was tipped off in Washington that the Federal agencies which were taking up such a disproportionate amount of space in the Mart and paying low rentals were scheduled to move out upon the expiration of their leases. Kennedy offered to buy the Mart with the virtual guarantee he would be able to secure private tenants at much higher rentals. Other real estate dealers were not privy to Uncle Sam's plan to move government offices out of the Mart, and they assumed that the building was doomed to depressed rentals for the foreseeable future. Accordingly they had not bid for the property, leaving Kennedy a free hand to arrange his own price.

The bargain was a spectacular one even for a wheeler-dealer who had become legendary for extracting fat bargains. Kennedy obtained the Mart for $12.5 million, borrowing $12 million of this on a mortgage from an insurance company. Four years after the purchase he was able to negotiate for the original $12 million mortgage, another one for $17 million, boosting the value of his property by almost $5 million at a stroke. Within fifteen years the book value of the Mart had quadrupled.

The audacity of Kennedy's deal would undoubtedly have stirred the admiration of that maestro of all bargain hunters—old Marshall Field himself, if he had been around to witness it. Along had come a parvenu outsider who had roundly outsmarted his heirs—and in his own backyard—Chicago.

6

FLORIDA, A SCANDAL IN THE SUNSHINE

"You Can Go Nuts on the Land"

Major economic trends frequently have been set in motion by crowd psychology. One student of mob behavior observed some time ago, "Have you ever seen in some wood, on a sunny quiet day, a cloud of flying midges—some thousands of them—hovering, apparently motionless, in a sunbeam? . . . Well did you ever see the whole flight—each mite apparently preserving its distance from the others—suddenly move, say three feet, to one side, or the other? . . . What made them do that? A breeze? I said a *quiet* day."

At certain mysterious moments in history, as Dr. Charles Mackay wrote in his book *Extraordinary Popular Delusions and the Madness of Crowds,* a delusion has swept the multitudes of mankind, triggering irrational behavior. In the fifteenth and sixteenth centuries, swept by a paranoiac fear of the Devil, mobs set upon and hung thousands of women on the charges they were witches serving Beelzebub. Also, in medieval times, alchemists cozened the masses with the claim they could make gold out of dross, and that by possessing a philosopher's stone, one could insure himself of everlasting life. During the sixteenth century a sudden craze swept Europe for murdering one's enemies by administering slow-acting poison. Fashionable ladies, who would

176

have shuddered at the idea of strangling or stabbing anyone to death, thought nothing of slipping a vial of poison into the drink of somebody who had earned their displeasure. Delivering a slow dose of poison to one's rival in society or love became the in thing to do.

The phenomenon of mass hysteria has nowhere been more apparent than in the field of monetary investment and most strikingly in real estate. Points out Charles MacKay: "Men . . . think in herds . . . they go mad in herds, while they recover their senses, one by one."

In this sentence lies the story of that land of coruscating dreams—Florida—where time after time the masses of money hunters have done their thinking in herds only to recover their senses one by one.

While Florida as a whole has been a most tempting area for real estate speculations, Palm Beach in particular has had an extravagant history. It was first discovered as a paradise for land peddlers in 1867 when an explorer, George Sears, heading along the Florida east coast for Miami, an old bartering area for the Seminole Indians, stumbled upon what seemed an uninhabited sandbar. The passageway led into a gorgeous lake whose shores were lined with jungle vines, overhanging trees, and semitropical foliage. There were two inhabitants in the area, deserters from the Confederate Army who had fled under gunfire and weren't aware that the Civil War had been over for two years. When Sears returned home, he spoke glowingly about the "paradise" he had stumbled upon, and others went to visit, and in some cases to dwell, in what came to be called the Lake Worth area.

An early settler was Robert McCormick, heir to the Harvester fortune, who bought several tracts and built a winter home on the lake. Other Americans, mostly Midwesterners, freezing in winter blizzards and hearing about this Utopia down south, flocked to Lake Worth. By the middle 1870s a community had sprung up on the east side of the lake, sizable enough to warrant the building of a post office. The postman delivered the mail to the lake dwellers by rowboat.

The inhabitants acquired in a highly curious fashion the coconut groves which became their proudest possession. A ship, the *Providencia,* sailing from the West Indies to Spain and loaded with a cargo of coconuts, was hit by a hurricane while passing through the Lake Worth area. As the ship sank, thousands of nuts floated up from its hold and were carried by a strong tide onto the beach. The settlers planted them and they sprouted into Palm Beach's ubiquitous groves.

This wasn't the only hurricane to benefit these acquisitive settlers. Once a ship went down yielding up a cargo of exquisite sherry, and for weeks Palm Beach residents went around gloriously drunk.

The first man to launch large-scale real estate operations in Florida was Henry Flagler. The son of a Presbyterian minister, he did zealous missionary work converting dollars into his bank account. Flagler was as weirdly ambivalent as he was ruthless. He would crush a competitor as casually as if he were an insect at a picnic. Yet he was at the same time overweeningly pious. He blanched at the use of swear words. He wouldn't touch a drop of whiskey. The strongest expression he allowed from his lips was "By thunder." When he really got angry, he'd stamp his cane on the floor with an "Oops" or an "Oh, my." Meanwhile, he cut the throats of his business rivals with the mien of a virgin reciting the Lord's Prayer.

Along with the network of lavish hotels he built in Saint Petersburg and Palm Beach, Flagler, his eyes rolling heavenward, put up a string of churches, each on a corner next to his latest hostelry. To make certain the dollars rolled in, he put next to each church a gambling casino.

Although he kept his gambling halls open around the clock, this pietist was violently opposed to anybody sipping intoxicating beverages on his premises. He inserted in all his real estate leases the decree that not a drop of liquor could be sold, and once he took out an injunction closing down a property when the lessor tried to sell whiskey in defiance of his orders.

Flagler displayed a brisk no-nonsense attitude early in life. At the age of fourteen he renounced the idiocy of spending more time for an education and quit school, going to work for his half-brother in Ohio. He had an educated noggin for making money, and to further ensure success he married a girl whose uncle was a wealthy whiskey manufacturer.

At this point Flagler became friendly with an aggressive young grain merchant who was dabbling part-time in the oil business, John D. Rockefeller. Rockefeller liked Flagler and admired his family connections even more. When he learned that Stephen V. Harkness, the whiskey mogul, was Flagler's uncle, Rockefeller assiduously cultivated him. In this case, whiskey and oil mixed magnificently. Harkness was induced to put up $100,000 to establish Rockefeller in the oil business, provided his nephew went in as a partner.

Flagler turned out to be a veritable Fortunatus. John D. pressed him again and again to get more cash out of his uncle, and the money was always forthcoming. The two men lived like Siamese twins; they sat in the same office, their desks only a few feet apart; they walked to work together in the morning and back home again in the evening. It is difficult to determine which was trickier, the son of the minister or his equally God-fearing partner.

When Flagler entered his sixties, his influence in the enterprise began to deteriorate. The Standard Oil Company had become a corporate titan and young men jostled Flagler in a struggle for power. Realizing he no longer had a role in the inner circle of Rockefeller advisers, Flagler quit the company. This wasn't exactly a tragedy for him. He took out $150 million which was his share of the profits the firm had made since he first induced his relative to put money into it. Such a nest egg could find widespread employment in the rapidly burgeoning America of the post-Civil War era. It could buy a large slice of the United States outright.

The project in which Flagler decided to pour his currency opened up rather casually. In 1874, like other midwesterners lured by tales of the wonders of Florida, Flagler took his wife, an invalid, on a vacation there. At the time of his visit, Florida was still quite primitive. There was no railroad south of Jacksonville. Miami was relatively unchanged from its original status as an Indian bartering place. Flagler, however, was captivated. He decided that this peninsula presented absolutely the finest chance for real estate investment that a benevolent destiny could have dumped into his lap. He proceeded to plunge money into building a vast complex of new communities linked by railroads, sparkling with lavish hotels, gambling casinos, and all the enticements necessary to lure tourists.

Flagler started his operations by erecting a hotel in Saint Augustine for Northerners yearning to come south for a frolic. This wasn't designed to be just another hotel; that wouldn't suit the man who cofounded the world's biggest oil imperium. This was to be one of the most elegant hostelries anywhere. He called it the Ponce de Leon after the legendary seeker of the Fountain of Youth, and it was built at a cost of $1.3 million to provide wealthy, elderly vacationers with the illusion they were recapturing their youth. Nowadays, the elderly rich regain their springtime via the cosmetic surgeon's knife in a Swiss clinic or the injection of hormones by a Yugoslavian sex doctor, but in that less sophisticated era, the oldsters hied themselves to Flagler's hotel.

The Ponce de Leon was designed in Spanish Renaissance architecture, featuring 540 rooms. It was one of the first large buildings in the United States to be made of poured concrete. This was a major technological innovation spawned of necessity. There wasn't any natural building-stone in the region. Flagler had to ship tons of coquina gravel from a Caribbean island to the Flagler mainland where twelve hundred laborers were hired to trample on the mixture to harden it into concrete.

The hotel was opened in January 1888. Electric lights, a novelty to many of the guests, were installed in every room. There were two miles of halls and corridors leading to the main lobby. The rooms were paneled in imported rosewood, mahogany and walnut, set against fancy draperies and Brussels carpets.

The Ponce de Leon set a standard in American architecture, for Flagler had the wisdom to hire the best brains available, Carrère & Hastings, a New York architectural firm, whose success with this hotel thrust it into the forefront of the profession. Subsequently the firm designed the interior of the old Metropolitan Opera House, the New York Public Library, the U.S. Senate Office Building, and the Arlington Memorial amphitheater.

The Ponce de Leon Hotel was an auspicious start. The alumnus of the hard-knocks school of oil was not content to rest with it. Flagler was determined to memorialize himself as the leading land developer and builder in the state. Even before the Ponce de Leon was finished, he sank money into a hotel across the street, the Alcazar, also dedicated architecturally to Old Spain.

One venture led to another. In order to crowd his hotels with revenue-bearing guests, Flagler figured he had to provide a railroad to bring them in. He realized that the single narrow-gauge railroad linking Jacksonville with Saint Augustine was inadequate to carry the heavy traffic he envisaged for his hostelries. He tried to convince the owners of the Jacksonville-St. Augustine and Halifax River Railroad that they should spend money to expand their line, but the railroad brass wouldn't put a nickel into the venture. So Flagler purchased the stocks and bonds of the railroad, becoming its new owner and expanding its traffic-carrying capacity.

In the early 1890s he visited Palm Beach and surveyed its possibilities for absorbing some of his loose cash. It was still a rural village, but Flagler sensed he could reap a financial harvest from this semitropical sandbar. McCormick, the reaper king, had bought property on the ocean side of the lagoon and Flagler wheedled him into selling out for the incredibly cheap price of $75,000. When the other inhabitants of the sandbar heard about this, figuring that Flagler would now expand his railroad south to Palm Beach, they rushed in to grab acres around the site of this purchase. Prices climbed from $150 to $1000 an acre in no time.

Meanwhile, Flagler built on the location a hotel that was even larger than his previous two in Saint Augustine. It was the largest wooden structure put up anywhere. Called the Royal Poinciana, it had accommodations for two thousand guests with acres of hallways leading to the main rotunda. Then Flagler built a hotel across the street—the Palm Beach Inn—directly facing the ocean.

Inexorably, Flagler expanded southward. Until 1903, Miami

was the southern terminus of Flagler's railroad. He pushed the road farther south as quickly as the wilderness was cleared by his engineers. The land adjacent to the tracks was sold to developers, and towns rapidly sprang up.

As Flagler's real estate operations grew in complexity, so did his private life. A Bible-quoting teetotaler who displayed an unflagging spirit of self-righteousness, Flagler pursued one rather unorthodox hobby—collecting expensive wives. Unfortunately, the church allowed him to collect only one at a time, but Flagler made the most of his opportunities. He stepped up his proclivities when other men had long retired from the pursuit.

The first Mrs. Flagler died when he was fifty-one. Two years later, Flagler hustled to the altar with the nurse who had taken care of his wife during her final illness. Alice Flagler was thirty-five and turned out to be psychotic.

Flagler became worried over his wife's mental condition, and he called in his personal physician to examine her. Alice showed him a pebble and told him it would make her pregnant if she kept it in her mouth long enough. She confided to the doctor she was madly in love with Czar Alexander of Russia and that her Ouija board reported the czar returned her passion. She announced she planned to marry His Majesty the day after her husband expired. One afternoon Mrs. Flagler bought a $2000 cat's-eye ring in Tiffany's which she mailed to the czar.

Mrs. Flagler's delusions became violent. She locked herself in her room, barricaded the door, and screamed that the house was loaded with Russian spies trying to prevent her marriage to the czar, but all the same she was getting messages to her beloved through her Ouija board. Flagler had papers drawn up for his wife's commitment to a sanatorium. She attacked a doctor in the institution with a pair of scissors, slashing his hand.

Ironically, while she remained in the asylum, imprisoned in her fantasies, Mrs. Flagler's wealth steadily increased, thanks to the Standard Oil stock she inherited from her husband. She outlived him by twenty years and when she died in 1930 in the asylum, she was worth over $50 million with nowhere to go and no way to spend it.

Undeterred by this marital experience, the aging multimillionaire tried again. The new Mrs. Flagler was formerly a Miss Lily Kenan whom Flagler met while she was visiting friends of his in Saint Augustine. He was seventy-one and she was thirty-four when they decided to marry.

One obstacle to the nuptial bells was that his second wife, Alice, happened to be languishing in an insane asylum. The law in New York, which was his legal residence, did not permit even a wealthy pasha to divorce a wife on the grounds of insanity. So Flagler moved to Florida, a state whose politicians he had in his hip pocket. He moved there, he told his friends, to avoid paying New York's steep inheritance taxes.

The moment Flagler took up residence in Florida, the State Senate introduced a bill to change its law and permit a severance of marriage on the grounds of insanity. The bill was rushed through in two weeks. Some irate citizens complained that Flagler had greased the palms of the legislators and gossips referred to the bill as "Flagler's Divorce Law." However, most Floridians took the bribery in stride. Indeed, the cause of education actually gained a victory, for Flagler handed over part of his bribe money to the Florida Agricultural College to build a student gymnasium. Two years later the college received another $10,000 from Flagler for good measure.

Fifteen days after "Flagler's Divorce Law" was passed, the elderly tippybob appeared at the altar to marry his thirty-four-year-old sweetheart. Lily Flagler in many ways proved to be the toughest dame of the lot. She wheedled her husband into lavishing money on her, and as he staggered deeper into senility, he yielded more readily to her caprices.

She demanded a marble palace to live in, and Flagler obliged by building a $2.5 million home, Whitehall. It was begun a few months after the marital knot had been spliced and was finished in the remarkably brief period of eight months. The building was fancy enough to have taken several years to complete, but Lily Flagler was an impatient wench and had wanted her whims gratified immediately. Flagler himself felt he hadn't much time left, so he drove and bullied his workers into putting up this Floridian Taj Mahal virtually overnight.

Whitehall featured a main rotunda lined with panels of black and white marble. Its acres of land were shaded by stately Australian pines set in splendacious gardens. As the years piled up, Flagler became so obsessed with the brevity of time, he installed in a huge foyer a clock that stood nine feet high to remind him constantly of the relentless ticking away of the hours.

One day in January 1913, when he was eighty-four, Flagler stumbled while walking down his grand staircase in the hall and he never left bed again. His son by his second wife had been infuriated over his father's abandonment of his mother and he had refused to speak to him for years, but now he relented to the point of paying him a visit. Flagler, however, was in a delirium and didn't recognize him. The old multimillionaire was buried in a mausoleum he had built years before in Saint Augustine. Four days after the ceremony, on May 27, 1913, his will was made public. It astonished many people. In providing the foundation for Florida's development into America's leading playground, Flagler had spent more money than he had taken in. (He had millions tied up in projects that were unfinished when he died and other real estate operators moved in to harvest his seedlings.)

Flagler's will disclosed an estate of nearly $100 million, $50 million less than when he had left the Standard Oil Company to enter the real estate business, but this wasn't peanuts. The bulk of his inheritance was passed on to his wife, Lily, under a trusteeship. She didn't live long enough really to enjoy it, dying four years after her husband on July 27, 1917. The preceding December she had married Robert Bingham, a Louisville, Kentucky, newspaper publisher. Six weeks before her death, she had added a codicil to her will by which her husband of less than a year inherited $5 million. The bulk of her fortune went into a trust fund from which payments were made to various Flagler business enterprises. Bingham did exceedingly well with his suddenly acquired wealth. He became a major financial contributor to the Democratic campaign which reelected Wilson president, and he was made an ambassador to England.

After Flagler's death, Florida continued to blossom as a seductive watering hole for leisure-minded Americans. Palm Beach, in particular, developed into a haven for the ultrasnobbish rich. It subdivided itself into a rigid caste system that would have made a Brahmin blanch. There were hotels for the Christian blue bloods and hostelries for the Jewish dukes of New York's Our Crowd fraternity. There was even a hotel for the chauffeurs who drove fancy Rolls-Royces that were coming into style for the rich.

One story passing the rounds concerned a tourist who asked for a room at the Breakers Hotel, a leading hostelry. When he said he was Jewish, he was politely told by the room clerk that the Breakers catered only to a Christian clientele. The guest applied at another hotel posing as a Gentile. The desk clerk replied that the hotel was reserved for Jewish gentry only—the Otto Kahns, the Lehmans and the like. "Well," exploded the irritated tourist, "I'll be a son of a bitch." "If you can prove that," replied the clerk, "I can get you in anywhere."

There was a quick dollar to be made in Florida land, and following Flagler, speculators swarmed in for the pickings. At the turn of the century, a retired Congregational minister by the name of George Merrick bought acreage dirt cheap outside of Miami. He built a multiple-gabled house out of the coral rock and called it Coral Gables. His son added parcels to his father's holdings and sold lots for what he advertised would become "America's most beautiful suburb." There were other toilers turning the wilderness into a land of milk and honey. One, D. P. Davis, snapped up two small islets in the Bay of Tampa. They were sand bars covered with marsh and mangrove that regularly disappeared under a high tide. Davis put money into raising an Aladdin-like island of fashionable hotels and homes. The first day he offered lots to the public he sold $3 million worth.

The pioneer promoter of Miami was Carl Fisher, an Indianan who started business as a storekeeper, then went into the fledgling new auto industry, forming the Fisher Automobile Company. In 1904 he launched with associates the Presto-O-Lite Corporation of America which developed an auto headlight that used acetylene to give off an especially bright glow. The product overnight made obsolete all lights powered by kerosene, and the Fisher syndicate reaped heaps of money. It sold out to Union Carbide for $9 million. Fisher received $7 million as his personal share.

In 1910 Fisher and his wife vacationed in Miami when it was little more than a mangrove swamp. As an ex-auto man he fully appreciated that the horseless carriage would become a major catalyst setting off a real estate boom in Miami, since it would bring middle Americans en masse to the winter playground.

Fisher filled the mangrove swamps with sludge dredged up from the bottom of Biscayne Bay, felled trees, built lagoons, put up artificial islands sparkling with hotels and villas. He made over $30 million in selling off lots to other speculators.

The development of Florida was stamped by the imprint of speculators, land developers, and builders who were as bizarre a cast as ever cavorted in the business arena. Once acreage was peddled and the money raised for building, architects were called in to apply the façade makeup. The cosmeticist who virtually single-handedly changed the landscape of Palm Beach was the architect Addison Mizner.

A blond strapping fellow over six feet, who in his prime weighed 240 pounds and carried every inch with bravura, Mizner, like Stanford White, reaped booty from beauty, yet he had only a half-baked training in architecture and very little general education. He was a baffling mixture of charlatanry and genius.

Palm Beach at the close of the First World War was jammed with the rich, many of whom had been in the habit of vacationing in the Riviera before the war. But four years of combat had shut off the south of France, so they seized on Florida, realizing it had the makings of Nice and Monte Carlo rolled into one and within easier reach of their homes.

But outside of a handful of hotels built by Henry Flagler, most of Florida had not yet been developed to its potential. The wealthy came with narrow cultural prejudices. They hired architects who built them homes similar to those they lived in up North. Comfortable with familiar surroundings, it did not occur to them to make use of Florida's splendid environment. Architects built structures duplicating the frame hotels of Saratoga, the Queene Anne cottages of New England, and the Middle West. They hauled down the wood from Northern pine instead of using the coral and the coquina rock native to Florida. They ignored the coconut groves, the poinsettia, and the bougainvillea, transplanting maples, lilacs, and woodbines for their landscapes.

Addison Mizner changed all this. All his life he had responded to rococo backgrounds. A gifted merchandiser, he was able to broaden the horizons of his clients while selling his fantasies, and Mizner's customers had limitless money to indulge his and their extravagances. They were enthralled with his plans to turn Palm Beach into a carnival city, part Spanish, part Moorish, sparkling with arabesques and minarets and spiced with the flavor of Gothic and Renaissance.

Explained Mizner: "My ambition [in building a house] is to make a building look . . . as though it had fought its way from a small unimportant structure to a great rambling house that took centuries of different needs and ups and downs of wealth to accomplish." He built history into the design and materials of his edifices. He sometimes started a house with a Romanesque corner, pretended that it had fallen into disrepair and that successive generations added to it in the Gothic spirit. Then, suddenly enriched by the wealth flooding in from the New World, a later generation incorporated into the mansion an ornate Renaissance-style wing.

One of the homes Addison built for a client was the Cosden villa, and it is typical of his freewheeling fancy. Wrote the journalist Ida Tarbell, "He does not miss a trick in getting the full value of the ocean—the very feet of the Cosden house are in the ocean—you sit on its balconies or walk its terraces and you seem to hang over the water. As you enter the front door, you have straight ahead, framed in a severe Gothic arch, a glimpse of the sea. It is managed by a tunnel which runs through the house and under the terraces above the seawall to the beach. Along these tunnels are doors into the bathing houses."

Together with his gifts, there was a crafty streak in Addison. To lure clients he started a side business, faking antiques to supplement his supply of the genuine article. Part of this was due to necessity, because during and immediately after the war, it was impossible to import the materials he needed for his "Old World" mansions, so he established his own workshops and taught local workmen to turn out ersatz "objets d'art." He trained a black-smith of West Palm Beach to become a Spanish wrought-iron "expert." Unable to get genuine ornamental cast stone, Addison assigned workers to bake powdered rock and glue in a backyard oven and ice the hot mixture to solidify it into a mold. This he passed off as genuine cast stone. As the demand for his services grew, he began to cheat more and more. He expanded his factory facilities, turning out a wider and wider range of phony "master-pieces." Bathing them with special acids, beating them with chains to age them properly, shooting them with BB guns to create wormholes, he simulated the patina of age and passed his junk off as centuries-old antiques on the culturally ignorant. Even when in a spasm of conscience he occasionally took trips to Europe to buy genuine art treasures, it was gossiped that his choicest items were smuggled into Florida duty-free by landing them in the Bahamas and sneaking them in hidden among kegs of bootleg whiskey. Displaying a piquant intermingling of knavery and genius, Addison wound up designing over $50 million worth of Palm Beach property.

The first "cottage" he built was for the Stotesburys, and it cost the banking family over 1 million. Called El Mirasol, it fronted the Atlantic Ocean and featured half a dozen patios, a swimming pool lighted from underneath, a forty-car garage, and a private zoo.

Almost entirely self-taught, Addison conjured up his designs from a study of old history books that featured pictures of Spanish castles and villas. These buildings had no bathrooms because toilets hadn't yet been invented, and the gentry used outhouses. Having no antique toilets to go by, Addison's inspiration halted at the bathroom door, and he let the plumbers take over the designing of the water closets.

An astute harvester of the money groves, Addison irritated, while at the same time he intrigued his clients, by deliberately leaving out some important features in the homes he built. In his first "cottages" he "forgot" to include a kitchen. Like the eye-patch in the Hathaway Shirt ad, forgetting a room or other architectural component became a promotional trademark. Addison's samples of "absentmindedness" became highly prized by his clientele.

One such oversight involved a house for George Rasmussen, a grocery magnate. Rasmussen came down from Chicago to visit it while it was being built, and he was astonished to find it had no staircase between the first and second floors. While the grocery king stood speechless, Addison solved the problem in his inimitable fashion. He refused to "ruin the beauty" of his conception with an inside staircase, he said, but he would compromise by building one on the *outside* of the house. This caused no particular difficulties when the weather was sunny, but on stormy days the Rasmussens had to put on raincoats to go up and down the stairs.

Some of Addison's clients were as zany as he was. A rich old eccentric, E. Clarence Jones, hired him to build a Palm Beach home as rapidly as possible. Jones, a bachelor in his seventies, looked forward to one great event each year, a marathon party he threw at which the booze flowed as freely as at a *festa* of Ovid Naso's. When Prohibition was passed, old Jones felt crushed. There was nothing left to live for, he decided, if he couldn't indulge in his once-a-year caper. He figured the only way out was to build a cellar and secretly hide enough whiskey in it to last him until he was ready to pass on. Jones hired Mizner to build such a basement and to construct over it a skimpy shelter just big enough for a single bed, to make it seem like a law-abiding residence. However, there was a problem. Since the ocean at Palm Beach rolls in as rapidly as one can dig into the ground, it's impossible to build a cellar underground.

Undaunted by this trifling obstacle of nature, Addison suggested he build it above the ground, and to disarm Prohibition agents of the notion that gallons of booze lurked inside, he designed it to look like a quaint old Chinese pagoda with five roofs curving entrancingly one above the other. The building cost three times the original estimate and old Jones screamed that he was being swindled, but the thirsty old coot was able to store enough moonshine to keep him in hilarious spirits, thanks to Mizner's legedermain, until he was called to his final accounting.

In addition to indulging in his cosmetic surgery, Addison took fliers into land speculation, and to facilitate the unloading of his properties, he enlisted a remarkably deft hustler, his own brother, Wilson, who had lived as variegated a life as his own. Wilson had been by turn a prospector in the Klondike, a ballad singer, a cardsharp, a hotel owner, a roulette wheel rigger, a prizefighter manager, and a Broadway playwright. The two brothers worked as a highly effective team. Addison developed the land, while Wilson shilled for the buyers.

And the pickings were lucrative indeed. While Palm Beach was the pasture ground for the wealthy, other Florida areas were beginning to attract people of more modest income desirous of aping the moneybags. America in the 1920s had become history's first society where the mass dared fantasize it was the class.

Middle America had been handed the technology to uproot itself from the hinterlands and savor the pleasures of mobility. For many the notion of God had been slain along with the young men in the trenches of the First World War. But if America had become a wasteland of the spirit, one was still entitled to a caper or two in Babylon. In a nation that strove to free itself from Inhibition as well as Prohibition, Florida was more than a place of perpetual summer sunshine. It was a state of mind. It was a symbol of defiance against the ethics that preached man's fate was to toil and shiver to win a toehold in heaven. To some puritan Marxists like Brecht, Florida was Mahagonny, the City of Nets. To real estate enthusiasts it was a utopia whose soil could be measured, sliced up, and ravaged for money. Technology and economic prosperity brought Florida within range of the humblest American from Bannock to Berkeley.

The advent of the low-priced Model T had revolutionized the life-style of Henry Ford's fellow citizens, who now found themselves able to travel anywhere at a moment's notice. The wealthy trekked to Palm Beach; the white-collar worker contented himself with going to Miami. National prosperity had lifted many into the brackets of the well-to-do. Investors had become affluent in the stock market. Crowds of Americans motored to Florida in their tin lizzies, picnicking and sleeping in camper sites along the way.

Ever since Flagler came to Saint Augustine, speculators had been reaping a harvest in Florida land. But speculation mounted to epidemic proportions in the mid-1920s. By 1925 the spirit of hedonism was at its peak. America had passed through an election in which the phlegmatic Calvin Coolidge won a second term as president. Clarence Darrow, the brilliant Socialist lawyer, had just saved Nathan Leopold and Richard Loeb from the electric chair for the murder of fourteen-year-old Bobby Franks. John J. Pershing had retired as general of the American armies. The airship *Los Angeles* on its maiden voyage from Puerto Rico to Lakehurst, New Jersey, made its appearance over Miami, and the huge cigar-shaped balloon drew crowds of rubbernecks gaping at the biggest thing they'd ever seen cruising in the sky. Pressured by ministers and women's clubs, the Miami Beach city fathers took a close look at bathing suits. Previously, they had ordered all female bathers to wear stockings, and rumors that males had been letting down their suits to their waistlines resulted in sharp police action. That spring the chemical industry had invented pyroxylin finishes and America's autos which had hitherto been turned out mostly in sober blacks burst overnight into a rainbow of colors ranging from wisteria white to canary yellow. Gene Tunney, who had narrowly won a bout, outscoring Jeff Smith in ten rounds at New Orleans, had arrived at Miami Beach to begin negotiating for his fight with Jack Dempsey for the world heavyweight title. The city fathers, to protect birdlife, decreed that all cats henceforth wear bells signaling their arrival. And in Dayton, Tennessee, Thomas Scopes, a schoolmaster, went on trial for daring to teach the theory of evolution in the heart of the Bible Belt.

In 1924 Florida revised its Constitution. Until then the state levied income and inheritance taxes, but now in a bid to entice wealthy migrants, the State Legislature canceled these.

Suddenly that year a strange, inexplicable thing happened. Charles Mackay's observation about extraordinary delusions and the popular madness of crowds was confirmed. Thousands of midges hovering, seemingly motionless in a sunbeam, suddenly shifted and fled toward a common target as if driven by a mysterious, unheard command. The stampede to Florida was on.

Prices of Miami real estate started climbing in 1925. Stories cropped up in newspapers about people who were becoming rich in land deals. One Miamian paid $1.75 million for three hundred thousand acres of swampland and forest in three counties south of Tallahassee, then turned around and peddled it within a week for a $250,000 profit. Another Miamian unloaded ten acres on Northwest Thirty-sixth Street to an ex-sheriff for $175,000. The seller had paid $250 for the property thirty years previously. A certain Ike Jones sold land near the Coco Lobo Kay Club for $250,000. He had bought it for $212. A shopkeeper peddled his store and surrounding land for $2 million and retired to enjoy his wealth. A month after the deal, his property was leased out for ninety-nine years on a $3 million appraisal. The president of the Miami Jockey Club bid $2 million for sixty thousand acres in Sumter and Hernando counties. The syndicate had bought the land unseen, believing it was located near Tampa several hundred miles away.

As early as February 1925, magazines around America were reporting that ordinary men and women with little or no capital were suddenly getting rich in Florida. The state census that year disclosed there were 103,000 year-round residents in greater Miami, but the city fathers predicted the population would jump to at least a million in ten years or less.

The speculative contagion mounted. Even the U.S. War Department became infected with it and decided to throw Chapman Air Field onto the market after giving a portion of it to the Department of Agriculture to use as an experimental farm. Leading Miami businessmen convinced the government it was wiser to keep the field as an air base in case of another war.

A phenomenon that mushroomed as a by-product of the speculative fever was the so-called "binder boys." Swarms of them poured into Florida to reap an overnight buck on land options. They jumped off trains, arriving from all directions, clad in golf knickers, rolled up their sleeves and went to work on the gullible. Knickers became the universal attire for the Miami hustlers.

The headquarters for the "binder boys" was the Biscayne Hotel, which was close to the major real estate offices. By the summer of 1925, the schedule of the hustlers was well established. They jumped from the train, looked around. "Is this Miami?" they asked. Then, "Where can I rent an office?" "What is the price of acreage?"

The binder strategy was highly lucrative. People contracting to buy a lot usually put up 10 percent or less of the established price until the arrangements could be undertaken to tie up the bargain formally. The purchaser received the binder and at the end of thirty days would pay another 15 to 20 percent upon the receipt of the lot after the title had been searched and the deed recorded.

But as the speculative craze spiraled, the county clerk became overwhelmed with work and there were long intervals between the down payment and the next one. During these interims, speculators could trade in options without putting up more cash, and the binder boys reaped a windfall. Initially they made small profits on the binders themselves, then they began working the business of running up the price of the lot through several transactions, while it was still on one binder. Properties were sold dozens of times before the first large payment fell due.

Profits mounted as the binder boys set a dizzier and dizzier pace. It wasn't unusual for a lot to change hands a half-dozen times from the day the first buyer received his binder until the deal was finally sealed. Often when the final buyer received the deed, there were a dozen mortgages attached to it "like ticks on a cow," each representing the profit of one of the traders along the way. The binder boys went around peddling from nine o'clock in the morning until two in the afternoon when the banks shut their doors. They rushed their checks immediately to depositories for the cash. Many a seat-pants plunger who had only enough money to buy a binder brazenly issued a subdivision brochure and sold enough lots to meet his first installment payment. He was careful to sell his lots only on the installment plan, for if a buyer had offered the total cash for a deal, he would have had to turn it down since he hadn't yet acquired the deed to sell it. He had to move quickly to stay one step ahead of his customers.

Meanwhile Americans poured in from all over. Asked by reporters why they came to Florida, they invariably replied they were seeking a way to "better themselves." Florida was the place where one could dine on lotus forever.

Newspapers around the country were crammed with reports on how ordinary folks living next door had suddenly struck it rich and would never have to work again. One newspaper wrote about a boilermaker from Buffalo who had worked hard all his life and despaired of getting ahead. He scraped up $1,000 and rushed to Florida in December 1924. There he accumulated $90,000 in cash and lots valued at $100,000. His employer offered him his job back. He wired, "Go to hell. I don't have to work!"

"The rush to Florida," argued one journalist, "has its rise in deep dissatisfaction with our economic situation, with the state of labor, with the physical limitations cities impose on the way we earn and spend our leisure."

The stories of people who had hit the jackpot continued to pour from the press. Around dinner tables, families discussed the latest tidbits—how the neighborhood butcher had shut up shop and moved his family to Florida, making $30,000 overnight in a property speculation. There was a story of a Columbia, South Carolina, stenographer who paid $350 for a Miami lot five years before and sold it—too soon alas—for a mere $65,000. There was the tale of James, a wealthy family misfit, whom relatives were sure would never amount to anything. He went to Florida in 1924, and, convinced millions could be made there, put $40,000 into property deals. When his family learned of this, they decided James must be saved from his disastrous speculation. They dispatched a battery of lawyers to Florida to extricate him from his binders, managing to free him after alienists testified he was insane. The $40,000 worth of land was released to another buyer who subsequently resold it for $400,000.

One minister was induced by the town undertaker to put his $2,000 of life's savings into Florida land. The mortician's son had just made $40,000 there in a month and had wired for $10,000 cash to swing more deals.

Exuberance in Miami was unbounded. One fellow called to see the head of a business concern. While he was waiting in the outer office, he overheard the office boy ask a stenographer if she thought the boss would pay their salaries on time this week.

"Gee, I hope so," said the girl. "I got to make another payment on those two lots I bought."

By the end of 1925, $7 billion worth of Florida real estate had changed hands. A full-page advertisement was carried in periodicals around the country showing a ragged breadwinner fighting off a pack of wolves while leading his wife and children toward a beacon light blazing from the doorway of a Miami real estate broker. The Miami newspapers churned out propaganda for the Chamber of Commerce. They played up the remarks of one New York businessman on Miami's precipitous growth. "Your skyline reminds me of New York." What the visitor had actually said was, "It compares with the skyline of *lower* New York."

A high-powered public relations machine headed by Steve Hannigan, who later turned up as President Franklin Roosevelt's press secretary, grounded out testimonials, interviews and speeches, and magazine articles to keep the ballyhoo going. Boasted Florida's Governor Martin, "We have a population of a hundred thousand, but we can support five million." Queried how long the Florida boom would last, a member of the Sarasota Chamber of Commerce replied, "As long as the sun shines, the birds sing and the children laugh and play." Financial pundits nodded their heads in agreement. Roger Babson, the investment adviser, predicted in *Forbes* magazine that the boom would persist for another five years at the very least.

The euphoria was breathtaking. Charles L. Apfel of Miami bought the entire town of Olympia in Martin County to use as the future capital of the world's movie industry. Eminent scientists had tipped him off, he explained, that a treacherous Arctic current had been discovered off the coast of California and in a few years it would freeze the California climate so severely that filmmakers would have to quit Hollywood and ship their studios to Florida.

For more than thirteen months, in 1925 and 1926, the *Miami Herald*, thanks to a flood of real estate advertising, became the world's largest newspaper in business volume, beating the *New York Times*, the *Chicago Tribune*, and the *Los Angeles Times* by a wide margin.

The boom brought to Miami a host of vaudeville headliners,

opera singers, and jazz bands. Real estate promoters put on lavish shows to entice crowds away from rival operators. Land peddlers and subdividers hired songwriters to compose music and lyrics, ballyhooing their properties. The offices of the bigger real estate promoters had the atmosphere of cabarets, with elaborate vaudeville acts presented between sales pitches.

Evelyn Nesbit, the ex-show girl who had been Stanford White's sweetheart, was hired to sing and lure the crowds into a leading real estate office. Feodor Chaliapin, the celebrated Russian opera basso who was touring the United States in *Boris Godunov*, was enticed by a fat salary offer to sing jazz songs for tired Miami businessmen relaxing after a hectic day's trading. Paul Whiteman, the band impresario, was hired to play fox-trots and pep up the flagging spirits of pitchmen. Gene Tunney, while awaiting his title fight with Jack Dempsey, entered the real estate business to reap a few dollars, becoming sales manager of an outfit called Hollywood Pines Estates.

William Jennings Bryan, the former secretary of state and perennial seeker of the presidency, turned up in Miami after a bruising Democratic Party convention which nominated John Davis instead of him. From the bandshell of the Royal Palms Park Hotel, Bryan made a tub-thumping pitch on the glories of Florida real estate, unloading 280 acres of property he owned in Dade County for $73,000. This erstwhile leader of the Free Silver Movement, the idol of Western liberals who headed the State Department in the Wilson presidency, now became a $100,000-a-year hustler for George Merrick, the Coral Gables land promoter.

The boom accelerated. By the middle of August 1925, real estate values on Miami's Flagler Street soared to $50,000 a front acre. Two weeks later a front acre went for $70,000. One businessman, I. C. Richmond, unloaded ten acres at N. W. Seventeenth Avenue and Thirty-third Street for $218,000. He had bought them twenty years before for $100.

The Miami Municipal Club sneered at the $50 million evaluation placed by tax officials on Dade County, calling it "ridiculously low" and complaining that such pikerish appraisal gave prospective purchasers an entirely false idea of what the property was really worth. Governor Martin added his scorn. No matter how high the evaluation was hiked, he predicted, the land's value would continue to skyrocket and the taxes would be a minimal burden upon the property owners.

With Miami bursting at the seams as speculators poured in by bus, tin lizzies, and on foot, rental space rose to a dizzy premium and widespread price-gouging took place. For five rooms in slum areas, $700 a month was being asked, with the first and last month's rent to be paid in advance. Many homeowners were reluctant to sell their houses no matter how high a price they were offered, because they were convinced they would have to pay even more for another shelter.

Traffic conditions became intolerable. Originally laid out for horse carriages, Miami's streets were too narrow to accommodate the stampede of autoists. They became hopelessly tied up for hours on end.

Most of the policemen, firemen, and other city employees had quit their jobs to strike it rich in the real estate business and there was a severe shortage of help to carry on essential services. Since virtually everybody in Miami was peddling real estate, the city's municipal fathers grabbed the most impoverished aspirants they could find, sharecroppers from the hills of Georgia, who wouldn't turn up their noses working for a modest city salary. These Georgia "crackers," many of whom had never before worn shoes let alone walked a city street, turned out to be rough customers. When they moved into the Miami police department and put on the uniforms of cops, they swaggered around, swinging their handcuffs and shaking their clubs menacingly at passersby. When one Miamian mistakenly crossed the street on the red light, a redneck whipped out his pistol and took dead aim at him, but he was a poor shot. He winged an elderly citizen who was shambling along the sidewalk a few hundred feet away. The Imperial Wizard of the Ku Klux Klan applied for the job as Miami's police chief, offering to install "law and order" in the city's emergency. But there was a limit to even Miami's fantasies. He was turned down.

The stampede to Miami threatened to depopulate a number of cities below the Mason-Dixon Line. *Billboard* and *Variety* reported a severe slump in the movie business because so many filmgoers had quit town heading for the lush pastures of Florida. The governor of Georgia told the Miami city fathers, "You're going to have a great state here in Florida—if the population in Georgia holds out." The Massachusetts Savings Bank Association disclosed that over one hundred thousand of its depositors had withdrawn their cash from the state's banks to plunge into Florida land. The *Indianapolis Times* complained, "Literally thousands of people are leaving our state in search of something for nothing in the land of oranges and speculators." Managers of warehouses in New York, Michigan, and Pennsylvania reported they were overwhelmed with the furniture of people who had pulled up their stakes and headed South, hoping to become so wealthy they'd never need return for their belongings. A conference of civic leaders in Virginia urged the state's Governor Trinkle to call a special session of the legislature and find ways to stop the outflow of citizens. The *Chicago Tribune* reported, "Florida, with its land boom and its bid for wealthy residents through exemption from state inheritance taxes, has helped stir up a political revolt out of the Missouri Valley that will be in evidence in Washington politics this year."

Around the nation, businessmen and civic leaders banded together for a vigorous counterattack. In September 1925, five Ohio banks, stung by the fact that millions of dollars were leaving their savings accounts, launched a campaign throughout the Middle West with full-page ads addressed to patrons thinking of rushing South. "You're going to Florida to do what? To sell lots to the other fellow who is going to Florida to sell lots to you. That's about all you can do in Florida—unless you want to work."

The Scripps-Howard newspaper chain, in September 1925, began printing articles from one of its top financial writers predicting that the boom was nearing its end, that Santa Claus was on his deathbed.

The Florida newspapers launched a bitter counterattack. The Clearwater Chamber of Commerce threatened to sue the Scripps-Howard chain for malicious slander. One top Miami businessman suggested that the City Council create the state post of "Fib-

Buster" to run down the derogatory stories and brand them as lies. When the sports editor of the *New York Herald* wrote a column kidding the boom, the Ku Klux Klan put on a parade in the streets of Miami carrying placards that warned him to watch his language. A Saint Petersburg newspaper printed an editorial entitled, "Shut Your God Damn Mouth." So worrisome did the anti-Florida publicity become that Herman Dann, president of the Florida Development Board, asked Governor Martin to propose a meeting in New York of leading Florida citizens with the nation's top newspaper and magazine publishers to urge them to stop printing "lies" about the boom. The meeting took place in October 1926, at the Waldorf-Astoria. Emotional speeches were made by Governor Martin and other Floridians. The newspaper publishers replied they had nothing against the state. They were printing the copy their reporters sent in because it was lively and attracted big readership.

The first sign of a crack in the upswing of real estate prices occurred in August 1925, seven months after the boom had begun. A hundred acres of sand and underbrush had been sold at Seminole Beach, north of Miami, and rumors spread that the beach would be subdivided by the new owners for development and that a portion of the undeveloped land would be put on the market. It was also rumored that Seminole Beach would be turned into a resort with a hotel, a casino, and stores. A mob rushed to the real estate offices, frantically demanding lots, and in seven hours $8 million worth of them were sold. Within a week speculators had unloaded them for $12 million, making a fortune merely by putting down a 10 percent deposit. Binder boys bought the lots, expecting to unload them on others. Before the month was over, trouble erupted. A few odds and ends of property near Seminole Beach were dumped on the market at 30 percent less than had been paid for the identical dirt on Seminole Beach. The unloading accelerated and panic set in. The binder boys who had stocked up heavily on Seminole Beach lots were cleaned out. Rumors spread that the unloading of the lots had been a deliberate ploy by major business interests in Miami to ruin the binder boys because they were annoyed with their shoestring hucksterism and the bad odor

199

they were giving Miami real estate. According to this gossip they unleashed properties near Seminole Beach at cut-rate prices to teach these carpetbaggers a lesson.

While the Seminole Beach debacle was the first major setback in the upward climb of real estate values, that same August other cracks appeared, warning of the queasy condition of the market. A dealer noticed that one of his lots which had been sold at a starting price of $10,000 and had soared to $60,000 on binders suddenly ran into trouble. The last bidder and the several below him had to sacrifice their binders, and the lot slid back to $30,000 where it was finally taken by a buyer.

Meanwhile other developments occurred. In August the Internal Revenue Service announced a ruling that was highly adverse for speculators. The commissioner decreed that henceforth the entire price of a real estate transaction must be reported as income, not merely the amount immediately picked up in cash. The impact was substantial. Suppose a man paid $200,000 in cash for property, and sold it for $500,000, receiving $100,000 in cash and $400,000 in promissory notes. Uncle Sam now demanded his share of the $300,000 profit, representing not only the cash, but also the notes. This meant that thousands of speculators henceforth had to raise cash by selling their properties or selling their promissory notes, frequently at a sharp discount. The IRS, to back up its tough new policy, dispatched a squad of twenty agents to the county court house in Florida to check on the profits of speculators.

In the meantime, shoestring plungers, who had rushed to Florida with high hopes, were drifting home, spreading stories of their disillusionment. The newspapers told about an elderly couple who had come all the way from Vermont. They lost their entire savings in Florida speculations and started the trip back to the New England hills in a tin lizzie, their last remaining asset. They got as far as North Carolina when they ran out of money. They tried to sell their car for $105, but the used-car dealer, after calculating their fare back to Vermont, offered them $75 and generously threw in another $10 for "incidentals."

Another blow struck Miami—a railway freight embargo. The

volume of merchandise pouring south had become so vast and unmanageable by August 1925, that just to ship a boxcar to Miami from Jacksonville took over a week, and when it arrived, the backlog was so huge it couldn't be unloaded. By mid-August, 900 freight cars were stuck in the Miami train yards and 1200 more were jammed back-to-back for miles to the north. Railroad officials stopped taking cars from other railroads and shut off incoming shipments on everything but perishables, livestock, and fuel. The freight embargo spread through Florida and serious shortages cropped up. Fresh milk virtually disappeared. Ice could be obtained only on a physician's prescription. The impact was devastating on the real estate business. Critical building materials no longer were coming into the city. Owners of buildings that were 90 percent completed became panicky. They were losing money by the minute, because they lacked a few bricks, boards, a small amount of glass necessary to finish their hotels or apartment houses.

The ingenuity used to obtain material was prodigious. One Miami contractor shipped a freightload of building bricks from a Northern city crated as "lettuce." The bricks were hidden under tons of ice, but the ruse was discovered and the contraband seized.

More troubles piled up. Steamship lines joined the railroads in declaring an embargo on Miami-bound goods. Milk became increasingly scarce and cows died of hunger at Florida dairies, because ships carrying grain feed from Europe couldn't deliver it. Bootlegging flourished. Contractors hired thugs to run the embargo and bring in urgently needed planks and beams. Hijacking became a lucrative trade. Bricks, lumber, and plumbing supplies couldn't be left unguarded at building sites because they would be stolen to finish off other structures.

Ships were anchored for miles off Miami, waiting their turn to thread their way through the tricky channel into Biscayne Bay and be unloaded. And even this outlet was suddenly shut off when an old Danish man-of-war capsized in the channel. The ship had been retired from naval service and was being towed to Florida to be converted into a hotel when the mishap occurred. The

Miami channel was only nineteen feet deep, and the ship flopped over on its side in the exact middle, blocking off sixty vessels ready to enter.

In March 1926, further bad news reached Miami. The New York Stock Market took its worse dive since 1920. In 1925, $500 million of Northern capital had poured into Florida land holdings. Now, wealthy Wall Streeters were strapped for cash.

The prospect that little money could be expected from Wall Street that spring made Miami business circles deeply uneasy. On the eve of Gene Tunney's bout in Miami, his manager had to abruptly cancel it because he couldn't find anyone willing to put up a guarantee for the boxer's $100,000 share of the purse. The promoters had a hassle with the bailiffs over a shipment of lumber that they had ordered for the seats and which had not been paid for.

Yet many Miamians still suffered from the illusion that the drop in real estate prices was only temporary. D. L. Hartman, Miami's strawberry king, held stubbornly onto twenty-six acres of land north of Seventy-ninth Street, rejecting a $1-million offer for them, convinced that the price would go higher. In the previous four years he had cleared $92,000 on his strawberry crops and he wanted to harvest one more crop before retiring. During the latter part of October he finally contracted to sell the strawberry patch to a corporation for $1 million to be subdivided into lots once it was harvested. But that year the harvest happened to be late, delaying the sale. By the time the strawberries were ready for shipping, the price had dropped well below $1 million. The corporation refused to take the property off Hartman's hands.

Still *gaieté de coeur* reigned among the credulous as 1926 began. Despite the tumbling stock market and freight shortage, the city outwardly put on a festive show. Although most property dealers were no longer willing to divulge to the newspapers the amount of daily business being transacted for fear investors would spot unfavorable price trends, one major promotor reported that his sales of $1.6 million for the first eight weeks of 1926 were substantially higher than the previous year. Nightclubs opened to a lively business. Fritz Kreisler and Mary Garden performed to sold-out houses. Al Jolson sang Gershwin for jazz aficionados. Red Grange, the star college halfback, joined the professional football ranks and made a dazzling debut in Coral Gable's new $25 million stadium amid wide ballyhoo in the sports pages.

Most Miamians declined to concede that the party was ending, for the city still seemed to be bursting with activity. The hotels were packed to the rafters with tourists. Miami and Seminole beaches swarmed with pleasure seekers. Feodor Chaliapin sang to SRO audiences at the Hotel Biscayne.

Disaster struck with a chilling decisiveness. On September 15, 1926, the weather report announced that a tropical storm was hurtling toward the Florida coast. On September 17 the news became more ominous. The hurricane was said to be bearing down at 110 miles an hour from Haiti straight for the heart of Miami. Shipowners were warned to batten down the hatches, residents on the coast to move their belongings inward. But the majority of inhabitants had never experienced a hurricane. They were relatively recent arrivals and were not aware of the battering the Florida coast had taken from tropical storms in the past.

In the early evening of Friday, September 18, the eye of the hurricane struck the tip of Florida at Key West and howled up the coast. Just before reaching Miami, the 100-mile-an-hour wind died down a bit as if to catch its breath and then resumed its fury, battering community after community with torrential rains and waves that reached twelve feet high as they smashed breakwaters and pounded inland. The winds, the rain, and the mountaineous waves roared up the coast, devouring people, homes, bridges, telegraph poles. The hurricane uprooted locomotives and railroad cars, flinging them hundreds of yards before depositing them head over heels in the mud.

By dawn on Saturday the entire coast from Key West to Miami was shut off from the rest of the nation as telephone wires and radio transmitters were put out of commission by the storm. The 400-foot tower of the radio station at Hialeah, which engineers boasted was able to resist winds of over 90 miles an hour, was totally demolished. Volunteers braved the storm to put up a temporary transmitting station on the deck of a vessel that miraculously still stood undamaged in the Miami River, and thus the news of the catastrophe that had overtaken Miami was broadcast to the world.

Martial law was ordered and the National Guard moved into the stricken city. Relief committees were set up to disburse food and medical supplies. One hundred and fifty bodies were dug from the wreckage. Five thousand homes were demolished; three thousand others suffered varying degrees of destruction. One hundred thousand Miamians were shelterless. Fifteen hundred homes in Hollywood were destroyed beyond repair; three thousand others, damaged partially. Two thousand homes were demolished in Fort Lauderdale. Trolley lines, telephone poles, lampposts were strewn for miles like broken matchsticks; bridges and causeways were uprooted. The Miami waterfront was an area of stark devastation. Yachts, motorboats, and other pleasure craft had been lifted by the winds from the waters of Biscayne Bay and flung hundreds of yards inland, landing randomly in front of hotels, office buildings, and in the backyards of the mansions of the wealthy. The hurricane was the greatest natural disaster the nation had suffered since the San Francisco earthquake.

The impact on the Florida economy was immediate. Unemployment was widespread. When one employer ran an ad for a night watchman, 150 men stood on line for twelve hours begging for the job.

Things became so bad that W. O. McGeehan, a New York sportswriter, in a dispatch from the camp of the New York Giants who were training in Sarasota for the start of the baseball season, wrote that real estate brokers who had been wiped out were disguising themselves as rookie players so they could obtain free meals at a restaurant serving the Giant team.

Virtually all the major real estate operators went broke. One of them, Charlie Ort, had started out owning a city dump. At the peak of the boom he had parlayed his winnings into $30 million. As prices started to tumble, his bankroll shrank to $500,000 and he was advised to take the cash and run while there was still time. "Hell, I can't do that," retorted Ort. "Someday this will all come back." Ort ended up without a cent.

Virtually all the other big fellows went down convinced to the last moment they would recoup their winnings. Carl Fisher, who had pioneered the development of Miami Beach and who could have sold out at the top with a fortune of $150 million, wound up leaving an estate of $40,000 when he died. George Merrick, who had built up Coral Gables and had been worth several hundred million, was completely wiped out. Joseph Young, who developed Hollywood-by-the-Sea into a lavish resort and parlayed his investment into $300 million, was left destitute. Barron Collier, one of the largest landholders in Florida, was buried under $20 million worth of debts. He had to get a special moratorium from the Federal courts to keep from bankruptcy. O. P. Davis, another spectacular operator whose financial coups were the talk of the town, vanished from an ocean vessel on the way to Europe. The gossip was he had jumped overboard.

Not only were individuals destroyed. The Brotherhood of Locomotive Engineers, which took $15 out of the union's treasury and plunged it into building an exotic Renaissance-style resort on the lower west coast, suffered disaster. Engaged in what they believed was a once-in-a-lifetime investment opportunity, the union officials purchased vast acreage from a local physician. When the crash came, the resort looked like a ghost town, strewn with deserted streets, unfinished hotels, and apartment houses for which there was not a single bidder.

One òf the gaudier victims of the crash was Addison Mizner, the eccentric Palm Beach architect. The flood of speculators' money that poured into Florida in 1925 proved too tempting for the old freebooter to resist and Mizner turned from building aeries for the wealthy to grabbing a hunk of Middle America's loot.

In those days of outlandish speculation, Addison had teamed up with his brother Wilson to promote the most garish project of all. The Mizners and their associates grabbed six thousand acres of land south of Miami at a site called Boca Raton, which in Spanish means "Rat's Mouth," so named since the inlet entrance to the property was shaped like the mouth of a rodent. There they planned to build a city which, according to their publicity releases, was to be a Florida version of Venice, complete with twenty miles of canals, topped off by a replica of the celebrated

Grand Canal and the Rialto Bridge. One hundred electrically driven gondolas were to ply the waterways. Addison rushed an order to the gondola makers in Venice to build the fleet and ship it quickly. The Italians who were experiencing a depression jumped at the chance for this business.

As an approach to this "Queen City of the American Adriatic," Addison planned to build the world's largest highway, El Camino Real (the King's Highway). According to the promotional brochures, it would have no less than twenty traffic lanes, wide enough to transport several thousand motorists daily into Boca Raton. With his typical flare for the *outré,* Addison planned to illuminate the highway indirectly, with lighting concealed in the curbs instead of from lampposts.

To be sure several problems arose. When El Camino Real was finally completed, it turned out that while it was unquestionably the *widest* highway in the world, it was also the *shortest,* for Addison's ambitions had outrun his finances. El Camino Real extended for less than a mile and it was freakishly lopsided. It had *twenty* lanes going into Boca Raton, but *only two lanes* going out of it. Addison figured the important thing was to bring the traffic in and not to worry about the eccentric few who wanted to leave his paradise.

No matter. El Camino Real wasn't meant from the outset to be a serious highway. It was as genuine as a road built on a Cecil B. De Mille movie set. What fueled and sustained the Florida boom was the power of suggestion. It wasn't what *was* but what *appeared* to be. The ballyhoo generated from the building of El Camino Real touched off a frantic bidding for property along the route. Ordinary folk figured that Boca Raton *had* to have a fabulous future if Addison was plunging money into constructing a twenty-lane highway into it. Neither Rome, Washington, or London had a twenty-lane highway going into *them.* How could anybody miss with Boca Raton?

The first day Addison put his property on sale, $14 million worth of lots were grabbed up. Checks were written so fast they were dumped into wastebaskets as they were received and counted at the day's end. Corner lots in Boca Raton zoomed from a few hundred dollars into $100,000 an acre.

In August 1925, while the highway was being dug, Addison let out $7 million in construction contracts. After the hurricane hit Florida, only a handful of buildings were finished in Boca Raton—these and a pathetic little street called Via Mizner. Along it, Addison had erected a cluster of shops and sidewalk cafés painted in bright pink, blue, and cream stripes. It was his farewell as an architect.

Boca Raton was well named. The rat's mouth had snapped up the cheese. Three thousand investors went broke in Addison's venture. Tumbling into bankruptcy, the project eventually was taken over by the Central Equities Company of Chicago, headed by Charles Dawes, who had been the vice president under Coolidge, and Dawes' brother, Rufus, a financier.

Addison Mizner had made the fatal mistake of becoming mesmerized by his own salesmanship. Extending himself financially, borrowing to the hilt, he went broke, losing every penny of the millions he had made.

He dragged on for another seven years until 1933, living off the handouts of friends, devoting most of his time to hiding away from subpoena servers. An old ailment, necrosis of the bone, cropped up. He suffered agonizing pain but his sense of humor remained. A great wit, he continued to be a deadly draw with the hilarious quip.

The uproarious quip was a family trademark. His brother Wilson, caught off guard and dragged into court by a subpoena server, was lambasted by a lawyer for having allegedly defrauded his client. "Didn't you tell the plaintiff he could grow nuts on the land you sold him," thundered the attorney. Wilson looked at him blandly. "The hell I did! I said he could *go nuts* on it."

The end to the boom was as far-reaching as it was unexpected. By 1927, virtually all the real estate offices that had mushroomed in Miami were closed. Many communities to the west and east were on the point of bankruptcy, unable to collect their taxes. In 1928, Henry Villard, the journalist traveling to Miami, reported, "Debt sub-divisions lined the highway, their pompous names half obliterated on crumbling stucco gates. Lonely white lights stand guard over miles of cement sidewalks where grass and palmetto take the place of homes that were to be."

207

Four years later, in 1932, the state had not yet recovered. A nationwide business recession following the stock market crash of 1929 left Florida's financial circles gasping for breath. Over twenty cities in the state went into default on the principal or interest on their bonds.

However, by the mid-1930s, Florida began to revive. Once the fantastically inflated land values had receded to realistic levels, people began to realize that Florida with its year-round sunshine *was still there.*

Ironically, the wild building spree left its impact on many a nook and cranny of America. Just as Paris fashions for the rich are copied by thrift designers for women in Podunk and Kalamazoo, so millions of white-collar families who had not been within a thousand miles of Florida moved into bargain versions of the grandiose architectural palaces Mizner and other architects had built for the wealthy in Palm Beach and Miami. Real estate promoters on Long Island, the outskirts of Philadelphia, and Connecticut went Italian Renaissance in a big way. Thirty miles from New York City, one enterprising realtor launched an American Venice for tired salesmen and middle-echelon executives to come home to after a long day's stint in their Manhattan offices. A bridge was built over a stream that was billed as a replica of the Deglia Paglia in Venice. The landscape, according to the promoters, "Recalls the famous city of the Doges only it's more charming and more homelike." Raved one of the advertisements, "To live in America's Venice is to quaff the very wine of life, a turquoise lagoon under an aqua marine sky. Lazy gondolas, beautiful Italian gardens and, ever present, the water of the South Bay lapping lazily all day upon a beach as white and fine as the soul of a little child"; and on Long Island, Jacob Frankel, a clothing business magnate, developed Biltmore Shores, a network of canals and waterways to whet the appetite of the dreamy *Hausfrau* and her vulnerable husband who could afford a small down payment.

This after all was America, the land of the spree and the home of the rave.

7

"MOMMA, DOES GOD
LIVE HERE?"

*The Movie Industry Joins the Land Barons to
Launch New Real Estate Empires*

Land is virtually indestructible, the oldest and most enduring source of wealth. Yet much of it is constantly changing in its nature of usage. And it is the impact of this conversion that frequently enhances its value and triggers the biggest profits reaped by real estate developers.

Land used for farming in an era when society is predominantly agricultural can be enormously revivified in value by being converted into the site for a supermarket in a society that has become highly automated. Indeed the use to which acreage is put at any given time as a result of popular demand tells the historian much about the aims, values, even the psychological hang-ups and temporary fads of that society.

One of the largest, most ambitious urban housing developments ever to be undertaken in the United States, Century City, was launched on acreage once used to turn out movies before the silver screen suffered the heat of competition from television. The land had been purchased in the days when moving shadows on the screen erupted as a sensational novelty entrancing millions of Americans and becoming for one gaudy decade, at least, the supreme form of entertainment from coast to coast.

The impact the movie syndrome had upon real estate activity and the subsequent financial bonanza reaped by land manipulators who converted old movie properties into new uses in demand by a changing society is a striking, if little discussed, chapter in the history of land development. Yet the evolution from Edison's movie kinescope to the development of Century City is labyrinthine and highly fascinating.

H. H. Wilcox and his wife, Davida, were a couple who lived in Los Angeles after the Civil War. Wilcox was an astute operator who invariably ferreted out a profitable real estate deal. He gobbled up ranchland on the outskirts of Los Angeles in 1888 and he bought 120 acres in a nearby valley aflame with berry bushes. He subdivided the property into blocks, put money into cutting roads through it, planted pepper trees, and called the place Hollywood, after the holly bushes that imparted the blazing color to the region.

Wilcox's investment turned out even more lucrative than he had foreseen. It was one of history's superbargains. The town, at first, experienced the slow, steady growth of a typical Los Angeles suburb, then something happened to revolutionize its future—the advent of the movie industry.

Fledgling movie producers were quick to seize upon Hollywood because it had sunshine all year round and pictures could be shot in the open air for less money than indoors back East.

The stampede to Hollywood began during the First World War. On open lots all over the community, barns served as studios, jammed with gingerbread sets. Fox snapped up a lot on Western Avenue. Jesse Lasky located his Famous Players studio in Hollywood. Carl Laemmle founded Universal City on acres of chicken farms beyond the Cahunga Pass. Sam Goldwyn's business expanded so rapidly, he was soon forced to add to his first barn, property near the ocean. Native Angelenos at first looked upon the moviemakers who trekked into Hollywood as if they were freaks in a traveling circus. At the first sign of business adversity, they expected them to fold up their carnival tents and sneak away, but they stayed. Producers, directors, actors moved in from New York and built stylish bungalow cottages along the beaches.

Movies were shot all over the place. Private residences were rented to use for elopement scenes in hearts-and-flowers sequences. Banks were taken over on Sundays for cinema hold-ups. Residents were recruited on the sidewalks to participate in mob scenes. Streets were hosed down with water, so that the autos would skid and overturn more easily in auto accident shots.

In the decade between 1910 and 1920, Hollywood's population skyrocketed from 5000 to 36,000. The cultivation of lemon grove trees and other agricultural pursuits had been virtually abandoned in favor of industrial and real estate operations. Farmland was replaced by business offices and expensive homes. In the six years between 1921 and 1927, bank clearings climbed from $133 million to over $400 million, thanks largely to the growth of the movie industry. By 1928, the average building permit valuation in Hollywood was $14,000, the largest of any urban property along the Pacific Coast.

As the movie producers grew from shoestring nickelodeon operators to executives of growing film empires, much of their success was due to their astute strategy of buying up real estate properties. Moviemaking in Hollywood was merely the tip of the iceberg. It wasn't enough to crank out celluloid fantasies. Theaters had to be built to draw in audiences and to serve as captive outlets for producers.

As the producers embarked on a vast power struggle grabbing up the choicest locations in cities and towns throughout the United States to build networks of theater outlets, a new kind of real estate enterprise mushroomed.

The times were ripe for it. Thirty million Americans stormed movie theaters weekly, enthralled by the antics of the celluloid mimes. Woolworth salesgirls and lonely old dowagers strayed for 25 cents into a world of meretricious make-believe.

The early 1920s was an America of Mah-Jongg, spiritualist seances, crossword puzzles, and a Utopia of technological equality. Not only did wealthy women wear silk stockings, but every shopgirl from Bangor to Podunk with an income of $1500 had discarded her cotton hose for silk. It was the age of sports spectacles in giant new coliseums. In Chicago, 140,000 people watched Dempsey fight Tunney for the heavyweight title, perched in an arena that was so cavernous two-thirds of the crowd couldn't see who had won the fight and had to turn on radios to find out. Radio listeners at home shared the excitement more intimately. Five dropped dead of heart failure.

It was a time when matters were definitely not as they appeared to be. There was a law on the books prohibiting whiskey from being consumed in America. Yet the production of corn sugar used for illicit stills rose 600 percent during the years of Prohibition.

Federal agents put wood alcohol and other poisons into industrial alcohol to discourage it from being drunk illegally, and outraged "wets" charged the government with murdering its citizens. Prohibition agents, frustrated by their inability to prevent liquor from flooding the country, shot to kill—frequently the wrong people. One eager revenue hunter pursued and sank a vessel two hundred miles off the U.S. coast, only to find it was a Canadian ship bringing Red Cross supplies to the Dominion. Scientific gadgets had replaced the bones of saints as society's idols of worship. So saturated had American life become with the cult of science that one New England clergyman told his congregation he thought of God as "a sort of oblong blur."

But if God was no longer in His heaven, all was still right with the world of free private enterprise which was providing the cornucopia of material plenty, sustained by its own mystique. Churchmen fell over one another to discuss their holy aims in the glowing parables of business enterprise. The Swedish Immanuel Congregational Church of New York, during a fund-raising campaign, offered to every parishioner who contributed $100 the greatest spiritual reward it could possibly conceive of, "an engraved certificate of investment in preferred capital stock in the Kingdom of God." The Rotarian Club had become the new grassroots congregation. American industry declared with priestly unction, "Let us prey."

In an era when millions renounced in their hearts the old theology and the power of science was as frightening as it was promising, Americans turned to a new mass diversion—the baroque world of escape conjured up by Hollywood. The modern house of worship was the movie palace. And a whole new strategy for real estate acquisitions was launched together with a bold new approach by the realty dealers' chief hireling, the architect.

The surroundings in which the films were shown grew to be as escapist as the scenarios flashed on the screen. As Hollywood increasingly whetted the lust for the exotic, a curious kind of rococo architecture swept the land.

Two basic schools of movie palace architecture were developed for the emporiums being built by the real estate sachems. One was the "hard-top" style which evolved out of the conventional vaudeville house. The second was the "stars-and-clouds" approach resulting from an architect's flinging stars, moons, landscapes about as if in a psychedelic dream.

The leading exponent of such extravaganzas was John Eberson, who stamped his imprint on scores of theaters from Skowhegan to San Diego. In the commercial heart of a city, next to the bank, a grocery store, or tailor shop, Eberson unveiled his "atmospheric" movie palaces that looked outlandishly incongruous in the drab context of American life. The 1920s was a period of grandiloquent kitsch. Eberson issued brochures describing himself ready to build for the highest bidder "a magnificent amphitheatre under a glorious moonlit sky . . . an Italian garden, a Persian court, a Spanish or a mystic Egyptian temple-yard . . . where friendly stars twinkled and wisps of clouds drifted."

Eberson's theaters were pop lessons in eclectic archaeology, landscape gardening, and Oriental architecture. An Austrian by birth, he cleverly exploited America's appetite for inspired vulgarity. While he may have deluded others, Eberson knew precisely what he was after. He enticed the Hollywood producers, those incomparable arbiters of American taste, by advertising that his aim was to "Prepare Practical Plans for Pretty Playhouses—Please Patrons—Pay Profits."

Eberson was a production as well as merchandising genius, for he was able to erect his mind-blowing edifices for less than it cost his competitors to build conventional movie houses. In reproduc-

213

ing "the art of Rome, Florence, the Acropolis and the Taj Mahal," Eberson used arches, cherubim, trellises, colonnades mass-produced by a firm he owned as a side business, which he named with lofty cynicism, "Michelangelo Studios." The clouds in the starry sky, alas, were simple plaster and the twinkling of stars was produced by cheap electric bulbs. Michelangelo, mass-produced more cheaply than a Model T Ford; it took the America of the 1920s to accomplish this lofty perversion of the artistic muse. Eberson's fabricated firmaments and peacocks popped up all over the nation in sizes 6, 7, and 5, like socks from Woolworth and nickel cigars.

For clients who were willing to pay more, Eberson upgraded his line and produced some mighty fancy bric-a-brac in a prestige "Cadillac" bracket.

As he grew increasingly successful, both in the schlock and the expensive, a horde of imitators sprang up who littered America with marble balustrades, crystal chandeliers, and Oriental domes. To stay ahead of the competition, Eberson constantly sprang new tricks. He designed the Majestic Theatre in Houston, Texas, a cow town of the old West, in a style that would have been eye-popping in Xanadu. Eberson built the emporium without any roof at all. The patrons were amazed to find themselves sitting in an Italian garden with the sky shining through. Vines tumbled languidly over the trellis and gorgeously stuffed peacocks stared down as the audience munched its popcorn, watching Mack Sennett cops scampering across the screen. The "sky" was engineered in blue plaster. Electric bulbs twinkled like a constellation of stars, and clouds gracefully floated by, thanks to an illusion induced by magic lanterns. It took God a week to create the world. Eberson didn't take very much longer to build the Majestic.

In designing the Loew's Paradise in the Bronx, Eberson was hampered by a local zoning law prohibiting the use of protruding marquees on the Grand Concourse. To compensate for this deprived opportunity for flamboyancy, he saturated the interior with a neo-Renaissance atmosphere, highlighting this with a replica of Michelangelo's tomb for Lorenzo di Medici in Florence, dutifully turned out by the Michelangelo Studios, Inc.

"Momma, Does God Live Here?"

Eberson also designed an emporium for Marcus Loew in Louisville, creating a ceiling for the foyer from which the heads of Dante, Socrates, and Beethoven peered down in bas-relief. Dominating this galaxy of super stars, in the very center of the ceiling were the sculptured features of John Eberson himself.

There were other necromancers besides Eberson peddling pretentious make-believe. One architect designed for a backwoods community in Minnesota a theater of only eight hundred seats, but it had ambitions as grandiose as those of its bigger sisters in New York and Los Angeles. Posted for the employees was a notice, "Please do not turn on the clouds until the show starts. Be sure the stars are turned off when patrons have left."

John Eberson's chief rival, who also reaped a fortune from movie palace kitsch, was Thomas Lamb, a native of Dundee, Scotland. Lamb received his first job from William Fox, the movie producer, to design a theater in Manhattan. Fox permitted him to employ whatever frills he desired just so long as he "allowed enough room for the projection booth." Three years later, Lamb designed an elaborate emporium in lower Harlem in neo-Renaissance, and on Broadway, he re-created the Parthenon of Athens. In San Francisco, he built a Fox theater, styled in French baroque.

As this phony grandiosity latched on across the land, *The New Yorker* magazine ran a cartoon by Helen Hokinson, showing a little girl walking with her mother into the grand foyer of a Manhattan movie palace. The child, wide-eyed, looks up and asks "Momma, does God live here?"

The architects for all their impact were merely the hirelings of the real estate moguls who financed the emporiums and reaped the bulk of profits. The rush of the Hollywood producers to build networks of captive theaters was a boon to real estate speculators, some of whom were scabby characters indeed. One top gamester was F. J. Gadsol, who, before he accumulated a fortune from movie houses, made money swindling the French government during the First World War. The French cavalry urgently needed horses, and Gadsol shipped aging, broken-down mules, billing the government for thoroughbred equines. He was sent to

215

jail for his fraud, and when he got out, he parlayed the money he had made with the mules into another fortune selling fake pearls.

Other dealers in movie houses had equally captivating if not quite as crooked backgrounds. Messmore Kendall, for instance, was a lawyer and man-about-town who boasted of his *Mayflower* lineage. After the World War, Kendall leased a plot of land from the Jacob Wendell estate on the corner of Fifty-first Street and Broadway. The property was occupied by a livery stable, a blacksmith shop, and, as a sign of the changing times, a gasoline filling station. Kendall bought the land for investment, but there was a quirk in the lease. It provided that no portion of the property could be sublet to any business engaged in making corsets or cosmetics. When the movies came to New York, Kendall decided the site would be ideal for a film theater, one that would outdazzle the extravaganzas being built elsewhere. To finance the undertaking, he put together a syndicate of partners with varying backgrounds. It consisted of General T. Coleman Du Pont of the Du Pont dynasty, who had recently run for the U.S. presidency; Frank Hitchcox, a former U.S. postmaster general; George Doran, a publisher; William Braden, a copper magnate; George Armstrong, a West Coast meat-packer; Robert Chambers, a popular novelist, who plunged a large part of his book royalties into the venture; and Major Edward J. Bowes, who later became a household name in radio entertainment.

Bowes, the son of an Irish dock laborer in San Francisco, early revealed a talent for making money. He acquired an extensive self-education, went into real estate, lost a fortune during the San Francisco earthquake in 1906, then proceeded to make another one by predicting correctly where the city's new business district would be located. He came to New York, invested in Broadway theater properties, took time out during the war to serve as an intelligence officer and then reentered the real estate business. He joined the Kendall syndicate to build a Manhattan movie house that would be the largest in the world, containing over five thousand seats and outdoing its rivals in architectural splendor. Tom Lamb was hired to design the Capitol Theatre and he utilized his entire bag of tricks. The lobby was lined in rich mahogany which was installed only after a heated battle with the New York Buildings Department, whose inspectors descended on the building site and scrutinized every inch of the structure to make sure it wouldn't be a fire hazard.

The boom in movie houses not only unleashed an army of real estate gamesters and their satellite architects, but also spawned a master showman who was to become the epitome of the Era of Kitsch. He was Samuel Rothafel, better known as "Roxy," who had once been a messenger boy, shined shoes, joined the marines, and fought in the Boxer Rebellion in China and climaxed his adventuring by becoming a troubleshooter in the movie theater business.

Roxy concocted shrewd stage and vaudeville presentations to bolster boring films and send box-office receipts soaring. A doctor of failing movie houses, he was called in everywhere to supply the hypo for luring in customers. He was summoned to revive the fortunes of the Strand at Forty-seventh Street in Manhattan, the Rivoli at Forty-ninth Street, and the Capitol—the house financed by Kendall, Major Bowes, and their cohorts. With deft showmanship, he turned a dying business venture into a highly successful one.

The silent films, for all their visual excitement, lacked the dimension of sound. Moreover, full-length feature films usually ran no more than sixty minutes, and the problem was how to hold an audience's attention for several hours so as to charge fancy admission prices. Roxy provided a solution.

He was unhampered by any elitist attitude toward the arts. While the moviegoing masses were looked upon by the highbrows of the 1920s as a hopelessly unsophisticated booboisie, Roxy handed them Culture Made Easy. Before the main picture went on at the Capitol, for instance, he presented excerpts from grand opera, hiring prima donnas from the Metropolitan Opera House to sing on the Capitol stage. He promiscuously interspersed opera with an orchestral medley of Irving Berlin songs followed by a ballet adapted from Chopin's *Les Sylphides*. He presented shortened versions of Gilbert & Sullivan operettas, violin solos by classical virtuosos, and saxophone pieces by popular jazz artists.

Roxy scavenged the entire universe of the arts with freewheeling eclecticism. Some of his adaptations were positively breathtaking. When the air dirigible, the *Los Angeles,* was shown arriving in Manhattan on its maiden voyage in a Fox Movietone newsreel, Roxy had the Capitol orchestra play Wagner's "Ride of the Walküres."

In addition to being an impresario, Roxy began broadcasting as a master of ceremonies from the Capitol Theatre, and his radio show, "Roxy's Gang," became a hit throughout the nation.

Roxy's chrome-plated showmanship wasn't confined to the entertainment field. During a trip to Chicago, he decided that the train he rode on, the Twentieth Century Limited, lacked sufficient glamour. When he got back to New York, he suggested to the president of the railroad that a red carpet be unrolled at the Grand Central Station platform for passengers. This, he said, would make the Century the most prestigious train in America and enormously boost its business. Roxy was right. New York Central officials were so delighted with the idea they gave him a lifetime pass on the road.

In 1926, a real estate syndicate got together to build still another theater in Manhattan, this one to be the largest and most lavish on earth, and Roxy was invited to join the venture, not only because his large following of radio listeners would be an ideal source for raising money through subscriptions, but Roxy's showmanship would guarantee additional success. Indeed, the promoters decided to call the theater the Roxy.

The project got rolling when H. Lubin and Arthur H. Sawyer, two aspiring real estate operators, acquired an option to buy for $3 million land on Fiftieth Street and Seventh Avenue, which had been the site of old trolley carbarns. Lubin and Sawyer were joined by the Chanin Construction Company, headed by the brothers, Irwin and Henry Chanin. Only seven years previously, they had started out scrounging for money to build two modest frame houses in the Bensonhurst section of Brooklyn. William Juthman of Bing and Bing, Inc., another realtor, joined the syndicate. Normally, when movie house realtors went to the banks for loans, they could obtain them only by promising to build a commercial structure as part of the theater complex, for bankers were leery about lending money solely on the prospects of a movie house. But on this occasion, a loan of $4.3 million was made by S. W. Straus & Co., a commercial factoring outfit, for a theater with no commercial building involved. Walter Ahlschlager, an architect, was chosen to design the theater which the promoters publicized would be the "Cathedral of the Motion Picture."

The syndicate erecting this behemoth poured in 250 tons of steel, 4 million bricks, 40,000 yards of burlap, 1000 tons of odd plaster and lime, 70 tons of modeling clay, and 700,000 feet of channel iron to hold the plaster in place. The newspapers chronicled item by item the vast amount of material that was plunged into the construction.

The wrecking of the carbarns commenced in November 1925 followed by the excavation work begun in December. The foundation was started the following March and the steel construction in April. It took a little over ten months to erect the mammoth theater, an extraordinary achievement for the times. As the building went up, the main truss, the largest ever fabricated, weighing over two hundred tons, was installed as the supporting structure covering over one and a quarter acres of land and provided a theater that would house ten thousand people under one roof.

Ahlschlager, the architect, faithfully adhering to the taste of the times, gave the Roxy the last full measure of his aesthetic devotion. He designed the interior in early Renaissance combined with a touch of Spain. Eight sculptors were hired along with three hundred mechanics who worked for five months on the art decorations. The team was headed by Pietro Ciavarra, a sculptor, who supervised the modeling of over one thousand designs for selection for the interior. Five men worked day and night for weeks to build the proscenium arch which consisted of a seventy-foot-long panel frescoed with sculptured figures twelve feet high. A similar period was spent in constructing the dome of the main foyer.

A devotion displayed by builders of the early Gothic cathedrals went into the erection of this twentieth-century equivalent, the movie theater. To paraphrase the historian Henry Adams, if the twelfth century was the Age of the Virgin, and the late nineteenth, the era of the Dynamo, then the twentieth was certainly the age of Cecil B. De Mille.

This cathedral for celluloid beatifics was built to seat over six thousand popcorn munchers. The foyer was designed to house four thousand additional people waiting for the show to change. A total of ten thousand people as noted were to be accommodated in the basilica.

The stage was the largest ever conceived. It was divided into four sections of which two were built on elevators that could be raised and lowered by hydraulic electric apparatus. The pit of the orchestra was engineered to hold three huge organ consoles, the largest in the world, to be played by three men simultaneously. High up in the proscenium were installed twenty-one bell tower chimes similar to those designed for open-air belfry use. So great was their vibration when rung, that the engineers had to place them behind massive shutters to control the volume of sound. The battery of musical devices was embellished by a Fanfare Chamber that simulated the sound of twenty-four trumpets and sixteen trombones. This, supplemented by one hundred musicians in the pit, plus a choir of one hundred voices, provided a rousing introduction to the latest Griffith or De Mille epic projected on the screen.

The Roxy's foyer and auditorium were decorated with replicas of art from ancient, medieval, and Renaissance times. The walls were festooned with spears and halberds of finely wrought brackets. A frieze design featured the Greek Muses of song. The electricity that powered the Roxy was sufficient to light a town of twenty-five thousand people. Roxy selected his ushers with the fastidiousness of a cardinal recruiting acolytes for a High Mass, and they were trained to perform their duties with the precision of a drill sergeant. They wore uniforms of blue trimmed with lace. The coat was cut in the fashion worn at Eton, England's posh school for aristocrats with the dress shirt, bow tie, and winged collar.

Ironically, the splendiferous opening of the Roxy on March 11, 1927, was the sheerest façade, for its promoters had scraped the bottom of the barrel for cash and were down to their last cent. So intoxicated had they become with their grandiose vision that they badly overshot their budget. The realtors had obtained a $4-million bank loan, and Roxy, peddling the project over the radio to his faithful listeners, had seduced thirteen thousand of them into buying $4 million worth of stock in the venture. But this was insufficient to pay the bills. The theater had been scheduled to open the previous Christmas. But this had to be postponed because Wall Street brokers were unwilling to provide any further funds. Ten days after their debut, the owners were so badly in need of cash that they were ready to unload their gorgeous edifice to the highest bidder. It was one of the most depressing boomerangs in the necrology of real estate.

A candidate promptly showed up with ready cash, William Fox, the movie producer, who was engaged at the time in aggressively accumulating a chain of movie houses in an effort to beat out Marcus Loew, his major competitor. Loew had amassed the industry's largest number of captive movie outlets, over twelve hundred. Fox, the next biggest operator, had a thousand theaters under his belt, and was rapidly closing in. The Roxy loomed as a prize catch. Located in the nation's largest market, it would be the crown jewel of Fox's network. So he bought the Roxy with its six thousand seats, its three console organs, and belfry chimes for $13 million. Samuel Roxy stayed on as Fox's hired hand to develop stage entertainments and lure the patrons in. But a clash between Roxy and Fox, two men of elephantine egos, was inevitable.

Fox had spent a lot of money developing a system to turn silent films into talking pictures and he installed it in his new showplace. With this technology, Fox could produce films with talking and singing actors and he had no need for the elaborate stage presentations and live background music that Roxy specialized in. Each time Fox booked a new sound film into the Roxy, Roxy complained that it was crimping his style as musical director. The canned, brassy music and dancing of the Fox films didn't gibe with his flesh-and-blood kitsch.

Fox and Roxy stopped speaking to each other. Finally, when one movie was about to be booked and Roxy again protested bitterly about being shorn of his talents, Fox turned to a business associate: "Tell that son of a bitch if he isn't out of this theater in twenty-four hours, I'll send someone over to throw him out."

Roxy received this message while sitting in his elegant office atop the theater, surrounded by his sculpture and library of musical scores. It was as if the chieftain of a barbarian tribe had broken into a holy sanctuary and smashed an image of the crucified Christ. Roxy, at first, was stunned. Then with a saintly shrug, he opened his desk and cleaned out all his belongings, those relics, souvenirs, and memorabilia that symbolized his achievements, and without once looking back he walked out of his splendacious tabernacle with its three console organs, its belfry chimes, its massage rooms, fifteen Steinway pianos, and closets loaded with his personal wardrobe of seventy dress suits.

William Fox, who kicked Roxy out of the house he had built, was more than his match as an egotist. He had parlayed a grubstake of $1600 into a $300 million business through rough-and-tumble manipulations. A lone wolf, a savage infighter, with piercing eyes, a beaked nose, and a crippled right arm, hanging limply at his side, he exulted in the struggle for power.

Fox didn't have a roster of big film stars like Metro, Loew's, First National, nor did he have their talented directors and scriptwriters, but he had a powerful chain of over a thousand theaters strategically located on virtually every main street in America. *He deeply appreciated that real estate holdings were a key to movie success.* The trick was to grab up valuable land locations for theaters that would act as captive outlets for the films cranked out by the Hollywood panjandrums and would lessen the gamble of making movies. At the time he acquired Roxy, Fox, as noted, was struggling with Marcus Loew for dominance of the movie theater field. Each was sending scouts all over America to snatch up locations in areas of the highest business traffic before the other could snatch the site.

Fox from the beginning had been forced to live by his wits, with his one good arm and overshrewd head. He had been born in the Hungarian village of Tulchva of German-Jewish parentage. His father operated a general merchandise store and, as a sideline, pulled teeth, advertising himself as a "Painless Dentist" and guaranteeing that nobody would feel the slightest twinge in his mouth as his tooth was extracted. The patient sat on a chair and stripped himself to the waist. Suddenly a sizzling hot iron was pressed to his back. Stunned by this distraction, he was oblivious to the yanking of his molar.

The family came to America when Fox was still a child. He trekked up and down the steps of old tenements on the Lower East Side where he lived, selling stove blacking for a nickel a can. He also peddled lozenges six for a nickel, and bought a stock of umbrellas which he sold on rainy evenings to ladies coming out of Broadway shows.

Thanks to his merchandising enterprise, Fox saved up several thousand dollars. In 1894, Thomas Edison, the inventor from Menlo Park, New Jersey, concocted a gadget he called a "kineto-scope." He had built a shanty inside which stood a camera, an awkward hunk of equipment, weighing over a ton, with a quickly moving shutter, through which one could take a series of action pictures provided that the field of vision didn't go beyond the lenses of the camera, which stood in a fixed position. To Edison's shanty trekked prizefighters, acrobats, and circus performers who did their thing before his lenses. Edison patented his kineto-scope, others used it, and before long, nickelodeons—arcades with a row of machines having eyepieces—sprang up all over America. A viewer dropped a nickel into the slot, looked into the eyepiece, and saw prizefighters slugging one another, acrobats turning somersaults, and dancers hoofing and pirouetting.

On Fourteenth Street in Manhattan, there was a shop called the Automat which, alongside punching bags and chewing gum machines, displayed the novelty kinetoscopes. Whenever Fox passed, he went inside, put a nickel into the slot, and was fascinated by what he saw.

He figured he would invest in the movie business. He learned there was another establishment at 700 Broadway in Brooklyn where the owner had gone a step beyond the nickelodeon operators. He was showing movie pictures flashed onto a sheet on a wall through a new machine called the Vitagraph. Fox made an appointment to inspect the operation. When he arrived, he found people gathered around the place. He visited a second time and found an even greater crowd. Figuring the business must be a lucrative one, he negotiated to buy it for several hundred dollars. On his first day as its new owner, only two people dropped in and he realized he had been bamboozled. The previous proprietor had stocked the joint with relatives and friends.

Fox cudgeled his wits figuring how to entice patrons. One evening a fellow in a cowboy hat walked in and noticing Fox's anxiety asked, "What's troubling you, pardner?" Fox told him he had invested his savings in the place and he wasn't doing any business. The Westerner replied he had some suggestions to offer and he would be back the next day to explain them. The following morning he appeared with three performers from a nearby circus, a swallower of swords, a fire-eater, and a magician who made coins disappear. Fox could hire any he chose, the Westerner said. Fox was afraid of involving himself with the fire-eater, for he carried no fire insurance on the premises. Swallowing swords was also dangerous; if there were an accident, he would be liable as the employer, but a coin manipulator seemed a safe trade. The magician put up a table in the doorway of Fox's premises and went to work making coins vanish. A crowd gathered to watch. The prestidigitator started an elaborate trick and announced he would finish it inside. The curious followed him up the stairs to a second-story room and were confronted with motion pictures projected on to the wall. They were enthralled. Within a week, so many people were lining up to see the movies, the police had to be called out to keep order.

Fox began renting other stores, borrowing money from the banks, putting an option on properties along the busy avenues of Brooklyn. As soon as he took an option for $100, he put up a sheet, assembled rows of chairs, and installed a projection machine. He couldn't put in more than 299 chairs in a room, for if he had more, he was considered a theater owner and the fire laws for theaters were stricter.

Borrowing money from the banks and friends, paying off his loans with cash that came in from the movie houses already operating, Fox, within a year, owned fifteen showhouses in Brooklyn and New York. Success depended on pouncing on a location where heavy crowds passed.

Operating the movie shows was not without headaches. The spectacle of dancers kicking their legs high, cars turning over and blowing up in flames, robbers holding up banks, shocked the better elements of the citizenry and raised the hackles of reform groups. By 1908, the nickel movies had acquired such a nasty reputation for depravity that New York's police commissioner urged Mayor McClellan to cancel the operators' licenses. On Christmas night, 1908, the authorities struck suddenly. At midnight, the police poured out of the station houses and pounced with swinging clubs on all the movie houses and nickelodeons in the city, closing them down and padlocking them. Manhattan's top moviemen, Adolph Zucker and Marcus Loew, got together with Fox and made plans to defend their business. They hired a lawyer, pressed injunctions against the license commissioner, and made a formal statement to the mayor, promising that henceforth they would refrain from showing violent train robberies and cops and robbers chasers and present only entertainment to which wives and children could be invited.

With New York's police commissioner off his back, Fox forged ahead. By 1915 he had a chain of movie houses blanketing the Greater New York area. Hundreds of thousands of patrons passed into his theaters to see the films he showed. With his business growing by leaps and bounds, it was a logical step to start making his own films.

In 1914 he went to Southern California to look over conditions and he bought twelve and a half acres for a studio to be built on Sunset Boulevard where it crossed Western Avenue. Meanwhile he plunged more and more aggressively into theater expansion because his competitors were closing in on him and if he stopped growing, he felt he couldn't survive.

His grasp stretched across America's heartland. He moved into the Middle West, wheeled and dealt all the way to California. In a predatory move, he grabbed a West Coast chain of 250 theaters; next seven movie houses owned by a realtor named Ascher, who controlled the Chicago market, fell into his grasp, followed by 50 theaters owned by the Saxe Circuit in Wisconsin and Iowa. Twenty Poli Houses in New England changed their name to Fox.

Fox accumulated his properties as if he were playing a colossal game of chess. Strategic pawns were snatched to get at more valuable pieces through intricate manipulations of leveraged financing. Local real estate dealers were made use of to wangle valuable properties and were cut in on the action for their services. Highly speculative and dangerous positions were taken with a minimum cash investment to leverage and grab the jackpot. Bargains were made with political powers. The infighting was savage.

As the decade of the 1920s neared its end, William Fox who had peddled stove blacking in the New York slums had become one of the richest and most powerful men in America. By 1927, he owned eight hundred movie houses, collecting them as other men bought neckwear. As an offshoot to his movie business he had become one of the nation's wealthiest real estate dealers. He was, moreover, a pioneer of talking pictures, introducing sound newsreels that brought events from around the world into ten thousand of the nation's theaters.

Thanks to Fox's Movietone newsreels, Bernard Shaw's witty conversation came live from the screens to millions of Americans. Fox's films showed Mussolini, the stocky little Italian dictator, speaking from the balcony of the Victor Emmanuel monument in Rome. Americans heard Lloyd George telling, in his clipped Welsh accent, how he bought a shepherd dog. King Michael of Rumania rode a lawn mower over his palatial grounds for the benefit of Fox cameramen. A new force had entered American life to compete with the newspaper.

The man who ruled over this dominion, with the crooked beaked nose, the suspicious eyes, and the crippled left arm, was a moody individual who eluded the attempts of the movie journalists and feature writers to analyze him. Wrote one columnist, "It is absurd to say that he is conceited, it is too puny a word. Megalomania afflicted with elephantiasis. That is the state of his self-esteem." At one point, Fox asked a political friend in Washington to wangle a colonel's commission for him, so that his employees would be compelled to salute him when they addressed him. When he was told he would have to go to Washington to be sworn in, he shrugged. "I'm too God damn busy—send them down to me."

When the Prince of Wales, the future Edward VIII, toured New York, it was arranged for him to visit the Academy of Music on Fourteenth Street where his grandfather, Edward VII, forty years previously had received the curtsies of the reigning New York beauties. (The Academy of Music had been sold to Fox who turned it into a movie theater and his press agent had arranged the Prince of Wales' visit). The day before the event, the agent explained to Fox that royal etiquette demanded he wear a morning suit and a top hat. "As the prince enters, don't extend your hand. You must bow to him." "That's out," retorted Fox. "I won't bow, God damn it." His staff pleaded with him. In vain. The last words he thundered as he strode out of the office, were "No bow, no damned bow."

The following day, the prince arrived at the Academy of Music with an impressive retinue. William Fox stood in the lobby in morning suit and top hat. Then as the cameras clicked and the news bulbs popped, a miracle happened. Reported a newsman, "The Fox torso twitched. It *actually twitched*. There was achieved involuntarily perhaps, a bow, a small but definitely visible *bow*."

Arrogant, secretive, and ruthless, Fox had a violent temper. Employees dreaded his anger. One high-ranking executive who displeased his boss was once knocked by him through a door into the next office.

While he lusted after publicity for his theaters and films, Fox hated personal ballyhoo and shunned the newspaper and magazine writers. He was positively paranoiac toward them. The major command given his staff was to keep William Fox out of the newspapers, and if, on occasion, it was absolutely necessary for his picture to be published, he insisted that the one used must be a photograph he had taken many years previously, showing him with a bristly black mustache. Shortly afterward, he had shaved the mustache off for good.

227

So aloof was Fox that only once in the four years from 1925 to 1929 did he inspect his huge Hollywood holdings. He never stepped foot on his new $10 million soundproofed stages nor saw a number of his million-dollar movie houses. Driven by a cupidity for power, he was unable to relax. He operated at such high tension that twice a year he entered a private sanatorium in secrecy to rest his shattered nerves.

So determined was he to persevere in whatever he attempted that, although he couldn't lift his left arm above his shoulder, he trained himself to play an excellent game of golf, using only his right arm.

He bossed his fiefdom with an iron grip. While other Hollywood sachems went into lengthy conferences to deliberate on important matters, Fox made his decisions alone, taking counsel of no one. There were definite advantages to this. On one occasion, a major chain of theaters on the West Coast was up for sale. First National Pictures ardently wooed it. The top brass met on a Friday, had a lengthy meeting, and decided to hold over the final decision until Monday morning, but on Saturday, William Fox, consulting nobody, wired an offer and snatched the chain from under the nose of his competitors.

This despotism continued even though Fox Films had become a public corporation responsible to shareholders. As early as 1915, Fox had made a public offering, transferring into a new corporation his assets, his leases, the ownership of ten theaters in New York, a dozen more in the suburbs and his real estate holdings in Hollywood consisting of twelve and a half acres along Sunset Boulevard and Western Avenue. In return for this, Fox raised enough money to step up substantially his acquisition program.

By 1928, Fox had over a thousand theaters, yet he continued his headlong expansion, dangerously overextending his credit. As the decade neared its end, his overweening ambition led him into trouble.

In 1928, during the peak of the tussle for control of the nation's theaters, Marcus Loew, Fox's chief rival, died suddenly, leaving a holding company that owned twelve hundred theaters, together with a valuable film production studio, Metro-Goldwyn-Mayer. Loew's widow inherited her husband's four hundred thousand shares of company stock which was almost a third of the total ownership and carried virtual control. This four-hundred-thousand-share ownership, which had a market price of $125 a share or $50 million for the block, was tempting bait for other Hollywood padishahs. Adolph Zucker, chief of Paramount Pictures, entered the bidding to grab the block and merge Loew's into his own combine; and Warner Bros. also sought the shares.

Fox, too, put in a bid. The advantages of a merger with his firm were obvious. Fox and Metro were rivals with similar plants and 115 marketing agencies doing the same job around the world. The elimination of such duplication from a corporate marriage would save $15 million a year. Fox was determined to get control of Mrs. Loew's stock.

In recent years to finance his expansion, Fox had gone into heavy borrowings from his bankers. Now to snap up ownership of Metro, he needed an additional $50 million, a sum too big for a single bank to handle by itself. It was necessary to approach a Wall Street investment banking house. Fox had a relationship with Halsey, Stuart & Co., and he contacted it to do some new financing for him. The Halsey brass advised Fox to approach the American Telephone & Telegraph Company, a $2 billion behemoth which owned the bulk of the nation's wire communications, and was also manufacturing the equipment for Fox's talking newsreels.

At the time, several of the major studios were experimenting with processes for getting the silent pictures to talk. Warner's had developed a system which was in competition with the equipment sold by the telephone company. AT&T was unhappy at the prospect of Warner Bros. getting control of Mrs. Loew's shares, for then the Metro firm would be eliminated as an outlet for its own talking equipment. Fox, on the other hand, was a customer for AT&T's hardware, and Ma Bell, anxious to block Warner's bidding, agreed to lend Fox $18 million for one year to help swing the Loew purchase. It also arranged for a bank it did business with to lend another $3 million. Halsey, Stuart & Co., for its part, offered to extend a $10 million loan, and the Bankers Security Company of Philadelphia, of which Fox was a director, prepared to lend another $10 million, taking a portion of the Loew's block of shares as collateral. Finally, Fox Theaters Corp. raised $18 million on its own, selling new shares to the public. The total sum raised amounted to over $50 million, and Loew and Fox entered negotiations for Mrs. Loew's stock.

Now that the marriage was on the point of being consummated, Fox arranged to have a round of golf with Nicholas Schenck, the Loew's president, at the Lakeview Country Club in Long Island on the morning of July 17, 1929. Fox drove in extremely high spirits to the club which was located in Long Neck, a few miles from his home. After months of arduous negotiations he had finally wangled the biggest prize of his career, Metro-Goldwyn-Mayer, which made him owner of the world's largest movie studio and theater combine. Reminisced Fox afterward to Upton Sinclair, "I was dreaming of the perfect conclusion. Life had just begun and this was to be the greatest stepping-stone of my career . . . at fifty one."

His chauffeur who was driving the limousine lost his bearings and turned into an unknown road. He approached a crossing moving cautiously at twenty-five miles an hour, not knowing which direction to take. There was a hill blocking the view of motorists moving in from the left. The limousine reached the crossing and was practically through the intersection when an auto driven by a woman motorist suddenly hurtled toward them and slammed into Fox's car, which went spinning into the air, landing on its roof. When Fox regained consciousness, he extricated himself from the wreckage. Nearby his chauffeur lay dead. The car had fallen on him, breaking his neck. Fox was rushed to the hospital where he underwent emergency surgery and a series of blood transfusions. For weeks he hovered between life and death. It took him six months to recover.

When he returned to the office, his business instincts which had been virtually infallible for so many years now turned sour. Fox continued to take heavy business risks, convinced that his credit was virtually unlimited and he would be able to pay off his debts from future earnings. Although he had for all purposes control of Loew's, warned by his investment counselors that he needed possession of an absolute majority of the stock to prevent from being ganged up on by other major shareholders and pushed out, he grew anxious and borrowed to buy 261,000 shares in the open market in addition to the 400,000-share block he had purchased from Mrs. Loew.

Because he had promised the government that Fox Films Corporation would own no more than 400,000 shares of Loew stock, he was compelled to buy the additional 261,000 shares in his own name and those of other members of his family and relatives. In this way, he gained absolute control of Loew's, but his indebtedness, much of it now personal, to Halsey, AT&T, and the bankers, had climbed to $70 million.

Then he was enticed into snapping up the Gaumont chain of three hundred theaters in Great Britain, increasing his indebtedness by another $20 million. Not only was Fox heavily leveraged and perilously overextended, but most of his collateral for the loans was involved in stock market operations. In the fall of 1929, misfortune struck suddenly.

On the evening of Monday, October 24, Fox, as he notes in his reminiscences, along with other business leaders, attended a banquet honoring the Republican Party and listened to Secretary of Commerce Robert P. Lamont deliver an ominous speech. When it was over, Fox, thoroughly shaken up, turned to an associate. "That fellow Lamont is either the biggest damned fool or the most intelligent man I've ever listened to. Which is it?"

Lamont had warned his distinguished audience that the nation's economy, which seemed on the surface to be so prosperous, was actually in jeopardy. Americans were overspeculating in the stock market and refusing to buy bonds upon which Lamont declared the real strength of the economy was based. The secretary painted so disturbing a picture that Fox shuddered at the thought of what would happen the following morning when the financiers who had attended the banquet reached their offices and the bell rang for trading on the stock exchange.

Lamont was correct, but tardy in the timing of his warning. The stock market had already begun its retreat from the peak of summer prices, a decline that was on the verge of turning into a stampede. It was too late for William Fox or anybody else who was heavily enmeshed in the market to extricate himself painlessly.

On the morning after Lamont's speech, stock prices continued to drop at the ringing of the bell; as the day wore on, the pace of the decline quickened and panic set in.

Fox was entrapped. He had 661,000 shares of Loew's stock for which he had paid more than $73 million to get majority control, and before the closing bell, its market price had tumbled to less than half its previous value. Sixty percent of the shares had been assigned to bankers as collateral for loans Fox had run up to finance his acquisitions. His brokers had possession of the remainder since he had plunged in on heavy margin in his own name and those of his relatives. The only way he could hold on to the Loew shares and not lose control of the company was to sell all the other stock he owned and hopefully use the money he received to pay off the margin on his Loew shares so that his brokers would not dump them on the market.

As panicky investors continued to unload stock, Fox held on to his Loew shares, shoring up his position with the sale of his other securities, but the price of Loew shares was deteriorating so rapidly, it was uncertain how long he could hold on to them.

Next morning, recalls Fox, he remained on his Long Island estate, trying to figure a way out of the looming disaster. His stock was in the hands of thirteen brokers. Shortly after ten o'clock, the telephone rang. One of the brokers was on the phone. "Fox, it's murder on the floor. Loew shares are diving like crazy. We need a check for two hundred and fifty thousand dollars to cover your margin or we'll have to sell you out."

Several minutes later, a second broker was on the phone, then a third and a fourth, each asking for additional margin. Fox added up the amount of the margin demanded. It was over $1.5 million. He phoned his secretary at his Manhattan office. "Make out checks for a million and a half and have them delivered by messenger."

Shortly after Fox hung up the phone, it rang again. It was the first broker. "We asked for two hundred and fifty thousand, but the price has fallen so damned fast, we need five hundred thousand now." Other brokers phoned. When all thirteen gentlemen had put in their calls, a stunned Fox realized that the margin money demanded amounted to over $4 million. He glanced at his wristwatch. Over $4 million and it was only noon. The market had three hours to run. He phoned his secretary. "Tear up the checks you've written. I am not sending a God damn cent to anybody."

Exhausted, he took the receiver off the hook and lay down to get some rest. After an hour's tossing, he was awakened by a business colleague who was staying at his home as a guest, shaking him by the shoulder. "I've just heard over the radio there's a panic. People on Wall Street are jumping out of office windows. Police have been called in to control the mob." The man paused. "I guess I'm over jittery. I've been looking all over the house for you. I noticed your boat wasn't tied up at the marina and I got the foolish notion you might have gone out and drowned yourself."

Fox's wife was ill and he didn't want to alarm her. He mumbled something about there being an emergency in Wall Street and he had to consult his brokers. He promised he would be home the following day. He didn't show up for six weeks.

That evening when he arrived in Manhattan, Fox found that the price of Loew shares had tumbled so low his margin obligations now had risen to $10 million. At nine the next morning he summoned his thirteen brokers to a meeting in his office, and told them bluntly, "I owe you ten million dollars, but I don't have the money. You are holding six hundred and sixty thousand shares of my Loew's stock. If you sell them, you'll drive the price down to nothing and lose your entire investment." He paused. "I have a favor to ask. Give me another twenty-four hours to come up with the money. Promise me you won't sell any stock until then. If you refuse, that's the finale of both of us."

The brokers replied they would go back to their offices and confer on the matter. When they had left, Fox paced the floor in a sweat. He hadn't the slightest idea how to raise the $10 million.

The phone rang. Fox picked it up. On the other end was Albert

Greenfield, a rich real estate dealer from Philadelphia, with whom Fox had engaged in a number of lucrative property deals. As Greenfield chatted about trivial matters, it dawned on Fox that the realtor wasn't aware of the desperate financial trouble he was in. This wasn't surprising. Fox had tried to keep his problems from everybody except those who absolutely had to know. Fox kept up a cheerful façade, exchanging pleasantries. While chatting, he casually recollected to Greenfield that a year ago he had closed a deal with him to buy a chain of 250 theaters on the West Coast, and that as part of the purchase price he had received, free of charge, a block of stock of First National Company, one of the major film studios. At the time Warner Bros. had also bid for the First National stock.

Now Fox reminded Greenfield of the transaction. "Al, remember that First National stock? I wonder whether Warner is still interested in buying it?"

"I don't know," replied the realtor. "In view of the trouble on Wall Street, I doubt if they would pay more than five million or six million dollars for it now. You'd be lucky to get even that."

In his need for cash, Fox would have unloaded the block at any price. "Nonsense," he exploded, displaying his shrewdest poker strategy, "five or six million is ridiculously low. Last year you remember, I asked Warner's for fifteen million. Because of the situation on Wall Street, I'd be willing to drop it to twelve and one-half million, but not a penny less."

Greenfield promised to contact the Warner people and next morning he phoned with incredible news. "Warner's are still interested in the stock. They are willing to buy it for ten million dollars." Apparently Warner Bros., like Greenfield, had no inkling of the mortal crisis Fox was facing.

The following day Greenfield closed the transaction. He brought Fox $8 million cash and $2 million in Warner Bros. notes for which he received a $500,000 commission. He went away with his cut in a jovial mood, unaware that he had rescued Fox from bankruptcy.

In the weeks after Fox paid his margin, the Loew stock began to rise. It went from $5 to $32, which was still only 50 percent of its price before the market crash, but the situation was temporarily salvaged. Fox had breathing time to continue his rescue operation.

This was no easy matter. He had gotten off the hook with the brokers, but there were still his bankers to deal with. He had retained his Loew stock, but he was still heavily in debt.

Fox went to the bankers, pleading for an extension of credit to give him time to settle his affairs. He was refused. Moreover his investment banker, Halsey, Stuart, replied that conditions were unfavorable for a new public stock offering. The commercial bankers turned a deaf ear. The man who had built the world's mightiest movie theater combine and whose real estate properties and other assets, while temporarily entangled, were potentially worth many millions more than his debts, became paranoiac. He felt that his bankers weren't really interested in getting back the money he owed them; they were embarked on a conspiracy to drive him to the wall and take over his business.

Failing to persuade the bankers to extend their grace, Fox tried to raise money from former business associates whom he had helped build fortunes in joint ventures. But Fox had hurt as many people as he had helped. In his climb to the top, he had smashed much crockery.

He notes in his reminiscences that he turned to one former colleague, Richard Hoyt, who had made several million dollars in deals with him, but who had also absorbed indignities from him during their years of affiliation. He phoned Hoyt, asking him to come over for a conference. Hoyt had been to a dinner party. He arrived at Fox's suite in the Ambassador Hotel in a top hat, white tie, and tails, swinging a cane.

Fox told Hoyt he was in deep trouble and desperately needed to raise money. He hadn't proceeded very far when he realized he might as well be talking to a barbed-wire fence. "I'm sure I can read your mind," he said. "The story of my troubles is music to your ears. What you would like to do is cut off my left ball."

"I'm glad you do your mindreading act so well," Hoyt retorted. "When you go broke, you'll be able to earn a living with it on the stage. You've made only one mistake. I don't want to cut off your left ball, I want *both* balls.'' Whereupon Hoyt put on his top hat, took up his walking stick, and strode out.

The end arrived on June 22, 1932. On that date the Chicago Title and Trust Company which held a personal note for $410,190, signed by Fox, called it in, and when he was unable to pay, petitioned to force him into bankruptcy. One property after another followed into receivership. In June, the Roxy, the jewel of Fox's empire, was thrown into the pot. The Irving Trust Company was appointed receiver for one Fox subsidiary, Metropolitan Playhouses, which operated 175 theaters in the New York area. The Fox chains in St. Louis and Detroit tumbled into bankruptcy. By June, the entire network of Fox theaters was in receivership.

In June 1936, having surrendered the last of his holdings, William Fox went into personal bankruptcy. The man who had amassed the world's most powerful theater combine and one of its most extensive real estate empires now walked into court and listed his total assets at $100 against personal liabilities of $10 million. Convinced he was the victim of a conspiracy to rob him of his properties, obsessed with the idea that the Ivy League financial institutions had squeezed the rack a little tighter because he was not one of their fraternity but a Jew who had risen from the Lower East Side, Fox used every means at his disposal to fend off the sharks.

After the bankruptcy proceedings, a district attorney brought charges that Fox had illicitly contacted the judge who was presiding over the court and offered him a bribe to be lenient with him. According to the allegations, His Honor, a venal official, met Fox in a side street and relieved him of $12,000 wrapped in a newspaper. Another $15,000 was allegedly handed to him through a third party.

A trial was held and Fox was found guilty of obstructing justice and he was sentenced to prison. Marshals escorted him to the jail in Lewisburg, Pennsylvania, put him in a convict's suit, shaved his head, and swung the bars shut behind him. He sat down to meditate on Gibbon's massive *The History of the Decline and Fall of the Roman Empire.*

Fox served for a year. Then he was handed a couple of dollars, a prison suit that was too small for him, and sent through the gates to try his luck in the world again. The ex-convict was sixty-five, but his head was still crammed with schemes. He was determined to regain the influence he once wielded.

But his plans proved to be completely visionary. The movie business had passed him by. It was concerned with new problems, attracted by new young faces. Fox lingered on another eight years in frustration and obscurity. When he died in 1952 none of the leaders of the movie industry bothered to attend his funeral.

The industry had passed William Fox by along with all those other egotistic, eccentric, hard-driving, immensely gifted founders of the movies, who opened up a new world of entertainment. Not only has William Fox become a footnote of history but, along with him, the era in which he reached the pinnacle of power—the age of the silent movies. When the talking pictures, which Fox helped pioneer through his newsreels, spread to full-length epics and captivated Americans, the quaint, inimitable industry built on silent pantomine went into a tailspin. When the public suddenly demanded talking pictures, the industry had sunk over $1 billion into the silent movies. It was caught with $100 million worth of negative film stocks. Hundreds of lavishly financed silent epics suddenly became obsolete even before their filming was completed.

In the space of a few months, the panjandrums of moviedom, who had made millions pantomiming their parts on the screen, were unceremoniously toppled from their thrones. What was suddenly needed were actors with good talking and singing voices, who had stage experience, to boot. To mimic was no longer enough. Clara Bow, the redheaded "It" girl, who had enticed the moviegoers, as the personification of the flapper, frightened by the trauma of having actually to speak her lines instead of relying on printed titles, quit at the zenith of her fame. Norma Talmadge, Florence Vidor, Colleen Moore, and others who had risen from nowhere to earn millions and live in rococo villas on Sunset Boulevard and Beverly Hills were nipped in their prime.

The most popular idol of all, John Gilbert, who had skyrocketed to prominence playing opposite Greta Garbo, was hit the most severely by the talking pictures. Audiences who had been enchanted by his charisma were appalled when they heard him speak from the screen. From Gilbert's lips emerged a squeaky, high-pitched voice that sounded like the eerie falsetto of a giggling adolescent girl. Audiences began to smile and the smiles turned into howls of laughter. Gilbert had been signed to make five pictures a year at a salary of over $1 million. The studio canceled them abruptly. One morning he walked into the library of his Beverly Hills mansion and shot himself.

Gilbert's suicide provided an appropriately baroque finale to the age of the silent movies. And with the passing of the silents, there also vanished those rococo castles of enchantment and escapism that supplied the atmospheric housing for the films. The architecture of Eberson and Lamb, and the freewheeling real estate dealers who had financed their gingerbread designs, disappeared with the onset of the Depression and a complete change-around in America's social values. In the midst of mass joblessness and breadlines, the Hoovervilles and apple sellers on street corners, the movie palaces, built in the 1920s with their Arabian domes, their Athenian colonnades, their French-sculptured fountains, and medieval armored knights, stood out with painful incongruity. America revolted against these vulgar monuments to profligate, witless living. In a few years, these movie palaces would become as obsolete as the Egyptian pyramids or the ruins of Pompeii. The vast majority of them were torn down by real estate men to make way for parking lots, restaurants, and high-rise apartment houses. Supermarkets replaced the domes of Granada and the spires of Seville. The machines that had once created magic clouds and propelled them across twinkling plaster skies have long since been thrown into the trash heap. The marble stairways that spiraled so grandiloquently up toward balconies festooned with medieval halberds have been hauled away by wrecking crews. In 1960 the most opulent monument to this bizarre, giddy past, the Roxy, was demolished. Tons of plaster casts, statuary, frescoed walls and ceiling were razed to rubble, to make way for the rise of a steel-cast office building.

238

Here and there, it is true, stand the remnants of those gaudy old movie palaces turned shabby and grotesque, with faded gold foliage and chandeliers tarnished with age, functioning now as third-run movie houses in cheap, down-at-the-heel neighborhoods, the last relics of an extraordinary era.

William Fox has passed into the realm of historical curiosa, but he guessed right in one important respect. Many of the real estate properties he so shrewdly selected have survived in other hands and become even more valuable than when he first snapped them up. To this extent Fox's career was one of high irony. He wanted to be the world's biggest theater owner. What survived him, however, were his shrewdly selected real estate holdings. The land that housed many of his theaters has been transformed into a burgeoning complex of office buildings, shopping centers, and apartment houses.

One property especially, located in Manhattan, that Fox latched onto in his salad days skyrocketed in value long after he had left the scene. Just before the stock market crash in 1929, when Fox was at the pinnacle of power, he bought two strategically located corner lots on Sixth Avenue between Forty-ninth and Fifty-first. The rest of the three square blocks in the area were owned by the Rockefeller family, and there were rumors that John D., Jr., planned to build a mammoth office complex to be known as Rockefeller Center which would include a movie theater even larger and more luxurious than the Roxy. Fox had moved in rapidly and snatched away the two corner properties for himself. The Rockefellers tried desperately to buy them from Fox because, without them, the lavish western façade of their center would be pinched inward instead of extending along the two-block area.

Fox resisted the offer. He enjoyed tweaking the noses of the Rockefellers. In addition, he didn't like the idea of their building a movie house to compete with his Roxy. To further embarrass them, Fox toyed with the idea of putting up two small buildings on his lots—an act of rank contemptuousness, for when Rockefeller Center was finally constructed, its grandiose front would be hemmed in embarrassingly by Fox's pygmy structures.

239

Before the stock market crash, the Rockefellers offered Fox $1.4 million for his corner properties. After the bust, when he urgently needed cash, Fox sounded out John D., Jr., and his sons to see if they were still willing to buy them at the $1.4 million figure. But, realizing they had him up a tree, they offered him only $800,000, this despite the fact that Fox's equity in the property, after subtracting the mortgage, was well over $800,000. Fox grimly held on to the property, refusing to give the Rockefellers the satisfaction of grabbing it at the shylock price.

Before going into bankruptcy, he managed to sign some of the properties he held in Manhattan over to his wife, keeping them from his creditors. Chief among these were the corner properties that were stubbing the toes of Rockefeller Center.

Twenty-five years after Fox's death, William Zeckendorf was looking for new areas in Manhattan to exploit. After squeezing the last mileage out of the East Side, he foresaw that a frontier of huge potential for a real estate revival was Sixth Avenue, which remained an old-fashioned, decaying bastion of nineteenth-century brownstone dwellings and small run-down shops and saloons. Zeckendorf envisaged razing entire neighborhoods revolving around the Sixth Avenue axis and putting up modern office buildings similar to those built on Park Avenue.

Searching the deeds of Sixth Avenue property title holders, Zeckendorf discovered that the two corner lots adjacent to Rockefeller Center were owned by Eva Fox, the widow of the film magnate, who had survived her husband.

Quick maneuvering was necessary, for the competition was heating up. Other realtors were vying to grab key frontage along Sixth Avenue to be in on the anticipated boom. Conrad Hilton and his associate, Henry Crown, were rumored to be angling for property to build a spanking new hotel near Rockefeller Center that would bring New York into the Hilton fold.

Seeking Mrs. Fox to bid for her lots, Zeckendorf, according to his memoirs, found she was living as a recluse wrapped in the misty past in a decayed old apartment that shut out the sunlight. Zeckendorf made friends with the widow. He discovered that she owned strategically located properties around town. In particular, Mrs. Fox owned the key corner properties on Sixth Avenue that Zeckendorf wanted as the foundation for the real estate project he had in mind.

At first Mrs. Fox refused to give up the properties. She was determined to hold on to them as a remembrance of her husband no matter how run down they had become. Zeckendorf finally persuaded her to sell him thirty thousand square feet of land, offering her a record price of $5 million. As the down payment, Zeckendorf reminisces, he presented a check for $500,000. Mrs. Fox glanced at it and tossed it into the wastebasket. The check had been drawn on the Chase Manhattan Bank and the widow contended that Chase was one of the "conspirators" that had sent her husband to prison. She accused the realtor of being an agent of her husband's enemies and slammed the door on him.

Zeckendorf made out a new check from Bankers Trust. It took days before he could get in to see Mrs. Fox again, but his persistence prevailed and the deal was consummated.

Mrs. Fox's property provided the toehold Zeckendorf needed to move in on Sixth Avenue along a broad front and launch a massive building revival. Part of the frontage the widow sold became the site for the new Time-Life office building, a gleaming complex of glass and steel that has arisen to dominate the corner of Sixth Avenue and Forty-eighth Street.

Out on the West Coast also, William Fox bought the acreage that has been converted into one of the biggest and most promising urban development projects in the annals of real estate.

After Fox went bankrupt, the owners who bought his properties merged them into a new combine, Twentieth Century-Fox, and Fox's successor, Spyros Skouras, stumbled into severe financial troubles of his own. The advent of television—a novelty which kept millions of Americans who formerly went to the movies at home glued to their sets—drastically cut film revenues. The Federal government's decree, separating the ownership of movie production from the theater chains, was a further blow. Moreover Fox had suffered heavy losses on a skein of films. The budget for its latest multimillion dollar epic, *Cleopatra,* had been overshot, thanks to Elizabeth Taylor and the star's dilatory work habits. Fox's shareholders were demanding Skouras' hide.

Up against the wall, Skouras suddenly saw a way to raise the millions of dollars that the company so urgently needed. The solution was to sell off the properties William Fox had bought forty years previously as the site of his movie studios, for development as commercial real estate. The movie operations weren't paying their freight, but the 260 acres of land on which they were located could be profitably converted in the current market into a community of hotels, shopping centers, and high-rise apartment buildings. Old William Fox had invested with uncanny, or lucky, foresight. The location of his property was supreme. It was just west of the Beverly Hills shopping district and south of the fashionable residential area of Beverly Hills. It was only a couple of miles from the campus of the University of California and conveniently close to the burgeoning new aerospace electronics industry that was mushrooming up in California.

William Zeckendorf, learning through the grapevine of Skouras' plans to sell his Fox properties, hopped a plane to Los Angeles. The wily producer announced that $60 million was his asking price. He wished to hold on to 75 of the 260 acres, he explained, and Zeckendorf immediately figured out an angle for himself. If Skouras agreed to lease back these 75 acres from him and pay him $1.5 million a year in rentals, he would be willing to talk turkey. He beat Skouras down to an asking price of $56 million, and he calculated that, since he was getting back $1.5 million in rentals which capitalized at 6 percent, would be worth $25 million to some insurance company who bought the deed from him, he was actually paying not $56 million but $31 million for the property.

Once the deal was struck, Zeckendorf was faced with the problem of raising the money to clinch it. Committed heavily to other ventures, he didn't have the cash to make the necessary $5 million down payment. He induced a broker, Lazard Frères, to put up $2.5 million on collateral provided by some of Zeckendorf's other properties with an option of a "put" to Zeckendorf. This meant that the broker had the right to walk out of the deal at any time, and Zeckendorf would have to give them back the money. Zeckendorf's firm, Webb and Knapp, put up the remaining $2.5 million, for a six months' option on the properties.

However, Zeckendorf got into further financial difficulties. At the time he negotiated the Skouras deal, he was also planning to build a luxury hotel in Manhattan, and this promised to soak up all the available cash he had. He realized he had to choose between the hotel or the Skouras investment, since he didn't have money for both. Reluctantly deciding to unload the Skouras property, he interested a New York real estate developer, Marvin Kratter, who at the last moment got cold feet and walked out of the venture. At the same time, another problem arose. Lazard Frères asked for their $2.5 million back.

But Zeckendorf was a resourceful man. He contacted Frank McGee, the head man of the Aluminum Company of America. Zeckendorf knew that Alcoa was deeply interested in promoting the use of aluminum as a major building product in homes and offices, and he pointed out to McGee that the best way for Alcoa to get its message across to America would be for it to go into its own real estate development, putting up apartments, hotels, and office buildings to showcase its aluminum products.

One morning, Zeckendorf went before Alcoa's board of directors. By this time, thanks to further hard bargaining, he had succeeded in getting Skouras' selling price down to $43 million. He pointed out to the Alcoa board that Skouras was willing to rent back seventy-five acres at $1.5 million a year in rentals, and this could be capitalized and sold to a financial institution, bringing Alcoa's exposure to only $18 million. The land could be developed, he insisted, at $4 per square foot, and could appreciate eventually to $50 a square foot.

The board was impressed. How much did Zeckendorf want? A check for $2.5 million immediately, Zeckendorf replied. The board said it needed time to deliberate. Zeckendorf, after all, had just made his presentation that morning. The New York real estate plunger responded that he was having lunch with a business associate but would be happy to come back in the afternoon for the check, and, incredible to relate, he got it. McGee contacted his treasurer and asked him to deliver the money to Zeckendorf. Afterward, Zeckendorf reminisced in wonderment, "We didn't have a contract, not a scrap of paper, and I had never met any of those men before in my life except for McGee."

The 260 acres of property Alcoa was committed to buying were rich with historic movie tradition. They included the land Tom Mix, the most celebrated cowboy of the old silent movies, had used as the ranch on which he had shot dozens of Western films with his horse, Tony. On William Fox's first visit to his Hollywood properties in 1916, he had observed a man sauntering outside the door of the studio wearing a ten-gallon hat. Each morning when Fox arrived, the bystander was decked out in a cowboy costume which was more flamboyant than the previous one. Finally the cowboy got up the courage to approach Fox and tell him he wanted to get into motion pictures. All he was interested in, he said, was money to take care of his horse, Tony. Fox was a little more generous. He gave Tom Mix $350 a week. Before he ended his tenure at Fox, the cowboy was earning over $7000 a week.

Also on the 260 acres Skouras sold Alcoa stood the set on which Theda Bara had shot the film, *The Vampire,* which launched her as the silent movies first major sex queen. She had been born Theodosia Goodman, the daughter of a Cincinnati tailor. William Fox introduced her to film audiences as an exotic Arabian beauty who couldn't speak a word of English and he promoted her to stardom. Here too was the set on which Shirley Temple, who would earn millions before she reached her teens, made *The Little Colonel,* and where Will Rogers, fresh from the Ziegfeld Follies, where he chewed gum, twirled his rope, and shook up the audience with his improvised jokes, made the movie that triggered his Hollywood career.

Alcoa's purchase of Fox's 260 acres turned out to be one of the most profitable real estate transactions in history. It planned a vast urban development project which, situated in the uptown area of Los Angeles, would compete for tenants with Los Angeles' burgeoning downtown section. Century City, as the venture was called, was projected as a half-billion-dollar complex featuring four million square feet of office space, five thousand high-rise luxury apartments, a fifty-acre shopping center, a theater, and a luxury hotel, The Century Plaza.

The development was designed by Minoru-Yamasaki, a Japanese architect who built the twenty-story hotel in the form of an arc, each room having a balcony with a complete view of the area. Half of the acreage was allocated to swimming pools, fountains, golf putting greens. A series of fashionable town apartments were built carrying rentals of from $400 to $4000 a month.

With the Los Angeles suburbs expanding at a tremendous rate, the demand for occupancy of Century City soon outpaced the speed of building it, and the price of land zipped from the $4 an acre purchase price to the over $40 an acre Zeckendorf had predicted. Moreover, Twentieth Century-Fox devoted part of the seventy-five acres it retained for commercial real estate development of its own, profiting by soaring land prices. Zeckendorf went in on the venture with Alcoa, putting up a third of the money, but eventually because of other commitments sold off his interest for $50 million to a British investment syndicate.

William Fox, the sharp-eyed, beak-nosed manipulator with the crippled arm, was vindicated in a most peculiar fashion. He had aimed to become big in the movie business, but he wound up achieving his most lasting memorial hustling acres of real estate.

8

SKYSCRAPERS, ORANGE GROVES AND BILL ZECKENDORF

Real Estate in the Era of Technology

Century City was, as noted in the previous chapter, one of the most ambitious residential complexes yet conceived for the American outer city. It marked the final flowering of generations of experimentation. Over the years, commercial building had developed independently of residential real estate. Now the trends were joined and blended into a unified, social community where Americans could live and work, shop and play. The path to this achievement was a steady, inevitable one. And before the current sophistication in suburban living was attained, the real estate industry had touched spectacular heights in changing the skyline of America's cities.

Over the years, the nation's real estate operators and their artistic hirelings, the architects, had continued to respond faithfully to the social changes in urban America. In the middle of the nineteenth century, as the nation increasingly became more mobile and *déclassé*, apartment houses or "flats," as they were called, sprang up in Boston and Manhattan, penetrating to the Middle West. Detroit and Chicago launched an apartment house boom, erecting flats modeled after those in the East. Besides the inevitable advances in the hardware of their trade, new techniques of real estate financing were promoted aggressively. Before the turn of the century, realtors began employing sales contracts for selling homes on the installment plan, thereby making their markets available increasingly to the masses of modest income buyers. By the 1890s, community planning became a serious concern. The restrictive gridiron pattern of property expansion, used for laying streets in most cities, was set aside in Baltimore, for example, and in its wooded outskirts, streets were laid out in curves, while plots were subdivided on the basis of these contours.

But despite these financing and engineering developments, and although certain sections of the nation enjoyed an undeniably charming native architecture—the Cape Cod and colonial houses of New England, the Spanish Mission architecture in California—the bulk of America's architects, especially in the commercial field, remained stodgy in their inspiration. When they weren't being downright ugly, they displayed the inferiority complex shown by America's writers and artists which impelled them to import culture wholesale from the Old World. Just as its novelists fawned on British writers, so the handful of architects who managed to resist catering to America's "libido for the ugly," in Mencken's phrase, sought their inspiration by imitating the Italian baroque, the English Georgian, the French Renaissance. Stanford White and Addison Mizner were prime examples of this towering inferiority complex.

However, toward the end of the nineteenth century, a highly industrialized America, which commercially and technologically was forging ahead of the rest of the world, began feeling its oats, acquiring increasing self-confidence, and it introduced to the bedazzlement of the world, its own unique contribution to architecture—the skyscraper.

Bradford Lee Gilbert, the architect who invented the skeletal-steel skyscraper, recalls in his reminiscences how he got the idea.*

*Smaller, metal-supported buildings were erected previously in Chicago, but Gilbert's is considered the first with all the basic characteristics of the modern skyscraper.

In the spring of 1887 a Manhattan realtor, John L. Stearns, owned a double plot off lower Broadway in New Street. The front plot consisted of only twenty-one feet facing Broadway, and because it was so hemmed in, Stearns found he couldn't sell it except at an unsatisfactorily low price. Hoping to build something on these plots which would bring him a decent income, he approached Gilbert with his problem. It wouldn't be economical to erect a high building on the Broadway frontage, since city law demanded that the walls be so thick a passageway on the Broadway side could be erected only a little over ten feet in width. Such a passageway, while providing an entrance for a higher building in the rear, would benefit only the latter. The former building would have to be constructed at a loss. The problem of what to do with the front lots while conforming to the building laws baffled Gilbert and at the same time intrigued him. He spent six months turning it over in his mind.

Then suddenly he arrived at the solution. It was to erect an iron bridge truss standing on its end. The laws didn't restrict or limit the height of the foundations of the building, either below or above the curb line. Why not carry the foundation up seven or eight stories in order to generate the floor space that was most desirable for the maximum occupancy and rentals? Why, in short, Gilbert asked, couldn't he begin the *superstructure* of the building several stories above the curb?

He made exhaustive tests which satisfied him as to the safety and feasibility of the concept from an engineering standpoint. Then he went to the New York head of the Buildings Department, Superintendent D'Oench, with his plan. The superintendent responded that it seemed practical enough, but no law existed under which such a construction could be approved. Gilbert and Stearns, the owner of the property, embarked on intricate negotiations with the Board of Examiners before the go ahead commitment was given.

Meanwhile, the New York newspapers had gotten wind of Gilbert's skyscraper project. They ran stories calling it an idiotic idea. Rumors of the plan swept across the nation and architects from all over called on Gilbert, scrutinized his plans, and denounced them as unsafe. The experts told him that if he ever succeeded in getting the building up, it would blow over in the first stiff wind that came up from the Bay at Sandy Hook. Newspaper and magazine editors repeated the warning that Gilbert's building would collapse at the first serious puffing of the wind.

Despite this ridicule, the architect proceeded with his plans. When he announced the actual specifications for the building, Gilbert evoked even more skepticism. The notion of a superstructure arising to a height of one hundred and sixty feet above the sidewalk horrified not only the professional architects, but also rank-and-file citizens. An engineer who had been an associate of Gilbert's begged him to abandon this outlandish plan. Gilbert brushed him off. The engineer wrote a letter to Stearns, warning him that if Gilbert's building blew over, he would be subject to heavy legal damages.

Upon receiving this letter, Stearns was ready to quit. Gilbert patiently went over his engineering plans with him, explaining that Stearns's fears were groundless. Due to a series of wind bracings from cellar to roof, it was a scientific certainty, Gilbert pointed out, that the harder the wind blew, the safer the building would be. If the wind reached the speed of seventy miles an hour, the structure would be amply protected by its footings. "You must trust somebody," Gilbert concluded, "and you'd better trust your architect for the sake of your peace of mind. To show my faith in the building I'll take my own offices in the two upper floors of the Broadway end. If the building falls, I'll go with it."

Reassured, Stearns allowed Gilbert to proceed with the work. The ground was excavated, the building begun; the walls rose thirteen stories into the air. Crowds of New Yorkers lined the streets three deep, watching nervously. The atmosphere was hostile. One Sunday morning when the architect was preparing to install his roof, the wind, which had been increasing in intensity for the past twenty-four hours, reached hurricane proportions. Gilbert rushed downtown to inspect his project. A huge crowd had gathered, behaving as if it were awaiting doomsday. People were laying bets as to the precise moment the building would collapse.

Gilbert turned to the foreman on the job and asked him for a plumb line. The workmen had left ladders in place for resuming operations the following morning. The architect began climbing up the ladder. Several people shouted out, "You damned fool. Are you trying to kill yourself?"

When Gilbert reached the thirteenth story, the wind was blowing so fiercely he was unable to stand upright. He got on his knees and began to crawl along the scaffolding. He dropped the plumb line, lowering it toward the ground. There wasn't the slightest vibration; the building stood steady as a rock. Exhilarated, Gilbert straightened up, waving exultantly to the crowd. Suddenly a puff of wind caught him and carried him headlong toward the end of the scaffolding. "It is in emergencies like this that a man prays, if he ever prays," Gilbert afterward recalled. As he hurtled toward the end of the platform, a rope swinging in the wind from an upright beam of the tower swept within his reach. He grabbed it, held on, went down on his knees, and crawled back slowly to the ladder. Then he descended to the street and, "walked up Broadway singing the Doxology."

America's first skyscraper built of skeletal steel made such ingenious use of the maximum space above ground that John Stearns reaped $90,000 a year more in rentals than he would have achieved from a conventional building. But Gilbert the architect had made a blunder. He had failed to take a patent on this audacious invention, allowing himself to be frightened off by eminent lawyers who told him that, if he were to become the legal owner of the skyscraper concept, the lawsuits that would bombard him charging damages to life and safety would far outweigh any possible remuneration he would achieve from the patent.

Never was an inventor more poorly advised. Had Gilbert patented his invention, he would have become a multimillionaire. For once he had proved that the skeletal-steel skyscraper was safe, other builders rushed in to erect their own superstructures. A mania for skyscrapers mushroomed up in Manhattan and spread across the nation. Within a generation there wasn't a major city in America that didn't boast of a cluster of skyscrapers in its downtown area.

In Manhattan, skyscraper building reached epidemic proportions. Variations were wrung from Gilbert's inspiration. Cage construction, for instance, was developed to supplement the basic steel frame structure and this served further to vindicate Gilbert's original judgment. Architects confirmed that the skyscraper was, indeed, one of the safest constructions ever devised, for the longer the steel or iron is buried in the cement the stronger it becomes.

Rivalry developed for the prestige of erecting the tallest building. Real estate operators vied to add more and more stories to their edifices.

In the spring of 1929, on the eve of America's worse stock market crash and the outbreak of the Depression, two skyscrapers were in the process of being erected in New York, both designed to outdwarf the Woolworth Building which at that time was the world's tallest structure. The Chrysler Building was rising in midtown on Lexington Avenue, and in the Wall Street area an edifice was being built for the Bank of Manhattan.

While these projects were still unfinished, New York's former Governor Al Smith announced to the press that a third venture was about to be launched, the erection of an even taller skyscraper, to be called the Empire State Building and soaring 102 stories into the air. It was to be built where the old Waldorf-Astoria hotel had been located on Fifth Avenue, between Thirty-third and Thirty-fourth streets. The Waldorf, as previously noted, had been financed in the nineteenth century by the Astor cousins as the result of a feud between William Astor and his aunt. It had in its day played host to visiting royalty, but in recent years it had run into financial difficulties. The current Astors, faced with the need for plunging money into remodeling and refurnishing it extensively or peddling it off, had sold it to the Bethlehem Engineering Company which a year later was approached by a syndicate headed by John Jacob Raskob who had become wealthy as a General Motors executive. He had also been chairman of the Democratic National Committee during Al Smith's losing race for the presidency.

Associated with Raskob were E. I. Du Pont, the chairman of the chemical firm, and two rich mining and banking executives.

251

The Raskob syndicate figured their location was a prime industrial one, predicting that the boom in commercial construction which had reached the southern edge of Central Park would spill back into the midtown and 34th street areas.

To finance the deal, Metropolitan Life Insurance advanced the consortium a $27-million mortgage, and it received an additional $25 million from several banking and mining groups. The Waldorf was demolished. (A new version was later reared on Park Avenue.) Meanwhile, on this site, which during the Revolutionary War had been a bloody field of combat between the Yanks and the Redcoats and which the first Astor had subsequently snapped up for $25,000, the Raskob syndicate launched its 102-story superstructure.

The laying of the foundation took place on St. Patrick's Day, March 17, 1930, as a tribute to Al Smith, the Irishman, who was named president of the Empire State Corporation. Construction proceeded at the rate of four and a half stories a week. The last fourteen stories were added in a final spurt of only ten working days. Sixty thousand tons of steel were used, enough to build a double track railroad from Baltimore to New York. Because of a shortage of storage space, the steel was set into place as soon as it was delivered from the trucks. To shuttle the massive amount of materials required around the project, a railroad was built and the workers were lifted to their places on a mine hoist. At various levels of the building, stations were installed to feed the workers.

The building was opened in May 1931 with elaborate ceremonies. President Herbert Hoover pressed a switch in Washington and lights went on in the Fifth Avenue superstructure. However, the optimism of the Raskob group proved unjustified. While the Empire State was being erected, the nation tumbled into its worst depression. Even after the bottom peaked out, the syndicate's prophecy, that commercial building would spill back south from Fifty-ninth Street, didn't materialize. During the 1930s the Empire State had heavy vacancies, and it came to be dubbed the "Empty State Building." New Yorkers wisecracked, "The only way the landlords will ever fill it, is to tow it out to sea." An anecdote was told about the king of Siam who, while on a state visit to America, toured the skyscraper. "Reminds me of home," he is reported to have remarked to a newsman, "we have white elephants too."

Despite the lack in revenues, the owners kept their cool. They insisted on maintaining rentals at the levels before the Depression and were willing to ride out a period of ten years, during which tenants renting above the sixtieth floor were scarce as hen's teeth. They looked upon the building as a long-term investment. Tongues wagged about the empty spaces above the sixtieth floor. There was gossip that a number of floors below the sixtieth were empty as well, and that the owners installed electric lights and left them blazing nights to pretend the offices were occupied.

The Empire State inevitably became an object of worldwide curiosity. Tourists bombarded the guides with questions. They asked if it were true the weight of the building was forcing Manhattan to sink lower into the water. Some wondered whether the superstructure had been built on steel springs to allow it to subside into the soil of Manhattan. Actually the building was constructed on bedrock and despite its weight of over 360,000 tons— the dirt and the rock excavated for the foundation alone dropped sixty feet below street level and weighed more than the building itself—it wasn't sinking into the ground. As for its behavior in a high wind, engineers have estimated it would sway a little more than an inch at the top if struck by a gale blowing one hundred miles an hour.

During the first sixteen years of the Empire State's existence, a dozen people committed suicide by jumping from its tower. To discourage this, a suicide rail was installed shortly after the Second World War. The building has inspired an outbreak of religious and mystical effusions. A number of people have requested that the ashes of their dead relatives be scattered from the Observatory Tower. On some occasions the building superintendent has obliged. In the early morning before the tower is opened to the public and when the wind is over thirty miles an hour, an attendant has on occasion allowed widows and widowers to scatter the ashes of their loved ones over the city. A female medium celebrated for her spiritual séances once asked permission to hold them in the tower so she could be nearer the dead.

One Saturday in July 1945, just after Germany surrendered to the Allies, the unthinkable happened. At ten in the morning, an army B-25 plane suddenly moved out of the mist only a thousand feet above ground, heading for the skyscraper. The pilot tried to pull out of the spin, but he crashed into the building, shearing off his wings. His gas tanks exploded, enveloping the tower in flames. The seventy-eighth and seventy-ninth floors were shattered. Thirteen people were killed, twenty-six injured. One of the bomber's two engines drove through two elevator shafts, cutting the cables and hurling the cars to the basement. But the Empire building survived this as it has survived everything else.

Before his death, Raskob, who was reputedly worth $100 million, bought the stock of his colleagues and wound up owning over 90 percent of the Empire State Building. After he died, his estate sold it to a new syndicate for $50 million, the largest price ever paid for a single building up to that time. A quarter interest in the new corporation was acquired by Henry Crown, a wealthy Chicago realtor. Ultimately he ended up as the sole owner.

Gradually the building was put on its feet financially. Close to $12 million was spent in remodeling and improvements and it ended up generating $12 million a year in rentals.

In 1961, the Empire State Building was sold again for another record price, $65 million.

The deal was a highly intricate one. The Prudential Insurance Company had for ten years owned the land on which the building stood and would have liked to have bought the building itself as an investment, but state law prevented an insurance company from putting more than $50 million into a single property. So Prudential worked out a sale and leaseback scheme with Lawrence Wien, a lawyer who was a freewheeling operator of real estate properties around the nation. Wien and his associates got together $39 million to buy a 114-year lease on the building for which the Wien group agreed to pay over $3 million a year in rent, this amount to be scaled down after thirty years. Wien technically became the buyer of the Empire State Building; he sold it to the Prudential and received it on a leaseback arrangement.

Apart from developments in the nation's cities, one significant trend that took place after the First World War was the move-

ment of millions of Americans to the suburbs. And two land jobbers who more than anybody else pioneered suburban real estate
on a large scale were the Van Sweringen brothers. The brothers
were a freakish duo. Two years apart in age, they went through
life as bachelors, resided in the same house, slept in twin beds,
and were as paranoiacally secretive about their business as their
daily life. When they reached the peak of power in Cleveland real
estate and a leading journalist sought to interview them for his
newspaper, they retorted, "Let the dead bury the dead; silence is
the key to survival."

Actually the Van Sweringens had much to be secretive about.
They were born *Sweringen,* but during the early years of their real
estate speculations they were unable to pay off on a property they
had optioned, and were dragged into court. Claiming they were
bankrupts, in order to avoid payment of their debt, they continued to buy and sell properties using the names of relatives as a
front. Then, as their ambitions grew larger, they decided to bury
the court records of their earlier indiscretion by changing their
name to Van Sweringen. This, hopefully, would throw alert
newsmen off the scent of embarrassing court records and would
also add a nice flavor of nobility to their lineage.

The brothers first moved into the real estate game by taking
temporary, speculative options on property and making quick
sales. Using the option and maximum leveraging technique in
their search for cheap lands, the Van Sweringens initially es-
chewed the downtown area of Cleveland, concentrating on the
suburbs where property was less expensive. Pyramiding their
money through a maze of clever option dealings, they bought
land and leveraged the deal into a massive residential and housing
development in the Shaker Heights area of the Cleveland suburbs. Realizing that the key to land development in the outskirts
of an urban center was to develop transportation to bring com-
muters into the inner city, the brothers got involved in laying trolley lines from downtown Cleveland to Shaker Heights. Coor-
dinating real estate and transportation transactions, they made
money in both areas by integrating them into a common program.

Virtually single-handedly, they developed the suburbs of

Cleveland for residential use; then they turned their attention to the downtown area of the city, which was in a shabby condition. They revamped it, building a brand-new railroad terminal, and alongside it, the tallest, most elaborate office building Cleveland had ever known, together with a retail store and a fancy hotel. Through their control of the trolley lines, the Van Sweringens linked their downtown real estate with their ventures in the outskirts so that a resident of Cleveland could live, travel, and work on properties owned by them.

As the sphere of their activities widened, the brothers became more and more heavily involved in railroad operations to link together their widely scattered properties. One highly strategic railroad, the New York, Chicago, and St. Louis, had key rights-of-way passing through Cleveland. Controlled by the New York Central and dubbed the "Nickel Plate," the line whetted the appetite of the Van Sweringens. By owning it they could control, in addition to the freight, the passenger business and steer prospects to their real estate holdings. The New York Central's owners were agreeable to selling the Nickel Plate since it was only marginally profitable. Their asking price was $8.5 million.

The Van Sweringen brothers, their capital committed to the hilt in a vast complex of real estate holdings, had no cash to spare. They couldn't scrounge up the $8.5 million demanded by the Grand Central, but their illiquid position didn't bother them one whit. They wangled from Cleveland bankers a $2 million loan in an odd fashion. They sold the bankers on the idea of accepting as collateral for the loan the stock in the Nickel Plate railroad *they were planning to acquire* although it was not yet in their possession. Then they handed over to the Grand Central owners the $2 million received from the banks, as a down payment for the railroad, and they persuaded them to accept the remaining $6.5 million in promissory notes to come due in ten years. In short, the astute brothers got hold of the Nickel Plate without putting up a cent of their own money.

The promissory notes, as noted, wouldn't become due for a decade, so the brothers weren't worried about that debt, but there still remained the little matter of paying back the banks the

$2 million lent them. This problem they solved neatly. They set up a corporation, the Nickel Plate Securities, Inc., and put into it the stock of the Nickel Plate line which they had just bought. The new corporation took over the $2 million debt and also the $6.5 million promissory notes. The brothers and several colleagues then bought a block of preferred stock in Nickel Plate Securities, Inc. for $1 million, half of which—$500,000—the brothers put up out of money they managed to wangle via still another bank loan. Then they unloaded an additional $1 million of preferred stock in the new corporation to the public. This made up the $2 million owed the banks on the previous loan. The brothers next took control of 50 percent of the preferred stock in their corporation, plus all the common stock—an easy enough thing to do since the common stock alone had the voting rights and they, as sole owners of the Nickel Plate Securities, Inc., had complete control of the railroad.

In short, the clever brothers had put up $500,000, every cent of which had been borrowed from the banks, to acquire a railroad whose mileage was greater than that of all of Great Britain and the Netherlands combined, together with a wealth of subsidiaries the road owned—including trucking firms, mining properties, dairy farms, pear and apple orchards, retail stores, office buildings, and a network of transportation terminals—adding up to an empire worth over $3 billion in paper holdings, all this controlled by the ingenious Van Sweringens.

The brothers used the same technique of pyramiding a shoestring investment, through the device of setting up a holding company, to acquire other railroads, together with their real estate properties and their commercial subsidiaries. In all cases they began with a piddling down payment (borrowed from the banks) to take an option or actual title to the new properties. They paid back the bankers by dumping massive flotations of stock, that had no voting power, on the gullible public. With incredible virtuosity they developed a combination of variations on this strategy, piling up their financial dominoes to a dizzy height. Sometimes they would conjure up a holding company to control the stock of a second holding company, or reverse the tactic and use one of their real estate properties to control the stock of a holding company. Their object was not only to make a shoestring investment perform the labors of Hercules, but also to so complicate the maze of their money flow that no investigator would be able to trace where the money came from and where it went—in case any unkind official ever got the notion of going through their books.

This pyramiding of holdings might have gone on endlessly as long as the economy in which the brothers were spinning their web remained prosperous, but the collapse of the stock market in 1929, followed by the Depression, triggered consequences even the shrewd brothers were unable to foresee. With money tightening drastically, rentals from their real estate properties tumbling, and the freight business from their railroads hitting the skids, the brothers found themselves highly vulnerable. Suddenly they could no longer pick the pockets of the public to pay off old ventures and finance new ones, and they ran short of new sources of cash.

The Cinderella story was to have a final tragic ending. Worn out with his financial tribulations, bombarded by creditors to whom he wound up owing $40 million, Mantis James Van Sweringen passed on in his early fifties. Within a year, the other half of the Siamese twins, his brother Oris, died as the result of a heart attack suffered in a train accident.

Most of the Van Sweringen real estate went to the government for failure to pay taxes; the rest was dumped on the market at bargain-basement prices. The lavish residence the brothers had maintained in Shaker Heights was reclaimed by the banks.

The Van Sweringens were classic victims of leveraging far beyond their means and going broke. But the real estate industry in general has always been featured by boom and bust. Credit greases the way for property transactions even more heavily than in the stock market. Although the market crashed severely in the fall of 1929, the real estate industry, while it continued solvent for a year or so after the market broke, when it finally tumbled fell even harder than Wall Street. The Depression of the 1930s hit the speculative builders very hard. The Uris Brothers, builders of a skein of Manhattan skyscrapers, were pushed into bankruptcy.

The Tishmans also suffered heavy financial reverses. (Both families made a comeback after the Second World War.)

The law served to aggravate the real estate slump during the 1930s. Taxes in most communities were based not on the price a building could command in the current marketplace, but what it previously cost to build it. Accordingly, when prices dove, many realtors were panicked into getting rid of their holdings at any price obtainable so as not to be hurt by taxes that were based on assessments made during periods of prosperity. At the height of the Depression, taxes in some cases were more than triple the market value of a property.

With the onset of the Second World War and the industrial boom that followed in its wake, the nation emerged from the economic doldrums and the real estate industry, always stimulated by cheap money and a mood of expansive optimism, responded like quicksilver to a fire lit under it. The stage was set after the defeat of Hitler and Japan for a vast new wave of land speculation. The Atomic Era had been launched, and along with it a rising obsession with tactics in place of teleological goals, with technology rather than spiritual pursuits. There were numerous diversions.

Dr. Alfred Kinsey wrote a book about the *Sexual Behavior in the Human Male* and overnight became the leading oracle in the field. The indefatigable doctor spent sixteen hours a day interviewing a variety of males about their habits of copulation. "I hardly ever see him at night anymore since he took up sex," bewailed Dr. Kinsey's wife.

Time magazine reported that film stars Sophia Loren and Gina Lollobrigida "were running chest and chest" in a race for Europe's number one box office attraction. In Ayot St. Lawrence, George Bernard Shaw died at the age of ninety-four. To the handful who gathered in his living room for a brief service, the Reverend J. Davis, the local Anglican pastor explained, "Mr. Shaw was not really an atheist. I would rather call him a skeptical Irishman."

Professor Norbert Wiener, a scientist, told the press that a newly emerging phenomenon—the computer—was human

259

enough to "suffer from typical psychiatric troubles; unruly memories sometimes spread through a machine as fears and fixations spread through a psychotic human brain."

People turned up in the news for odd reasons. Frank Buss, arrested in Detroit for biting a cop while intoxicated, received a suspended sentence when it was found he didn't have any teeth. In Las Vegas, Henry Beebe, seized for the illegal possession of dope syringes, insisted he was selling them to pay his way through Bible classes. George Taylor went to court to change his name to Pappados because his Greek friends couldn't pronounce Taylor.

The story of a Colorado housewife who insisted under hypnotism that she was the reincarnation of Bridey Murphy, a redheaded wench born 158 years previously in Cork, Ireland, touched off a boom in the supernatural. One California hypnotist advertised he would establish the preexistence of anyone for $25 a visit. American hostesses gave "come as you were" parties, and guests turned up on television talk shows insisting they had been medieval French queens, German Meistersingers, or ancient Roman Legionaires. One fellow insisted he had been a horse in a previous life. A piquant event occurred at the Broadway opening of Noel Coward's musical, *Sail Away*. Elaine Stritch, who played a shipboard hostess, appeared with a team of dogs for an airing on the sun deck. One of the canines mistook the stage for a gutter and proceeded to answer the call of nature. The next line of the play brought the house down. "I think we're getting near land. There's a change in the air."

In sophisticated Manhattan, vestiges of the old days cropped up from time to time. In 1950, the city was hit by a severe drought. The supply of drinking water from the reservoir dwindled dangerously. Air-conditioning machinery ceased to function. Cars went unwashed. Drinking water was rationed. The manager of a Park Avenue hotel remembered hearing that, years before his hostelry had been built, its site had been occupied by a nineteenth-century brewery which reportedly discovered beneath *its* foundation a spring-fed well of water which it used in its beer-making process. However, no one knew the exact location of the historic well, or whether it actually existed. The hotel manager hired a New Englander who specialized in finding forgotten spring wells. This "dowser," as he called himself, descended on Manhattan with his divining rod, and after poking around for a few days located the long-lost well. The exuberant hotel manager was able to restore the comforts of air conditioning for his guests. Restaurants, laundry operators, and other big industrial users of water immediately embarked on a search for dowsers, hoping to find wells located on their own premises. The Brooklyn Dodger baseball club dug for a well near first base in Ebbets Field to irrigate the grass infield. For a brief dizzy time the centuries-old trade of divining well-sites enjoyed a lively boom in Manhattan.

Not long afterward a new craze originated in the Southwest and spread over the country—rain making. Scientists and amateurs seized on the technique of spraying dried ice or silver iodine into clouds to unleash their watery vapor. General Electric technologists used the dried-ice technique to start a heavy blizzard in Schenectady. The storm snarled traffic, closed down factories, caused a drop in department store sales. Some lawyers warned rainmakers they were exposing themselves to an epidemic of law suits. Others wondered, Can a man really be sued for a storm?

Meanwhile as the 1950s drew to a close, the nation was treated to its typical quota of bright, nervy maneuverings and sleight-of-hand shenanigans in the real estate field.

Cheap bank money made leveraging a property investment highly tempting and profitable. In the cities, as industry grew increasingly affluent, there was a rising demand for office space, and commercial builders, forming syndicates using other people's money, put up edifices from Skowhegan to San Diego. At the same time a covey of residential builders sprang up to serve the needs of millions of urbanites fleeing to the suburbs. Moreover, staid old industrial firms and newly emerging conglomerate swingers alike moved into land acquisitions for their tax shelter benefits and as a hedge against rising inflation. And as always there were a skein of lone-wolf operators who played a bold unorthodox private game and emerged richer than all their brethren.

One plunger, Joseph P. Kennedy, amassed one of his several fortunes as easily as a corpulent man accumulates his many chins, by wheeling and dealing with gusto and skill in real estate after the Second World War. After making millions on Wall Street and from the movie and whiskey business, Kennedy turned to real estate in a modest way. Upon returning to the United States after serving as ambassador to England, he decided to move from New York to Florida to avoid income and inheritance taxes. Francis Cardinal Spellman, who employed John J. Reynolds as his real estate broker to manage the extensive properties of the New York Archdiocese, learned that Kennedy wanted to sell his Bronxville home, and he recommended Reynolds to handle the deal.

Kennedy had been pessimistic about the Free World's efforts to stop Hitler. He had wanted America to stay out of the war, but when the nation was in the thick of it, he was very bearish about the economic future. As a result he had built up a substantial cash position and he sought investments to put his money into for maximum returns. Manhattan real estate was a solution suggested by Reynolds. Prices had fallen steeply during the Depression. A man with cash could pick up fantastic bargains, he pointed out.

Kennedy moved into real estate operations by setting up two holding companies, Ken Industries and Park Agency, Inc. Leaning heavily on Reynolds's advice, he began buying and selling properties, closing in and moving out rapidly like a hit-and-run driver, taking quick profits. He came to the conclusion that the most underpriced area in Manhattan was midtown from Forty-second Street to Central Park South, east and west of Fifth Avenue. Kennedy utilized heavy leverage—the equivalent of a stock trader's buying up to his ears on margin. He purchased a building by borrowing 90 percent of the money from the bank at close to prime rates and wrested a handsome profit above interest charges from his rentals. He snapped up one property on the East Side, putting in 5 percent of his own money and selling it for three times what he paid for it. He peddled another one in the same area for five times his buying price. He grabbed an old mansion on the East Side for one-fifth of its assessed value and more than

262

doubled his money in selling it. He bought residences and office buildings in Manhattan and then penetrated into the suburbs.

He was not only shrewd but fantastically lucky. Toward the end of the 1950s he had unloaded most of his Manhattan properties but retained a single building on Columbus Avenue, which was in a rapidly deteriorating section of the city. His instinct told him to hold on to this building and sure enough, shortly afterward the city launched a project, the Lincoln Center for the Performing Arts, turning this shabby area at a stroke into one of the most valuable and attractive sections of the city. To provide space in the complex area not only for the Metropolitan Opera House, the New York State Theater, and Philharmonic Hall, but also for restaurants and high-rise apartment buildings that were expected to mushroom up as a result of the cultural rejuvenation, the city launched a massive slum clearance project, buying up properties that stood in the way of its plans. For a reason never satisfactorily explained to the public, the city fathers didn't sweep up Kennedy's building in the condemnation process which would have meant he would have had to surrender it for a relatively modest price. Kennedy held out stubbornly, refusing to yield the building, and the city wound up offering him a special deal to buy it at an inflated price. It had been assessed for $1.8 million, but the city paid Kennedy, out of the public purse, $2.5 million for the building. While properties lying around Kennedy's were snapped up by the city for under $10 a foot, it paid over $60 a square foot for Kennedy's holdings.

Newsmen pressed the politicians who run New York City to explain this discrepancy. They got no satisfactory answer. Shortly after this curious deal, Kennedy's son John became president of the United States. The younger Kennedy at the time of his father's transaction was already a power in the Democratic party and New York City's treasury was in the custody of Democratic politicians.

The irony was that while the city had previously assessed Kennedy's property for $1.8 million, old Joe had vigorously fought this as being too high. He resented paying taxes, he said, based on such a steep valuation. He maintained through his lawyers that his taxes should have been based on an assessment of only $1.1 million. Within a year after this argument, the city offered to buy his building. Now Kennedy suddenly changed his tune, finding that the "outrageously high assessment" of $1.8 million was a very convenient base upon which to figure his selling price. The matter was brought up in court. The judge decided that, although Kennedy had originally pressed for an assessment of $1.1 million before he realized he would be selling his property, this figure didn't represent the actual worth of his building but was merely Kennedy's dodge for avoiding higher taxes. The building was worth $1.8 million, and the judge in his infinite wisdom decreed that the city couldn't deprive Kennedy of the price he asked for just because he "was greedy enough to try and pay less than his fair share of taxes."

Another real estate operator, besides Kennedy, who kicked up a storm with his exuberant gamesmanship was William Zeckendorf, a Jew who boasted he may have inherited some Indian blood. (His ancestors lived in Arizona during its frontier days.) He first entered the real estate business in Manhattan, reorganized the Astor portfolio as noted elsewhere, and moved on to even bigger things. He was a master at exploiting those tax laws which were highly favorable to real estate investors. He was one of the earliest, for instance, to perceive the advantage of the tax-loss carry forward device. Under it a company that has gone into the red is given a tax allowance to enable it to get on its feet again. All the profits it makes for a specified number of years are tax exempt until its overall earnings equal its previous losses. Zeckendorf realized that by merging a profitable firm with one that had a substantial tax loss granted, the newly formed entity would enjoy this synergism reaped from the tax exemption of the unprofitable partner to shelter its own profits. Zeckendorf served for a time as consultant to the Rockefeller brothers, and preaching the strategy of acquiring tax credits through corporate mergers, he persuaded the Rockefellers to combine their personal holdings into a real estate company, thereby avoiding substantial taxes.

Zeckendorf had a mind that cut through grubby details to grasp the total potentials of a situation. As noted, he referred to his knack for buying undervalued properties and transforming them into the crown jewels of real estate as making "grapefruit out of lemons." For instance, he studied the East Side of Manhattan running from Forty-fifth to Forty-ninth streets, which was a shabby, evil-smelling stretch of land loaded with meat slaughterhouses that had run down the value of the surrounding acreage to $5 a foot, compared to acreage on the West Side selling at twenty times that amount. Zeckendorf sensed that the value of the land would skyrocket if the meat plants were razed and the acreage used for something audaciously new.

So he gambled on buying blocks of this property for the inflated $17 a foot the meat-packing owners asked for their properties. He also snapped up land around the slaughterhouses for $5 and less. Over sixty separate deals were made to accumulate the acreage Zeckendorf needed to put a scheme he had in mind into operation. One owner who held out stubbornly was an Italian fruit peddler who had sunk $10,000 of his savings into a house on the east side of First Avenue. The owner maintained he wouldn't sell for less than $12,000. When Zeckendorf agreed, the price suddenly went up to $13,000. The cat-and-mouse game continued until Zeckendorf had to pay $100,000 for the home. Yet, ironically, this turned out to be a bargain. Within twenty years the property, by Zeckendorf's own estimation, had skyrocketed to $500,000.

Upon putting together this property, Zeckendorf announced dramatically to the newspapers the great plan he had. New York was being slowly strangled because of its heavy traffic, he pointed out. To resuscitate it, he planned to erect a model community— he called it City X—that would be built on a foundation forty feet above street level, consisting of seven blocks long and two blocks wide. The "city" would include four office skyscrapers, on the roof of one of which would be a landing field for helicopters; a six-thousand-room hotel; three thirty-story apartment houses; a new home for the Metropolitan Opera House; a convention and a concert hall; a yacht basin along the East River, together with a marina and several floating nightclubs; and a parking space dug below the "city" for over four thousand cars.

Zeckendorf's concept of a platform over the city streets was designed to overleap the restrictions that had been forced on cities by the nineteenth-century habit of building streets in the pattern of a gridiron. The growth of traffic far exceeded the calculations of these planners.

Zeckendorf had snatched up the property, gambling he could unload it on developers at a heady profit. But while City X fired the imagination of news editors and Sunday-supplement readers, no contractor turned up to put hard cash into the venture. As Zeckendorf beat the bushes for prospects, without results, his concern mounted.

One morning at breakfast he noticed a piece of news. In the aftermath of the Second World War, America and the Free World had launched plans for an organization to be called the United Nations, designed to prevent a Hitler-type aggression from occurring again. Hopes were high for the United Nations, and it seemed appropriate that it should be located in the United States, which had led the Free World to victory. A number of cities had invited the UN to settle within their borders. To win UN approval would bring tremendous prestige.

Zeckendorf read that the United Nations was negotiating for its headquarters in Philadelphia. He was struck with the idea that the acreage he had accumulated on Manhattan's East Side would be an ideal site for the UN. He phoned Mayor William O'Dwyer and told him he could provide New York with the opportunity to prevent the UN from moving to Philadelphia and coming instead to Manhattan. Zeckendorf suggested to the mayor that he wire the UN officials, offering them the seventeen acres on the East River at any price they would deem suitable. O'Dwyer was flabbergasted. Zeckendorf told him he was willing to let the UN name its price, because the deadline for moving its headquarters was so close there was no time to haggle; the only way of inducing the UN to change its mind about Philadelphia was to make a dramatic counteroffer.

The strategy worked. When the UN got wind of Zeckendorf's generous proposal, they asked for an option on the Manhattan property, naming its own price—$8.5 million. Zeckendorf gave them a thirty-day option; the sum was advanced to the UN by John D. Rockefeller, Jr., and the deal was consummated.

To facilitate his expansion, Zeckendorf developed a strategy of applying the tools of corporate finance to real estate. An investment banker underwriting an industrial firm can peddle it in a number of ways. He can sell first mortgage notes, common stock, convertible and preferred stock, all on the same property and tailored to whet the appetites of different types of investors. Conventionally, a real estate property is peddled as a single entity. Zeckendorf's idea was to break it up into various subdivisions and peddle them as an industrial concern is peddled.

The various parts of a real estate property marketed separately (Zeckendorf figured) *are worth more potentially than if merchandised as a single entity.* Commercial properties, he calculated, can be divided up into sections—the title to the land is distinct from the lease which permits the use of the land. Why not offer several leases on the building—for example, an outer or operating and an inner sandwich lease? Why not attach different types of mortgages to a building, each with a specific risk, reward potential, and tax status and providing an appeal to a specific type of investor? In short, Zeckendorf began fractioning off his properties, making the whole substantially more valuable than some of its parts. Under his financial wizardry, two and two no longer equaled four, but five and six. Zeckendorf was not the first realtor to fraction off his properties, but he was a pioneer in launching a systematic strategy of dividing up properties to lure money from multiple markets simultaneously.

Zeckendorf was ahead of most of his business colleagues in his conceptual thinking. For example, he wished to raise the status of the architect from a commercial hack to the level of an artist free to carry out imaginative new designs. To this end he hired Ieoh Ming Pei, a talented Chinese professor at the Harvard Graduate School of Design, and gave him a free hand to develop revolutionary new concepts. Pei used his art skillfully to provide merchandising as well as aesthetic appeal. Zeckendorf and Pei pioneered in the use of aluminum construction for office buildings. They did so by inducing the Aluminum Company of America and its rivals to build offices with their own product as a showpiece. Pei sold the same bill of goods to the structural steel business, and he promoted the technology of poured-in-place concrete in structures to the point at which they became competitive, cost-wise, with curtain-wall construction in a number of uses.

Not all of Zeckendorf's stratagems—in other areas—worked. Occasionally he stubbed his toe. He entered the hotel business and tried snatching the queen of the covey—the Statler chain. It was a closely held company with absentee ownership, and Zeckendorf learned it was up for sale. With his flare for the spectacular, he offered to pay $110 million for the chain which would make it the biggest property deal ever transacted. He put up $1 million in cash as a binder, lined up his bankers for the additional money, and confidently waited for the deal to be ratified by Statler stockholders.

But the rug was pulled from under him. Word had accidentally reached Conrad Hilton, the world's largest hotel operator, that the Statler chain was up for grabs. Jimmy McCabe, the vice-president of the chain, happened to be a friend of Hilton's. He ran across McCabe during a plane flight and the latter suggested casually, "Why don't you buy the Statler Hotel?"

Although Zeckendorf had put up $1 million as a binder and was deep in negotiations, Hilton decided to outflank him by going directly to Mrs. Statler, the widow of the owner, who was a trustee for a large number of Statler shares her husband had left Cornell University.

From California, Hilton phoned one of his top executives in New York and told him to hunt up Mrs. Statler and tell her that he was leaving immediately by plane to talk to her about acquiring the chain, and would give her a better offer than his rival, if she would sit tight and wait for him to arrive. Hilton offered the same price as Zeckendorf, $110 million, but he sweetened it by promising to put up $7 million in cash instead of the $1 million dangled by Zeckendorf. Hilton was convinced that the fiduciary trustees under the prudent man rule couldn't refuse a $7 million over a $1 million cash offer.

Moving rapidly and secretly, the Hilton forces grabbed from Statler's widow and several other owners the controlling stock in the hotel chain. Zeckendorf woke up to find himself completely outmaneuvered. Rather than get embroiled in a rough-and-tumble battle, he wired Hilton his congratulations and turned to other schemes.

Zeckendorf didn't grub merely for dollars and cents. His ego demanded his involvement in ambitious social programs. During the Second World War, white laborers from the rural hinterlands and blacks from the South migrated to the cities to work in war plants, and wherever they settled slums developed. The white middle classes fled to the suburbs, leaving the cities increasingly to the poor.

As early as the 1950s it was apparent that the inner cores of America's cities were deteriorating drastically and that an urban crisis loomed. In 1949, Congress passed legislation to rehabilitate the slum areas. The law, which was a modern variation of the nineteenth-century land subsidy legislation launched for the nation's railroads, was called the Title I Urban Redevelopment Act. The concept was that a city, through its right of eminent domain, could acquire slumland, paying the owners a fair market price. The city would then clear the land and offer it to private developers who would erect low- and medium-priced housing. Two-thirds of the cost of the land would be borne by the Federal government, the remainder by the city.

However, since big builders and institutional investors were wary of becoming involved in politically sticky projects, many cities were unwilling to commit their money, and Congress, to spur activity, in 1954 passed legislation to allow the Federal Housing Authority to insure urban development projects by allocating the seed money for them. Matters were arranged so that a builder could undertake a project by putting up in cash only 5 percent of the total cost, and even though the returns were held to modest proportions, the small amount of cash needed to get into a deal offered tempting leverage for a big builder.

Zeckendorf became an enthusiastic advocate of urban redevelopment. One of the worst ghettos in the nation, and an especially embarrassing one because it existed within sight of the nation's Capitol, was a region along the Potomac. In this area, whose northern boundary was called, ironically, Independence Avenue, lived the black migrants from the South and other impoverished victims. The elevated tracks of the Pennsylvania Railroad, which ran south of the avenue, had divided the southwest slum from the rest of the city ever since Lincoln emancipated the slaves. A pleasant middle-class area in pre-Civil War days, most of its houses were now rotting away with age. One out of every three had no indoor toilets, half had no baths, four out of five had no central heating system, one out of five no electricity.

Washington planners hoped that under the new urban redevelopment legislation the area would be rejuvenated by putting up low-cost housing and revamping the business region to readmit the southwest as a respectable member of the city.

The project intrigued Zeckendorf. He announced to the press that he would like to take over the job and he submitted his ideas for the face-lifting. The heart of his scheme was to build a broad scenic mall at right angles to Independence Avenue, arching over the railroad tracks. (Again the device for overleaping the congestion generated by gridiron patterns of expansion.) Along the mall, Zeckendorf envisaged an entertainment and cultural center combined with government office buildings to be named L'Enfant Plaza in honor of the original planner of Washington. Below this plaza along the Potomac, Zeckendorf planned an elegant marina and town houses to induce Washington's wealthy to move into the area.

Zeckendorf plunged $500,000 into the project in its initial stages, only to become embroiled in the intrigue Washington excels in. Local builders and financiers, who had spurned previous schemes for reviving the southwest, seeing Zeckendorf going ahead with his own cash and realizing that development of L'Enfant Plaza could substantially boost property values in the long depressed neglected area, suddenly began pressuring politicians in Congress and the government to grab the action away from an outsider and give it to the native hustlers.

What happened to Zeckendorf is what happened to that other city planner almost two hundred years before, Pierre Charles L'Enfant. Local land speculators moved in and greased the palms of the political "stiffs" in government. They attacked Zeckendorf's concept of the mall, which was designed to be the lifeline of his project, and induced the government to whittle it down to an underground tunnel. They wanted the rest of the land for themselves.

Although Zeckendorf had signed a $60 million contract to develop L'Enfant Plaza, he was sandbagged so effectively by Washington politicians and by government agencies, who held up Uncle Sam's share of the financing, he was compelled to sell off his properties under development together with his plans for the plaza. Others took over and rehabilitated the area along lines very similar to his master plan. Twenty years after he was pushed out of Washington, L'Enfant Plaza was completed as Zeckendorf had originally conceived it.

Zeckendorf was finally toppled because he financially overreached himself, not only in Washington but elsewhere. His ambitions were greater than his pocketbook, and finally his troubles came home to roost. His urban redevelopment ventures ran late with skyrocketing costs. His hotel business went sour. (The emergence of speedy jets allowed businessmen to travel to New York and back to the West Coast in a single day without the need to stay overnight in hotels.) An amusement park in Westchester in which Zeckendorf had invested heavily turned into a dud, causing a severe drain on his finances.

As he plunged deeper into debt, he was forced to sell one property after another before it reached its maximum depreciation. Needing massive injections of borrowings when he used up his prime banking lines for collateral, he turned to loan sharks who charged him up to 18 percent on his short-term borrowings. "I'd rather be alive at eighteen percent than dead at six percent," he replied philosophically to those who criticized his borrowing practices. As long as he remained in business, there was a hope, he felt, of recouping his fortunes by a shrewd or lucky stroke.

During the final eighteen months of his ordeals, any of the over seventy-five creditors to whom he owed money could have pushed him into bankruptcy, but none of them made a move to foreclose on him, hoping he would be able to bail himself out and pay them off. The move came from a relatively minor creditor, the Marine Midland Trust Co. of New York, which held a note for $8.5 million on a building Zeckendorf's company had bought on lower Broadway years before. There was a clause in the agreement which promised that Midland could demand full payment before the maturity date if it discovered that Zeckendorf wasn't meeting his other debts. Over $4 million was still outstanding on the loan, and in May 1965, Marine Midland notified Zeckendorf that the debenture was in technical default and it demanded immediate payment of the principal. Zeckendorf was unable to meet this call and the bank forced him into bankruptcy.

In the long run, Zeckendorf achieved a curious vindication. Even though he was forced to abandon many of his grandiose projects in midstream because he ran out of cash, a number of his works—in Washington, at Century City, California, in Montreal, in Denver, Colorado—were finished according to his plans. Observes Chris Welles, the financial writer, "[Zeckendorf] was the creator of all these projects and in his mind they are his—forever."

Zeckendorf, as noted, was deeply concerned by the implications of the flight of the middle classes from the nation's cities. Since these are the centers of culture and finance, draining them of their energy and resources, he felt, is a serious matter. Writing of this problem in the *Yale Review*, Zeckendorf made the point that many of the satellite towns resulting from the flight to the suburbs are, in fact, parasites. The cost of maintaining the central core supporting the suburban area is borne by the city, but the revenue and benefits go to the towns on the periphery.

Zeckendorf cited New York as a classic example of a city that is collapsing under the strain of paying not only for its own services, but also for those rendered to millions of people who use New York as a place to earn their living, but spend their money elsewhere. At the same time, New York is expected to—and continues to provide—the sports arenas, museums, and other cultural activities that benefit the entire metropolitan community.

When a satellite town saps off the buying power, the taxing power, and the other vital factors that make for a cohesive, comprehensive, healthy city, Zeckendorf argues, it is as though the United States has lost the taxing power in California and New

York through their setting up of independent operations but continues to have the cost of maintaining the central governments, the army and navy and so on. "It wouldn't take very long for the United States to go broke on such a basis, and as long as this sort of thing can be done by the satellite towns around the mother city we are jeopardizing the entire fiscal and political future of our great municipalities."

Zeckendorf concludes that parasitic towns and the urban metropolis must be brought together into a single organism so that the suburbs will be governed by the city off which they live. Only those communities which are truly independent should be spared from being incorporated into the center city. The test of independence is simple. Can a community survive—socially and economically—without the benefits it derives from the mother city?

One real estate promoter, a contemporary of Zeckendorf who disagrees vigorously with his commitment to the inner city, is William Levitt, whose family developed a concept for residential building that not only generated a great personal fortune, but also enabled masses of Americans, after the Second World War, to move out of the city into the suburbs and the countryside. Bill Levitt is convinced that the cities offer no real future. "If we dump any more people on the streets of [New York] it will get to the point where it will be physically impossible to carry on any normal semblance of comfortable or efficient social or business life." He feels that to rehabilitate a city is like trying to cure a cancer. America's big cities are beyond help. He realizes that moving more and more Americans out of the city presents a difficulty. One can't dump people on the plains of Nebraska or Minnesota and tell them to earn a living. Whole new communities have to be built up with the facilities for work, schooling, entertainment. In short, Levitt envisages as the solution bigger and better (but perhaps more sophisticated) Levittowns, the trademark under which he became famous and rich as a builder.

The Levitts became wealthy applying the principles of mass production to house building. They entered the real estate business by accident. In the mid 1920s, Abraham Levitt, a Long Island lawyer, had an interest in some property owned by his clients in Rockville Centre. The politicians decided to install a sewage system for the community. These politicians, bribed by the leading real estate operators to keep the sewage disposal plant as far away from their properties as possible so that the value of their acreage wouldn't nosedive, selected a twenty-acre tract next to the property of Levitt's clients who didn't have the political muscle of the competitors. His clients panicked, believing no builder would buy their land once a sewage disposal plant was erected, and Levitt, to salvage his own investment in the acreage, went into the real estate business, managing to sell off his property without losing his shirt, and he began to build houses for others.

He took in his two sons and they did a brisk business on Long Island. Gradually they hatched a new concept to meet the inadequacy of contemporary building practices. Real estate was the only major business in America dominated by thousands of small craft operations out of touch with the new technological age. The Levitts calculated that if they constructed homes on an assembly-line basis they could cut building costs by 30 percent or more and give millions of middle- and lower-class Americans the chance to own their own homes.

An opportunity to put their theories into practice occurred during the Second World War. After the attack on Pearl Harbor, the government looked for a builder to put up sixteen hundred homes to rent to officers of the navy at the nation's largest naval base in Norfolk, Virginia. The Levitts placed the lowest bid, figuring they would try to do the job by mass-production methods which had never been tested before, but which they had thoroughly discussed among themselves. It was a gamble. Their bid price was so low it could ruin them if they had to use conventional procedures and absorb normal costs. Moreover, Uncle Sam wanted the houses as quickly as possible. To do the job along conventional lines would take three or four years, so the incentive to use the new methods was substantial.

Adopting the concepts of the assembly line, the Levitts framed an entire wall on the ground and raised it into place. They bought lumber and other materials in mass volume at low costs. They used machines to cut the lumber instead of having craftsmen saw it by hand. They got plumbing and electrical supplies at bargain rates because of the volume orders they offered.

One problem bothered them at first. Under normal conditions it took at least a half day to install a septic tank in the ground, and this operation didn't seem susceptible to assembly-line techniques. Then one of Levitt's engineers got the offbeat notion of employing burial vaults. He contacted a manufacturer of these vaults, directed him to make a few changes in his production techniques and then turn out septic tanks of precast concrete. Using this mortuary technique, the Levitts found that instead of installing one septic tank they could put in twenty in a half a day.

After the war, the market for the Levitts boomed. Little private building had taken place during war time, and there was a pent-up demand for housing. The Levitts developed a highly sophisticated strategy. They broke the job of building a house down into twenty-six basic steps ranging from the "digging of footings to the painting of the outside trim." "Each step," William Levitt explained in an interview, "was handled by a different crew especially trained in the particular operation." They made studies of time and motion and divided carpenters into two groups, those who were skilled in the roofing and those who performed interior, exterior, and framing operations. They found as did Henry Ford I, who pioneered the concept, that putting workers to work on a single operation saved time and money.

The Levitts' first major postwar project was Levittown on Long Island. Several thousand acres of land that had been devoted to the growing of potatoes was bought, and in four years the Levitts built seventeen thousand houses, sheltering seventy thousand people, and selling in a price range from $8,000 to $10,000. Critics claimed that these houses, each one looking like the other, were aesthetically ugly, that the Levitts were creating slums in suburbia.

To this, Bill Levitt, who is the only one of the brothers still alive, replies that whatever the critics may say, the value of these homes has steadily increased over the years. Far from being jerry-built shacks, he insists, they have withstood the test of time.

Twenty years after they were built, a home that originally sold at $7999 was bringing in $35,000.

Besides the Long Island complex, the Levitts built a Levittown in Bucks County, Pennsylvania, and launched one in New Jersey. In 1960, because land large enough to build tract houses was growing scarce and perhaps becoming sensitive to the criticism of the purists, the Levitts modified their approach and began building smaller housing communities. Moreover, they broadened their price line and diversified their model homes. By the mid 1960s, William Levitt reported, "We have all kinds of models just like General Motors. Thirty models to be exact. They sell from thirteen thousand, five hundred to thirty-one thousand dollars, with everything in between."

Levitt insisted that he didn't consider himself to be in the real estate business at all, but was a manufacturer of housing. "We manufacture roads, water distribution lines, sewage disposal systems, schools, shopping centers. We use lumber, nails, cement, and real estate as well as a hundred other items." He didn't trade, buy, or sell real estate properties in any different way, he insisted, than he bought cement, lumber, nails.

In 1967, his cup of good luck brimming over, Levitt sold his company to International Telephone and Telegraph, a freewheeling conglomerate. As a result of an exchange of stock, Levitt was given almost nine hundred thousand shares of ITT worth over $90 million, and he walked away from the real estate business, which his family had entered in the 1920s, richer by $100 million.*

Levitt and Zeckendorf represent two completely opposite philosophies about communal living. Just as the one, who is urban-oriented, disagrees vigorously with the other who believes the suburbs and rural America hold the greatest promise for future living, so the nation reflects this basic rift in its own thinking. The dilemma is unresolved and may be for years to come.

While the issue of urban rehabilitation versus suburban development continued to plague the 1960s, there was another side to

---

*Finding it unsuitable to its own activities, ITT subsequently resold the business to Levitt.

the coin. Large sums of money continued to be made by real estate operators in an area untouched by the urban-suburbia brouhaha, an area that continued to grow along with the nation's increasing affluence. This was the market for agricultural real estate.

For one thing, the vast old-time cattle spreads of the nineteenth century, which had been subsequently converted to farming and residential real estate, were providing increasing opportunities, after the Second World War, for imaginative land gamesters.

For another, during the middle 1960s, Florida, the site of the 1925-6 boom-and-bust, became the vehicle for new maneuverings to turn a rapid dollar. Taxes were soaring and an increasing number of people were becoming highly vulnerable to the meat cleaver of the tax collector. A slew of peddlers emerged to sell enticing tax shelters. Florida was lavishly endowed with orange groves. At first blush it didn't seem possible an orange could be of much help to a harassed taxpayer; but some lads who were sharp with a pencil disclosed the hidden opportunity in a citrus tree. Any hardworking American, who planned to retire in ten years, they averred, could buy undeveloped land in Florida and plant orange, lemon, or grapefruit tree groves on it. He could do this with 15 percent down in cash, paying the balance of the price over ten years. It took about half that long, alleged the promoters, for the grove to begin bearing fruit, during which period it would be under professional management. The absentee owner residing on Park Avenue or in Chevy Chase could take business losses that would substantially reduce his tax liabilities; then when he was ready to retire and his taxable income dropped, the trees would be bearing fruit in droves, providing him with a nice tidy profit.

Under the law, pointed out the promoters, a citrus grove could enjoy a 7 percent investment tax credit which the investor could deduct during the first year his trees started to yield fruit. He also enjoyed depreciation allowances that provided a handsome annual charge-off, until he was able to recoup his investment. This was ironic, for, far from depreciating, the citrus grove *multiplied* in value as it began bearing fruit. Some groves, alleged the promoters, bore fruit for as long as seventy-five years and had been known to yield financial returns as high as 50 percent annually.

Finally there was the prospect of a capital gains profit if and when the owner decided to sell. And as a lush fringe benefit, the absentee owner, if he decided to take a trip to Florida to inspect his groves and soak himself in the sun, could charge this off as a business expense.

Of course, the more candid promoters disclosed, there were some risks involved in Florida grove investments. The trees were at the mercy of uncertain weather; hurricanes and frost could wipe out a grove overnight. For those who survived, however, the results could be heady indeed. In 1962 a severe freeze created such an acute shortage of oranges that prices for the remaining crop shot up over 200 percent. In any case the idea of owning, "a beautiful, picturesque orange grove in sun-blessed Florida," as one brochure rhapsodized, seemed to have an irresistible appeal to people. Among those who snapped up the bait were big-name athletes whose brief careers, combining high income and early retirement, seemed especially tailored for citrus grove deals. One investor was a star football quarterback who feared that injuries would force him to the sidelines sooner than he had intended. He gave a ringing endorsement to orange groves, advertising them from coast to coast.

Ownership in Florida groves appealed especially to affluent foreigners, many of whom had never tasted an American orange. Shrewd Europeans noted that Florida was one of the nation's fastest-growing states, and that land prices, while high on the heavily developed East Coast, inland, and on the West coast, were still cheap compared with California. Consequently, investors from Germany, France, Greece, and even trust fund managers in Scotland, the canniest investors on the planet, rushed into Florida citrus groves. One *grande dame,* descended from a family founded during the Austro-Hungarian Empire, and now residing in Switzerland, became one of Florida's most enthusiastic investors, plunging a large slice of her inheritance into orange groves.

To serve this growing demand, grove salesmen cropped up all over the place, buying land and parceling it out on the installment plan to eager customers. Many hustlers assumed the job of planting the trees and running the operation for the starry-eyed absentee owners.

Amidst this frenetic plunging lay pitfalls for the unwary. One exuberant hawker of land in South Florida issued a deed which disclosed in fine print that the property was "subject to easement by the Central and South Florida Control District." That meant in plain English that the state reserved the right, anytime it desired, to inundate the property under ten feet of water.

An especially ambitious, fast-growing venture was launched by two brothers who were accountants from New Jersey, and who snapped up on a shoestring land far enough south to minimize the risk of freezes and peddled it for $1700 an acre, 50 percent down, the balance payable in monthly installments running up to ten years. The firm received a commission of 10 to 12 percent on the net returns of the grove owner in return for picking, packing, and marketing the fruit for him.

So great was the appetite for its groves, American Agronomics, as the Freemans named their business, soon launched a public offering to raise money for more land acquisitions. With these public funds, it bought 50,000 acres of real estate, taking an option on 11,600 more in De Soto County in the southern part of the citrus belt.

The firm also started selling pistachio nuts, peddling contracts for nut orchards as a new tax shelter.

But the Securities and Exchange Commission looked into the operations of American Agronomics with a jaundiced eye. It filed charges that the firm was conducting a boiler shop operation, telling prospects that an orange grove could be producing $2800 in income by the time it was five years old, while, in fact, the groves the firm owned for its own use were producing substantially less. The promoters also assured prospects, the SEC charged, that they were the "ideal age" for maximum tax benefits, no matter how old the prospects actually were. Moreover, according to the SEC, the firm hired "ostensibly independent professional advisors including accountants and tax attorneys" to recommend the orange groves without disclosing to would-be customers that American Agronomics was paying them commissions for each client they lured into a contract.

As soon as the SEC charges against the real estate firm became public, its profits took a nosedive, and class-action suits were

279

filed on behalf of the three thousand investors who had bought over twenty-five thousand acres of orange groves during the four years the firm has been operating, demanding $50 million in damages and recission of all sales contracts. Battered by lawsuits and sliding profits, the owners resigned from the helm and new management took over.

Meanwhile a new development occurred in the tangled affairs of American Agronomics. Although the company was reeling from SEC action, investor lawsuits, and tobogganing earnings, rumors suddenly spread that two individuals in Florida, a Mr. and Mrs. James Corr, had suddenly started buying shares in the firm which was listed on the American Stock Exchange. The spectacle of the husband-and-wife team avidly snapping up stock of a company whose prospects were clouded with tumbling earnings and perhaps years of litigation ahead seemed to defy reason. Yet in a period of sixty days from October 1 to December 3, it was disclosed that the optimistic Corrs latched onto over 250,000 shares of the real estate firm. Then word came from the West Coast that a California lawyer was also frenetically buying up shares in American Agronomics, garnering 175,000 by the end of December.

Students of stock raids on Wall Street began studying the Agronomic situation a little more closely. The situation was a highly piquant one. As the firm's troubles with the SEC and the investors' lawsuits became widely publicized, a number of professional bears on Wall Street had begun selling the stock heavily short, expecting the sliding prices to drop still further. (They were selling borrowed stock in anticipation that they would be able to buy it back at a much lower level and reap a handsome windfall.) By early December the short sales waiting to be covered had reached a peak of 90,000 shares. However, a study of the balance sheet indicated that there might not be enough floating stock available from which the short sellers would be able to buy back their shares. The stock available for trading turned out to be less than 350,000 shares and of this, 90,000 were short sales needing to be covered. In the historic words of old Daniel Drew, a notorious nineteenth-century plunger, "He who sells what isn't his'n, must pay it back or go to prison!"

In short, the conditions were present for something that had not happened on Wall Street for generations—a classic "corner" of the stock of a firm. A "corner" meant that a trader or a ring of traders buys up all the floating supply of a company's stock in order to force all the short sellers to settle at any price the ringleaders peg it at. Corners were a regular weapon of the nineteenth-century Wall Street raiders. The pundits had proclaimed they could never be achieved under modern SEC rules. Yet right before the eyes of astonished Wall Streeters, an attempt to corner the market seemed to be under way by the Corrs of Florida and the West Coast lawyer. Triggered by this massive bull buying, the price of American Agronomics stock, which had been dawdling along at 1 ½ in October surged to over 18 by January. By then the Corrs had bought up 400,000 shares in the open market, while the California lawyer had acquired over 170,000 shares, amounting to a combined 60 percent of the total stock outstanding.

The SEC struck quickly, placing a ban on all the trading of the stock. After an intensive investigation, it filed charges against the Corr group, claiming they were allies in a pincer operation designed to run the price up for a financial fleecing. Noting the heavy volume of short selling and knowing the float was excessively small, the ring decided to buy all it could lay its hands on to corner the stock operating (according to the SEC) through a network of brokers from coast to coast, employing nominee purchases to disguise their buying, and with a flurry here, a cadenza there, to lure other traders into grabbing the stock on the way up.

The story of citrus groves, pistachio nuts, Addison Mizner, and Boca Raton goes on and on through infinite variations. And it will continue to do so as long as there are dollars to be made and the gullible to be inveigled.

9

TODAY

AND TOMORROW

*The Bust of the Trusts; Lucrative Farm
Acres; Battling Over the Environment*

As the nation passed into the 1970s, the gyrations of the real estate industry served once again, as so often previously, as a mercilessly revealing mirror of the strength and weaknesses of the American society. The behavior of land and property investors drowned out all the rhetoric of the social scientists, recalling the words of Bert Lahr, the comedian, "Your actions speak so loud, I can't hear your words."

America entered the current decade out of breath from a prolonged industrial boom and a protracted bull market in Wall Street. Prices got out of hand as the volume of paper money outpaced physical productivity. The frightened Federal Reserve tightened up on the money supply, interest rates went through the roof, stocks dove through the floor, and industry, suffering from an unaccustomed capital squeeze, opened its maws and regurgitated millions of workers into the unemployment insurance lines. Real estate has historically thrived on cheap money like a lighted match on kerosene, and the severe tightening up of capital threatened to strangle the highly leveraged field.

A dramatic saga that neatly encapsulated the brief joys and subsequent jolts of the land hustlers over the last five years has been the rise and fall of a brand-new instrument that was joyously concocted for moneymaking and which, like Humpty-Dumpty, eventually toppled from the wall—the real estate investment trust (REIT). The career of the trust ironically underscores how something that starts out as a useful, even noble experiment can, when let loose on the stage of human trial and error, run into disaster.

Vast, socially oriented real estate projects, especially in the field of urban redevelopment, have always suffered from a lack of capital.

The trust was incorporated into law as an amendment to the Internal Revenue Code to tap fresh new sources of capital for the real estate field and to give small investors in America the opportunity to buy a share of real estate via mortgages or equity participations in the same way that investors were able to buy stocks in mutual funds. The trust was designed to be exempt from income taxes, but in order to qualify in this way, it had to be unincorporated and its board of trustees represent "transferrable shares of beneficial interest." The tax exemption was to be on the portion of income that was distributed as dividends to the shareholders. There had to be at least one hundred such beneficial owners with no one block controlling 50 percent. Three-quarters of the gross income of the trust had to be derived from real estate and a minimum 75 percent of assets had to be held in real estate, government securities, or cash. Most important of all, the trust was required to distribute no less than 90 percent of its net income annually to its shareholders. The independent management company, which originated the loans in the trust and serviced the portfolios, usually had a contract not unlike those in the mutual fund industry. Its fee was based on a fixed percentage of the trust's asset value—typically between 1 percent and 1½ percent.

The concept behind the trusts was both sound and useful. It was, as noted, a vehicle which would allow the nation's smaller shareholders to invest in a diversified portfolio of real estate ventures while providing a substantial new source of capital for large-scale developments like urban renewal.

What made the trusts especially intriguing was the role they were designed to play in periods of tight money. When the pressure is on the commercial banks to cut down their business loans, the first borrowers to feel the pinch are typically real estate builders who are the riskiest customers. When the banks withdraw, a wide-open opportunity is provided for a trust to move in and build its portfolio of construction and development loans. So thought the pundits.

The trust concept became the hottest property on Wall Street. Analysts gleefully called them "perpetual moneymaking machines." The effect of leverage on their earnings could be amazing. For instance, if a trust were earning $1.50 a share and its stock was selling at 20, it would go to the public market to obtain new capital cheaply and expand its lending operations. Suppose it sold a hundred thousand shares for $2 million; it would put these funds immediately to work in construction and development loans that yielded, in a period of tight money, 14 percent, generating for the trust new earnings of $280,000. In short, the hundred thousand shares of new capital would return $2.80 a share, boosting overall earnings as well as book value. Then the trust would come to Wall Street for still another public stock offering at an even higher price, boost its earnings again—and so on and on. That, at least, was the theory.

Not surprisingly, as noted, the potential of the trust excited the imagination and the greed of Wall Streeters. Borrowing cash at 10 percent and lending it at 14 percent, returning at least 90 percent of their tax free profits as dividends to shareholders, while the price of their stock continued to soar to increasingly higher multiples—how could an investor go wrong with them?

A crowd of wheeler-dealers, outside the real estate field as well as in it, rushed headlong to set up their own trusts. "People with no background whatsoever in the business came to me and demanded that I raise fifty million to start an REIT," reported one leading underwriter in Wall Street. "I asked them what they knew about real estate; and their answer was that they didn't have to know a damn thing about it. They could always hire a mortgage man from a bank." Most underwriters in those euphoric days needed no further persuasion. Some of the latter got involved in promoting trusts of their own.

By 1969 the trusts were by all odds the glamour equities of Wall Street. The stock of almost any new REIT that came to the market was snapped up and a cinch to climb 100 percent or more in price without scarcely a pause. A huge rash of trusts were launched on the premise that the boom in real estate—in shopping centers, commercial buildings, residential apartments—would go on indefinitely. Within a period of six years, industry volume rose from a mere $1 billion to almost $20 billion. By the early 1970s the trusts were accounting for over 20 percent of all the construction and development loans to the real estate industry.

The risks of this speculative jamboree were steadily accelerating, and, enhancing the danger, were foolish laws passed by many of the states. New York, for instance, required that before a trust could raise money through a stock offering, it must show in its prospectus that it already had negotiated commitments for 60 percent of the money it wished to raise. In short, if anyone wished to start a trust and raise $40 million from the public, he had to have at least $25 million of that amount already committed to loans. The quickest way for a newcomer to load up his books with this 60 percent loan quotient was to rush hat in hand to the nearest bank. The bankers were only too happy to offer participation in loans they had on their books, for they would receive their cut on the business, and the newcomer would have to do all the grubby work of servicing it. However, they invariably handed over the least attractive, most unprofitable loans in their portfolio—the veritable dregs of their business. And the newcomer, pressed to meet the qualification for going public, found himself with old mortgages that yielded 6 percent interest at a time when newer mortgages were bringing in twice that amount. But the trust managers remained optimistic. They were sure they could raise the return on their wretched portfolios by rolling over their bad loans as quickly as possible once they had raised money from the public.

And for a time prospects seemed bright. Indeed the banks which initially had handed over their portfolio junk to the trusts soon became so enamored with the prospects of the field, they decided to elbow their way into it on their own, rather than let the trusts run off with all the profits. The prestigious Chase Manhattan launched a trust with a $50 million line of credit and announced, with fanfare, a public offering of $112 million worth of shares and debentures. Chase's idea was to get into the field of risky, short-term, high-interest loans, designed to yield quick profits, by wearing the hat of its REIT affiliate—a game it wouldn't dare play under its own parent name. What was good for Chase looked even greater to its rivals. The Bank of America, Wells Fargo, on the West Coast, such insurance titans as Connecticut General, Mutual of New York, and Massachusetts Mutual, and oddly, even the Holiday Inns of America—rushed in to set up trusts of their own. In a few months these financial behemoths managed to wangle over $600 million from the public, and their success lured other financial institutions in to join the fun.

As the number of financial Johnny Appleseeds increased, the pressure to hand out more and more money and take riskier and riskier loans accelerated. But there is no such thing as a free lunch in the financial world. A highly leveraged operation like an REIT, to work successfully, must hustle for business primarily in the construction and development mortgage field which, while yielding the highest profits, is the most speculative area of real estate. As one expert observes: "The field is loaded with booby traps. There's often a great variance between the 'appraised' value and the actual value of a property. A builder can get virtually any 'appraisal' he wants, and it's up to the trust manager to verify the property's true worth." To be sure, some trust managers were prudent. They refused to make a loan unless a permanent lender (i.e., an insurance firm) committed himself to taking over the long-term mortgage once the construction job was completed, from which the advances on the construction loan could be repaid. But the danger was that if the builder defaulted at any stage of the construction, the permanent lender could withdraw from his commitment, leaving the trust holding the bag. And builders were prone to defaulting for any number of reasons—a sudden turn for the worse in the economy, an overnight reduction in the demand for real estate, poor management of the budget, bad weather suddenly intervening to delay the construction schedule.

In addition to these risks, there were flaws in the way many trusts did business. So eager were they to put out loans as competition mounted, in many cases they not only lent builders money covering 100 percent of the construction costs *but they subsidized all the interest payments on the loan until the final payment when both the principal and the accumulated interest became due.* In short, not until the date the loan matured and the builder was required to pay back the principal was he also obligated to pay the accrued interest. At the same time, many trusts indulged in a bit of cosmetic accounting. They kept their books as if the builder were paying his monthly interest installments on his loan, reporting earnings that would not be forthcoming until the loan's maturity date.

This procedure was especially perilous because the trusts by law had to distribute 90 percent of their income each year to their shareholders, if they wished to keep their exemption from Federal income taxes. Since many of them were subsidizing the interest payments of their borrowers, they were, in effect, *distributing their profits to their shareholders before they had actually received them*—distributing money generated from previous loans or from public offerings on Wall Street.

Here is an example: suppose a trust gave a builder a $2 million loan at 10 percent interest for a period of twenty-four months. The first year, $200,000 of interest payments become due, but the trust funds the builder the amount and does not receive it as income. Nevertheless it distributes 90 percent of this as income to its shareholders—$180,000. The same procedure is adopted the following year. In the meantime, the builder encounters bad weather or he's hit by a strike and is unable to pay back either the loan or the accumulated interest. The trust has distributed to its shareholders $360,000 of income it hasn't earned. If this experience is repeated with many more builders, the trust is on the road to bankruptcy.

With practices like this prevailing, it was inevitable that the first major downturn in real estate would bring down the REIT industry with a crash. In December 1974, the collapse of a major builder who had borrowed heavily from a number of trusts started the dominoes tumbling. Walter J. Kassuba Realty, a Florida-based corporation, which had a $550-million investment in 119 properties around the nation, including 35,000 apartment houses and a wealth of offices and shopping centers, suddenly filed for bankruptcy under Chapter XI. Caught up in the tight money squeeze, beset by shortages of materials and cost overruns, thinly capitalized and dangerously overextended, the thirty-nine-year-old Mr. Kassuba ran out of cash, stranding over two thousand secured and two hundred unsecured creditors, including some of the nation's biggest mortgage bankers and insurance companies. In addition to such victims as John Hancock, Connecticut Mutual Life Insurance, Northwestern Mutual Life Insurance Company, and Chase Manhattan, which was a trustee for clients who lent Kassuba money, no less than a dozen real estate investment trusts were stuck with $110 million in bad loans.

Kassuba was not the only big builder to fall victim to the money squeeze and inflationary construction costs. John Jamail Builders, Inc. of Texas and Urbanetics Communities of Southern California also filed under Chapter XI, and scores of smaller contractors went broke from coast to coast as the real estate industry became engulfed in its worst recession since the end of the Second World War.

The impact on the industry's almost two hundred REITS, worth on paper over $17 billion, was tremendous. A survey undertaken shortly after the Kassuba collapse revealed that over 10 percent of the industry's portfolio represented delinquent loans. The trusts sharply reduced their dividends, and a number of major ones stopped paying them altogether. One, Associated Mortgage Investors, filed for bankruptcy under Chapter XI. The response on Wall Street was equally drastic. Within six weeks after the news broke on the Kassuba debacle, the stock prices of 130 REITs tumbled 50 percent. Shares of the average trust plummeted to 40 percent below its book value.

In addition to hapless Wall Street shareholders who had invested so euphorically in the trusts, another group left holding the bag were the banks. Faced with having to write off their massive loans to the trusts with frightful results to their balance sheets, the majority of bankers stood fast, giving the REITs an extension on their loans, doing everything possible to keep their clients afloat to prevent their own investment from going down the drain.

However, what is bad news for some turns out to be happy news for others. Stuck with a default on billions of dollars worth of properties, the banks and the trusts have been forced to repossess a mammoth inventory of shopping centers, commercial buildings, and residential developments. The most fascinating story in real estate today is what will happen to these foreclosed properties? If they were suddenly dumped onto the market en masse, they would push a reeling real estate industry into complete disaster.

But while the bulk of the property has been held off the market, so as not to shake the boat any further, a growing number of deals are being quietly offered to buyers with the proper contacts. Those with a knowledge of where the bodies lie are snapping up real estate at incredibly low prices. One affiliate of Smith, Barney, the Wall Street broker, SB Partners, has emerged as a leader in the trade of gobbling up foreclosed properties disgorged by the real estate trusts, the savings banks, and life insurance companies who have been hit with an avalanche of delinquent loans.

The business of unloading and buying distressed properties is being conducted in the most discreet way possible. Like a family which refuses to admit that one of its members has died and keeps the corpse embalmed in the living room rouged by a make-up specialist, so the trusts and the banks who are unloading their properties are pretending that nothing out of the way is happening, for if the actual prices at which some of these properties were being sold were widely known, the current decline in real estate could turn into an utter catastrophe.

The real estate trusts and other financial institutions have been dumping their properties by using an ingenious cosmetic device. They are persuading buyers to pay the highest possible price *on paper,* so that they will look as good as possible on the deal. For example, a real estate trust has sunk $14 million into a real estate property; it is reluctant to sell out for anything less than that figure, for it will have to disclose in its records that it has taken a loss. The trust manager, accordingly, begs would-be buyers to pay the $14 million price. The buyers are usually willing to oblige—on one condition. They'll pay the asking price for the record, but in return they want a thirty-year mortgage at an abnormally low interest rate, drastically below the current market. They demand, for instance, a 4½ percent interest compared with 7 percent or 8 percent being asked by everybody else. Explains one buyer, "For us to pay the current interest rate, the seller would have to offer the fourteen million dollar property to us at its true market price today, say nine or ten million."

Everything may look fine for the moment. The seller is protected with the $14-million price which goes into the record for the transaction. This is all the shareholder sees; he is unaware that the seller has been forced to make the concession of taking mortgage paper bearing 4½ percent. At some point in the future, when he's hard pressed enough financially so that he has to sell this mortgage paper to a bank, he'll be clobbered with a drastic discount that will have to show up on his books. In short, the true severity of the crisis following the bust of the real estate trusts has so far been camouflaged. But the delayed reaction, when it hits the public, could be traumatic. Traumatic, that is, for the losers, not for the ingenious few who, amidst the doom and gloom, are finding—and will continue to ferret out—once-in-a-lifetime buying opportunities in massively underpriced properties.

In addition to aggressive bargain hunting for properties dumped by the REITs, there has been another area where plungers have been enjoying a spectacular rise in fortunes in recent years. That is in agricultural real estate. One branch that has traditionally provided a hedge against galloping inflation is America's ranchland, which from pioneer times has generated fortunes for ambitious real estate families.

While many of the older cattle ranches have been turned into residential developments, a few have continued to ply their original trade. The most successful of these is the King Ranch, which is the largest privately owned piece of real estate on earth.

Launched over a century ago by the King family, it covers a territory of a million acres, bigger than the state of Rhode Island, twice the size of the Grand Duchy of Luxembourg. It is so huge that a dozen different kinds of climate are experienced by the cowboys working in its different sectors. For over a century the ranch has been owned by the King-Kleberg clan which has maintained its suzerainty against bandits, lawsuits, hurricanes, taxes, and epidemics. Within this fiefdom several hundred Mexican and American cowboys have worked for four generations, handing down their jobs from father to son to their grandchildren.

This walled-off empire at one time was a puzzle to the communities surrounding it. For many years no outsider was allowed to enter on the threat of being apprehended as a trespasser. In the 1920s several residents in the neighborhood vanished mysteriously amidst rumors that they had strayed onto the ranch grounds and were killed by guards. A fierce public outcry was raised against the King family, but no evidence was turned up indicating that the ranch was responsible for the disappearance of the Texans.

Richard King, the ranch's founder, was of Irish descent who was born in Manhattan in 1824. At eleven he ran off to sea, rose from a cabin boy to become a captain on the riverboats carrying cargo in the Gulf of Mexico. In 1852, King, noticing that cattle and horses increase their value by reproducing themselves while boats ran the hazard of getting wrecked, quit his job as river captain and started buying acreage in the wilderness below the Nueces River. On the advice of a close friend, Colonel Robert E. Lee, later to become commander of the Confederate Army, King snapped up fifteen thousand acres of ranch land from a Spanish owner for $300, which worked out to less than 2 cents an acre.

From then on, King's strategy was "Buy land and never sell." Eventually he accumulated six hundred thousand acres. Before he died, he possessed the biggest spread anywhere, employing one thousand people and grazing one hundred thousand head of cattle.

Not surprisingly, when one takes into account the extent of the grubstake, the family's inheritance has touched off a spate of

291

acrimonious lawsuits. Dissension broke out with the passing of Henrietta King, widow of the founder, who lived to the ripe age of ninety-two, functioning as the iron-willed matriarch of the dynasty. At her death cowboys from remote corners of the spread converged on the headquarters to pay their respects to the body that lay in a simple bronze casket surrounded by lilies. Some hands spent two days of hard riding before they reached headquarters. When the home services were concluded, the *kinenos* jumped into the saddle and trotted around the grave, waving their hats in a salute to *La Padrina,* who had dressed in widow's mourning from the day her husband died.

Several King heirs have made news headlines with their eccentric behavior. Alice Atwood, one collateral descendant, lived into the nineties as a solitary shut-in and amazed her neighbors by leaving millions to a Chicago cop who had quietly befriended her. Another heir willed $20 million to a crazy monk of the Trappist Order.

To obviate future wrangling among descendants, Bob Kleberg, whose father had married Henrietta King's daughter and who inherited the management of the ranch until his recent death, organized the business into a family corporation, each of whose four branches (consisting of some fifty heirs) has a one-quarter interest in the ranch holdings. Each votes fifteen thousand shares of stock. The entire clan gathers once a year for the annual corporate conclave. The youngest shareholder in the corporation began attending the meetings as a stockholder, an infant sitting in the lap of his mother.

The Klebergs have made a major contribution to Texas agriculture. The difficulty of growing, in South Texas, which lies under a steaming sun, a species of grass that does not shrivel from the heat has been increasingly vexatious. King Ranch scientists spent years importing grasses from all over the world and cross breeding them with the Texas variety to produce a durable strain. Finally they came across a Rhodes grass in Africa which seemed the answer until it was discovered that it was vulnerable to a Japanese parasite that attacked and destroyed it. Threatened with the destruction of their pastureland, King agronomists looked for ways to combat the death-dealing parasite. Finally they came up with a wasplike parasite in India that miraculously was found to feed upon the Rhodes grass bug. But the Indian wasp was in very scarce supply, and the King scientists were forced to grow a special culture of it until it multiplied sufficiently so that it could be tried out on the ranch. Since this wasp creeps less than half a mile during its entire life-span, to hunt out and destroy the Japanese parasite King agronomists came up with the inspired idea of dropping armies of them from low-flying planes, camouflaging the bug in the nodules of the Rhodes grass. They made their first drop over a hundred thousand acres of the ranch and in so doing saved not only the grassland of the King Ranch but much of South Texas, which has learned to use the Indian parasite to restore its pastureland to a fertile-yielding forage for cattle.

The Klebergs have operated their spread with a deep-seated cockiness as if it will endure forever. To a reporter who asked if he believed there would be a King Ranch in the year 2000, Bob Kleberg, Sr., retorted, "Absolutely—if there is a world."

There are other areas besides ranchland that have become lucrative operations not only for Americans but for "smart money" from abroad which since the start of the 1970s has joined the rush into American farmland.

Recently members of the Burda family, which owns one of West Germany's biggest publishing houses, plunged over $9 million into three choice parcels of U.S. farm- and ranchland, including the 2500-acre Schuster Farms near Gower, Missouri, one of the world's largest hog producers. Moreover, Tria Holding Corp., an Arabian enterprise, has acquired a substantial stock interest in the Arizona, Colorado Land and Cattle Company, while a syndicate of Hong Kong Chinese businessmen has bought the 200,000-acre Deseret Ranch, one of Utah's biggest. Also, a business group from Japan has acquired a stake in a large Iowa farm and has snapped up additional rural real estate near Salinas, Kansas. Other syndicates of Argentinians, Austrians, Swiss, and Kuwaitis have also been avidly bidding to acquire a stake in U.S. agricultural estate.

This inrush of rich foreigners has been one cause for a massive boom in farming real estate, sending acreage prices skyrocketing to an all-time high. Since 1972, when U.S. farmers negotiated the first large-scale grain deal with the Russians, triggering an upsurge in wheat prices, and America rapidly expanded its role as the breadbasket for the world, not only farmers themselves, but also hordes of outside investors, managers of pension funds, gold bugs, and other fiscal pessimists have been gobbling up acres of bottom croplands in the Midwest and elsewhere.

Spurring this land rush has been the erratic performance of the stock market, the upsurge of inflation, the mounting concern over the dollar, together with the warnings of bearish investment advisory services that farmland provides the best hedge against the collapse of U.S. currency, and an ideal retreat from the violence "certain to break out" in the streets of the nation's cities when urban society finally collapses.

The upshot of these jeremiads has been to set off a rise in prices that has shattered all previous records for farm real estate. By 1976 they had zoomed to over two and a half times the level of 1967. In some areas of the Midwest, choice cropland has soared in value to over $3000 an acre. The average price of Iowa farmland is double that of three years ago. Last year's (1976) increase over the previous year—$232 an acre—was more than the total price Iowa land sold for fifteen years ago.

The motives for getting into farmland seem sound enough. The United States has the world's largest contiguous mass of fertile soil and an excellent growing climate. Since 1970, while world food supplies have dropped to 69 million tons, U.S. food stocks have soared to over 30 million, and by 1975 the United States was selling half of all the grain that was exported over the world. The Soviet Union, which several years ago began committing itself to expanding its livestock production and putting more meat on the dinner table for its people, has emerged as a major customer for American grain. The Japanese also are eating more meat and have become a rapidly expanding customer for American feed grains and soybeans. Triggered by rising world demand, U.S. agricultural exports have been setting new records.

Apart from American farmers who have been adding substantial acreage to their holdings since the costly, sophisticated new tractors and other equipment now becoming available can only be utilized at their greatest efficiency on large-scale farm tracts, the runaway inflation of recent years has been a big factor in luring nonfarmers into rural acreage. Also the tumbling stock market disgorged disenchanted investors into farmland.

Not only have individual investors from Wall Street been trying their luck in the corn belt, but big institutional money managers have been vying for a slice of the action. One major Midwestern bank has been acquiring New Jersey farmland for its pension accounts. Another bank, in Chicago, has bought farms in the Midwest, Texas, Arkansas, and Mississippi for its trust clients. Explains one buoyant money manager: "Our chief purpose in buying this land is for capital appreciation." Iowa, thanks to the sensational rise in its land prices, has been an especial cynosure of investors. The New York Stock Exchange reported that by the end of 1975 the state had led the nation in the percentage of shareholders who quit the stock market since 1970 to sink their cash into farm acreage.

The enthusiasm for U.S. farmland has been tremendous, but what about its future? Are prices already too high? One indicator of continuing confidence is the behavior of the wealthy foreign dynasties—the Krupps, Oppenheimers, Agnellis—who are concerned not with getting a fractionally higher return on their investment today or tomorrow, but with protecting their multimillion-dollar fortunes in a world of political change and inflationary perils over the next fifty years at least. They want to make sure their huge wealth will be transmitted to their grand- and great-grandchildren in the twenty-first century as unimpaired as possible.

These dynasties have hired the most expert investment counselors money can buy to explore financial hedges all over the world. It was only after a careful study of the situation that a number decided that the best long-term hedge against global inflation and social change was American farmland. As U.S. labor costs continue to soar more rapidly than elsewhere, theorize these pundits, American industrial goods are threatened with becoming increasingly uncompetitive in world markets. But at the same time, America's food exports will become the single most important generator of foreign exchange currency for the U.S. economy. Accordingly, the prices of farm real estate should continue to climb steadily and the U.S. government will be increasingly compelled to favor agriculture with tax and other legislative benefits.

Analyzing the future for farmland investment, Harry Oppenheimer, the head of a leading rural land management firm and a top investment counselor, concedes that while $3000-an-acre cropland may be inflated, there is still a major investment play to be made in ranchland which, due to the severe collapse of cattle prices when the beef market went on the skids in 1973, is still selling at depressed prices (as low as $30 an acre, compared with $3000 an acre for top cropland). Ranchland, Oppenheimer insists, will be the big sleeper buy in real estate in the years ahead.

One specialized branch of farmland that is currently being exploited by a handful of selective investors are properties that are neither wholly agricultural nor wholly rural but lie on the outskirts of urban areas to which an overflow population is expected to spill into in the near future. Much of this land is used for truck farming, and an increasing number of farmers, finding it tough to operate profitably on small acreage so close to urban centers, are only too happy to sell out to land developers who aim to upgrade the land for suburban residential living.

A highly successful operator in this field is John Hannon, a former top money manager on Wall Street, connected with the T. Rowe Price Fund, who, losing faith in the ability of the stock market to provide an effective hedge against inflation, has turned to real estate as the solution. Hannon points out that for long periods of time wisely selected real estate investments have returned double the amount of money wrested from the best-performing stocks, low-grade bonds, and Aaa corporate bonds.

In short, while many real estate operators have been hard hit in recent years, what's poison for some is meat for others. America since the Second World War has been going through a period of rapid social change marked by the burgeoning of civil rights, Women's Lib, etc. And this has had a significant impact on the property market. The fortunes of real estate, after all, are a major barometer of social trends.

One group that is currently developing a strongly aggressive stake in the ownership of real estate is the much exploited American Indian. Litigation by Indians is sweeping the nation. Over 170 land claims are currently pending before the U.S. government's Indian Settlement Committee, promoted by tribes who are demanding title to land they argue was stolen from them by the white man.

The Western Shoshones, for instance, are laying claim to 86 percent of the entire state of Nevada. They demand that fourteen million acres be returned to them, yielded by their ancestors under a treaty signed with the U.S. government in 1863. Uncle Sam claims it took the land by the right of eminent domain. The Shoshones insist they were robbed. After prolonged wrangling, the U.S. government has agreed to compensate the Shoshones for the land at a price of $1.05 an acre, which was the value of the land at the time the treaty was signed. The traditionalist or die-hard wing of the tribe has been urging its brethren not to accept the offer. Considering how land in the United States has skyrocketed in price since 1863, it argues that $1.05 is an outrageously low offer. Indeed, this faction of the tribe doesn't want any money at all, it insists, but outright title to the land so that it can fish and hunt as its ancestors had done on their ancient terrain. Some irreverent observers feel that these Shoshones want title to the land not to go fishing on it, but to turn around and sell it off at today's inflated market prices.

One tribe that has been only too willing to terminate its argument over an ancestral treaty by accepting a cash payment from Washington are the Indians of Klamath Falls, Oregon. Uncle Sam, not long ago, sold off to a third party the tribe's reservation lands which contained some of the finest pine timber in all of North America. From the proceeds, they paid over a thousand Klamath Indians with lush chunks of cash. Donald Schonchin, a tribal brave, received special satisfaction from the reparations deal. In 1877 the brother of Schonchin's great-great-grandfather was hanged by the U.S. army on the charge he had taken part in the murder of a general during treaty negotiations to end the Modoc Indian Wars. Schonchin for years had been attempting, with no results, to acquire the skull of his great-great uncle which had been sent after the hanging to the Smithsonian Institution for the edification of scholars. Now Schonchin has pocketed Uncle Sam's cash with the satisfaction that he has received at least partial payment for the abuses his ancestors had been subjected to.

Meanwhile, there has been a bitter racial contretemps at Palm Springs, where Hollywood movie stars and other swingers sun themselves beside their pools and play at being celebrities. The Agua Caliente Indians, a tribe of thirty families constituting 170 members in full, has grown rich through its ancestral holdings, the proceeds of which, unlike those of other tribes, Uncle Sam has allowed them to enjoy. (Over eighty years ago the U.S. government handed over the 31,500 acres of land to the Indians under a trust agreement.) As a result, the tribe's thirty families have title to land valued at over $90 million and they share in common an income of over $2 million a year. Major hotels, banks, office buildings, and apartment houses in the center of Palm Springs are located on land leased out by these Indians.

Besides the cash flow from the leases, the Indians have garnered additional money, selling over $18 million worth of property, including a chunk of acreage to the municipal fathers on which to build the Palm Springs Municipal Airport.

Since they are wards of the government, the Agua Calientes are exempt from all Federal, state, and local income and property taxes. Some of them live as opulently as the pale-faced Hollywood stars who cavort in this Far West playland. They drive around in air-conditioned Jaguars and Cadillacs and live in homes costing $150,000, complete with lavish swimming pools. A large percentage of the tribe are children who are independently wealthy. One child received over $250,000 when she was six as her share of the land sale for the city airport.

Despite such largesse, the Agua Caliente tribe has launched a lawsuit against the municipality, charging the Palm Springs city fathers with a conspiracy to pass zoning laws preventing them from employing their land in a fashion to reap the maximum profits. The Indians argue that when Palm Springs was incorporated as a city in 1958, the municipal fathers illegally annexed the best portions of land the Indians were entitled to under the government trust agreement, and that only a fraction of the acreage they retain from the original grant is providing decent revenues. Moreover, the tribe claims that, far from being wealthy, a number who drew allotments of property away from the center of Palm Springs' commercial growth—in the canyons of the San Jacinto Mountains surrounding the city—are struggling to make ends meet.

Moreover, the Indians are challenging the attempt of Palm Springs authorities to bring their territory under tax regulations. The city fathers retort that because of the soaring expenses of running the government, they desperately need tax revenues from this land. They want the Indians' trust status abolished so that levies can be made. Indeed the White Fathers warn that if the Agua Calientes win in court, the resort's role as a vacation playground will be doomed and the city's thirty thousand permanent inhabitants will have been victimized by a "handful of Indian agitators." The braves retort, "We're not agitators, we're patriots."

In addition to the crusade of minority racial groups for greater land ownership, there are social pressures that paradoxically present a growing threat to private land ownership no matter who possesses the deed.

The most recent onslaught is by powerful environmentalist lobby groups who, in addition to attacking the quality of the nation's air and water and pushing through Congress legislation on pollution control, have also set their sights on controlling the usage of land throughout the United States. As an editorial in the *Sacramento Union* put it: "The environmentalists argue that land can no longer be considered as only a commodity to be bought, sold and used freely within the framework of a community plan. It must be 'managed' in the public interest—the way we manage our

299

water and mineral resources, to conserve them and make sure they will serve the public good."

A number of states have passed "wet land" legislation to restrict the use of acreage within their domain. But nowhere is the issue being more hotly debated than in California. In 1970, the state legislature passed the California Environmental Quality Act, which decreed that an environmental impact report must be issued on private as well as public land projects.

This coastal commission was set up with the aim of preserving the panoramic view of the California coast for motorists driving along the shore route. Anybody who desires to build within a thousand yards of the coastline must apply for a permit to erect his or her home and to plant trees on his or her property. It is up to the commission to decree whether motorists should look at the Pacific Ocean with trees, without trees, or through trees. The bureaucrats decide the aesthetic value of one alternative over another, while the applicant for a deed to the property sweats it out.

While sympathizing with many of the goals of the environmentalists, real estate interests in California and elsewhere have become increasingly worried over this assault on the right of the private landowner, particularly since the California coastal legislation, like similar laws elsewhere, makes no provision for monetary compensation to the landowner. Not only private land interests, but also numbers of people concerned philosophically as well as practically with the property rights of the individual, have become embittered over the views of the social activists. They challenge the notion that the right to use privately owned land belongs to the state, not the individual. Observes one critic: "The environmentalists say the cost of purchasing the land that society wants to save is far greater than the amount of money society can pay. No doubt that is correct, but it is also prima facie evidence that society gives higher ranking and priority to alternative uses of its public funds. In other words, the public wants the environmental preservation of private lands—but only if it is free." The landowner need not be compensated whatsoever for the expropriation of his property.

Not surprisingly, under the spreading impact of environmental regulations, real estate prices along the California coast have dropped sharply.

One case that made the newspapers recently involves Carl Scheffler and his wife who in 1971 bought a $12,000 lot on the California coast to build a home for their retirement. Shortly afterward, the Coastal Zone Act was passed, placing the Schefflers' property within the zone needing a permit from the commission. After they had spent $4500 in architectural fees, the Schefflers' permit to build their house was denied by the commission on the grounds it would impair the ocean view for autoists driving along the highway. Meanwhile the Schefflers, who were continuing to pay the State of California taxes on their property, took the case to a higher authority and were told that their permit would be denied for at least a year since the state or some other agency might *possibly* wish to buy the property for a public park. Only after prolonged petitioning by the Schefflers and interminable bureaucratic foot-dragging did officialdom finally lift its ukase. By that time the costs of constructing the house (since the Schefflers had bought the property) had skyrocketed. Meanwhile, their investment had been frozen without any return to them, and, to add insult to injury, they were forced to pay taxes which, in effect, subsidized the motorist's view of the ocean from the highway.

Another victim of an overzealous bureaucracy, who made the newspapers not long ago, is a physician who for twelve years had owned coastal property in Humboldt County, planning someday to build a retirement home. A trail ran through his property which the public used to get to the beach, and it was covered by a thicket of underbrush threatening to trip up and injure the unwary passerby.

A year ago, the doctor began clearing away his underbrush when a leading member of a local environmentalist group drove up in his auto and told the doctor he had no right to clear off his land unless he obtained a permit from the Coastal Commission. Section 27103 of the law, he proclaimed, prohibited the homeowner from removing "major vegetation" on his grounds without permission. The doctor, upon being reported to the authorities, argued that he was clearing the shrubbery and dead trees to prevent injury to innocent passersby, and he didn't consider he was violating the law by going out of his way to protect the public from accidents. In vain. The state attorney general brought charges against him, demanding that he pay not only a fine for "breaking the law," but also, since he had the temerity to insist on fighting the matter legally, the state attorney's fees and other costs incurred by the state in bringing the action against him. Only when the doctor agreed to undertake the costs of "the necessary corrective work to mitigate and prevent damages" in connection with "his breaking the law," did the attorney general cease his harassment.

A related challenge to real estate is the decision by a growing number of municipalities to pass laws putting limits beyond which they will not permit population growth. One of the earliest examples of such a "no growth" policy is again in California, in Petaluma, a rural community where environmentalists wield great political clout. Petaluma is adjacent to the San Franciso Bay area and has been threatened with being turned into a "bedroom" for the overflow of the city's population. The municipal authorities unleashed a computer to calculate for them that Petaluma's population, which is currently at 50,000, would grow, under normal conditions, to about 77,000 by 1984. The authorities passed a law arbitrarily limiting the population growth to 55,000 by, among other things, limiting the number of houses that can be built in any one year to five hundred units.

The real estate industry is fighting the ban on homes and legal groups are battling the limitation on population growth on the grounds that, if it prevails, thousands of people will be arbitrarily prohibited from moving into Petaluma. The lawyers argued that the law violates the right of Americans to travel freely and a U.S. district judge, agreeing with the plea, struck down the Petaluma action. However, the decision was reversed by the Appeals Court on technical grounds and the case has been appealed to the Supreme Court.

Recently two other areas in California, Santa Barbara and Orange County have unveiled "no growth" legislation of their own. In battling these decrees, several shrewd lawyers have turned the favorite weapon of the environmentalists—the environmental impact statement—against them. In seeking to restrict population growth, these lawyers argue, Santa Barbara and Orange County have failed to take into account the impact their decree will have on their communities' environment. "Environment," points out one legal plaintiff, "is not only flora and fauna, but man's environment, his right to quality living."

Keeping people out of one area, he argues, will lead to a rash of overbuilding elsewhere to compensate for this, causing over-congestion, substandard housing conditions, and a poor standard of living.

The spread of environmentalist programs obviously poses a growing threat to the real estate industry. The issue of protecting the earth, water, and the atmosphere is a highly complex one and promises no easy solution. But then, America today is going through the crucible of social ferment, and out of this will be shaped the community of tomorrow. Whatever compromises are worked out, whatever accommodations are arrived at with the forces that oppose it, the real estate industry will undoubtedly survive and prosper, since land, after all, is the most indestructible element on the planet.

Moreover, the social dimensions of private property ownership are changing in many ways. Today for instance, unlike the past, land ownership is no longer enjoyed by a wealthy few. The American masses have a large and growing stake in private property. Millions of our people own their homes and the land around them. The money invested in real estate is, in many cases, the most significant source of equity Americans have. And it is an investment whose value has been steadily appreciating since the Second World War.

This evolution of millions of white- and blue-collar Americans into a property owning class is perhaps the most important social development that has taken place in this century. It is the nation's irrefutable answer to the challenge of Marxism. This rapidly expanding democratization of real estate could well be the subject for historians of the future. The age of the land barons will be as remote to these scholars as the eras that preceded the Pharaohs and the Mayans are to us.

But for the present, all of us with a feeling for the epic and the baroque, and a sense that history belongs not only to blocs of people acting as mass economic units—a concept so dear to the hearts of our social engineers—but to aspiring individuals who, for all their failings insist on expressing themselves as individuals, must pay at least some grudging tribute to the ambitious, incorrigible old nabobs of real estate. For as long as they held stage center, they put on a virtuoso performance.

SELECTED BIBLIOGRAPHY
AND REFERENCE NOTES

Chapter 1   *The Magnificent Bankrupts*

For the history of early American land speculation, the author is indebted, among other sources, to a landmark study—A.M. Sakolski, *The Great American Land Bubble* (Harper & Bros., 1932). For the old Northwest land swindle, the author has referred to *Passages from the Journal of Rev. Manasseh Cutler,* in the New Jersey Historical Society Collection, 1874; *Manasseh Cutler and the Settlement of Ohio,* by Robert Elliott Brown, 1938; and collected papers on Cutler in the Essex Institute, Historical Collections, Salem, Massachusetts. For real estate transactions in Washington, reference has been made to Wilhelmus B. Bryan's *History of the National Capital* (Macmillan, 1914–16); Elizabeth Sakolski Kite's *L'Enfant and Washington* (The Johns Hopkins Press, 1920); *The Great American Bubble;* The James Dudley Morgan collection of L'Enfant's papers, United States Catholic Historical Society, New York, 1920; and in the Columbia Historical Society, 1944. Sources on the career of Robert Morris include *Letters,* Robert Morris, *Bulletin of the Historical Society of Pennsylvania,* 1845; the Morris correspondence in the New York Historical Collection, New York Public Library; Eleanor May Young's *Forgotten Patriot, Robert Morris,* (Macmillan, 1950); Charles Henry Hart's *Robert Morris, the Financier of the Ameri-*

can *Revolution; Pennsylvania Magazine of History and Biography,* 1877; Clarence L. Ver Steeg, *Robert Morris, Revolutionary Financier* (University of Pennsylvania Press, 1954).

Chapter 2   *The Little Foxes in Old Manhattan*

Sources for the history of nineteenth-century Manhattan include *The Diary of Philip Hone, 1828–51* (Dodd Mead, 1936); Lloyd Morris, *Incredible New York* (Random House, 1951); Michael and Ariane Batterby, *On the Town,* (Scribner's, 1973); B.A. Botkin, *New York City Folklore* (Random House, 1956). A basic study of the Astor fortune is Gustavus Myers, *The History of the Great American Fortunes* (H. Kerr & Co., 1911). Other Astor sources include Arthur Douglas Howden Smith, *John Jacob Astor, Landlord of New York* (J. Lippincott Co., 1929); Kenneth Wiggins Porter, *John Jacob Astor, Businessman,* 2 vols. (Harvard University Press, 1931); Calvin I. Hoy, *John Jacob Astor, an Unwritten Chapter* (Meador Publishing Co., 1936). An analysis of White's architecture appears in *The Bulletin of the Museum of the City of New York,* March 1942, and *Architectural Record,* Aug.–Oct. 1911; also Frederick Lewis Collin's *Glamorous Sinners* (Long & Smith, 1932). A source for the management of the Astor fortune in the twentieth century is William Zeckendorf's *Autobiography* (Holt, Rinehart, Winston, 1970).

Chapter 3   *"Where in the Lord's Name Is Tucson?"*

A basic source for early San Francisco and its society has been H. H. Bancroft, *History Of California,* 7 vols. (San Francisco History Co., 1890); also David Lavendar, *California: Land of New Beginnings* (Harper & Row, 1972); Stephen Birmingham, *The Right People* (Little, Brown, 1968); Dana L. Thomas, *The Story of American Statehood* (Wilfred Funk, 1961). Sources for the Spreckels Family story include Jacob Adler, *Claus Spreckels, the Sugar King in Hawaii* (University of Hawaii Press, 1966), and Lincoln Steffens, *Upbuilders* (Doubleday Page & Co., 1909). For Nicholas Longworth, reference has been made to Clara Chambrun's *The Making of Nicholas Longworth: Annals of an American Family* (Long & Smith, 1933); also *"Old Nick" Longworth, Cincinnati Historical Society Bulletin*, Oct. 1967; Charles Theodore Greve's *Centennial History of Cincinnati and Representative Citizens*, 2 vols., 1904. A source for the Austin Capitol story and the XIT Ranch is James Evetts Haley's *The XIT Ranch of Texas* (The Lakeside Press, 1929). Sources for the Myra Gaines' case include Nolan Bailey Harmon, *(The Famous Case of Myra Clark Gaines* (Louisiana State University Press, 1946); John S. Kendall, *The Gaines Case*, in the *Louisiana Historical Quarterly*, Sept. 1937; Anna Clyde Plunkett, *Corridors by Candelight: A Family Album* (Naylor Co., 1949). Material for Train is partially based on his autobiography *My Life in Many States and in Foreign Lands* (D. Appleton Co., 1902), and Thornton Willis, *The Nine Lives of Citizen Train* (Greenberg, 1948); Clark Bell, *Speech to the Jury* (At Sanity Hearing), 1873. For the Black real estate experiment, the major source is W. E. B. Du Bois, *Black Reconstruction in America* (Harcourt, Brace, 1935).

Chapter 4 *"I Believe in the Northern Pacific as I Believe in God"*

Basic sources for Jay Cooke and the Northern Pacific are Jay Cooke, Papers in the Historical Society of Pennsylvania and the Baker Library, Harvard University. A major biography to which the author is indebted is Ellis Paxson Oberholtzer's *Jay Cooke, Financier of the Civil War,* 2 vols. (Burt Franklin, 1907). Other sources include Henrietta Larson, *Jay Cooke, Private Banker,* Harvard Studies in Business History, 1936; Matthew Josephson, *The Robber Barons* (Harcourt, Brace, 1934); John L. Harnsberger, *Jay Cooke and Minnesota* (University of Minnesota, 1956); *The Northern Pacific Railroad's Land Grant and the Future Busi-*

ness of the Road (issued by Cooke & Co., Bankers, New York, 1870). For Cooke's bribery of journalists, partial reference has been made to the testimony of the Northern Pacific President Smith before two Congressional Investigation Committees, 1872. For the immigration to Duluth, sources include *Cooke Papers, Book of Reference, N.P. Railroad, Meeting of Directors* (cited by Henrietta Larson). For fund-raising activities abroad, Oberholtzer; also the *Book of Reference* and *Cooke letters to Baron Gerolt and others,* 1872–3. For analyses of Cooke's bond-selling strategy, sources include Oberholtzer; also *Report of the Trustee . . . In the Case of Jay Cooke & Co., Bankrupts—Statement of the Bankrupts as to the Causes of Insolvencey* (Allen, Lane & Scott's Printing House, Philadelphia, 1878). Fahnestock's disagreements with Cooke and his reasons for breaking with him are suggested in a key letter to Cooke, June 8, 1872, and by Larson, *Jay Cooke, Private Banker,* pp. 390–93. For statistics on overbuilding of railroads, a key source is *Poor's Manual of Railroads,* 1874–75. Sources for the 1873 Panic include the *New York Times* and *Tribune,* Sept. 17–22, 1873; *Banker's Mag.,* New York, 1891; Edmund Clarence Stedman, Ed., *The New York Stock Exchange, Its History,* 2 vols. (New York Stock Exchange Historical Co., 1905); Dana L. Thomas, *The Plungers and the Peacocks* (Putnam, 1967).

Chapter 5   *The Grand Dukes of Chicago*

Chief source material for the early history of Chicago real estate includes *One Hundred Years of Land Values* (Chicago Real Estate Board Historical Records); Charles Cleaver, *Early Chicago Reminiscences* (Fergus Printing Co., 1882). For an eyewitness report of the Chicago Fire, *The Great Conflagration—Chicago, Report of the Fire Commissioner of the City of Chicago,* 1873–75. For a later review, Stephen Longstreet, *Chicago, 1860–1919.* A valuable study of the Field fortune is Gustavus Myers, *History of the Great American Fortunes,* (H. Kerr & Co., 1911); also S. H. Ditchett, *Marshall Field & Co: The Life Story of a Great Con-*

cern, *Dry Goods Economist,* 1922, and Robert W. Twyman, *History of Marshall Field* (University of Pennsylvania Press, 1954). An excellent biography of the Fields family is John William Tebbel's, *The Marshall Fields, a Study in Wealth* (E. P. Dutton, 1947). A lively account of the Field merchandising business is Lloyd Wendt and Herman Kogan's *Give the Lady What She Wants* (Rand McNally, 1952). Data on the Field trust has been based, among other sources, on *The Marshall Field Trust,* Rand McNally's *Banker's Monthly,* 1906. Sources for the career of Marshall Field III include Stephen Becker's *Marshall Field III, a Biography* (Simon & Schuster, 1964); *Current Biography,* March 1952; *The Saturday Evening Post,* Dec. 6, 1941; *Coronet,* Feb., 1949; *Life,* Oct. 18, 1943; *Newsweek,* Aug. 4, 1947; *Business Week,* August 16, 1974; *Time,* March 22, 1948.

Chapter 6   *Florida, a Scandal in the Sunshine*

Sources for Flagler's real estate activities include Sidney Walter Martin's *Florida's Flagler* (University of Georgia Press, 1949); Nathan D. Shappee, "Flagler's Undertakings in Miami," *Tequesta,* Nov. 19, 1959; *A Brief History of the Florida East Coast Railway,* St. Augustine, 1936. Anecdotal material has been cited from Cleveland Amory's *The Last Resorts* (Harper & Bros., 1952); *Harper's Weekly,* Nov. 2, 1907, and Nov. 21, 1908; *Palm Beach News,* 1903; *Palm Beach Post-Times,* Nov. 17, 1940. Major sources for Addison Mizner are his autobiography, *The Many Mizners* (Sears Publishing Co., 1932); Alva Johnson, *The Legendary Mizners* (Farrar, Straus & Young, 1953); Ida M. Tarbell, *The Florida Architecture of Addison Mizner* (W. Helbburn, 1928). The writer has been indebted to a highly valuable source for the Florida boom and bust, especially regarding the prices of individual property sales, Kenneth Ballinger, *Miami Millions* (The Franklin Press, 1936). Other sources have included Theodore Pratt, *The Story of Boca Raton* (Great Outdoors, 1963); Frederick Lewis Allen, *Only Yesterday* (Harper, 1931); Robert

Sobel, *The Money Manias* (Weybright & Talley, 1973). For anecdotes and other details of the boom and bust, references have been cited from numerous newspaper and magazine articles including *The Miami Herald, The New York Times,* Nov. 19, 1925; *The Literary Digest,* March 7, June 20, Oct. 24, April 17, 1926; *Harper's,* Jan. 1926; *World's Work,* Sept. 1926; *Review of Reviews,* May 1927, Nov. 1928; *Saturday Evening Post,* June 20, 1925; *Nation,* June 6, 1928.

Chapter 7   *"Momma, Does God Live Here?"*

A basic source for Hollywood's early real estate boom has been Edwin O. Palmer's *History of Hollywood,* 2 vols. (A.H. Cawston, 1937); also Bosley Crowther, *Hollywood Rajah, the Life and Times of Louis B. Mayer.* For the business psychology of the 1920s, see Dana L. Thomas, *The Plungers and the Peacocks* (Putnam, 1967). A major source for the movie theater architecture has been Ben H. Hall, *The Best Remaining Seats* (C. N. Potter, 1961). Sources for Roxy's career have been *A History of Roxy,* New York Public Library Theatre Collection; also, news clippings from the Collection. A prime source for the building of the Roxy has been *Roxy, a History, Film Daily,* 1927, pp. 4–32. The most valuable source for William Fox's career is Fox's own account as told to Upton Sinclair in *Upton Sinclair Presents William Fox,* Los Angeles, California, 1933. A biography by a business associate is Glendon Allvine's *The Greatest Fox of Them All* (Lyle Stuart, 1969). Additional material on Fox's career has been culled from Fox Theatre Corp., *The Story of Motion Pictures and the Fox Theatres Corp.,* Booklet No. I, 1929, New York Public Library Theatre Collection; also, Fox Film Corp., *William Fox Press Services,* New York, 1916–22, 12 vols; *Publicity Sheets from the Advertising and Publicity Dept.,* New York, 1927; *Fox News, 1905–19,*—all from the New York Public Library Theatre Collection. Further details and anecdotes about

Fox have been based on *World's Work*, Feb., 1923; *Outlook and Independent*, April 8, July 31, 1929; *Business Week*, April 16, 1930, June 23, 1934, March 9, 1935; *Newsweek*, Feb. 25, Dec. 2, 1933, and Oct. 20, 1934. Material on Mrs. Fox's property purchase and on Century City comes from Zeckendorf's *Autobiography*, (Holt, Rinehart, Winston, 1970); *Business Week*, July 23, 1966; *Architectural Record*, August 1966.

Chapter 8   *Skyscrapers, Orange Groves and Bill Zeckendorf*

A reference source for Gilbert's skyscraper has been "The Birth of Gilbert's Skyscraper," *New York Times*, May 21, 1905. Material on the Empire State Building has been derived partially from B. A. Botkin's *New York City Folklore* (Random House, 1956); source for the Van Sweringens has been Dana L. Thomas, *The Plungers and the Peacocks* (Putnam, 1967), and for Kennedy's real estate operations, Richard Whelan, *The Founding Father* (New American Library, 1965). The chief source for Zeckendorf's career is his *Autobiography* (Holt, Rinehart, Winston, 1970); other sources include *Time*, June 12, 1964; *Architectural Forum*, Aug. 1963; *Business Week*, March 16, 1963, May 15, 1965; Dana L. Thomas, *Barron's National Business and Financial Weekly*, Aug. 5, 1974; Eugene Rachlis and John E. Marques, *The Landlords*, (Random House, 1963); Gilbert Burck, *Fortune*, July 1960. Zeckendorf's views on urban development are cited from his article in the *Yale Review*, Sept. 1958. A source for the Levitts is an interview with William Levitt in *Nation's Business*, Feb. 1967; also Max Gunther, *The Very Rich and How They Got That Way* (Playboy Press, 1972). Material for Florida's tax shelters comes from Dana L. Thomas, *Barron's* Aug. 19, 1968. For the story of American Agronomics, reference has been made to Thomas, *Barron's*, Oct. 6, 1969, and to various articles in *The Wall Street Journal* from 1972 to 1975.

Chapter 9   *Today and Tomorrow*

A comprehensive study of the Real Estate Investment Trusts has been made by Dana L. Thomas in *Barron's,* Oct. 28, 1968, July 7, 1969, Aug. 24, 1970, and July 22, 1974. A source on the King-Kleberg family is Tom Lea's *The King Ranch* (Little, Brown, 1957). Source for the farm land boom includes Thomas, *Barron's,* March 1, 1976. Reference to the Klamath Indians is based, among other sources, on the *New York Times,* Dec. 5, 1974; a source for the Palm Springs lawsuit is the *New York Times,* Dec. 12, 1973. Material on the California environmentalist challenge is derived from *California Real Estate Magazine,* Feb. 1975; also *Pacific Legal Foundation, Legal Activities Report 1973–75.*

INDEX

313

Index

Index

315

Index

Index

Index

O'Dwyer, William, 266
Oklahoma Territory, 60
O'Leary, Patrick, 146, 153
O'Leary, Mrs. Patrick, 146
Olmstead, Frederick, 42
Olympia, Fla., 195
Omaha, Nebr., 86–87, 89, 93, 94
Oppenheimer, Harry, 296
Orange County, Calif., 302–3
Oregon, 59
Ort, Charlie, 204

Paine, Thomas, 14
Palm Beach, Fla., 177–78, 181, 184–85, 186–90
Palm Beach Inn, 181
Palmer, Potter, 137, 142–43, 144–46, 154
Palm Springs, Calif., 298–99
Panic of 1873, 126–35, 136
Paramount Pictures, 229
Park Agency, Inc., 262
Parkhurst, Dr. Charles, 54
Patti, Adelina, 153
Pei, Ieoh Ming, 267–68
Pennsylvania, 25, 88
Pennsylvania Railroad, 129
Perier, Emile, 88
Pershing, John J., 191
Petaluma, Calif., 302
Petersburg, Ill., 33
Philadelphia, Pa., 35, 266; Morris mansion, 28–29
Philadelphia and Erie Land Company, 103
Philadelphia *Inquirer*, 127
Philadelphia *Press*, 110
Philadelphia *Public Ledger*, 117–18
Philadelphia Stock Exchange, 128
Pico, Pio, 62
P.M. (newspaper), 172
Pocket Books, 173
Poe, Edgar Allan, 41
Polignac, Prince de, 88
Ponce de Leon Hotel (St. Augustine, Fla.), 180–81
Poor Richard's Almanac (Franklin), 158
Pottawatomie Indians, 139
Presto-O-Lite Corporation, 185
Primogeniture, 34
Prohibition, 212
Providencia (ship), 178
Prudential Insurance Company, 254
Pullman, Goerge, 159–60, 164, 172
Pullman City, Ill., 159

Railroads, 87, 88–89, 100–3, 123; Miami freight embargo, 200–1
Ramsey, Alexander, 105–6

Ranches, 290–92, 296
Raskob, John Jacob, 251–52, 254
Rasmussen, George, 189
Real estate: agricultural, 277–81, 290–96; black ownership, 95–99; environmentalism and, 299–303; family dynasties, 11–12, 33–35; political theory of, 14–15; speculation methods, 12–14, 61–62, 100–2; taxes, 55, 264; and urban architecture, 51–52
Real estate investment trusts (REITs), 283–90
residential builders, 261
Revolutionary War, 23
Reynolds, John J., 262
Rhinelander, Frederick, 36
Rhinelander, William, 36
Rich and the Super Rich, The (Lundberg), 34
Richardson, Henry, 52
Richardson, Joseph, 50–51
Richardson, William, 133
Richmond, I.C., 196
Robert Thode and Company, 116
Rockefeller, John D., 179
Rockefeller, John D., Jr., 172, 239–40, 266
Rockefeller Center (New York, N.Y.), 239–40
Rockefeller family, 167, 264
Rogers, Isaiah, 41
Rogers, Mary, 41
Rogers, Will, 244
Roosevelt, Franklin D., 171, 195
Roosevelt, Theodore, 75, 94
Root, Elihu, 166
Rotarian Club, 212
Rothafel, Samuel "Roxy," 217–18, 221–22
Rothschild, Baron Guy de, 115–16
Roxy Theatre (New York, N.Y.), 218–21, 236, 238
Royal Poinciana Hotel (Palm Beach, Fla.), 181

Sacramento, Calif., 63, 102
Sacramento *Union*, 299–300
Sail Away (musical), 260
Saint Augustine, Fla., 180, 184
St. Paul and Pacific Railroad, 115
Sampson, Henry, 118–19
Sandburg, Carl, 167
San Diego, Calif., 67
San Francisco, Calif., 11, 35, 63, 64–67, 68–70, 102, 137; earthquake of 1906, 152
San Francisco *Chronicle*, 66
Santa Barbara, Calif., 302–3
Sargent, George, 118–19

318

Index

Sarner, Hyman, 50–51
Sasoon, Sir Philip, 160
Sawyer, Arthur H., 218
Saxton, Gen. Rufus, 97
SB Partners, 289
Scheffler, Carl, 301
Schell, Richard, 129
Schenck, Nicholas, 230
Schermerhorn family, 45
Schlesinger and Mayer, 157–58
Schonchin, Donald, 297–98
Schuster Farms, 293
Scopes, Thomas, 191
Scott, Thomas A., 129
Sears, George, 177
Securities and Exchange Commission
  (SEC), 279, 280, 281
Seminole Beach, Fla., 199–200
Sexual Behavior in the Human Male
  (Kinsey), 259
Shaker Heights, Ohio, 255, 258
Sharkey, Jim, 91–92
Shaw, George Bernard, 226, 259
Sherman, Gen. William T. 96–97
Sherry's Hotel (New York, N.Y.), 53
Shoshones, 297
Simon and Schuster, 173
Sinclair, Upton, 230
Skouras, Spyros, 241–42, 243, 244
Skyscrapers, 247–54
Smith, Al, 251, 252
Smith, Governor, 109
Smith Jeff, 191
Sonoma Valley, 64
Spellman, Francis Cardinal, 262
Sprague, William, 134
Sprague Concerns, Inc., 134
Spreckels, Adolph, 66–67, 68
Spreckels, Claus, 66–67
Spreckels, John, 67, 68
Spreckels, Rudolph, 35, 67–68
Spreckels family, 137
Squatters, 32, 61–62
Standard Oil Company, 179, 182
Stanton, Edward, 96–97
Statler, Mrs. (wife of hotel magnate),
  268
Stearns, "Horseface," 64
Stearns, John L, 248, 249, 250
Stedman, Clarence, 123
Stevens, Thaddeus, 95
Stock market crash of 1929, 231–33,
  239, 258
Stockton, Calif., 102
Stokes, Edward, 91
Stotsbury family, 188
Stritch, Elaine, 260
Stuyvesant family, 44
Suburbs, 255–56, 261, 296; effect of, on
  cities, 272–73

Sullivan, Dennis "Peg leg," 146
Sumner, Charles, 95
Sutro, Adolph, 70
Swedish Immanuel Congregational
  Church of New York, 212
S.W. Straus & Co., 219

Talmadge, Norma, 237
Tarbell, Ida, 187
Taylor, Abner, 76
Taylor, Elizabeth, 241
Taylor, George, 260
Temple, Shirley, 244
Texas, 75–79, 292–93
Texas and Urbanetics Communities of
  Southern California, 288
Thaw, Harry, 54
Tiffany's, 53, 54
Time, 170, 259
Tishman family, 259
Titanic (ship), 56
Title I Urban Redevelopment Act, 269
Train, George Francis, 86–90, 91–95
Tria Holding Corp., 293
Trinkle, Governor, 198
T. Rowe Price Fund, 296
Tunney, Gene, 191, 196, 202, 212
Tuscon, Ariz., 60
Twain, Mark, 101
Tweeddale, Marquis of, 77–78
Twentieth Century-Fox, 241–42, 245.
  See also Fox Films Corporation
Twentieth Century Limited (train), 218

Uncle Tom's Cabin (Stowe), 90
Union Banking Company, 130–31
Union Carbide, 185
Union National Bank, 147
Union Pacific Railroad, 87–89, 93, 115,
  142
Union Trust Company, 131–32
United Nations headquarters, 266
U.S. Cabinet, 107
U.S. Congress, 20–21, 24, 33, 79, 87;
  and California land grants, 62–63;
  and L'Enfant Plaza project, 269–71;
  and Northern Pacific land grant, 104,
  105–6. *See also* Continental
  Congress
U.S. Department of Agriculture, 192
U.S. government: and black land
  demands, 95–99; and Chicago
  Merchandise Mart, 174; and Indian
  land claims, 297–98; and Louisiana
  Territory, 79; and public land
  settlement, 14–15; and railroad land
  charters, 101–2, 105–7; and
  squatters, 61–62; and Texas public
  lands, 75; and Washington, D.C.,
  20–22

319

Index